朱争平 著

朱争平人文历史随感集

GROWTH
RING
OF
SHANGHAI

ZHU ZHENGPING

上海文艺出版社
Shanghai Literature & Art Publishing House

朱争平

中国国际文化传播中心艺术总监、上海总部部长，《红蔓》杂志创始人。长期从事军队思想政治工作，近些年致力于上海近现代历史文化的研究和传承。曾任南京军区宣传部部长，装甲10师政委，第1集团军政治部主任、副政委，江西省军区政委、中共江西省委常委，上海警备区政委、中共上海市委常委等职。出版著作有：《不能忘却》《信笔摩风云》《绿色时空》《实践与思考》《艺海钩沉》等。研究生学历、少将军衔。

目 录
Contents

6 序：年轮所及长情长忆
   Preface: Recollection of Old Shanghai's Vicissitudes

16 老上海的月份牌
   Calendar Poster of Old Shanghai

24 老上海的古玩店
   Antique Shop of Old Shanghai

32 老上海的电影业
   Film Industry of Old Shanghai

40 老上海的舞厅
   Ballroom of Old Shanghai

48 老上海的话剧
   Drama of Old Shanghai

56 老上海的影楼
   Photographic Studio of Old Shanghai

64 老上海的越剧
   Yue Opera of Old Shanghai

72 老上海的戏院
   Theater of Old Shanghai

70 老上海的评弹
   Pingtan of Old Shanghai

88 老上海的连环画
   Comic Strip of Old Shanghai

96	老上海的茶楼	
	Teahouse of Old Shanghai	
104	老上海的沪剧	
	Shanghai Opera of Old Shanghai	
112	老上海的淮剧	
	Huai Opera of Old Shanghai	
120	老上海的爵士乐	
	Jazz of Old Shanghai	
128	老上海的唱片	
	Jazz of Old Shanghai	
134	老上海的昆曲	
	Kun Opera of Old Shanghai	
142	老上海的金曲	
	Golden Oldies of Old Shanghai	
150	老上海的琴行	
	Musical Instrument Stores of Old Shanghai	
158	老上海的滑稽戏	
	Burlesque of Old Shanghai	
166	老上海的报业	
	Newspaper Industry of Old Shanghai	
174	老上海的书业	
	Book Industry of Old Shanghai	
182	老上海的京剧	
	Peking Opera of Old Shanghai	
190	老上海的装帧业	
	Bookbinding Industry of Old Shanghai	
198	老上海的服饰	
	Costume of Old Shanghai	

206 老上海的广告
Advertising of Old Shanghai

214 老上海的旗袍
Cheongsam of Old Shanghai

222 老上海的广播
Broadcasting of old Shanghai

230 老上海的期刊
Periodicals of Old Shanghai

238 老上海的跑马场
Racecourses of Old Shanghai

246 老上海的教堂
Church of Old Shanghai

254 老上海的西餐
Western Food of Old Shanghai

260 老上海的女校
Girls' School of Old Shanghai

268 老上海的小吃
Snacks of Old Shanghai

276 老上海的银楼
Jewelry Stores of Old Shanghai

284 老上海的花园洋房
Garden House of old Shanghai

292 老上海的石库门
Shikumen of Old Shanghai

300 老上海的电信
Telecom of Old Shanghai

308 老上海的旅馆业
Hotel Industry of Old Shanghai

316　老上海的慈善业
　　　Philanthropy of Old Shanghai

324　老上海的邮政
　　　Postal Industry of Old Shanghai

332　老上海的钱庄
　　　Money Shops of Old Shanghai

340　老上海的租界
　　　Concession of Old Shanghai

348　老上海的体育
　　　Sports of Old Shanghai

356　老上海的路名
　　　Road Names of Old Shanghai

364　老上海的中医
　　　Traditional Chinese Medicine of Old Shanghai

372　老上海的公园
　　　Parks of Old Shanghai

380　老上海的城厢
　　　Urban Area of Old Shanghai

388　老上海的车
　　　Vehicle of Old Shanghai

396　老上海的寺庙
　　　Temples of Old Shanghai

404　老上海的商会
　　　Chamber of Commerce of Old Shanghai

412　写在后面
　　　Postscript

序：年轮所及　长情长忆

何　菲

总有种直觉：朱争平将军偏爱有江河湖海的都市，水的开放性和流动性给了探究欲强烈者源源不断的动力，也给人适当的疏淡冷感，此间澎湃着人生至味，让寸心终有了一点安放之处，虽然关于这个话题我们从未聊起过。有些都市，注定是被聚焦、玩味和效仿的对象，西方有巴黎，东方有上海。它们的共同特点：有江河，有码头，是过客的驿站；有文艺气息和生活质感，能做跌宕起伏的人生大梦。能在此地有所作为者，没有一个人内心是安分的，都有着不可言说的神奇。它们的一切都在传达着四个字：聚散离合。

读罢朱争平历时五年半创作而成的力作《上海年轮》，感觉虽然"传奇"这顶帽子很重，上海却扛得起。这座城市有着浑然天成的整体优雅，有着来自根部的生命力和聚合力，且极具吸收力和同化力，既纷纭又规范，有型有款有格有调，更吸引有着细腻追求的人。新旧空间在此互动，横街窄巷也有见惯世面的眼锋急智，盖因自开埠以来她就享有城市发展的天时地利人和。上海的年轮算不得幽深，却瞬息万变难以描述，因此是复杂的、3D的、演进的，承载某些秘密且不容易被定义的。也因此它让烟火日常拥有了价值，让现实变

Preface: Recollection of Old Shanghai's Vicissitudes

He Fei

Although General Zhu Zhengping and I have never talked about cities, an intuition has been always haunting me: He prefers cities with rivers, lakes and seas, because water can empower people with strong desires for exploration inexhaustibly by its openness and flowability, while leaving a proper sense of alienation and coldness. What surges between this fire and ice is the real meaning of life that the heart can finally count on. Some cities are destined to be focused, playful and imitated like Paris in the West and Shanghai in the East. They are commonly characterized by their rivers, wharves, stations for passers-by with an atmosphere of literature and art and a sense of life quality, and dramatically great dreams can be imagined. All of those that can make a difference here undoubtedly have an ambitious heart with unspeakable magical power. Everything about them shows us a person's life through Home and Away conveyed in four words.

After reading Zhu Zhengping's masterpiece Growth Ring of Shanghai that took him five and a half years to finish, my idea is that although "Legend" is a big word, Shanghai totally deserves it. This city boasts natural elegance, vitality and convergence rooted with extremely absorptive and assimilated power, both diverse and standardized in styles and tastes, which makes it more attractive to people pursuing delicateness. New and old spaces interact here with cross streets and narrow lanes indicating sophisticated persons' quick-wittedness with sharp eyes, which has benefited from its development (favorable climatic, geographical and human conditions) since its port opening. The growth ring of Shanghai is not long, but difficult to describe because of its fast changing nature. It is complex, three-dimensional and evolutionary, embracing certain secrets that are difficult to define, thus making the daily life worthy of experiencing. Zhu Zhengping, with his ability to comb the

得值得去生活。有能力剥丝抽茧梳理出这魔幻之姿前世今生经络的朱争平，其实早已打通了上海的任督二脉，成为掌握了都市掌纹与脉息的人，能告诉那些业已感觉到魔都韵律却苦无密钥进入的人们，什么是上海。

　　《上海年轮》无疑是一本大书，为上海幽昧流动的旧时光定位、为正在经历的当下造影。它由 50 篇散文组成，梳理了上海自开埠 170 多年来的历史人文生态情态，涵盖艺术、文化、建筑、休闲、风尚等众多领域，以冷静磅礴的笔触，还原百年都市生活里真正的醇美与辛辣所在，珍存在东方大都会发展进程中无法忽视的文脉、史脉和人脉，成为近年来海派文化单行本中涉及面最广的集大成之作，并为城市研究者提供了扎实准确的索引。终归是男性手笔，而且是干过并干着大事业的男性手笔，老上海，大时代，上天入地，年华内外，林林总总在书里纠缠明灭，仿佛全景时光照相机，即使急流险滩也随岁月之河不疾不徐的潺潺向前。它是一部真正平视的作品，没有站在洋房露台上睥睨脚下老式里弄众生时微蹙眉头的悲悯自得，最终却形成了另一种境界的俯瞰……多少红尘深景，都恍如隔世花影，裹在作者内心的江湖，终在此书中无缚无脱。

　　大上海需要大散文，否则将会以个人经验限制客观提炼，使得人们对上海的理解偏于感性化、碎片化。相对于私上海小记忆的写作，《上海年轮》具备了上乘城市散文的几大要素：史实感，故事感，结构感，节奏感，交响力，观点，趣味，精炼和优雅。全书调动了朱争平大量的知识储备和创作热情，理性精神和人文精神交融，

past and present of this magical city, has in fact already got a comprehensive understanding of Shanghai. As the person who has mastered the development rules of the city, he can narrate what is real Shanghai for those who have already sensed its lingering charm but found no way to get entirely acquainted with this magical city.

Growth Ring of Shanghai, as an undoubtedly masterpiece, has both fixed the correct direction for Shanghai's old obscured time river and created a phantom for its present. Consisting of 50 essays, it has narrated logically Shanghai's historical, humanistic and ecological modality for over 170 years since its port opening in many fields such as art, culture, architecture, leisure, fashion, and so on. With a calm and majestic attitude in writing, it has remained the real mellow beauty and bitterness of the urban life of a century as they were, and revealed literary rules, historical rules and human connections that cannot be soaked and ignored in the course of the development of the Eastern Metropolitan. It has been considered as the most extensive masterpieces among the Shanghai culture monographs in recent years and also provided a solid and accurate index for urban researchers. As it was created by a general who had done and is doing a great job, it seemed as if a panoramic time camera reproducing Old Shanghai, the Great Times and its vicissitudes. As a work created in a genuine equal angle of view, Growth Ring of Shanghai has not shown any sense of pity with a slight frown, which is a kind of feeling produced as if standing on the Western-style terrace to look scornfully down at all people living in the old lanes, but outlined from a different view... No matter how many worldly impressive things there are, all that would be like the shadow of flower in another world, with the author's feelings unrestrainedly expressed in this book.

The reason why Great Shanghai needs great proses is that personal experience will limit the extraction in an objective way and give people only an emotional and fragmented understanding of Shanghai. Compared with the small private writing of recollecting Shanghai, Growth Ring of Shanghai has several important elements of the quality city prose: sense of historical facts, sense of story, sense of structure, sense of rhythm, symphony force, point of view, interest, refinement and elegance. The book has arranged Zhu Zhengping's large amounts of knowledge reserves and creative enthusiasm, where

是其知性与智性的延展。每一处看似点到为止的细节，都有海量史实研究作支撑。每篇动笔前他需要看上百万字的史料，然后消化、梳理、思考与提纯，最终创作成1500字左右的散文。单看每篇标题注定了这不是普通写作者有心力驾驭的入口，也就注定了里面捣腾得更大，取舍更多。他用历史纵深开阔的眼光和理解幽微致密的心情，解析了城市文化与物质形态、人与城之间的关系，将浩瀚体量融于简练圆通的文字中，写意与探微双管齐下，却也让人感到了水面之下的体积，以期在有限中体会无限，这需要极大的掌控力。老上海百年都市生活渐渐从一堆抽象概念中走出来，变成真实可感的土地，变成一段段史海钩沉与折叠，变成一个个出现又湮没在城市江湖中的上海人。

《上海年轮》的每篇文章就是一个领域的历史，皆可单独成册，选材当属稳、准、狠，让人受益匪浅，适合反复重读，所有题材都百川归海地指向老上海何以会成为今日之魔都。书中展现了上海是个大而细的城市，此中劲道、门道，可谓上海之"道"。对于个体，无论身处哪个领域、何种境遇，唯有精准捕捉到这座城市特有精神函数，才能迅速找到适合自己各个时期发展的坐标和思路。若无融入，上海永远是身外之物。

十里洋场，浪奔浪流。上海是个大码头，苏州河汇入黄浦江最终奔流入海在地理与文化上的双重意象，使得唯有上海才能被称为"滩"。在《上海年轮》里，石库门、花园洋房、旗袍美女、唱片金曲月份牌等等迷人元素轮番登场，让人目不暇接之外，更心生喟叹：在老上海石库门弄堂里生活过的人，把他放到全世界任

rational spirit and humanistic spirit were integrated, representing the extension of his intellectual and intellectual nature. Every detail that seemed to not express clearly can find a great deal of historical research support. Before each prose writing, he needed to read, digest, sort out, think and refine historical materials with a total of millions of words, so as to create a final prose with 1500 words. It can be seen from each title that an ordinary author cannot easily control such an exquisitely created article where a variety of elements have been used. With a historical deep and open view and an attitude for subtle understanding, he analyzed the relationship between city cultures and material forms and that between human beings and cities, integrating a vast deal of implications into the flexibly concise words. The combination of spontaneous expression and subtle exploration has surfaced such implications that unfold an infinite picture from a finite point of view, which requires powerful control. A pile of abstract concepts on Old Shanghai's urban life has gradually come out and turned into a reality: an epitome of Old Shanghai undergoing the ups and downs where Shanghainese witnessed changes of generations.

Every prose in *Growth Ring of Shanghai* embodies history of a certain field that can be made into a single book, and its stable, accurate, overwhelming selection can benefit readers a lot, which makes it suitable for repeated reading. All subjects have inclusively focused on the reasons why Old Shanghai can become today's magical city. What this book presents us is a large but small city of Shanghai, with its rules and laws described as the "Way" (survival law) of Shanghai. Individuals from all walks of life can find their positions and thoughts suitable for their own development only by accurately capturing the specific spiritual implications of Shanghai. If they are unable to fit in here, Shanghai will be always unrelated to them.

Old Shanghai was a West-affected metropolis with ebb and flow. Shanghai, as a big wharf where water from the Suzhou River flows into the Huangpu River and finally rushing into the sea, indicating a double image in geography and culture, which makes only Shanghai qualified as the title for "Beach". Growth Ring of Shanghai has depicted us such charming elements as Shikumen, Garden House, cheongsam beauty, calendar posters with golden hits, etc., which can dazzle us and arouse our thinking. For people who lived in the

何地方都能生活得很好,他看得懂很多东西,这是环境所给予的能量。这个逼仄又开放的空间十足考验着生存智慧和向美本能,使他们天然形成复杂多元、柔韧硬挣的心智,生活便有了无限可能性;而上海女人的情商亦如她们穿的海派旗袍,在秘实与显露的分寸里游走,在优美曼妙中流露出运筹帷幄的柔韧与自信,擅长与时代讲和,与内在的自己斡旋……沿岁月年轮,上海滩的风景、风物、风俗和风情,在书里纤毫毕现,且足以满足一部大型纪录片的总体构成,也使得这座移民城市具有了蜿蜒迭代的审美意味、抒情意味和乡愁意味。在我看来,《上海年轮》最大的价值并非那些风云际会、姿态万千的历史,而是使人们渐渐开悟:海派文化是一种强势文化。这绝非中西文化简单粗放的结合,而是中国江南文化的灵动纤秀与西方欧陆文化的高雅精致的一拍即合,是东西方文化中最精美的两大分支文化的精准卡位。当然,如果将强势文化聚焦在一个个小人物身上,必然会产生不同程度的矛盾与压力,却也能渐渐打磨出属于各自圆满的价值体系。从老上海到魔都,亦步亦趋不见得是最好的步伐,而成为自己又是个浩瀚渐进的功课,该如何自处关乎个体化的黄金把握。历史与当下,上海与世界,规则与人性由此被打通!

在我眼中,《上海年轮》是一部并不涉及爱情却非常浪漫的作品。浪漫是情有所用,心有独钟,是敢去打一场世俗眼中性价比不高的美好的仗。可以感觉到朱争平对于此书持久的创作热情,文字却干净而节制。这形成某种摧枯拉朽的吸引力,来势汹汹又不动声色。巴金曾说,"我之所以写作,不是因为我有才华,而是

old Shanghai Shikumen lane could live well anywhere in the world, because they could gain insights into a lot of things well, which was empowered by their surroundings. The narrow and open space is a complete challenge for survival wisdom and aesthetic instinct, which makes their mindset naturally complex: both pliable and tough with a firm belief in infinite possibilities in life... While Shanghai women have an EQ just like the Shanghai-style cheongsam they wear, planning and preparing between proper limits invisible and those visible, revealing their flexibility and self-confidence in full charge gracefully and beautifully. They are good at keeping peace with the times and mediating with their own inner self... The scenery, beauties, customs and glamour of Shanghai Beach are unfolded before readers' eyes in the book, enough to compose a large documentary from overall, thus making this immigrant city have a sense of aesthetics, lyricism and homesickness in the course of its history. In my opinion, what is the most valuable for Growth Ring of Shanghai refers not to its dramatic and colorful history but to its influence on people's gradual enlightenment: Shanghai-style culture is a dominated culture. This is not simply and extensively combined by the Chinese culture and Western culture, but the perfect match of the smartness and delicacy of Chinese Jiangnan culture and the elegance and refinement of Western European culture and a precise integration of the most exquisite branch of eastern culture with that of Western culture. Small photos who are focused on by the dominated culture will inevitably face different degrees of contradictions and stresses, but can also form their own perfect value systems by gradually increasing their willpower. Following others cannot be necessarily seen as the best step from old Shanghai to the magical city, while staying true to itself is considered as a vast and gradual effort. It is thought-provoking how it can deal with the matter of the critical mastery of individualism in which its past and present, Shanghai and the world as well as humanity and rules will be linked.

In my eyes, Growth Ring of Shanghai is a very romantic work that doesn't involve love. Its romance can by embodied by the author's deep emotions and unique focus, courage to announce a romantic fight not cost effective in secular eyes. Although Zhu Zhengping's lasting passion for writing can be felt from the book, the words what he used

我有感情。"想来上海留下了朱争平将军人生中最重要的职业与事业履痕,他对上海有大深情和自始至终的赤子之心。有深情者,必有愉色,无畏于时流,有道于高峰。同时他与上海之间,也是不断拓展彼此生命维度的凤缘相遇。足迹所经,年轮所及,弹指芳华,长情长忆。

2018 年 8 月于上海

are clean and restrained, which generates an overwhelming attraction that is both aggressive and quiet. Referring to Mr. Ba Jin's saying, "The reason why I write not because I am talented, but I have emotions", it can be seen that General Zhu Zhengping's most important career and cause path in his life has been kept in Shanghai. He had strong affections for this city with man's natural kindness. Those who with deep affections must boldly face up to hardships and difficulties with a pleasant temperament. Meanwhile, it is a destiny for he encounters Shanghai, which has constantly expanded mutual dimensions of life. Every footprint marks the growth ring with the passage of time, beckoning a recollection of Old Shanghai's vicissitudes.

August 2018, Shanghai

老上海的月份牌

月份牌是旧上海政治、经济、文化相互作用的产物,对研究我国近代史、绘画史、商业史以及戏剧、影视、烟草、服饰等有着不可替代的重要价值。

鸦片战争后,上海被迫作为通商口岸开埠,渐成商业繁华之地。随着先进彩印技术的传入以及外国商品的输入,新生的民族资本家仿照洋商在商品中附带印有美女、风景、静物等外国画片进行商业宣传的做法,开始大量印制融中国传统文化和民俗风情于一体的年画,与洋行竞争商品销路。月份牌由此应运而生。

实际上,在1906年清廷发布《政治官报章程》中,已使用"广告"一词,宣告了中国现代广告的诞生。而月份牌则是老百姓喜闻乐见的中国最早的广告形式。月份牌画的题材和内容主要是美女,亦有风景,同时还有古典人物、历史故事、时代女装。西施、杨贵妃、王昭君、貂蝉等古代四大美女以及旧时名伶、名模、名演员在月份牌上最为常见。广告的商品大多是香烟、电池、百货、保险、肥皂、酒类等。这种广告既满足了市民对美的欣赏,又促销了产品,因而在上世纪20、30年代,月份牌的绘画艺术达到了前所未有的

Calendar Poster of Old Shanghai

The calendar poster is the product of interaction of politics, economy and culture in old Shanghai, which is of irreplaceable importance to the study of China's modern history, painting history, commercial history, drama, film and television, tobacco, clothing and so on.

After the First Opium War, Shanghai was coerced to open its port as a trading port and gradually became a prosperous place for business. With the introduction of advanced color printing technologies and the import of foreign goods, the new-generation national capitalist imitated the foreign businessmen to advertise by printing beautiful women, scenery, still life and other foreign pictures on the goods and began the business competition with foreign businessmen by printing a large number of calendar posters with an integration of traditional culture and folk customs. Therefore, the calendar poster emerged.

Actually, in the *Constitution of the Political Organ* issued by the government of the Qing Dynasty in 1906, the word "advertisement" had been used, which announced the birth of China's modern advertising. The calendar poster was the earliest form of advertising in China, whichwas favored by ordinary people. The theme and contents of the pictures on the calendar posterswere mainly beautiful ladies and sceneries, as well as classical persons, historic stories and fashionable women's dresses. The most common pictures on the calendar posters were the four ancient beauties such as XI Shi, YANG Yuhuan, WANG Zhaojun and DIAO Chan, as well as reputeddrama actresses, models and actors.

ZHOU Muqiao was the early representative figure of calendar poster creation. He

高峰。

周慕桥是月份牌创作的早期代表人物。他传统画功力深厚，对古装人物画情有独钟，后在传统画的基础上糅入了西画造型和透视，画面视觉效果特别，作品很受欢迎。郑曼陀是中国近代广告擦笔绘画技法的创始人。他特别注意画人物的眼珠，使观众与画中人的视线接触时，产生"眼睛能跟人跑"的效果，因而名声大振。不少人仿效他的画风，以使擦笔水彩时装美人月份牌画成为

← 杭稚英　弹琵琶女郎

had profound skills in traditional painting and showed special preference to ancient-costume figure painting. Later, he integrated the modeling and perspective of western painting into traditional painting, thus presenting distinctive visual effects, which was very popular. ZHENG Mantuo was the founder of brush-rubbing painting technique of China's modern advertising. He paid special attention to the eyes of the characters, making the audience experience the effect of "eyes can run with people" while contacting with the eyes of the people in the paintings and become very famous for it. Many people imitated his painting style, which made the brush-rubbing watercolor painting of fashion beauty calendar poster become a popular form of advertising paintings. HU Boxiang was a characteristic calendar poster painter. He was the only designer at the time who insisted on the traditional ink style and then applied the watercolor cover dyeing, instead of the brush-rubbing technique. With the use of translucent watercolor cover dyeing, the characters in his paintings owned delicate and tender skin, showing the sweet, waxy, satay and tender charm, so he was the highest paid calendar poster painter of the year. HANG Zhiying owned the unique position in the history of calendar poster creation. He founded China's earliest modern advertising company and designed more than 1600 kinds of calendar posters. His works, such as *My Dear Cigarettes* and *Two Girls Floral Water*, swept the county and formed the "Hang School" of calendar poster creation. The representative figures of calendar poster creation in old Shanghai also included XIE Zhiguang, YUAN Xiutang, NI Gengye and LIANG Dingming, etc. They all had profound painting skills with pristine painting styles and different characteristics.

After the founding of the People's Republic of China, the calendar poster underwent socialist transformation and gradually became the calendar-poster New Year picture with Shanghai style, commonly known as "Shanghai-style New Year picture". Its theme and content mainly reflected the industrial, agricultural and military figures and new development of socialism in the new life. In the 1950s and 1960s, it was the peak period of new calendar poster creation. In the beginning of "the Cultural Revolution", calendar poster, as the "four old ideas and old culture", was banned and experienced decline from then on. After the reform and opening up, with the rise of wall calendars and pure

广告画的一种流行形式。胡伯翔又是一个富于个性特色的月份牌画家。他是当时唯一不使用擦笔技法而坚持传统水墨造型再敷水彩罩染的设计师。他笔下的人物在半透明的水彩罩染下形成细致柔嫩的肌肤感觉，传递出甜、糯、嗲、嫩的风韵，因而他是当年薪酬最高的月份牌画家。杭稚英在月份牌创作史上地位独特。他开创了中国最早的现代广告公司，设计的月份牌超过 1600 种。他的作品《美丽牌香烟》、《双妹牌花露水》等风靡全国，形成了月份牌创作中的"杭派"。老上海月份牌创作的代表人物还有谢之光、袁秀堂、倪耕野、梁鼎铭等，他们个个笔力深厚、画风纯朴、特色各异。

← 胡伯翔月份牌作品

advertisements, as well as the rapid development of science& technology and media, the calendar-poster New Year picture gradually withdrew from the historical stage. However, as the old urban landscape slowly disappeared, nostalgia rekindled. In some hotels and restaurants in Shanghai, replicas of old-style calendar posters have become a fashionable decoration. It seems that those ethereal and attracting beauties in the old calendar posters are telling people the beautiful totem of commerce in old Shanghai. People look for romance and memories from these old calendar posters. And the authentic works of

先施化妆品有限公司　作者：杭穉英　年份：1935　尺寸：53×77cm
上海杨培明宣传画收藏艺术馆提供

→ 月份牌

新中国成立后，月份牌经历了社会主义改造，逐渐成为具有上海风格的月份牌年画，俗称"海派年画"。其题材和内容主要反映新生活中的工农兵人物和社会主义新景象。上世纪50、60年代，是新月份牌创作的鼎盛阶段。"文革"初期，月份牌被作为"四旧"受到禁止，从此衰亡。改革开放后，随着挂历和纯广告的兴起以及科技和媒体的迅速发展，月份牌形式的年画逐渐退出了历史舞台。然而，随着城市旧景观的慢慢消失，怀旧情愫复燃。走进上海的一些宾馆饭店，各种旧式月份牌的复制品成为一种时尚装饰。那些飘渺在老月份牌里的香鬓云衫、韵致天成的淑女，仿佛在向人们诉说着旧时上海商业的美丽图腾。人们从这些老月份牌中寻找一份浪漫和对往事的回忆。而月份牌真迹，已成为难觅的收藏种类，备受藏家们的推崇。

月份牌作为一种民族绘画形式，记录着一个时代的历史与文化。繁荣和发展社会主义大文化，我们不应该忘记月份牌所作的贡献。

2012年4月

calendar posters have become rare collections and are highly respected by collectors.

As a national form of painting, calendar posters have recorded the history and culture of an era. We should not forget the contribution of calendar posters to the prosperity and development of the big socialist culture.

April 2012

老上海的古玩店

老上海的古玩业是海上文化市场的重要组成部分。

上海开埠后，渐成为中国文物贸易的主要集散地，形成了当时中国最大的古玩市场。1853年，为避太平军兵火，由南京、苏州等地迁沪的一批古玩商在原南市区侯家路设立的玉业汇市公所，在城隍庙花园开业的四美轩，在新北门开业的天宝斋等是上海最早的古玩行业组织和古玩店。进入19世纪后，社会动荡，战火不断，古玩货源开始多起来，使得上海古玩市场颇显起色。一大批逃难上海的前清遗老、失意军阀等携带大量古玩细软来到租界做起了寓公。为了维持奢侈的生活，他们将一件件古董送进店铺。在上海的外国人发现很容易就能买到中国古物，因而形成了一支收藏中国古董的洋人队伍。在租界与旧城相接的老北门、新北门一带成为上海开埠后最大的古玩业汇市，从古斋、辟玉林、仪古斋等当时上海最有影响的古玩店铺都集中于此。上世纪20年代后，上海的古玩业日趋繁荣，至40年代，古玩店铺多达数百家。

老上海的古玩店有的是兼营，但大多是专营。如专营字画，专

Antique Shop of Old Shanghai

The antique industry of old Shanghai is an important part of Shanghai-style cultural market.

After Shanghai opened its port, it gradually became the main collecting and distributing center of trade for China's cultural relics and formed the largest antique market in China at that time. In 1853, in order to avoid the warfare of the Taiping Army, a group of antique dealers moved from Nanjing, Suzhou and other places to Shanghai and then set up the Foreign Exchange Association of Jade Industry at Houjia Road of the former Nanshi District, Simeixuan at City God Temple Garden and Tianbaozhai at New North Gate, which were the oldest antique trade organizations and antique shops in Shanghai. In the 19th century, due to social instability and ongoing wars, the supply of antique goods began to increase, which brought significant improvement to the antique market in Shanghai. A large number of old adherents of the Qing Dynasty and frustrated warlords fled to Shanghai Concession and brought a large number of antiques and valuables. In order to maintain luxurious life, they sold the antiques to the shops. Foreigners in Shanghai found that it was easy to buy Chinese antiques and then there formed a team of foreigners who focused on collecting Chinese antiques. Therefore, the largest antique industry foreign exchange market since Shanghai opened its port, had emerged in the areas of Old North Gate and New North Gate, the junction of the Concession and the old city. The most influential antique shops in Shanghai at that time, such as Congguzhai, Piyulin and Yiguzhai, were located here. Since the 1920s, the antique industry in Shanghai began to boom. By the 1940s, there were hundreds of antique shops.

Some of the antique shops in old Shanghai were concurrently engaged in multiple fields, but most were specialized in one field. For example, there were antique shops

营玉器，专营青铜器，专营瓷器、木器、象牙、钱币、景泰蓝等。当时比较出名的字画专营店有达永清、杨大记、集宝斋等，玉器有瑞文斋、彝古斋、马呈记等，象牙有黄鹤记、王永记、同兴斋等，瓷器有王少泉、童庆记、李昌记等。还有一些古玩店专营出口业务，旅法华商卢芹斋与上海古玩商人吴启周等联合创设的卢吴公司，是中国开办最早，向外国贩运珍贵文物数量最多、经营时间最长、影

老上海的古玩店　贺竹元绘

specialized in calligraphy & painting, jade ware, bronze ware, porcelain, woodware, ivory, coin and cloisonné, etc. Prestigious antique shops specialized in calligraphy & painting included Dayongqing, Yangdaji and Jibaozhai, etc. Reputed antique shops specialized in jade ware included Ruiwenzhai, Yiguzhai and Machengji, etc. Renowned antique shops specialized in ivory included Huangheji, Wangyongji and Tongxingzhai, etc. Famous antique shops specialized in porcelain included Wangshaoquan, Tongqingji and Lichangji, etc. And there were some antique shops specialized in export businesses. LU-WU Company, jointly founded by Chinese French businessman LU Qinzhai and Shanghai antique dealer WU Qizhou, was China's earliest private company that exported the largest number of precious cultural relics to foreign countries and boasted the longest operating time and the greatest influence.

In order to protect the interests of the industry, some antique dealers with legal awareness launched and established a variety of industry organizations. Shanghai Special City Antique Trade Association, located at No. 67, Jiangxi Road, had recruited more than 200 members at its peak period and specially hired the lawyers of Citibank. Shanghai Antique Commercial Trade Association consisted of teams including general affairs, communication, investigation, accounting, evaluation and identification, thus assisting the members in resolving disputes. These industry organizations played a positive role in normalizing the antique market order in Shanghai.

The antique dealers in old Shanghai were many industrialists with lofty patriotic spirit. YAN Huiyu, the founder of Kunban of New Yuefu, was one of them. During the Anti-Japanese War, the wealthy Jiangnan region was occupied by the enemy, and people with some fortunes fled to the isolated island of Shanghai for refuge. Many people without a source of livelihood depended on the sale of antique paintings and calligraphy to make a living. YAN Huiyu was very sad to see a large number of antique paintings and calligraphy be acquired by foreigners and resold overseas. In order to protect Chinese cultural relics, he opened an antique shop "Yunqilou" at Shaanxi North Road. He invited the famous publisher and collector QIN Gengnian and the famous calligrapher & painter and collector TANG Dingzhi as the managers and specially invited the three famous painters and

响最大的私人公司。

为了保障同业权益，一些具有法律意识的古玩商发起成立了各种不同的行业组织。位于江西路67号的上海特别市古玩业同业公会，鼎盛时会员有200多人，还专门聘请了花旗银行律师。上海市古玩商业同业公会设总务、交际、调查、会计、评议及鉴定各组，协调会员解决纠纷。这些行业组织，对正规当时上海古玩市场秩序起到了积极作用。

老上海的古玩商不少是具有崇高爱国气节的实业家，新乐府昆班的创始人严惠宇就是其中一位。抗战期间，富有的江南地区沦陷，稍有家产的人都逃难到孤岛上海避难，许多没有生活来源的人靠出卖古董字画维持生计。严惠宇看到大量的古董字画被外国人收购，转售海外，心情十分沉重。为了保护中华文物，他在今陕西北路开设了古玩店云起楼。他请印坛名宿兼收藏大家秦更年，书画家兼收藏家汤定之为掌眼人，又聘潘君诺、刘伯年、尤无曲三位名画家兼鉴定家专门修复古字画，为上海地区文物、字画的保护起到了重要作用。全国解放后，严惠宇将5000余件珍藏全部捐献给上海、南京、镇江3家博物馆。

新中国成立后，上海古玩商业系统实行全行业公私合营。以后由于政治运动不断，古玩市场逐渐萎缩。上世纪80年代后，中国进入改革开放的盛世，上海古玩市场开始复苏。如今，除上海文物商店、朵云轩、上海古籍书店等老牌文物店外，形成

↗ 古董店

appraisers—PAN Junnuo, LIU Bonian and YOU Wuqu to restore the ancient calligraphy and paintings, which played an important role in the protection of cultural relics and paintings in Shanghai. After the liberation of China, YAN Huiyu donated more than 5000 pieces of treasures to three museums in Shanghai, Nanjing and Zhenjiang.

After the founding of the People's Republic of China, Shanghai antique commercial system implemented public-private partnership in the whole industry. Since then, as a result of the political campaigns, the antique market has gradually declined and fallen. After the 1980s, China entered the heyday of reform and opening-up and the antique market in Shanghai began to recover. Nowadays, besides the Shanghai Cultural Relics Store, Duoyunxuan, Shanghai Ancient Bookstore and other old-line cultural relics stores, there have formed the antique market, including Yunzhou Antique City, Cangbaolou at City God Temple, Zhongfu Antique City, Antique Street at Dongtai Road, etc. Thousands of private and folk antique shops with different characteristics have various kinds of antiques and crafts showcased, becoming a beautiful landscape of Shanghai's cultural market.

Culture is the most vivid reflection of social life. The history of Shanghai antique industry, from one perspective, has reflected the political, economic and social

了云洲古玩城、城隍庙藏宝楼、中福古玩城、东台路古玩街等古玩集市。千余家各具特色的民营和民间古玩店铺鳞次栉比，林林总总展示着各式各样的古玩工艺品，成为上海文化市场一道靓丽的景观。

　　文化是社会生活最生动的反映。上海古玩业的历史，从一个侧面，折射出近代上海政治、经济、社会的发展变迁。乱世黄金，盛世古玩。愿上海的古玩市场长盛不衰。

2012 年 5 月

development and changes of modern Shanghai. Gold is favored by collectors in troubled times, while antique is favored in prosperous times. We wish the antique market in Shanghai would be prosperous forever.

May 2015

老上海的电影业

　　老上海的电影业是中国近代民族电影发展史的一个缩影。

　　1913年，中国第一部故事片《难夫难妻》在上海问世。由此，改写了自19世纪末电影进入中国后上海虽有影业但都是外国人所为的历史。上世纪20年代，明星公司等一批电影公司纷纷在上海成立，掀开了中国电影发展史的重要一页。30年代，上海影业步入黄金时代，被誉为"东方好莱坞"。中国"左联"在上海成立后，党领导的进步文化人进军电影阵地。第一部左翼影片《狂流》和《渔光曲》、《十字街头》、《马路天使》等一批爱国进步电影的诞生，使得电影不再沉湎于家庭伦理、儿女私情、滑稽打闹，而是直面阶级矛盾，关注民族生存。孤岛时期及上海沦陷后，爱国影人顶住重重压力，拍摄出了《木兰从军》等一批具有民族气节的影片。抗战胜利后，上海影业同国民党反动派的文化施压进行了针锋相对的斗争，拍摄了《八千里路云和月》、《一江春水向东流》等具有巨大社会反响的进步影片。《乌鸦与麻雀》是上海解放前拍摄的最后一部影片，成为迎接新曙光的最佳电影。新中国成立后，上海影业在复杂的政治环境中曲折发展，生产出了一批深受广大观众喜爱的优秀影片。

　　老上海电影公司林立，鼎盛时多达140多家。上世纪20、30年

Film Industry of Old Shanghai

The film industry of old Shanghai is an epitome of the development history of modern Chinese national film industry.

In 1913, the first Chinese feature film *Die for Marriage* was launched in Shanghai. Therefore, the history of "all films are produced by foreigners" in Shanghai film industry had been rewritten since the introduction of films into China at the end of the 19th century. In the 1920s, a number of film companies such as Star Film Company were founded in Shanghai, which opened an important page in the history of Chinese film development. In the 1930s, Shanghai film industry entered the golden age and was praised as "Oriental Hollywood". After the establishment of China's "League of Left-Wing Writers" (Left League) in Shanghai, the progressive intellectuals marched into the film industry. There emerged the first left-league film *Raging Waves* and many patriotic progressive films, including *Song of The Fishermen*, *The Cross of the Street* and *Angels on the Road*, etc., thus making the films no longer focus on family ethics, love affairs and funny slapstick, but more concern the class contradictions and national existence. During the Isolated-Island period and Shanghai's occupation by the Japanese, patriotic film works withstood the heavy pressure and produced a number of films with national integrity, such as *Mulan Joins the Army*. After the victory of the Anti-Japanese War, Shanghai film industry fought against the cultural pressure from Kuomintang reactionaries and produced lots of progressive films with great social response, such as *Eight Thousand Li of Cloud and Moon*, *Spring River Flows East*, etc. *Crow and Sparrow* was the last film shot before the liberation of Shanghai, becoming the best film to embrace the new dawn. After the founding of the People's Republic of China in 1949, Shanghai film industry experienced

代，明星、联华、天一三家公司最负盛名。由张石川、郑正秋、周剑云等人组建的明星公司坚持"教化社会"的宗旨和电影与民族文化传统结合的艺术主张，公司成立15年间共拍摄影片200余部。由黎民伟、罗明佑、吴性裁、但杜宇联合组建的联华影业公司，以"提倡艺术、宣扬文化、启发民智、挽救影业"为口号，将影片内容从家庭伦理转向社会问题，拍摄出了一批优秀影片。由邵醉翁兄弟创办的天一公司拍摄的《电影女明星》，成为中国第一部发行海外的影片。老上海有影响的电影公司还有长城、神州、新华、国泰、昆仑、文华、艺华等，它们为中国民族电影事业的发展作出了重要贡献。

老上海影业刷新了中国电影多个零的纪录。中国第一部有声片《歌女红牡丹》、第一部武侠片《女侠李飞飞》、第一部反帝片《黑籍冤魂》、第一部体育片《二对一》、第一部彩色戏曲片《生死恨》、第一部动画片《大闹画室》等都诞生在上海。

老上海影坛造就了一批著名电影编导。郑正秋是中国第一代电影编导的杰出代表。他与张石川合作拍摄的《难夫难妻》，为中国电影奠定了现实主义基础。应云卫导演的《桃李劫》是中国第一部真正的有声电影，影片插曲《毕业歌》极大地鼓舞了当时的热血青年。田汉、夏衍、许幸之编导的《风云儿女》激发了救亡图存的民族精神，影片插曲《义勇军进行曲》建国后成为国歌。洪琛、蔡楚生、史东山、阳翰笙、郑君里、孟君谋、卜万苍、孙瑜、汤晓丹、沈西苓、袁牧之、沈浮、费穆、司徒慧敏、于玲、吴永刚、陈鲤庭等都是应该重重书上一笔的电影艺术大师。

↑《八千里路云和月》海报

→《电通》画报第2期（1935年6月1日）为影片《风云儿女》特辑

↑ 阮玲玉

tortuous development in a complex political environment and there produced a number of excellent films favored by the audience.

There were many film companies in old Shanghai, with more than 140 ones at its peak period. In the 1920s and 1930s, Star Film Company, Lianhua Film Company and Tianyi Film Company were the most prestigious film companies. Star Film Company, jointly founded by ZHANG Shichuan, ZHENG Zhengqiu and ZHOU Jianyun, adhered to the tenet of "civilizing the society" and the artistic concept of combining film with national culture and tradition. During the 15 years since its establishment, the company produced over 200 films. Lianhua Film Company, jointly founded by LI Minwei, Luo Mingyou, WU Xingcai and DAN Duyu, upheld the slogan of "advocating art, promoting culture, enlightening people's wisdom and saving the film industry" and produced a number of excellent films by transforming the film contents from family ethics into social issues. *The Movie Actress*, produced by Tianyi Film Company (founded by Runje Shaw and his brother), was the first Chinese film to be released overseas. The influential film companies in old Shanghai also included Great Wall, Shenzhou, Xinhua, Cathay, Kunlun, Wenhua and Yihua, which made important contributions to the development of Chinese national film industry.

The film industry of old Shanghai set several new records for Chinese films., including China's first sound film *Sing-song Girl Red Peony*, China's first swordsmen film *Lee Fee-Fee the Heroing*, China's first anti-imperialist film *Victims of Opium*, China's first sports film *2 VS 1*, China's first color opera film *Regrets of Life and Death* and China's first animated film *Studio Scen*e, which were all produced in Shanghai.

The film industry of old Shanghai cultivated a number of reputed film directors. ZHENG Zhengqiu was an outstanding representative of the first-generation film directors in China. He cooperated with ZHANG Shichuan in producing *Die for Marriage*, laying a realistic foundation for Chinese film industry. *Plunder of Peach and Plum* produced by the director YING Weiyun, was the first real sound film in China and its film interlude— *Graduation Song* greatly encouraged the young people of that era. *Children of Trouble Time*, jointly directed by TIAN Han, XIA Yan and XU Xingzhi, inspired the national

老上海影坛星光灿烂。明星公司"四大金刚"王汉伦、杨耐梅、宣景琳、张织云,"电影皇帝"金焰、"电影皇后"胡蝶、一代影星阮玲玉、歌影双星周旋,以及赵丹、石挥、舒适、金山、陈玉梅、邬丽珠、殷明珠、王人美、舒秀文、吴茵、白杨、张瑞芳、上官云珠、黄宗英、秦怡、王丹凤……犹如一颗颗闪亮的明珠,永远镶嵌在银幕上。

如今,中国进入盛世,电影业却遇到了市场经济和新兴媒体的挑战。振兴影业,需要弘扬老上海影人忠诚影业、不甘人后、勇于担当、敢于创新的革命精神和艺术勇气。只要我们殚智竭力,再铸上海影业的辉煌应是可期的。

2012 年 6 月

spirit of saving the nation from subjugation and its film interlude— *March of the Volunteers* became the national anthem after the founding of People's Republic of China. There were also many other renowned film masters, including HONG Chen, CAI Chusheng, SHI Dongshan, YANG Hansheng, ZHENG Junli, MENG Junmou, BU Wancang, SUN Yu, TANG Xiaodan, SHEN Xiling, YUAN Muzhi, SHEN Fu, FEI Mu, SITU Huimin, YU Ling, WU Yonggang ad CHEN Liting, etc.

There were many film stars in old Shanghai, including the "Four Guardians" of Star Film Company— WANG Hanlun, YANG Naimei, XUAN Jinglin and ZHANG Zhiyun; the "King of Film" JIN Yan and the "Queen of Film" HU Die; the famous film star RUAN Lingyu; the film star and singer ZHOU Xuan, as well as ZHAO Dan, SHI Hui, SHU Shi, JIN Shan, CHEN Yumei, WU Lizhu, YIN Mingzhu, WANG Renmei, SHU Xiuwen, WU Yin, BAI Yang, ZHANG Ruifang, SHANGGUAN Yunzhu, HUANG Zongying, QIN Yi and WANG Danfeng, etc. They were like the shining pearls inlaid on the screen forever.

Now, China has entered its golden age, but the film industry is confronted with the challenges of the market economy and emerging media. To revitalize the film industry, we need to carry forward the revolutionary spirit and artistic courage of the old Shanghai film workers who are loyal to the film industry, unwilling to lag behind, and brave in undertaking and innovation. As long as we do our best, the revival of Shanghai film industry should be expectable.

↗ 胡蝶

老上海的舞厅

奢靡浮华的老上海舞厅是时人神往的去处。透过这风花雪月的休闲场所，可以窥见上海娱乐业发展的历史轨迹。

上海开埠后特殊的政治格局，形成了以英租界为核心的市中心区域，西藏路沿线成为上海的中央娱乐区。位于西藏路巴黎饭店内的黑猫舞厅诞生于上世纪20年代，是老上海第一家独立经营的舞厅。此后，月宫、老大华、安乐宫、圣爱娜等舞厅相继开张。30年代，上海经济畸形繁荣，奢靡之风盛行，舞业迅速发展，西藏路被称为"舞场路"。

百乐门、大都会、仙乐斯、新仙林是当时最具代表性的舞厅，被称为老上海的"四大歌舞厅"。中国商人顾联承于1932年投资70万两白银建造的百乐门舞厅号称"东方第一乐府"，最大舞池500多平方米，大舞池周围有可以随意分割的小舞池，供舞客习舞和幽会。舞池的地板用汽车钢板支托，富有弹性。室内冷暖空调，陈设豪华。广东商人江耀章1934年营建的大都会舞厅是老上海夜生活的地标之一，建筑风格自成一体，外呈八角形，里面正中一个穹窿顶，顶下正对圆形舞池，四周雕梁画栋，古色古香，与洋派的百乐门舞厅风格迥异。英籍商人沙逊建造的仙乐斯舞宫，将古典风格与现代气派

↑ 当年舞会场景

Ballroom of Old Shanghai

The luxurious and buckish ballrooms of old Shanghai were an attractive place for people of that era. This romantic leisure land testified to the development history of Shanghai's entertainment industry.

Due to the special political pattern after Shanghai opened its port, there formed the downtown area with the British Concession as the core and the Central Entertainment District along Xizang Road in Shanghai. The Black Cat Ballroom, located at Paris Hotel, Xizang Road and founded in the 1920s, was the first independently operated ballroom in Shanghai. Since then, the Moon Palace, Old Dahua, Pleasure Palace, Saint Ana and other ballrooms has opened one after another. In the 1930s, Shanghai's economy underwent abnormal prosperity and the trend of extravagance prevailed, thus bringing about the rapid development of the dance industry. Therefore, Xizang Road was called "Ballroom Road".

融为一体，被时人称为远东一流舞宫。新仙林舞厅前面有一个大花园，每逢夏季，花园里霓虹闪烁，红男绿女，美酒咖啡，轻歌曼舞，成为老上海最迷人的露天花园舞场。

　　交谊舞随西方冒险家进入上海，因而老上海舞厅既有洋派的豪华富贵又有海派的优雅情调。当时舞厅乐队主要来自南洋和西洋。百乐门舞厅30年代就由卡拉扬爵士乐团演奏，钢琴、单簧管、萨克斯、低音提琴、号、鼓、沙槌、打击乐等合成的西洋乐演奏着《夜来香》、《玫瑰玫瑰我爱你》等金曲，加上周璇、白光、吴莺音等海上红歌星的伴唱和红舞女的伴舞，舞池充满柔情似水的话旧轻愁。派拉蒙电影里有句旁白："老百乐门爵士乐队响起了，你无法拒绝华

↖ 百乐门舞厅内景

Paramount, Metropolitan, CIROS and New Xianlin were the most representative ballrooms, known as the "four major ballrooms" of old Shanghai. Paramount, founded by the Chinese businessman GU Liancheng in 1932 with an investment of 700,000 liang of silvers, was known as "the largest oriental ballroom". Its largest dancing floor boasted an area of more than 500 square meters. Around the large dancing floor, there were small dancing floors which could be divided at random for the dancers to dance and date. The floor of the dancing floor was supported with auto steel plates, full of flexibility. There were indoor air conditioning and luxurious furnishings. Metropolitan, founded by a Guangdong businessman JIANG Yaozhang in 1934, was one of the landmarks of night life in old Shanghai. Its architectural style was unique. It looked like an octagonal outside and had a dome on the center inside with the round dancing floor just below and carved beams and painted pillars all around. Its antique beauty made it very different from the exotic Paramount. CIROS, founded by a British businessman Sassoon, integrated the classical style into the modern style, which was known as the "first-class oriental dance palace". There was a large garden in front of New Xianlin. Every summer, the garden was neon-lit and people were enjoying wine and coffee, singing and dancing here, thus making it become the most attractive outdoor garden dance venue in old Shanghai.

Social dancing was introduced into Shanghai by the western adventurers, so that the ballrooms of old Shanghai were both full of the luxurious exotic style and the elegant Shanghai style. At that time, the bands of the ballrooms mainly came from Southeast Asia and the Western world. Paramount had the famous songs performed by Karajan jazz band with a combination of piano, clarinet, saxophone, contrabass, horn, drum, maracas and percussion, such as *Evening Primrose* and *Rose, Rose, I Love You*. Moreover, there were reputed singers including ZHOU Xuan, BAI Guang and WU Yingyin to perform vocal accompaniment and famous dancers to be the dancing partners, thus making the dancing floors full of romance and sentiment. A narratage in a Paramount film said, "When the jazz band in old Paramount began to perform, you can't refuse the resplendent turn-back." The ballrooms of old Shanghai were the first choice for Chinese and foreign

丽转身"。老上海舞厅是中外显贵巨商夜生活的首选之地,蒋介石、张学良、黄金荣、杜月笙、徐志摩等都曾光顾。世界著名影星卓别林夫妇访问上海仅留一晚,特为到百乐门一展舞姿。陈香梅与美国飞虎将军陈纳德的订婚仪式也在百乐门举行。

老上海舞厅见证上海经济社会的历史变迁。上世纪30年代是上海舞场的全盛时期,职业舞女数千人,舞厅与影院、戏院在娱乐界形成三足鼎立之势。曹禺的《日出》、于伶的《花溅泪》都是以舞女生活为素材写的著名剧作。抗战期间,一些国人为逃避现实,舞厅成为他们今朝有酒今朝醉的去处。抗战胜利,上海光复,舞厅更加热闹起来。1947年国民党政府因内战失利,为整饬军纪,限令国内

← 舞厅中伺候舞女的童仆,又名小郎

dignitaries and businessmen to enjoy their night life. Chiang Kai-shek, Chang Hsueh-liang, HUANG Jinrong, DU Yuesheng and XU Zhimo had ever visited Paramount. The world-famous Chaplin couple visited Shanghai for only one night and specially visited Paramount to have a dance. The engagement ceremony of CHEN Xiangmei and the American Flying General Chenault was also held in the Paramount.

The ballrooms of old Shanghai witnessed the historical changes of Shanghai's economy and society. The ballrooms in Shanghai experienced the heyday in the 1930s, when there were thousands of professional dancers. The ballrooms, the cinemas and the theaters formed a situation of tripartite confrontation in the entertainment industry. CAO Yu's *Sunrise* and YU Ling's *A Dancing-girl's Fate* are famous dramas based on the life of a dancing girl. During the Anti-Japanese War, the ballrooms became the places for some Chinese people to drink and escape from the reality. With the victory of the war and the recovery of Shanghai, the ballrooms became more popular. In 1947, due to the defeat in the civil war, the Kuomintang Government overhauled the military discipline and closed down all the domestic ballrooms. A large number of people in the dance industry were unemployed. As a result, the "dance-strike case" in Shanghai shocked the whole country, and the ban on dancing was canceled. Up to the eve of liberation, there were more than 100 dancing venues in Shanghai, ranking top in China's major cities. After the founding of People's Republic of China, the dance industry was able to renovate. Due to ongoing political movements, the once prosperous Shanghai dance industry had gradually declined. In the mid-1980s, social dancing became a new fashion with the spring breeze of reform and opening up, first popular in university campuses and later on in offices and communities. Old ballrooms such as Paramount and Metropolitan, which had been closed for many years, resumed business, and lots of new ones had opened one after one. But with the development of economy and technology, new forms of entertainment such as karaoke and KTV emerged. The single-phase corridor, padauk dancing floor, spiral stair, jazz band and nostalgic golden melody of Paramount had become the epitome of the history and culture of old Shanghai. People came here just wanting to experience the Shanghai charm in the past. The nightclubs, KTV and discos were the really popular places

舞场全部停业，大批舞业人员失业，致使上海发生震惊全国的"舞潮案"，禁舞令被迫取消。至解放前夕，上海舞场计100多家，居国内各大城市之首。新中国成立后，舞业得以整治。随着政治运动不断，曾经盛极一时的上海舞业逐步衰落。上世纪80年代中期，交谊舞随改革开放的春风，先是在大学校园，后又延伸到机关和社区，成为新的时尚。歇业多年的百乐门、大都会等老舞厅恢复营业，新舞厅纷纷开张。但随着经济和科技的发展，出现了卡拉OK、KTV等新的娱乐形式。百乐门的回马廊、紫檀木舞池、旋转楼梯、爵士乐队、怀旧金曲已成为老上海历史与文化的缩影，人们来这里只是想体验一下昔日的上海风情。而华灯初上的夜总会、KTV，劲歌劲舞的迪斯科舞厅才是当下年轻人夜生活的真正去处。目前，上海注册的夜总会、迪厅等娱乐场所已逾2000家，娱乐业呈现空前的多彩与繁华。

老上海的舞厅，海上娱乐业曾经的辉煌。这段历史，将永载老上海的风情画卷。

2012年6月

for young people to enjoy their night life. At present, there are more than 2,000 entertainment venues registered in Shanghai, such as nightclubs and discos. The entertainment industry was undergoing unprecedented abundance and prosperity

The ballrooms of old Shanghai have represented the glory of Shanghai's entertainment industry in the past. This part of history will be drawn on the scroll of Shanghai charm forever.

June 2012

老上海的话剧

老上海的话剧史是中国近现代话剧史的缩影。在上海话剧舞台日趋繁荣的今天,我们不能忘记老一代剧人曾经创造的辉煌和留下的传统。

1907年9月在上海由春阳社演出的《黑奴吁天录》,标志着话剧在中国的开场。此后,被时人叫做"新剧"的文明戏即早期话剧在上海兴起。文明戏大大改变了中国人的戏剧观念,真实地表现了当时急剧变革的社会现实,为中国话剧的民族化提供了最初的经验。"五四"新文化运动掀开了中国戏剧史新的一页。为了改变由于戏剧商业化使得文明戏日渐衰败的局面,上海进步剧人在"新青年派"戏剧改革理论的感召下,尝试通过非盈利的演剧形式摆脱商业化的桎梏,重振新剧的雄风,上海话剧进入"爱美的"戏剧时代。爱美剧运动有力扭转了民初以来文明戏衰退的趋势,奠定了健康的现代话剧发展方向。1930年前后,正当爱美的戏剧完成它的历史使命之际,中国共产党领导的第一个剧团——艺术剧社宣告成立,鲜明提出了"无产阶级戏剧"的口号。这是现代话剧史上具有划时代意义的重要转折。由此,掀起了轰轰烈烈的左翼戏剧运动。左翼戏剧工作者们提出了"国防戏剧"的口号,旗帜鲜明地反对国民党政府专

Drama of Old Shanghai

The drama history of old Shanghai is the epitome of modern Chinese drama. Today, with the increasing prosperity of Shanghai dramas, we cannot forget the glory and tradition created by the older generation of drama workers.

Life Among the Lowly, performed by Spring Sun Society in Shanghai in September 1907, marked the beginning of dramas in China. Since then, the so-called "modern drama", or early drama had prevailed in Shanghai. Modern dramas greatly changed the Chinese people's theatrical concept and truly manifested the then drastically revolutionary social reality, providing the initial experience for the nationalization of Chinese dramas. The "May 4th" New Culture Movement opened a new page in the history of Chinese dramas. In order to change the declining situation of modern dramas caused by the commercialization of dramas, the progressive drama workers in Shanghai, inspired by the drama reform theory of "new youth school", tried to get rid of the shackles of commercialization through the non-profit drama performance, and revitalized the vigor of new dramas. Shanghai dramas entered the era of "amateur" dramas. The "amateur drama movement" had effectively reversed the declining trend of modern dramas since the early period of the Republic of China and established a healthy development direction for modern dramas. Around 1930, just as the "amateur" drama completed its historical mission, the first modern drama troupe led by the Communist Party of China — the Art Drama Society, was founded and clearly put forward the slogan of "proletarian drama", which was an important turning point with epoch-making significance in the history of modern drama. Therefore, the left-wing drama movement was launched. The left-wing drama workers put forward the slogan of "defense drama" to clearly oppose the Kuomintang Government's

制独裁和消极抗日政策。在"国防戏剧"的旗帜下,上海迅速掀起了新一轮的话剧活动浪潮。党领导下的以上海为核心的左翼戏剧和国防戏剧运动,给内忧外患的中国人带来了信心和希望,现代话剧走向成熟。抗战八年直至新中国成立,上海话剧发挥了革命文艺的重要作用,创造了话剧史上的战斗辉煌。新中国成立后,上海话剧在曲折中发展,走过了一段极不平常的历程。改革开放的春风,使上海话剧走进新世纪。

老上海话剧发展的每个历史阶段,都有一批代表性的话剧社和话剧作品。谈到中国话剧在上海的诞生,就不能不提到春阳社和《黑奴吁天录》、《迦茵小传》。谈到文明戏的兴衰,就不能不提到新民社、启民社、民鸣社、民兴社、开明社、春柳剧场和《爱海波》、

←《保卫卢沟桥》在上海首演

despotic dictatorship and passive anti-Japanese policies. Under the banner of "defense drama", there quickly set off a new wave of drama activities in Shanghai. Under the leadership of CPC, the left-wing drama movement and defense drama movement with Shanghai as the core brought confidence and hope to the Chinese people who suffered from both internal and external troubles, thus making the modern drama become mature. From the Anti-Japanese War to the founding of People's Republic of China, Shanghai dramas played an important role in revolutionary literature and art and created the fighting glory in the history of dramas. After the founding of People's Republic of China, Shanghai dramas experienced tortuous development and underwent a very unusual course. The spring breeze of reform and opening-up brought Shanghai dramas into the new century.

In each historical stage of the development of the old Shanghai drama, there were a number of representative drama societies and drama works. When it came to the birth of Chinese dramas in Shanghai, we cannot help but mention the Spring Sun Society and its works including *Life Among the Lowly* and *Joan Haste* . When it came to the rise and fall of modern dramas, we cannot help but mention the Xinmin Society, Qimin Society, Minming Society, Minxing Society, Kaiming Society, Soring Willow Theater and their works including *Love Haibo*, *Turn Head Strongly*, *Bloody Coir Raincoat* and *Long Live of Republicanism* . When it came to "amateur drama", we cannot helpbut mention the Mass Drama Society, Cooperative Theater Association, Nanguo Society, Xinyou Drama Society and their works including *The Young Mistress' Fan*, *The Most Important Thing in Life*, *The Death of the Famous Drama Actor* and *A Peasant's Tragedy* . When it came to the left-wing drama and defense drama, we cannot helpbut mention the Art Drama Society, Alliance of Left-Wing Drama Troupes, Travel Drama Troupe of China, Amateur Drama Workers' Association and their works including *Roar, China!*, *Thunderstorm*, *Sunrise*, *Sai Jinhua*, *Put Down Your Whip* and *Under the Roofs of Shanghai* . When it came to Shanghai drama during the period of the Anti-Japanese War, we cannot helpbut mention the13 salvation dram troupes consisting of drama workers in Shanghai drama circle, Shanghai Drama Art Society, Kugan Drama Troupe, Shanghai Art Troupe and their works including *Defend the Lugou Bridge*, *Apartment for Ladies*,

《猛回头》、《血蓑衣》、《共和万岁》。谈到爱美剧,就不能不提到民众戏剧社、戏剧协社、南国社、辛酉剧社和《少奶奶的扇子》、《终身大事》、《名优之死》、《山河泪》。谈到左翼戏剧和国防戏剧,就不能不提到艺术剧社、左翼剧团联盟、中国旅行剧团、业余剧人协会和《怒吼吧,中国!》、《雷雨》、《日出》、《赛金花》、《放下你的鞭子》、《上海屋檐下》。谈到八年抗战时的上海话剧,就不能不提到上海戏剧界人士组成的13个救亡演剧队以及上海剧艺社、苦干剧团、上海艺术剧团和《保卫卢沟桥》、《女子公寓》、《花溅泪》、《葛嫩娘》。谈到解放战争时的上海话剧,就不能不提到上海电影戏剧协会、中国演剧社、观众戏剧演出公司、青春剧艺社和《夜店》、《升官图》、《大地回春》、《丽人行》、《风雪夜归人》。

老上海话剧舞台造就了灿若群星的艺术剧人。"新剧鼻祖"王钟声,进化团派新剧的开拓者任天知及徐半梅、陆镜若、黄喃喃、刘艺舟,"新剧中兴功臣"郑正秋及朱双云,爱美戏剧的发起者汪仲贤、陈大悲,被誉为"中国话剧的三个奠基人"洪深、欧阳予倩、田汉,"专演难剧"的朱穰丞、应云卫、袁牧之、马彦祥、王莹,职业话剧的创始人唐槐秋,剧作家和戏剧导演夏衍、宋之的、陈鲤庭、郑君里、刘保罗、白薇、陈白尘、于伶、章泯、阳翰生、石凌鹤、熊佛西、黄佐临、费穆、吴仞之、朱端钧、阿英、李健吾、杨绛、顾仲彝,表演艺术家唐若青、金山、赵丹、舒绣文、石挥、黄宗江、章曼苹、孙道临、丹尼、白杨、张瑞芳、黄宗英……这里虽然不能一一列举老上海优秀剧人的名字,但历史将记住他们。

自中国话剧在上海诞生后的数十年内,上海一直是中国话剧无

↗《黑奴吁天录》全体演职人员合影

A Dancing-girl's Fate and *Ge Nenniang*. When it came to Shanghai dramas during the period of the War of Liberation, we cannot helpbut mention Shanghai Film& Drama Society, China Drama Show Society, Audience Theatre Company, Youth Drama Society and their works including *Nightclub*, *Dream of Promotion*, *Spring Returns to the Good Earth*, *Three Ladies for the Road* and *Returning Home on a Snowy Night*.

On the stage of old Shanghai drama, there emerged a batch of excellent artistic drama workers, including the "founder of new drama" WANG Zhongsheng, pioneers of the evolution group school of modern dramas REN Tianzhi, XU Banmei, LU Jingruo, HUANG Nanan and LIU Yizhou, "modern dramareviving heroes" ZHENG Zhengqiu and ZHU Shuangyun, initiators of amateur drama WANG Zhongxian and CHEN Dabei, the "three founders of Chinese dramas" HONG Shen, OUYANG Yuqian and TIAN Han, "professional actors specializing in difficult dramas" ZHU Rangcheng, YING Yunwei, YUAN Muzhi, MA Yanxiang and WANG Ying, "founder of professional dramas" TANG Huaiqiu, dramatist and drama director XIA Yan, SONG Zhidi, CHEN Liting, ZHENG Junli, LIU Baoluo, BAI Wei, CHEN Baichen, YU Ling, ZHANG Min, YANG Hansheng, SHI Linghe, XIONG Foxi, HUANG Zuolin, FEI Mu, WU Renzhi, ZHU Duanjun, A Ying, LI Jianwu, YANG Jiang and GU Zhongyi, performing artists TANG Ruoqing, JIN Shan, ZHAO Dan, SHU Xiuwen, SHI Hui, HUANG

可争议的中心。在当代话剧走向多元的今天，重铸上海话剧的辉煌，需要我们解放思想，积极探索话剧的市场化道路。同时，老上海话剧的现实主义战斗传统、人文精神和社会责任感也绝不可或缺。

2012 年 7 月

Zongjiang, ZHANG Manping, SUN Daolin, DAN Ni, BAI Yang, ZHANG Ruifang and HUANG Zongying, etc. It is impossible to list all the names of the excellent drama workers of old Shanghai, but they will be remembered by history.

Shanghai has been the undisputed center of Chinese dramas for decades after the birth of Chinese dramas in Shanghai. Nowadays, modern drama is becomingmore and more diversified. For the resplendence of Shanghai dramas, we needto emancipate our minds and actively explore the market-oriented road of dramas. Meanwhile, the realistic fighting tradition, humanistic spirit and social responsibility of the old Shanghai drama are also indispensable.

July 2012

老上海的影楼

老上海的影楼是上海开埠后市井文化的独特景观。

自 1839 年 8 月法国布景画师达盖尔发明银板照相法，1840 年美国人率先在纽约创办全球第一家照相馆后，随着鸦片战争爆发、外国资本主义势力入侵，照相机和摄影技术开始传入中国。虽然在中国最早引进摄影技术的是广州和香港，但上海却是开展摄影活动最活跃、发展最快的城市。在上海开影楼先是西人所为，但不久就有了国人自己开的影楼。广东人罗元佑原是上海道台吴健彰手下的会计，被革职后随外国人学摄影，成为上海滩最早的职业摄影师，并于 19 世纪 50 年代在上海开了一家专业影楼。据史料记载，19 世纪中期在上海比较活跃的影楼有公泰、苏三兴、森泰、宜昌、丽珠等。止 19 世纪末，上海开设的影楼约 50 多家，大多集中在今南京东路到广东路一带。

早期的照相使用的绝大部分是玻璃底片（湿片），感光速度很慢，当时又没有灯光和其他人造光，必须利用日光，摄影室一般都在楼上开设，所以影楼当时也叫照相楼。在摄影术进入中国之前，人们要把自己的形象保存下来只能到画像馆请画师画。摄影术进入中国初期，由于照相技术和设备尚不成熟，画像馆和影楼并存了很

Photographic Studio of Old Shanghai

The photographic studio is a unique landscape of urban culture after Shanghai's port opening.

Since the French scene painter Daguerre invented the daguerreotype in August 1839 and the American opened the world's first photo studio in New York in 1840, and with the outbreak of the First Opium War and the invasion of foreign capitalist forces into China, the camera and photography began to be introduced into China. Although Guangzhou and Hong Kong were the first to introduce photography in China, Shanghai was the most active and fastest-growing city for photography activities. The first people who opened the photo studio in Shanghai was a westerner and Chinese people opened their own photo studio soon. The Cantonese LUO Yuanyou was once an accountant under the leadership of Shanghai Taotai WU Jianzhang. After he was dismissed, he studied photography with foreigners and became the earliest professional photographer in Shanghai. And in the 1950s, he opened a professional photographic studio in Shanghai. According to historical records, there were several famous photographic studios in Shanghai in the middle half of the 19th century, such as Gongtai, Susanxing, Sentai, Yichang, Lizhu, etc. There were about 50 photographic studios opened in Shanghai by the end of the 19th century, most of which were located along the area from West Nanjing Road and Guangdong Road.

In the early days, glass negative film (wet film) was the most commonly used, the photosensitive speed of which was very slow. At that time, there was no light or other artificial light, so it was necessary to use the sunlight. Therefore, the photographic studio was always on upstairs and also known as "photo studio". Before the introduction of

20世纪初,上海富商家庭祖孙三代在影楼拍摄全家福

长一段时间。到19世纪70年代后,随着摄影技术的发展,画像业逐步萎缩。玻璃干片发明后,摄影师可以走出摄影室摄影,并大规模印制所拍照片。一些反映风景民俗的照片可以向旅游者出售,摄影商业色彩日渐凸显。

19世纪80年代后至民国前,上海的影楼多达百家,其中宝记、耀华、同生等尤为出名。宝记创办于1889年,1925年停业,是当时上海地区活动时间最长的影楼。创始人欧阳石芝被时人称为"最有书卷气的影楼老板"。由于宝记几十年如一日视顾客为上帝,因而博得沪上众多普通人家的青睐,康有为曾说:"沪上之为摄影久且世而今妙者,应无出欧阳生。"创办于1892年的耀华,除了摄影技术精

photography into China, people who wanted to save their own portraits could only go to the portrait gallery and ask the painter to draw their portraits. In the early days of photography in China, the portrait gallery and the photographic studio co-existed for a long time due to the immature photographic technology and equipment. By the 1870s, with the development of photography, the portrait industry shrank progressively. After the dry glass film was invented, photographers could step out of the studio to take photographs and print them on a large scale. Some of the photographs reflecting the customs of the landscape could be sold to tourists, and the commercial trend of photography was increasingly prominent.

From the 1880s to the early period of the Republic of China, there were hundreds of photographic studios in Shanghai, among which Baoji, Yaohua and Tongsheng were especially famous. Founded in 1889 and closed in 1925, Baoji was the oldest photographic studio in Shanghai. Its founder OUYANG Shizhi was known as "the most bookish photographic studio owner". As Baoji had adhered to Customer First for decades, it was greatly favored by many ordinary people in Shanghai and KANG Youwei also spoke highly of Baoji. Founded in 1892, Yaohua not only possessed exquisite photography skills, but also paid special attention to advertising, thus becoming the photographic studio that made the most advertisements. In addition, SHI Dezhi, the boss of Yaohua, asked his eldest daughter to set up the Yaohua West Branch adjacent to Shanghai Race Club at Nanjing Road, which aimed to provide photography services for females and became very popular among the females. Tongsheng Photographic Studio was located at Fuzhou Road today. Its boss TANG Jintang made friends widely and was well connected in official circles. In the early years of Xuantong, Tongsheng was invited to Beijing to take photos for the funeral of Emperor Guangxu and Empress Dowager. The photos in the *Commemorative Book of the Prime Minister's Grand Funeral* published in 1929 were all taken by Tongsheng. The 160 photos vividly recorded the whole process of Sun Yat-sen's coffin moving from Temple of the Azure Clouds in Beiping to Sun Yat-sen Mausoleum in Nanjing, which has become important, precious and rare historical document today.

湛，还特别注重广告宣传，是当时做广告最多的一家影楼。耀华老板施德之还让长女在南京路跑马厅旁设耀华西号，"专拍女照，以便闺阁"，致使慕名而去者络绎不绝。开设在今福州路上的同生影楼，因老板谭京唐交友广泛，在官场中极有人脉。宣统初年，同生被聘进京拍摄光绪帝和西太后葬礼的照片。1929年出版的《总理奉安纪念册》中的照片都由同生拍摄，160幅照片生动记录了孙中山灵柩从北平碧云寺起灵到南京中山陵止的整个过程，成为今天珍贵难觅的重要历史文献。

上世纪20年代后，随着电光日夜拍照技术的使用，拍照价格大

← 老上海的影楼　贺竹元绘

After the 1920s, with the use of electro-optical day and night photography technologies the price of photographing was greatly reduced, hencethe photographic studios not only provided services for the dignitaries, celebrities, debutantes, rich and powerful people, but also for the ordinary citizens. In addition, some photographic studios also took news photos for newspapers, hence the photographic studios developed rapidly. At that time, there were many famous photographic studios such as Huifang, Baofang, Zhaofang, Pingfang, Weixin, Jinghua, Meihua, etc., but the most famous one was Wangkai, which is still well known today. Wangkai was first opened in Beijing and moved to Shanghai in the 1920s. It has been adhering to the tenet of "Innovative Idea, Exquisite Technology, Customer First and Quality First", thus standing out in the fierce market competition. In that very year, Sun Yat-sen and his wife Soong Ching-ling once went to Wangkai and took photos. After the fall of Shanghai, in order to adapt to the requirements for the photos on the "Police Clearance Certificate", photographic studios in Shanghai were expanded again. After the victory of the Anti-Japanese War, the United States dumped its wartime surplus materials and sold a large numberof photographic materials. Moreover, the Kuomintang received high-ranking officials to Shanghai and rich businessmen returned to the city, so the photographic studios then underwent the deformed development. According to the member list compiled by the trade association in 1948, there were 382 registered photographic studios in Shanghai.

After the liberation of Shanghai, the photographic industry underwent the reorganization and transformation in the 1950s, and experienced serious blocks during the ten years of the Cultural Revolution and several important periods of restoration and development after the Cultural Revolution. After the entry into the new century, with the development of the market economy, there emerged various forms of economic competition in the photography market, and the photographic studios also moved from scale operation to collectivization management. At present, Shanghai has more than 1000 photographic studios, photo studios and modern photography studios registered for industry and commerce.

Photos are the expressions of an era and the most real memory of time. While

幅降低，影楼服务对象由达官显要、名伶名媛、新生豪富普及至普通市民，加之部分影楼还兼为报馆拍摄新闻照片，影楼迅速发展。当时有名的影楼有汇芳、宝芳、兆芳、品芳、维新、京华、美华等，但名声最大的还是今天人们熟知的王开。王开最早开设于北京，20年代迁移上海。它以"人无我有，人有我精，顾客至上，质量第一"为宗旨，在激烈的市场竞争中独占鳌头。当年，孙中山先生携夫人宋庆龄曾去王开留影。上海沦陷后，为适应拍摄"良民证"照片的需要，上海影楼又有扩展。抗战胜利后，由于美国倾销战时剩余物资，大量抛售照相材料，加之国民党接收大员到沪，富商巨贾回城，影楼畸形发展。据1948年同业公会编印的会员名册载，上海在册影楼达382家。

上海解放后，照相业经历了50年代的改组改造，"文革"十年的严重阻滞，"文革"后的恢复发展几个重要时期。进入新世纪后，随着市场经济的发展，照相市场出现多种经济形式竞争局面，影楼也由规模经营走向集团化。目前，上海在工商注册的影楼、照相馆、摄影工作室达1000余家。

照片是一个时代的表情，是时光最真实的记忆。在研究老上海影楼发展史的同时，迫切需要我们抢救搜集散落民间的不计其数的老照片，并加以社会学和历史学意义上的解读。这应是历史赋予我们的责任。

2012年8月

studying the development history of photographic studios in old Shanghai, we urgently need to collect countless old photographs scattered in the world and endow them with sociological and historical interpretation, which shall be our responsibility that history has bestowed upon us.

August 2012

老上海的越剧

抒情动听、唯美典雅的越剧是上海艺苑的奇葩。

越剧源于浙江嵊州,发祥于上海。1852 年,嵊州西乡马塘村农民金其柄所创的曲艺"落地唱书"为越剧的起源。这种在农村草台演出的戏曲形式曾称小歌班、的笃班、绍兴文戏等。1917 年,小歌班初进上海,两年后在上海立足。上世纪 20 年代初,越剧艺人吸收海派京剧和绍剧的表演程式,使越剧由简单小型的戏曲表演向古装大戏发展。当时小歌班编演的《梁山伯与祝英台》、《碧玉簪》、《孟丽君》等新剧目,适应了"五四运动"后争取女权和男女平等的思潮,受到观众欢迎。1923 年,嵊州商人王金水请男班艺人金荣水回乡办第一个女班,翌年 1 月 22 位赛姓女生在上海升平歌舞台演出,称"髦儿小歌班",开始了由男子越剧向女子越剧为主的历史演进。1925 年 9 月 17 日上海《新闻报》演出广告中首次以"越剧"称之。

1928 年起,女班蜂拥来沪。上海几乎荟萃了当时女子越剧的所有著名演员,报纸评论称"上海的女子越剧风靡一时,到近来竟有凌驾一切之势"。女子越剧在上海立足后,为适应形势、环境和观众的需求,以姚水娟为代表的一批越剧人对越剧进行了改革,时称"改良文戏"。姚水娟、樊迪民等以古诗《木兰辞》为内容,参照梅

Yue Opera of Old Shanghai

The lyric, beautiful, aesthetic and elegant Yue Opera is a miracle of Shanghai art.

Yue Opera was originated in Shengzhou of Zhejiang Province and prospered in Shanghai. JIN Qibing, a farmer at Matang Village, Xixiang Township, Shengzhou City, created the "Chinese folk rap", which was the origin of Yue Opera. This form of opera performed on the rural grass terraces was known as "little song troupe", "folk song troupe" and "Shaoxing literary opera". In 1917, "little song troupe" was first introduced into Shanghai and developed steadily in Shanghai two years later. In the early 1920s, Yue Opera artists absorbed the performance form of Shanghai Opera and Shaoxing Opera, thus making Yue Opera develop from a simple and small opera performance to an ancient-costume drama. At that time, the new operas compiled and performed by "little song troupe", such as *The Butterfly Lovers*, *The Emerald Hairpin* and *Li-Jun Meng*, adapted to the ideological trend of fighting for women's rights and equality of men and women after the May 4th Movement, so that they were warmly received by the audience. In 1923, Shengzhou merchant WANG Jinshui invited the male artist JIN Rongshui to return to his hometown for the purpose ofsetting up the first female class. In the next year, 22 girls whose family names were SAI performed in Shanghai, known as "Mao-Er little song troupe", thus starting the historical evolution from male Yue Opera to female Yue Opera. On September 17, 1925, it was first known as "Yue Opera" in the performance advertisement on *The News* of Shanghai.

Since 1928, female troupes had flocked to Shanghai. Almost all the famous actress of Yue Opera gathered in Shanghai so that the newspaper commented that "the female

前排左起：
徐天红 傅全香 袁雪芬
竺水招 范瑞娟 吴小楼
后排左起：
张桂凤 筱丹桂 徐玉兰
尹桂芳

兰芳的京剧《木兰从军》，改编演出了越剧《花木兰代父从军》。当时，抗日烽火正在中国大地燃烧，花木兰的形象正体现了人们的爱国情绪，演出激起强烈社会反响。姚水娟塑造的裙钗佩剑、挥戈歼敌的花木兰成为观众心目中的英雄，她因此当选为"越剧皇后"。这次改良，使越剧从农村传统文化走向都市文化，越剧的面貌发生了历史性变化。1942年，袁雪芬等有志之士开始了"新越剧"的探索和实践。改革主要是编演新剧目，建立剧本制，废除幕表制，改革唱腔曲调，注重剧目的社会效应，主张给观众以积极有益的影响。经过改革，涌现了一大批反对封建思想、揭露社会黑暗和宣扬爱国

↖ 1947年7月越剧十姐妹合影

troupe of Yue Opera in Shanghai prevailed and seemed to overwhelm all others." After the female Yue Opera rooted in Shanghai, a group of Yue Opera artists represented by YAO Shuijuan reformed Yue Opera to adapt the situation, environment and the audience's demands, which was known as "reforming opera". YAO Shuijuan, FAN Dimin and other people took the ancient poem *The Ballad of Mulan* as the contents and referred to Peking Opera MEI Lanfang's *Mulan Joins the Army*, thus adapting the Yue Opera *Miss Hua Mulan's Military Legend*. At that time, the flames of Anti-Japanese War were burning in China. Hua Mulan's image reflected people's patriotism so that the performance aroused strong social response. The role Hua Mulan played by YAO Shuijuan was very vivid and became the heroine of the audience, thus makingYAO Shuijuan known as the "Queen of Yue Opera". This reform enabled Yue Opera to move towards urban culture from rural traditional culture and undergo historic changes. In 1942, YUAN Xuefen and other people with lofty ideals started the exploration and practice of "New Yue Opera". The reform mainly involved the compilation and performance of new plays, the establishment of script systems, the abolition of the scene plot system, the reform of vocal music and tone, the emphasis on the social effect of plays, and the advocacy of positive and beneficial impacts on the audience. After the reform, there emerged a large number of operas which fought against feudalism, exposed social darkness and advocated patriotism. In 1946, Xuesheng Opera Troupe adapted LU Xun's novel *Blessing* into the opera *Mistress Xiang Lin*, starred by YUAN Xuefen. This attracted the attention of ZHOU Enlai and the underground organization of the Communist Party of China on Yue Opera. QIAN Yingyu, Liu Housheng and other members of CPC were sent to the circle of Yue Opera as editors and directors, which brought Yue Opera into a new era. *Mistress Xiang Lin* was praised as the milestone in the reform of Yue Opera in the 1940s.

At each historical stage of the development of the old Shanghai Yue Opera, there wererepresentative outstanding actors. The most famous ones were the "three Hua, one Juan and one Gui" in the 1920s and 1930s, namely, SHI Yinhua, ZHAO Ruihua, WANG Xinghua, YAO Shuijuan and XIAO Dangui. In the 1940s, there were the "ten

精神的剧目。1946 年，雪声剧团将鲁迅小说《祝福》改编为《祥林嫂》，袁雪芬领衔主演。这引起了周恩来和中国共产党地下组织对越剧的重视。钱英郁、刘厚生等中共党员被派往越剧界担任编导，使越剧跨入一个新的时期。《祥林嫂》被誉为 40 年代越剧改革的里程碑。

老上海越剧发展的每个历史阶段，都有其代表性的优秀演员。最著名的是 20、30 年代的"三花一娟一桂"，即施银花、赵瑞花、王杏花、姚水娟、筱丹桂。40 年代的"越剧十姐妹"，即袁雪芬、尹桂芳、筱丹桂、范瑞娟、傅全香、徐玉兰、竺水招、张桂凤、徐天红、吴小楼。"越剧十姐妹"为反抗社会恶势力联合义演的《山河恋》声震沪上。

老上海越剧在表演和唱腔上，形成了异彩纷呈的宗师流派。其中生角流派有：由尹桂芳创立的以聪颖不佻、潇洒不飘、深沉隽永、缠绵柔和为特色的"尹派"；由徐玉兰创立的以华彩俊逸、洒脱流畅、奔放高亢、感情炽热为特色的"徐派"；由范瑞娟创立的以朴素大方、咬字坚实、旋律多变、阳刚之美为特色的"范派"；由竺水招创立的以细腻妩媚、清新脱俗、甜润柔糯、扮相俊美为特色的"竺派"等。旦角流派有：由袁雪芬创立的以从容自如、婉转圆润、深沉含蓄、韵味醇厚为特色的"袁派"；由傅全香创立的以唱腔俏丽、跌宕婉转、表演充沛、细腻有神为特色的"傅派"；由王文娟创立的以自然流畅、情深意浓、婉转回荡、富于韵味为特色的"王派"；由吕瑞英创立的以质朴细腻、委婉深沉、绚丽多彩、雍容花俏为特色的"吕派"等。

sisters of Yue Opera", namely, YUAN Xuefen, YIN Guifang, XIAO Dangui, FAN Ruijuan, FU Quanxiang, XU Yulan, ZHU Shuizhao, ZHANG Guifeng, XU Tianhong and WU Xiaolou. In order to fight against the evil forces in the society, the "ten sisters of Yue Opera" jointly performed the *Memory of My Country*, which shocked Shanghai.

The Yue Opera of old Shanghai consisted ofvariousschools according to the style of performance and singing, including male role schools: "YIN School" founded by YIN Guifang and featured by smartness, richness, profoundness and softness; "XU School" founded by XU Yulan and featured by prettiness, fluency, boldness and passion; "FAN School" founded by FAN Ruijuan and featured by simplicity, strong pronunciation, diversified melodies and manly beauty; "ZHU School" founded by ZHU Shuizhao and featured by delicate charm, grace, sweetness and beautiful appearance; female role schools: "YUAN School" founded by YUAN Xuefen and featured by ease, round pronunciation, profound implication and lasting appeal; "FU School" founded by FU Quanxiang and featured by pretty tones, diversified emotions, abundant performances and exquisite expressions; "WANG School" founded by WANG Wenjuan and featured by natural fluency, strong affections, diversified emotions and lasting appeal lingering charm; and "LV School" founded by LV Ruiying and featured by simplicity, exquisiteness, euphemistic implication, gorgeousness and elegance, etc.

After the founding of the People's Republic of China, there launched a series of reform movementsinvolving "opera reform, performer reform and system reform", thus bringing about profound changes of epoch-making significance to Yue Opera. During the golden period of Yue Opera from the 1950s to the early 1960s, a large number of influential art masterpieces emerged and won great reputation for Yue Opera at home and abroad. During the Cultural Revolution, Yue Opera was severely damaged and forced to be suspended. After the ending of the ten-year unrest, Yue Opera was revived.

Now, Yue Opera is facing the challenges of market economy and modern media. It will be a daunting task to reshape the image of Yue Opera in Shanghai. As long as we carry forward traditions of the old Shanghai Yue Opera artists while keeping pace with the

新中国成立后，经过以"改戏改人改制"为内容的戏曲改革运动，越剧发生了时代性深刻变革。上世纪50年代至60年代前期是越剧的黄金时期，一大批有重大影响的艺术精品应运而生，使越剧在国内外赢得了巨大声誉。"文革"期间越剧受到严重摧残，被迫停演。十年动乱结束后，越剧得以复兴。

而今，越剧遇到了市场经济和现代传媒的挑战，重塑越剧在上海的形象任重道远。只要我们发扬老上海越剧人贴近时代、勇于改革，携手团结、优势互补，注重社会效益、积极影响观众的传统，努力探索越剧的市场化路子，越剧一定会辉煌再现。

↖ 袁雪芬徐玉兰《西厢记》
　　1955年

2012年8月

times, daring to reform, joining hands, complementing each other's advantages, emphasizing the social benefits and influencing the audience positively, and strive to explore the market-oriented development of Yue Opera, we will reproduce the resplendence of Yue Opera.

August 2012

老上海的戏院

老上海的戏院是近现代上海文化发展史的见证。

清代后期,上海逐渐诸腔杂陈。士大夫和豪富蓄养家伎,或请戏班唱堂会演昆曲,戏院应运而生。当时上海城厢里的戏院都称"园"。创办于1851年的三雅园是上海最早的营业性戏院,由上海县一座顾姓住宅改建而成。此后,一桂轩、满庭芳、丹桂、景芳、金桂茶园等一批戏园陆续兴起。京朝名角竞相南下上海,丹桂、金桂、天仙、大观成为当时上海四大京班茶园。每当上灯时分,各戏园门前车马纷来,绮罗云集。"桂园观剧"成为时尚,被列为"沪北十景"之首。止19世纪末,上海各类演出场所近百家。

随着上海的开埠,西风渐入,园林茶座式的小规模戏园逐步演进为剧场式的戏院。由英侨集资创建于1867年的兰心大戏院,是中国最早的欧式剧场。中国第一部话剧《黑奴吁天录》在兰心首次公演,梅兰芳抗战辍演八年后首次复出也在这里。建于1909年的文明大舞台、1926年的天蟾舞台、1927年的共舞台、1930年的中国大戏院是老上海著名的四大京剧舞台。文明大舞台首演曾邀"内廷供奉"的刘永春、吕月樵等名角。天蟾舞台曾有"远东第一大剧场"之誉,是当时上海最主要的京剧演出场所,观众席位3917座,有

Theater of Old Shanghai

The theaters of old Shanghai have witnessed the cultural development of modern Shanghai.

In the late Qing Dynasty, there were various kinds of operas in Shanghai. The scholar-officials and the wealthy kept private singers and dancers or invited theatrical troupes to perform or sing Kun Opera, which led to the emergence of the theaters. At that time, the theatres in Shanghai were called "gardens". Founded in 1851, Sanya Theater was the first commercial theater in Shanghai, which was rebuilt from a residence of GU Family in Shanghai. Since then, a series of theaters, such as Yiguixuan, Manting Fang, Dangui, Jingfang, and Jingui Opera Theater, prevailed one after another. The famous opera performers in Beijing raced south to Shanghai, and Dangui, Jingui, Daguan and Tianxian became the four major Peking Opera theaters in Shanghai. Every night, the theaters were full of people. "Watching opera in Guiyuan" became the fashion, ranking the first among the "ten sceneries in north Shanghai". By the end of the 19th century, there were nearly 100 performing venues in Shanghai.

With the opening of Shanghai's port and the introduction of Western styles, the small-scale garden and teahouse gradually evolved into the theater. Lyceum Theatre, founded in 1867 by British Born Chinese, was the earliest European-style theater in China. China's first drama *Uncle Tom's Cabin* premiered at Lyceum Theatre, where MEI Lanfang returned for the first time after he had dropped out for eight years because of the war. The four most famous Peking Opera theaters of old Shanghai were Wenming Theater founded in 1909, Tianchan Theater founded in 1926, Gong Theater founded in 1927 and Grand China Theater founded in 1930. For the premiere of Wenming Theater, the

"北有长安，南有天蟾"，"不进天蟾不成名"之说。欧式建筑的共舞台以机关布景和演出长篇连台本戏的海派京剧著名。中国大戏院原名三星舞台，京朝名家都曾在此登台献艺。建于1923年的长江剧场，是话剧《原野》的首演剧场。1930年初建成开业的黄金大戏院，为青帮头子黄金荣所建，后改名为兰生影剧院。建于1941年的美琪大戏院是美式建筑，定名美琪，原是取其"美轮美奂，琪玉无瑕"之意，戏院开幕时曾首映美国电影《美月琪花》。这座融现代美与古典美之精华，风格典雅独特的戏院，是上海近代优秀历史建筑。老上海著名的戏院还有：西班牙商人雷玛斯于1914年在南京西路创办的夏令配克大戏院，广东人曾焕堂于1917年在四川路虬江路创办的上海大戏院，浙江商人徐颂新于1923年在六马路北海路创办的申江大戏院，魔术大师张慧聪的父亲张志标于1925年在乍浦路建的好莱坞大戏院，广东商人何挺然等人于1926年在贵州路创办的丽都大戏院，英商买办潘志衡于1939年在延安东路建造的沪光大戏院，宁波商人柳中亮、柳中浩兄弟于1940年在延安中路创办的京都大戏院，以及东湖路的杜美大戏院、南京西路陕西北路的平安大戏院、海宁路乍浦路的虹口大戏院等。有资料显示，上海解放时中心城区正规的戏院达110多家。

老上海的戏院好戏连台，明星荟萃。清咸丰、同治年间的"梨园三绝"程长庚、徐小香、何桂三，京剧四大名旦梅兰芳、荀慧生、程砚秋、尚小云，四小名旦张君秋、毛世来、宋德珠、李世芳，越剧四大名旦施银花、赵瑞花、王杏花、姚水娟，名优名伶谭鑫培、李少春、马连良、麒麟童、盖叫天、谭富英、周信芳以及"越剧十

famous imperial performers including LIU Yongchun, LV Yueqiao and others were invited. Tianchan Theater, known as "the largest theater in the Far East", was the most important performing venue for Peking Opera in Shanghai, where there were 3917 audience seats, just as the sayings went, "There is Chang'an in the north while Tianchan in the south" and "You must give performances in Tianchan Theater to be famous". The European-style Gong Theater was famous for its machine-operated stage scenery and the performance of Shanghai Peking Opera with complete long series. For Grand China Theater, formerly called Sanxing Theater, lots of famous Peking opera artists had given performances on this stage. The Yangtze Theater, founded in 1923, was the premiere theater of the drama *The Savage Land*. Grand Golden Theater, founded in early 1930, was established by the leader of Green Gang — HUANG Jinrong, and was renamed Lansheng Cinema later. Majestic Theatre, founded in 1941 and derived from "extremely beautiful and flawless", was an American-style building, where the American film *Moon Over Miami* was premiered at the opening ceremony. This theater, which combined the essence of modern beauty and classic beauty, with its unique and elegant styles, was an excellent modern historical building in Shanghai. Other famous theaters of old Shanghai included: The Grand Olympic Theater founded by the Spanish merchant Ramos at West Nanjing Road in 1914, Grand Shanghai Theater founded by the Cantonese ZENG Yutang between Qiujiang Road and Sichuang Road in 1917, Grand Shenjiang Theater founded by Zhejiang merchant XU Songxin between Beihai Road and Liuma Road in 1923, Grand Hollywood Theater founded by ZHANG Zhibiao (the father of the famous magician ZHANG Huicong) at Zhapu Road in 1925, Grand Rialto Theatre founded by the Cantonese HE Tingran at Guizhou Road in 1926, Astor Theatre founded by the British merchant and comprador PAN Zhiheng at East Yan'an Road in 1939, Grand Jingdu Theater founded by Ningbo brother merchants LIU Zhongliang and LIU ZHonghao at Yanan Road (Middle) in 1940, and Grand Doumer Theatre at Donghu Road, Grand Uptown Theatre betweenShaanxi North Road and WestNanjing Road, Grand Hongkou Theater between Zhapu Road andHaining Road, etc. According to the data, there were more than 110 formal theatres in the downtown area during the period

姐妹"等都曾在老上海戏院各显英姿。当时的上海戏院天天开业,夜夜有戏,占据了国内演出业的半壁江山,享有"东方百老汇"的美誉。

老上海的戏院也曾拥有过政治辉煌。建国之初,美琪大戏院一度成为上海重要的政治活动场所。1954年8月,上海市第一届人民代表大会在美琪举行。周恩来曾在美琪向参加全国省委书记会议的干部作关于知识份子改造的重要讲话。兰心大戏院是上海解放后党

↖ 老上海的戏院　贺竹元绘

of liberation of Shanghai.

In the theaters of old Shanghai, there emerged many excellent plays and stars, including the "three operatic masters" during Xianfeng's and Tongzhi's reign of the Qing Dynasty CHENG Changgeng, XU Xiaoxiang and HE Guisan; the four famous Dans in Peking Opera — MEI Lanfang, XUN Huisheng, CHENG Yanqiu and SHANG Xiaoyun; the four young Dans in Peking Opera — ZHANG Junqiu, MAO Shilai, SONG Dezhu and LI Shifang; the four famous Dans in Yue Opera — SHI Yinhua, ZHAO Ruihua, WANG Xinghua and YAO Shuijuan; famous actors and actresses TAN Xinpei, LI Shaochun, MA Lianliang, QI Lintong, GAI Jiaotian, TAN Fuying, ZHOU Xinfang and the "ten sisters of Yue Opera", had all showed their performances in the theaters of old Shanghai. At that time, the Shanghai theaters were open every day and had performanceson every night, occupying half of the market of the domestic performance industry and enjoying the reputation of "Oriental Broadway".

The theaters of old Shanghai had also enjoyed reputation in the political circle. At the beginning of the founding of the People's Republic of China, Grand Majestic Theatre

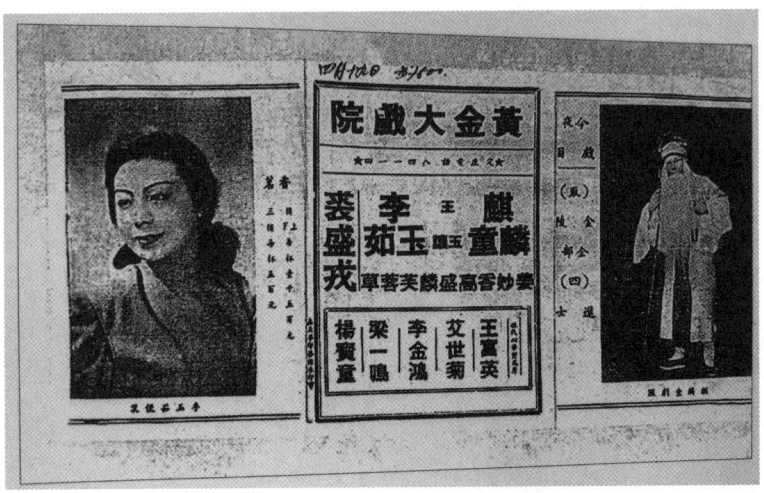

→ 黄金大戏院(西藏路)戏单

和国家领导人会见外国元首、接待各国友人的重要场所。1960年1月，毛泽东、刘少奇、周恩来等在兰心观看了上海实验歌剧院演出的舞剧《小刀会》。1964年7月，刘少奇、陈毅等在兰心观看上海人民淮剧团演出的现代戏《海港的早晨》。

老上海的戏院是上海宝贵的历史文化遗产。在演艺业日益繁荣发展的今天，如何在建好用好一批现代化剧院的同时，挖掘修缮利用好一批承载着上海文化历史沧桑的老戏院，形成现代和经典交相辉映的演出场馆，并使剧院本身成为艺术的象征和殿堂，应是亟需研究解决的文化建设课题。

2012年9月

once became an important place for political activities in Shanghai. In August 1954, the First People's Congress of Shanghai was held in Grand Majestic Theatre. ZHOU Enlai delivered an important speech on the transformation of intellectuals to the cadres attending the secretary meeting of national provincial party committees in Grand Majestic Theatre. Lyceum Theatre was an important place for CPC and national leaders to meet with foreign heads of state and receive friends from all countries after the liberation of Shanghai. In January 1960, MAO Zedong, LIU Shaoqi, ZHOU Enlai and others watched the dance drama *Small Swords Society* performed by Shanghai Experimental Opera House in Lyceum Theatre. In July 1964, LIU Shaoqi and CHEN Yi watched the modern drama *Morning of the Harbor* performed by Shanghai People's Huai Opera Troupe in Lyceum Theatre.

The theaters of old Shanghai are valuable historical and cultural heritage of Shanghai. Nowadays, the performance industry becomes more and more prosperous. The cultural construction projects that need to be studied and solved urgently are how to build and utilize the modern theaters and at the same time how to explore, restore and utilize a number of old theaters bearing the cultural and historical vicissitudes of Shanghai, thus forming the performance venues where the modern and classic charm enhance each other and making the theatres become the symbol and the palace of art.

September 2012

老上海的评弹

吴侬软语娓娓动听的评弹是老上海人的最爱。

评弹起源于苏州,兴盛于上海。早在明代苏州地区就有说书活动。据吴县志记载:"明清两朝盛行弹词、评话,两者截然不同,而总名兼曰说书,发源于吴中。"上海开埠后,经济文化迅速发展,人口日益膨胀,大批苏州人创业上海,一度上海出现"街头巷尾尽吴语"的情景,评弹随之而入。进入20世纪后,上海逐渐成为中国的商业、金融、贸易中心,文化消费需求急剧上升。抗战爆发后,上海成为孤岛,经济出现畸形繁荣局面。在经济、文化等诸多条件的综合作用下,到上世纪30、40年代,从苏州传入上海的评弹进入鼎盛时期,上海成为评弹活动的中心。

书场是评弹繁荣的标志。上世纪30年代后,上海的专业书场遍布城厢,成为独特的文化景观。老城隍庙内就有得意楼、怡情处、四美轩、逍遥楼、蠡园、明园、柴行厅等多家。随着评弹艺术的发展,出现了舞厅书场、饭店书场、游艺书场、茶楼书场、公园书场、旅馆书场等一批新书场。当时著名的舞厅书场有米高美、仙乐斯、新仙林等。饭店书场有东方、沧州、远东、南京等。福建北路玉茗楼、四马路青莲阁、广东路万云楼、东棋盘街春江花月楼、十六铺

Pingtan of Old Shanghai

Pingtan, a kind of storytelling and ballad singing in Suzhou dialect, was the favorite for Old Shanghai people.

Pingtan was originated in Suzhou and prospered in Shanghai. As early as in the Ming Dynasty, there were storytelling activities in Suzhou region. According to the records in the annals of Wu County, it said, "In the Ming and Qing Dynasties, the ballad singing and Pinghua were very different, but they all called storytelling, originated in Wuzhong." After Shanghai opened its port, its economy and culture developed rapidly with the increasing expansion of population. A large number of people from Suzhou started a business in Shanghai so that people could hear Suzhou dialect everywhere in Shanghai and pingtan was introduced into Shanghai. After entering the 20th century, Shanghai gradually became China's commercial, financial and trade center, and the cultural consumption demand increased greatly. After the outbreak of the Anti-Japanese War, Shanghai became an isolated island, and its economy was in a state of abnormal prosperity. Under the comprehensive effect of economy, culture and many other conditions, by the 1930s and 1940s, pingtan that was introduced from Suzhou into Shanghai experienced its heyday, and Shanghai became the center of pingtan activities.

The storytelling house was the symbol of the prosperity of pingtan. After the 1930s, professional storytelling houses were scattered all over Shanghai, becoming a unique cultural landscape. In the Old Town's God Temple, there were Deyilou, Yiqingchu, Simeixuan, Xiaoyaolou, Liyuan, Mingyuan, Chaixingting and many other storytelling houses. With the development of pingtan, there emerged a number of new storytelling houses, such as the ballroom storytelling house, restaurant storytelling house,

称心如意楼、西康路明月楼、牯岭路湖园等是当年最热门的书场。福州路山西南路的也是楼是上海第一家女书场。老上海人把泡上一壶茶听评弹看作是最惬意的享受。值得一提的是，当时上海数十家民间电台竞相开设空中书场，街头巷尾的收音机里弦索叮咚、昼夜不辍。据1938年11月29日《申报》的统计，全市20多家电台每天播放评弹节目达103档，每档40分钟，影响可见一斑。

上海巨大的演出市场，吸引了江浙等地众多的评弹艺人。评弹演员进上海并在上海立足，成为衡量其艺术水准的标准。红飞蔓茂的演出市场，争奇斗艳的艺术竞争，加上听众的追捧，上海涌现了一批艺术精湛、富有创新意识的评弹艺术家。夏荷生、周玉泉、徐云志被称为"三大单档"。蒋如庭、朱介生，朱耀祥、赵稼秋，沈俭

← 蒋月泉、江文兰演出《玉蜻蜓》

entertainment storytelling house, teahouse storytelling house, park storytelling house and hotel storytelling house. At that time, the famous ballroom storytelling houses included MGM, CIROS, New Xianlin, etc. The restaurant storytelling houses included Dongfanyg, Cangzhou, Yuandong and Nanjing, etc. The most popular storytelling houses were the Yuminlou at Fujian North Road, Qingliange at Sima Road, Wanyunlou at Guangdong Road, Chunjianghuayuelou at East Qipan Road, Chenxinruyilou at Shiliupu, Mingyulou at Xikang Road and Huyuan at Guling Road, etc. Yeshilou between Shanxi South Road andFuzhou Road was the first female storytelling house in Shanghai. For old Shanghai people, the most comfortable thing was to drink tea andwhile enjoyingpingtan. It was worth mentioning that at that time, dozens of folk radio stations in Shanghai were competing to open the air storytelling house so that people could enjoy pingtan through the radio day and night. According to the statistics of *Shun Pao* on November 29, 1938, more than 20 radio stations in the city broadcast 103 pingtan programs every day and each program lasted for 40 minutes, which was of great influence.

The huge performance market in Shanghai attracted numerous pingtan artists in Jiangsu and Zhejiang. Pingtan artists entered Shanghai and rooted in Shanghai, which became the standard to measure their artistic level. Because of the prosperous performance market, the fierce artistic competition and the audiences' passion, there emerged a batch of excellent pingtan artists with exquisite technique and innovative consciousness. XIA Hesheng, ZHOU Yuquan and XU Yunzhi were known as "three major stand-up artists". JIANG Ruting, ZHU Jiesheng, ZHU Yaoxiang, ZHAO Jiaqiu, SHEN Jianan and XUE Xiaoqing were known as "the three major pairs of partners of Pingtan". The "seven most famous pingtan operas" at that time included the *Jade Dragonfly* of JIANG Yuequan and WANG Baiyin, the *Ten Beauties* of ZHANG Jianting and ZHANG Jianguo, the *Pearl Pagoda* of ZHOU Yunrui and CHEN Xian, the *Invincible Knights Errant* of HAN Shiliang, the *Hero* of ZHANG Hongsheng, the *Three Kingdoms* of TANG Gengliang and the *Zhang Wenxiang Stabbed the Horse* of PAN Boying. The most reputedfemale pingtan artists included XU Xueyue, FAN Xuejun, HUANG Jingfen and ZHU Huizhen,

安、薛筱卿被称为"三大双档"。蒋月泉、王柏荫的《玉蜻蜓》,张鉴庭、张鉴国的《十美图》,周云瑞、陈希安的《珍珠塔》,韩士良的评话《七侠五义》,张鸿声的评话《英烈》,唐耿良的评话《三国》,潘伯英的评话《张汶祥刺马》是当时有名的"七煞档"。徐雪月、范雪君、黄静芬、朱惠珍等是当时女演员中的佼佼者。范雪君先后两次荣登"弹词皇后"宝座。

随着书情内容的变化、听众审美的需要,以及各种艺术的相互影响和交流,老上海评弹在清嘉庆、道光年间陈调、马调、俞调三大流派的基础上,创新形成了众多特点各异的风格流派。其中弹词流派的唱腔发展尤为突出,成为当时评弹繁荣的又一个重要标志。由夏荷生所创的以响弹响唱、挺拔遒劲为特色的夏调,由徐云志所创的以清悦甜润、旋律软糯为特色的徐调,由蒋月泉所创的以雍容华美、潋滟浓彩为特色的蒋调,由沈俭安所创的以清雅飘逸、苍劲柔美为特色的沈调,由薛筱卿所创的以明快爽利、咬字铿锵为特色的薛调,由张鉴庭所创的以苍劲厚重、力度强烈为特色的张调,以及严雪亭所创的严调,杨振雄所创的杨调,祁莲芳所创的祁调等,可谓精彩纷呈。与此同时,《描金凤》、《隋唐》、《包公》、《顾鼎成》、《长生殿》、《啼笑因缘》、《秋海棠》、《雷雨》等一大批评弹书目演为经典。

全国解放初期,上海市人民评弹工作团等专业演出团体相继成立,集中了当时评弹界的精英,编演了一大批优秀作品,把评弹艺术推向了新的境界。此后,由于各种原因,评弹经历了艰难曲折,出现了式微的征候。进入新世纪后,由于文化产业和现代传媒的多

↗ 评弹《蝶恋花》

etc. FAN Xuejun was rated as "the queen of pingtan" twice.

With the changes of book contents and audience aesthetic needs, as well as the mutual influence and exchange of various arts, there emerged a variety of styles and schools with different characteristics, which were based on the three major pingtan schools in Jiaqing and Daoguang reign of the Qing Dynasty — CHEN School, MA School and YU School. Among them, the vocal music development of pingtan schools was particularly prominent and became another important symbol of the prosperity of pingtan at that time. There were all kinds of different pingtan schools, including XIA School founded by XIA Hesheng and featured by loud sing and strong voice; XU School founded by XU Yunzhi and featured by sweet sound and soft melody; JIANG School founded by JIANG Yuequan and featured by magnificent charm and attractive colors; SHEN School founded by SHEN Jianan and featured by elegant style and vigorous

元发展,评弹听众锐减,书场萎缩,艺人流失,生存和发展面临新的考验。

评弹,作为国家级非物质文化遗产绝不能让它琴声远去。在文化市场日益繁荣的今天,应当给评弹创造发展的空间。同时,评弹自身也应发扬老艺人们勇于改革创新的精神,吸收姐妹艺术的营养,运用现代科技等手段丰富表现形式,使弦琶琮铮、轻清柔缓的评弹再展风采。

2012 年中秋节

melody; XUE School founded by XUE Xiaoqing and featured by refreshing styles and sonorous pronunciation; ZHANG School founded by ZHANG Jianting and featured by vigorous and thick tones and intense strength; as well as YAN School founded by YAN Xueting, YANG School founded by YANG Zhenxiong and QI School founded by QI Lianfang, etc.

In the early stage of national liberation, professional performing groups such as the Shanghai People's Pingtan Working Group were set up successively. The elites of the pingtan industry at that time were gathered together tohave compiled and performed a large number of excellent plays, whichpromoted the pingtan art to a new level. Since then, due to various reasons, pingtan had experienced a difficult and tortuous development and underwent the decline. After entering the new century, as a result of the diversified development of cultural industry and modern media, the audience of pingtan declined greatly, the storytelling housesdecreased and the artists left the industry, thus making the survival and development of pingtan face new challenges.

Pingtan, as a national intangible cultural heritage, shall not disappear. Today, the cultural market is more and more prosperous. We should create space for the development of pingtan. Meanwhile, we should carry forward the reform and innovation spirit of the old-generation pingtan artists, absorb nutrition from other similar art and utilize modern technologies and other means to enrich the forms of expression, thus reproducing the resplendence of pingtan.

Mid-Autumn Festival, 2012

老上海的连环画

连环画作为一种艺术形式走过了漫长的发展道路。上海是中国连环画的诞生地,在连环画创作经历了前一段低谷重又回暖的今天,回顾老上海的连环画史颇有意义。

连环画是用多幅画面连续叙述一个故事或事件发展过程的独特绘画形式。中国古代故事壁画、故事画卷及小说戏曲中的"全相"等都具有连环画的性质。但"连环图画"即连环画名字的正式起用,是上世纪20年代上海世界书局出版的《连环图画三国志》等5套演义故事。这种具有连续性、通俗性、普及性等特点的连环画,成为海派文化的一个独特衍生物。1928年以后,连环画的样式逐渐完善,加上东南亚发行网初步形成,国内各大城市的发行网也逐步增加,连环画的发行量急剧上升,一般从每种几百本上升到2000本左右。上世纪30年代,上海连环画出版商达30多家。抗战爆发后,为满足群众文化上极端饥渴的需要,连环画出版商增至近百家,上海连环画进入繁荣时期。

老上海的连环画以64开本为主要版式,先是上文下图,后为上图下文。受有声电影影响,一度人口"冒气"添加人物对白的"口白"成为连环画又一构图形式。当时连环画的题材除传统的古典文

Comic Strip of Old Shanghai

As an art form, comic strip has undergone a long road of development. Shanghai is the birthplace of Chinese comic strips. It is of great significance to review the history of old Shanghai's comic strips after the previous decline of comic strip creation and its recovery today.

  Comic strip is a unique form of painting in which multiple frames are used to describe a story or the development of an event. Chinese ancient story frescoes, story scroll painting and "holograph" in novels and operas all have the characteristics of comic strips. The name "comic strip" was first officially used in the five books of *Comic Strips of Warriors of Fate* published by Shanghai World Publishing House in the 1920s. This kind of comic strip with the characteristics of continuity, popularity and universality became a unique derivative of Shanghai-style culture. After 1928, the style of comic strip was gradually improved. And the distribution network of Southeast Asia was initially formed while that of major cities in China was also gradually increased. The circulation of comic strips increased greatly, generally from several hundred copies to about 2,000 copies. In the 1930s, there were more than 30 comic strip publishers in Shanghai. After the outbreak of the Anti-Japanese War, the number of comic strip publishers increased to nearly 100 in order to meet the urgent cultural demands of the masses, thus making Shanghai comic strip enter the period of prosperity.

  The comic strips of old Shanghai were mainly in the format of 64 folios, first with texts above and pictures below, then with pictures above and texts below. Under the influence of the sound film, it became a compositional form of comic strips to use "speech bubble" to add the character dialogue "uttered words". Besides the

学和神话传说外，舞台戏剧场面和故事也是重要内容。上世纪40年代，《海国英雄》、《雷雨》、《天堂与地狱》等一批进步连环画作品诞生，成为唤醒民众的重要力量。这是老上海连环画发展中极其宝贵的革命传统。

老上海连环画造就了一大批艺术家。刘伯良、李澍承、朱润斋、陈丹旭等是早期知名的连环画家。沈曼云、赵宏本、钱笑呆、陈光镒被誉为老上海连坛的"四大名旦"。赵三岛、笔如花、颜梅华、徐宏达被誉为"四小名旦"。老上海著名的连环画家还有严绍唐、何庙云、张龟年、李铁生等。周云舫、赵宏本、杨青华等受中共地下党和进步文化的影响，针对当时一些连环画内容低俗的状况，勇于改革，创作了一批宣扬爱国主义精神和揭露社会黑暗的革命连环画。

《铁道游击队》连环画

traditional classical literature, myths and legends, the dramatic scenes and stories were also important contents of comic strips at that time. In the 1940s, a number of progressive comic strips such as *Heroes of the Sea*, *Thunderstorm*, *Heaven and Hell* emerged and became an important force to awaken the public, which was an extremely valuable revolutionary tradition in the development of old Shanghai comic strips.

Then, a large number of comic artists of old Shanghai emerged. The early famous comic artists included LIU Boliang, LI Shucheng, ZHU Runzhai and CHEN Danxu. SHEN Manyun, ZHAO Hongben, QIAN Xiaozhi and CHEN Guangyi were praised as the "four major famous comics artists" of old Shanghai. ZHAO Sandao, PEN Ruhua, YAN Meihua, XU Hongda were known as "four young famous comics artists". Prestigiouscomic artists in old Shanghai also included YAN Shaotang, HE Miao yun, ZHANG Guinian, LI Tiesheng and so on. Influenced by the underground Communist Party of China and the progressive culture and in order to fight against the vulgar content of some comic strips at that time, ZHOU Yunfang, ZHAO Hongben and YANG Qinghua created a number of revolutionary comic strips to promote patriotism and expose social darkness. Due to the special function and influence of comic strips, some artists who were not professional in comic strips were also involved. Many comic strips had a positive and extensive influence, such as FENG Zikai's *The True Story of Ah Q*, YE Qianyu's *Mr. Wang* and ZHANG Leping's *Winter Of Three Hairs*, etc.

In order to support the popular art form of the comic strip, LU Xun, QU Qiubai, MAO Dun and other people focused on the issues of comic strips and had a controversy with HU Qiuyuan and SU Wen in 1932. LU Xun's articles about comic strips included *Debating for Comic Strips*, *Detailed Discussion on Comic Strips*, *The Adoption of Old Forms* and *Preface to "Suffering of the Person"*. With powerful examples, he refuted the argument that some people were trying to obliterate comic strips and pointed out, "comic strip has not only been the art, but has already been in the palace of art." He hoped that the comic artists should pay attention to making the masses "understand and

由于连环画的特殊作用和影响，一些非连环画专业的画家也参与了进来。丰子恺的《漫画阿Q正传》、叶浅予的《王先生》、张乐平的《三毛流浪记》等，都产生过积极广泛的影响。

为了支持连环画这一通俗的艺术形式，鲁迅、瞿秋白、茅盾等曾在1932年围绕连环画问题与胡秋原、苏汶展开了一场论战。鲁迅论述连环画的文章有《连环图画辩护》、《连环图画琐谈》、《论旧形式的采用》、《〈一个人的受难〉序》等。他以有力的例证批驳了一些人企图抹杀连环画的论调，指出连环画"不但可以成为艺术，并且已经坐在'艺术之宫'的里面了"。他希望连环画工作者既要注意使群众"能懂、爱看"，又不迎合和媚悦大众，坚持"前进的艺术家正确的努力"。

上世纪中叶出生的人，大多对连环画有着特殊的感情。当年多数少年儿童和平民无钱买书，都是租书看书，有的把买早点的钱省下来看连环画。花几分钱租几本连环画坐在小板凳上阅读，是最快乐的文化享受。朱润斋的代表作《天宝图》出版后，民间流行一句顺口溜："看了《天宝图》，忘了肚皮饿"。茅盾在《连环图画小说》一文中写道："上海的街头巷尾像步哨似的密布着无数小书摊。这些小书就是所谓连环图画小说。"老上海的小书摊是最受欢迎的流动图书馆，连环画成了最普遍的民众教育工具。

上海解放后，经过整合改造，一大批连环画家云集上海人民美术出版社。老连环画家重新焕发了艺术青春，其它画种的画家顾炳鑫、程十发、陆俨少、刘旦宅、米谷、黎冰鸿等加入连环画创作队伍，贺友直、华三川、王仲清、丁斌曾、韩和平、韩敏、戴敦邦、

love to read", instead of catering to and flattering the masses, and adhere to "correct efforts of advancing artists".

Most people born in the middle of the last century had special feelings about comic strips. In those days, most of the children and civilians had no money to buy books so that they had to rent books for reading. Some people even saved money on breakfast to read comic strips. It was the happiest cultural treat to rent several comic strips and read them sitting on small stools. After the publication of ZHU Runzhai's masterpiece *God Treasure Map*, the doggerel became popular among people, "Reading the *God Treasure Map* makes you forget the hunger." MAO Dun said in *Comic Strip Novel*, "There were numerous small bookstalls in the streets and lanes of Shanghai and the books just referred to the comic strip novels." Small bookstall in old Shanghai was the most popular mobile library, and comic strips had become the most popular public education tool.

After the liberation of Shanghai and through integration and transformation, a large number of comic artists gathered in Shanghai People's Fine Arts Publishing House. The old comic artists rekindled their artistic vitality, and other painters such as GU Bingxin, CHENG Shifa, LU Yanshao, LIU Danzhai, MI Gu and LI Binghong also joined the production team of comic strips. HE Youzhi, HUA Sanchuan, WANG Zhongqing, DING Binzeng, HAN Heping, HAN Min, DAI Dunbang, WANG Guanqing, and ZHENG Jiasheng stood out in the field of comic strips. There emerged lots of classic comic strips, including the stories reflecting the revolutionary war, such as *Railway Guerrillas* and *Tracks in the Snowy Forest*, and masterwork-themed comic strip *Water Margin*, thusmaking the creation of comic strips enter the peak period. Since the beginning of the Cultural Revolution, the creation of comic strips had suffered a serious setback. The reform and opening-up brought new life to comic strips. In the mid-to-late 1990s, the comic strip dwindled and even became collectibles due to the influence of new media and cartoon.

Recently, it is glad to hear that Shanghai has launched the project to revitalize comic strips, and Shanghai Comic Strip Center has been unveiled. Nowadays, the creation of

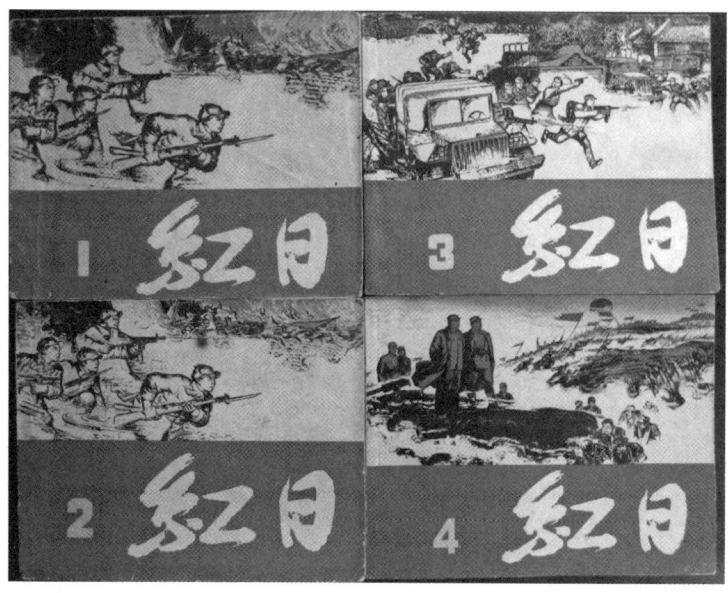

汪观清、郑家声等崭露连坛。《铁道游击队》、《林海雪原》等反映革命战斗故事和《水浒传》等名著题材的经典作品应运而生,连环画创作进入高峰期。"文革"开始后,连环画创作受到严重挫折。改革开放使连环画迎来新生。上世纪90年代中后期,由于新兴媒体和动漫等影响,连环画逐渐萎缩,以至只成了收藏品。

最近,欣闻上海启动连环画振兴工程,海派连环画中心揭幕。在连环画创作走向主题化、规模化、专业化、集成式的今天,需要我们传承弘扬老上海的连环画传统,使新时期的连环画真正成为民族的、大众的美学。

2012年10月　　汪观清《红日》封面

comic strips has been theme-oriented, large-scale, professional and integrated. It is necessary for us to inherit and carry forward the tradition of the comic strips of old Shanghai, thus making comic strips in the new era truly become the national and popular aesthetics.

October 2012

老上海的茶楼

茶楼，老上海精致的风情旧景。在茶生活成为一种文化时尚的今天，回顾老上海茶楼的历史别有意味。

老上海茶楼兴盛于清同治初年。《清稗类钞·茶肆品茶》中记载："上海之茶馆，始于同治初三茅阁桥沿河的丽水台。其屋前临洋泾浜，杰阁三层，楼宇轩敞。"自丽水台茶楼之后，老上海茶楼由南市向北市一路发展，一洞天、湖心亭、怡兰、桂芳阁、香雪海、鸿福楼、一壶春、得意楼等颇有诗情画意馆名的茶楼纷纷开张。至清宣统元年，上海约有茶楼60余家，上世纪20年代增至160多家。当时，沪城内外、南市北市、河沿桥旁、十字街头茶楼林立、茶客如云、茗香醉人。时人去宝善街松凤阁茗饮为"沪北十景"之一。

老上海是五光十色的老上海，茶楼自然也五花八门。四面八方的人创业上海，开出了特色各异的茶楼，有苏浙风味，有南国风情，也有日式欧派。同芳居是当年小有名气的广式茶楼，南社的苏曼殊是广东人，在异地他乡的上海见到同芳居，他有如回故乡如见亲人的感觉，许多诗文在品茶时抒发写就。"在这个古老的茶馆中，我们不难会见一两个有学问有身份的中国人，他们一面喝着香茗，一面神游故国，追念着这古老中国的过去的光荣，一面向往着凤凰的再

Teahouse of Old Shanghai

Teahouse is the exquisite old scenery of old Shanghai. Nowadays, drinkingtea has become a kind of cultural fashion so that it is of special meaning to review the teahouse history of old Shanghai.

The teahouse of old Shanghai prospered in the early years of the Tongzhi's reign in the Qing Dynasty. The records in the ancient document said, "The teahouse of Shanghai was originated in Lishuitai along Sanmaoge Bridge in the early years of Tongzhi's reign, where there was a river in front of the spacious and bright building with three storeys." From then on, the teahouse of old Shanghai had developed from the south of the city to the north of the city, and teahouses had opened one after one, such as Yidongtian, Huxinting, Yilan, Guifangge, Xiangxuehai, Hongfulou, Yihuchun and Deyilou, the name of which were very poetic and artistic. In the first year of Xuantong reign in the Qing dynasty, there were about 60 teahouses in Shanghai and it increased to over 160 ones in the 1920s. At that time, teahouses were everywhere in Shanghai and people loved drinkingtea in the teahouses. It was one of the "ten sceneries in north Shanghai" to enjoy tea at Songfengge in Baoshan Street.

The old Shanghai was multifarious, so was the teahouse. People all around the country came to Shanghai and started a business here. Various styles of teahouses were launched in Shanghai, including Suzhou style, Zhejiang style, Cantonese style, Japanese style and European style. Tongfangju was one of the famous Cantonese style teahouses. SU Manshu of the South Society was a Cantonese. He came to Tongfangju and felt as if he returned to his hometown and stayed with his relatives. Lots of his poems were created while tasting tea at Tongfangju. "In this ancient teahouse, it is not difficult for us to meet

生。"这是美国作家爱狄密在《上海——冒险家的乐园》一书中写下的文字。老上海的茶楼不像北京茶馆那样泾渭分明,各有其不同的娱乐形式,而是多种功能圆融,光怪陆离。当然,因茶客不同茶楼也分高低两档。高档茶楼大多开在繁华市面或风景幽静之处,是要人显贵、社会名流、文人学士、阔佬商贾聚会之所。低档茶楼遍布市井里弄,茶客为社会的普通百姓。"老虎灶"则是后者的代表。底层百姓劳作之后来此歇脚,泡上一壶廉价的热茶,边饮边说笑逗趣,传播社会各类消息和奇闻,甚以为乐。

老上海茶楼不仅仅是啜茗,多数茶客是以茶楼为场地交流信息

← 上海老城隍庙茶楼

one or two learned and respectable Chinese. They are tasting the tea, thinking about the country, reviewing the glory of this ancient China and looking forward to its revitalization." It was written by the American author Addimillar in his book *Shanghai: The Paradise of Adventurers*. The teahouse in old Shanghai was different from that in Beijing where the teahouses had different kinds of entertainment activities. In old Shanghai, the teahouses integrated various functions, bizarre and motley. Of course, due to the difference in customers, the teahouses were divided into two levels — high-end and low-end. The high-end teahouses, mainly located in the downtown area or a quiet place, were the gathering places for dignitaries, socialites, literati, rich businessmen. The low-end teahouses, mainly located all over the streets and lances of the city, were the gathering places for common people. "Laohuzhao" was one of the representatives of the low-end teahouses. People at the bottom of society came here to rest after work. They made a pot of cheap hot tea, talked and laughed while drinking tea and discussing various

→ 上海天韵阁茶楼

洽谈生意。晚清的营造商大多在福州路青莲阁举行茶会，建筑商常聚于福州路长乐茶楼，小包工则在湖北路天香阁及附近的一乐天茶楼活动，花卉行业在老西门外阿德茶楼设台交易，品芳楼是旧汽车配件的交易场所，四美轩是珠宝玉器市场之一，浙江路萝春阁是木业集散地，一洞天茶楼则是报人的新闻聚会中心。争执双方议和一般也在茶楼进行，旧时叫做"吃讲茶"。即发生纠纷的双方请第三者一起到茶楼调停，如果双方同意和解，调解人就把红绿两种茶混在一起，双方一饮而尽，事情就算解决。

← 老上海的茶楼　贺竹元绘

social news and anecdotes happily.

The teahouse in old Shanghai was not only the place for people to taste tea, but also for people to exchange information and negotiate business. The contractors in the late Qing Dynasty always held tea party at Qingliange of Fuzhou Road. The builders always gathered together at Changle Teahouse of Fuzhou Road. Small labor contractors always got together at Tianxiangge of Hubei Road and the Yiletian Teahouse nearby. People of the flower industry set up trading desks at Ade Teahouse outside the Old West Gate. Pingfanglou was the trading place for old auto parts. Simeixuan was one of the jewelries and jade markets. Luochunge at Zhejiang Road was the distribution center for the wood industry. Yidongtian Teahouse was the gathering place for the newspaper industry. Teahouse was also the place for both sides of the dispute to negotiate peace, namely, the so-called "peace-making tea". The two parties of the dispute invited a third party to come to the teahouse for mediating. If the two parties agreed to reconcile, the mediator would mix the red tea and green tea, then the two parties drank the tea together, and the matter was solved.

"Opera is a kind of art that is cultivated by tea", which illustrates the indissoluble bond between tea houses and culture. The earliest theater in old Shanghai — "Sanyayuan", was actually a teahouse for people to drink tea and appreciate operas. Literati and masters of painting and calligraphy also liked to gather at the teahouse for tea-tasting, art discussion and creation. In those days, the famous lantern riddles association "Ping Society" often held activities in the teahouse. The lantern riddles hung in the teahouse added profound folk-art charm to the teahouse. Many teahouses had storytelling houses for pingtan artists to give performances and tell various stories. Many pingtan artists became famous in the teahouse.

The teahouse of old Shanghai was also the news center. The customers in the teahouses were always well-informed so that reporters of the newspaper offices, patrols of police stations, undercover detectives often patronized the teahouses. Some reporters heard the interesting news in the teahouse, then immediately wrote the article and sent to the newspaper offices, so many newspaper tidbits were produced in this way. Patrols and

"戏曲是用茶叶浇灌起来的一门艺术",这句话说透了茶楼与文化的不解之缘。老上海最早的戏院"三雅院"就是吃茶带看戏,实际上是个茶楼。文人雅士、书画墨客也都喜欢到茶楼雅集,煮茶论艺、泼墨挥毫。当年著名灯谜社团"萍社"常借茶楼举行活动,茶座间悬挂着灯谜,给茶楼增添了浓厚的民间艺术色彩。许多茶楼还辟有书场,长枪袍带、公案侠义,或弦索悦耳,或惊堂醒目,不少评弹艺人是由茶客泡成名的。

老上海茶楼也是新闻集散地。因茶客杂消息多,故而报馆的记者、巡捕房的巡捕、便衣侦探都经常光顾茶楼。有的记者在茶楼听到消息趣闻后,当场草就文章发往报馆,许多报纸的花边新闻就是这样炮制出来的。巡捕房的巡捕、侦探不仅常从茶楼中得到破案线索,有时干脆在茶楼办案,所以老上海有包打听茶会之说。不过,这种茶客从不付茶资,茶楼老板需依仗他们的势力维持市面。

抗战的孤岛时期,老上海的茶楼逐渐萎缩,一些晚清极负盛名的老字号茶楼因门庭冷落纷纷关门。上海解放后,受"左"的思想影响,茶楼茗饮被视为旧社会生活方式遭到批判,老茶楼所剩无几。改革开放后,茶文化复兴。一些老字号茶楼恢复营业,各种新茶楼、茶艺馆和茶室如雨后春笋遍布街市,传统茶文化进入城市的慢生活。人们在这里品茗休闲,享受浪漫和温馨。

茶楼,上海人心目中永远不会消失的风景。期待今天的茶楼能为这座城市拂去一份喧嚣,平添一份静气。

2012 年 10 月

detectives not only came to the teahouses to get clues and solve the cases, and even sometimes handled the case directly at the teahouse. Therefore, the teahouse of old Shanghai was also called "nosy parkers' tea party". Nevertheless, this kind of customers never paid for the tea because the owner of the teahouse relied on them to maintain the market.

During the isolated period of the Anti-Japanese War, the teahouses in old Shanghai gradually shrunk, and some famous teahouses in the late Qing Dynasty closed down due to the lack of customers. After the liberation of Shanghai, under the influence of the "left-wing" ideology, teahouses were regarded as the lifestyle of old society and criticized, thus making the old teahouses nearly disappear. After the reform and opening up, the tea culture revived. Some time-honored teahouses resumed business. New teahouses, tea culture centers and tearooms have sprung up all over the city. Traditional tea culture became a part of the urban slow lifestyle. Here, people can taste the tea and enjoy leisure, romantic and happy times.

Teahouse is the scenery that will never disappear in the minds of Shanghai people. We sincerely expect that the teahouses today can flick away the noisein the city and bring some quietness to the city.

October 2012

老上海的沪剧

沪剧是唱出来的上海话，是代表上海城市独特形象的戏剧。

被列入第一批国家级非物质文化遗产名录的沪剧，渊源于浦江两岸的民歌俚曲，后受其它民间说唱及戏曲影响进入花鼓戏时期，清末形成上海滩簧。文明戏时代，发展成为小型舞台剧申曲。1941年上海沪剧社成立，申曲正式改称沪剧。上海解放后，沪剧创作和演出进入新的繁荣期，剧目丰收、人才辈出，舞台艺术水平大大提高。1960年4月，上海市人民沪剧团晋京展演，获文化部和中国剧协表彰并被授予坚持编演戏曲现代戏的"四面红旗"之一。"文革"中，沪剧遭受严重摧残，所有剧团编导演人员几乎全部遭到冲击和批判，剧团被迫停演或解散。改革开放后，沪剧逐步恢复生机，创作演出了一大批深受观众欢迎的新剧目。进入新世纪后，受都市文化大环境的影响，沪剧面临新的困难。从最早的花鼓戏到当代沪剧，沪剧走过了200多年艰辛发展的历程。

沪剧是从田头山歌发展而来的戏曲剧种。在漫长的发展过程中，它逐步形成了重视深入生活，抒发内心世界，形体塑造人物，表现时代气息的艺术特色。在各个不同的历史时期，涌现了一批优秀剧目。如花鼓戏和滩簧时期的《女看灯》、《卖红菱》、《拔兰花》等，

Shanghai Opera of Old Shanghai

Shanghai opera, sung in Shanghai dialect, represents the unique image of Shanghai.

Listed in the first batch of national intangible cultural heritage, Shanghai Opera is originated from the folk songs and tunes in Pujiang districts. Influenced by other folk raps and operas, it entered the period of flower drum opera and then developed into Shanghai Tanhuang in the late Qing Dynasty. In the era of modern dramas, it developed into the mini living theater "Shenqu" (another name of Shanghai Opera). In 1941, the Shanghai Opera Society was founded and the "Shenqu" was officially renamed "Shanghai Opera". After the liberation of Shanghai, the creation and performance of Shanghai Opera entered a new period of prosperity. There emerged lots of excellent plays and talents of Shanghai Opera, and the level of stage art was greatly improved. In April 1960, Shanghai People's Shanghai Drama Troupe gave performances in Beijing and was awarded one of the "four red flags" by the Ministry of Culture and China Theater Association for its adhering to compiling and performing modern operas. During the Cultural Revolution, Shanghai Opera was severely damaged and nearly all the directors and actors of the troupes were attacked and criticized. The troupes were forced to suspend or disband. After the reform and opening up, Shanghai Opera gradually recovered its vitality and a large number of new popular plays were created and performed. After entering the new century, influenced by the metropolitan cultural environment, Shanghai Opera faced new difficulties. From the earliest flower drum opera to the contemporary Shanghai Opera, it has gone through more than 200 years of difficult development.

Shanghai Opera is a kind of opera developed from folk songs. In the long process of development, it has gradually formed the art characteristics, including paying attention to

丁是娥主演沪剧《罗汉钱》

申曲时期的《离婚怨》、《杨乃武与小白菜》、《阮玲玉之死》等,上世纪40年代的《魂断蓝桥》、《骆驼祥子》、《家》、《雷雨》等,全国解放后的《白毛女》、《罗汉钱》、《赵一曼》、《金黛莱》、《母亲》、《星星之火》、《鸡毛飞上天》、《芦荡火种》等。改革开放后,《金绣娘》、《张志新之死》、《一个明星的遭遇》、《东方女性》等一批新剧目在历届上海戏剧节和全国汇演中获奖,其中《清风歌》、《今日梦圆》分别获文化部新剧目奖和"五个一工程"奖。

在沪剧的发展过程中,出现了一批有影响的班社剧团,涌现了一大批优秀演员。20世纪比较有影响的班社剧团有:成立于20、30

plunging into the thick of life, expressing inner world, shaping characters vividly and expressing the spirit of The times. In different historical periods, there emerged a batch of excellent plays, such as *Women Watching Lanterns*, *Selling Chestnut* and *Picking Orchid* in the periods of flower drum opera and Tanhuang, *Complain of Divorce*, *Yang Nai-wu & Hsiao Pai-tsai* and *The Death of RUAN Linyu* in the period of Tanhuang, *Waterloo Bridge*, *The Ricksha Boy*, *Home* and *Thunderstorm* in the 1940s, and *White Haired Girl*, *Luohan Coin*, *ZHAO Yiman*, *JIN Dailai*, *Mother*, *Sparks of Fire*, *Feather Fly* and *Flames of War* after the national liberation. After the reform and opening up, a batch of new plays, such as *JIN Xiuniang*, *The Death of ZHANG Zhixin*, *The Encounter of a Star*, *Oriental Woman* and other plays won awards successively at Shanghai Theater Festival and national joint performance, among which *Song of Integrity* and *Reading the Dream Today* respectively won the New Opera Award of Ministry of Culture and the "Five-One Project" Award.

In the development process of Shanghai Opera, there appeared a group of influential troupes and a large number of excellent actors. In the 20th century, the influential Shanghai opera societies and troupes included the Big Abo Troupe, Shaolan Society, Fuying Society, Ziyun Society, Xinya Society, the Children's Shenqu Class of Wan Society, SHI Family Troupe and Wenbin Troupe founded during the 1920s and 1930s and the Shanghai Opera Society, China Art Troupe, Shanghai Art Troupe, Qinyi Art Troupe, Nuli Art Troupe, Yihua Art Troupe and Aihuahu Art Troupe founded in the 1940s. After the liberation of Shanghai, besides Shanghai People's Shanghai Opera Troupe and Yangtze Shanghai Opera Troupe, etc., lots of district-level Shanghai opera troupes were re-established in Baoshan, Xuhui, Changning and other districts on the basis of some old Shanghai opera troupes. There also emerged lots of famous artists who had made important contributions to the inheritance and development of Shanghai opera in different historical periods of the development of Shanghai opera, such as SHI Lanting, SHAO Wenbin, DING Shaolan, FAN Zhiliang, XIAO Wenbin, SHI Chunxuan, YANG Yueying, DING Shie, GU Yuezhen, XIE Hongyuan, SHAO Binsun, SHI Xiaoying, WANG Pansheng, YANG Feifei, WANG Xiuying, WANG

卫鸣歧、石筱英主演时装沪剧《黄陆恋爱》

年代的大阿宝班、少兰社、新兰社、福英社、紫云社、新雅社、婉社儿童申曲班、施家剧团、文滨剧团等，成立于40年代的上海沪剧社、中艺剧团以及上艺、勤艺、努力、艺华、爱华沪剧团等。上海解放后，除上海市人民沪剧团、长江沪剧团等外，宝山、徐汇、长宁等区都在一些老沪剧团的基础上重新组建了区级沪剧团。施兰亭、邵文斌、丁邵兰、范志良、筱文滨、施春轩、杨月英、丁是娥、顾月珍、解洪元、邵滨孙、石筱英、王盘声、杨飞飞、汪秀英、王雅琴、马莉莉、茅善玉、孙徐春、陈瑜、吕贤丽、钱思剑等是沪剧发展不同历史时期涌现出的著名艺人，他们为沪剧的传承和发展作出

Yaqin, MA Lili, MAO Shanyu, SUN Xuchun, CHEN Yu, LV Xianli and QIAN Sijian, etc.

Shanghai Opera regards long-cavity long board, triangle board and poem board as basic music for voices. The melody is beautiful and full of the Jiangnan charm. Shenqu was an important stage during the development of music for voices in Shanghai opera, which has changed the defects of the flat narration in the early years. After shenqu was renamed Shanghai opera, with the development of plays, there formed different schools of music for voices in Shanghai opera. After the liberation of Shanghai, music for voices in Shanghai opera received reform and innovation in the aspects of basic board cavity system application, inheritance and development of traditional Qupai tones, and absorption and integration of music for voices insimilar operas, resulting in an unprecedented prosperityof various schools. The representative schools included SHI School founded by SHI Xioaying and featured by euphemistic emotion expression, DING School founded by DING Shie and featured by magnificence and variety, YANG School founded by YANG Feifei and featured by dignified and intense feelings, WANG School founded by WANG Xiuying and featured by liveliness and fluency, GU School founded by GU Yuezhen and featured by sadness and steadiness, SHAO School founded by SHAO Binsun and featured by loudness and passion, XIE School founded by XIE Hongyuan and featured by vigorousness and strength, WANG School founded by WANG Pansheng and featured by elegance and naturalness, ZHAO School founded by ZHAO Chunfang and featured by the integration of strength and ease, and YUAN School founded by YUAN Binzhong and featured by sweetness and romance, etc. After the reform and opening up, a number of rising stars of Shanghai opera made new innovations to the music for voices in Shanghai opera and brought new features to Shanghai opera.

After the entry into the new century, the development of Shanghai opera encountered severe challenges due to the multiple impacts of the film, television and network. As the world's cultural metropolis, Shanghai shall not lose its traditional native culture. Shanghai opera needs reform and innovation, but it is also very important to create a good development environment for native culture. Shanghai should provide more

了重要贡献。

沪剧以长腔长板、三角板、赋子板等为基本音乐唱腔，曲调优美，富有江南乡土气息。申曲是沪剧唱腔发展的重要阶段，改变了滩簧早期唱腔平铺直叙的缺陷。申曲改名沪剧后，随着剧目的发展，不同流派的沪剧唱腔开始形成。上海解放后，沪剧音乐在基本板腔系统的运用方面，在传统曲牌小调的继承发展方面，在吸收融化兄弟剧种的唱腔音乐方面等都有了改革与创新，出现了流派纷呈、盛况空前的局面。代表性的有：石筱英创造的以抒情委婉为特色的石派，丁是娥创造的以瑰丽多变为特色的丁派，杨飞飞创造的以凝重深沉为特色的杨派，汪秀英创造的以活泼流畅为特色的汪派，顾月珍创造的以哀怨刚稳为特色的顾派，邵滨孙创造的以激昂高亢为特色的邵派，解洪元创造的以浑厚苍劲为特色的解派，王盘声创造的以飘逸潇洒为特色的王派，赵春芳创造的以刚中有柔为特色的赵派，袁滨忠创造的以滋润甜糯为特色的袁派等。改革开放后，一批沪剧新秀对沪剧唱腔又有新的创造，呈现了新的特色。

进入新世纪后，面对影视网络等多重冲击，沪剧的发展遇到了严峻挑战。上海作为世界性文化都市，绝不可缺失传统的本土文化。沪剧自身需要改革创新，但为本土文化营造良好的发展环境也极为重要。上海应该为用本地母语表达思想感情、反映生活的沪剧提供更大的空间。

期望沪剧这朵奇葩在上海这座世界语言文化日趋多元多样的百花园中永远绽放！

2012 年 11 月

space for Shanghai opera to express feelings and reflect life in Shanghai dialect.

We expect that Shanghai opera will prosper forever in Shanghai, the world's cultural metropolis where languages and cultures become increasingly diverse.

November 2012

老上海的淮剧

淮剧作为苏北地方剧种在上海的代表,已经成为海派戏剧不可分割的组成部分。

淮剧,又名江淮戏,起源于清代中叶苏北一带,由流行的家民号子和田歌雷雷腔、栽秧调逐渐发展而成,距今已有200多年历史。1906年,淮河洪水泛滥,大批苏北难民和淮戏艺人逃荒进入上海。为了生存,流落上海的淮戏艺人自由组合演唱卖艺,使得当时被称为"盐淮小戏"的淮剧从"路头戏"发展到"拉围子",直至1916年上海第一家淮剧剧场"群乐戏院"诞生,淮剧迈出了从苏北农村的草根文化向城市剧场进军的第一步。上世纪20年代末,著名京剧演员高雪樵、赵松樵等先后参加淮剧班同台演出,从而有了"京淮不分家"、"一台淮戏半台京"之说,历史上称为"京夹淮"。在京剧等剧种的影响下,淮剧从剧目、表演艺术、音乐伴奏到舞台美术,逐渐步入全新的戏曲表演新境界,形成了既不同于北方剧种的阳刚,又不同于江南剧种的阴柔的刚中有柔、柔中有刚的独特审美气质,给上海剧坛带来了一股充满生活质感的艺术冲击力。当时上海的淮剧演艺团体多达十多家。田汉、洪深和欧阳予倩等一批进步艺术家对淮剧给予了支持,大批戏剧界优秀艺人为淮剧的魅力所吸引,纷

Huai Opera of Old Shanghai

As the representative of northern Jiangsu operas in Shanghai, Huai Opera has been an inseparable part of Shanghai-style opera.

Huai Opera, also called Jianghuai Opera, was originated in northern Jiangsu in the middle period of the Qing Dynasty and developed from the popular farmer work song and tunes of farming songs and sowing songs. It has a history of more than 200 years. In 1906, due to the flooding of Huaihe River, large numbers of refugees in Northern Jiangsu and artists of Huai Opera fled to Shanghai. These Huai Opera artists cooperated with each other and made a living as performers, thus making Huai Opera, which was called "Yanhuai Operetta" at that time developed from "street opera" into "cooperative opera". In 1916, the first Huai Opera theater "Qunle Theater" was founded in Shanghai, which made Huai Opera take the first step in moving into the urban theater from the grass-roots culture in northern Jiangsu. In the late 1920s, the famous Peking Opera artists GAO Xueqiao, ZHAO Songqiao and other performers took part in the same performance of Huai Opera troupes successively. Therefore, there were sayings like "Beijing Opera and Huai Opera are inseparable" and "Half of a complete Huai Opera consists of Peking Opera", which was the so-called "Peking Opear integrated in Huai Opera" in the history. Under the influence of Peking Opera and other operas, Huai Opera gradually developed into a new stage of opera performances in the aspects of opera plays, performing arts, music accompaniment and stage art and formed its unique aesthetic charm — solidness in softness, and softness in solidness, which was different from the manly solidness in the northern operas and the feminine softness in Jiangnan operas, which brought the artistic impact with sense of life uponShanghai opera circle. At

纷加盟淮剧剧目的创作，最终形成了有别于苏北淮剧的海派淮剧。

新中国成立后，淮剧焕发出全新的活力，赢得了广阔的发展空间。上海淮剧团是上海成立最早的国家院团之一，毛泽东、刘少奇、周恩来、朱德、宋庆龄等老一辈中央领导都先后观看过上海淮剧团的演出。改革开放使淮剧获得新生。1985年，时任上海市市长的江泽民观看了淮剧《水漫泗洲》。1993年，时任中央政治局常委的胡锦涛观看了都市新淮剧《金龙与蜉蝣》，极大鼓舞了淮剧的发展。

淮剧艺术特色鲜明。它的音乐属于多声腔综合系统，具有苍劲质朴、婉美抒情的特点。《淮调》、《拉调》、《自由调》为三大基本声腔，又辅以几十种民间小调，唱腔丰富多彩。它的表演能文能武，既能演古装戏，又能演现代戏，可塑性、适应性很强，为广大观众所喜闻乐见。

在海派淮剧100多年的发展历程中，积累了一大批优秀剧目。如《白蛇传》、《千里送京娘》、《兰桥会》、《九件衣》、《海港的早晨》、《八女投江》等。特别是都市新淮剧《金龙与蜉蝣》、《西楚霸王》、《千古韩非》的创作演出，成为淮剧史上新的里程碑，为戏曲改革创新提供了宝贵经验。吕秉仁、吕世凤、骆有贵、骆保杭、何廷裕、何孔标、武旭东、顾汉章、谢长钰、孙东升、何益山、马麟童、何叫天、徐桂芳、杨占魁等是淮剧历史上重要的代表人物。筱文艳、马秀英、武筱凤、顾少春、何双林、梁伟平、施燕萍等则是淮剧代表性传承人。

在长期的艺术实践中，淮剧形成了多彩的唱腔流派。如，筱文艳创立的以细腻柔美、爽朗动听为特色的筱派旦腔，何叫天创立的

that time, there were more than ten Huai Opera performing troupes in Shanghai. A group of progressive artists, including TIAN Han, HONG Shen and OUYANG Yuqian, gave support to Huai Opera. And a large number of outstanding artists in the opera circles were attracted by the charm of Huai Opera and joined in the creation of Huai Opera, thus finally forming the Shanghai-style Huai Opera which was different from the Huai Opera in Jiangsu.

After the founding of the People's Republic of China, Huaiju Opera gained new vitality and won broad development space. Shanghai Huai Opera Troupe was one of the earliest national-level opera troupes in Shanghai. MAO Zedong, LIU Shaoqi, ZHOU Enlai, ZHU De, SONG Qingling and other central leaders of the older generation watched the performance of Shanghai Huai Opera Troupe. The reform and opening-up brought new life to Huai Opera. In 1985, JIANG Zemin, then the mayor of Shanghai, watched the Huai Opera *Flooding Sizhou*. In 1993, HU Jintao, then member of the Standing Committee of the Political Bureau of the CPC Central Committee, watched the new urban Huai Opear *Golden Dragon and Ephemera*, which greatly encouraged the development of Huai Opera.

The artistic features of Huai Opera are distinctive. Its music belongs to the multi-tune synthetic system which is vigorous, plain, graceful and lyric. It consists of three basic systematic tunes, namely, Huai tune, pulling tune and free tune, and dozens of folk tunes, which are very diversified. Its performance is very flexible and adaptable, involving not only the classical operas, but also the modern ones, thus being favored by general audience.

In the 100-plus-year development history of Huai Opera, it has accumulated a large number of excellent plays, such as *Madam White Snake*, *Emperor's Lover*, *Dating at Lanqiao Bridge*, *Nine Pieces of Clothes*, *The Morning of the Harbor* and *Eight Women Fighters*, etc. Especially, the creation and performance of new urban Huai opera, such as *Golden Dragon and Ephemera*, *Overlord of Western Chu* and *The Historic Figure HAN Fei*, became a new milestone in the history of Huai Opera and provided valuable experience for the reform and innovation of operas. The important representative artists in

何叫天、筱文艳《三女抢板》

以吐字清晰、音韵纯正为特色的何派生腔，马麟童创立的以节奏分明、跌宕有致为特色的马派自由调，李玉花创立的以句急而气不乱、腔紧而字不糊为特色的李派旦腔，杨占魁创立的以韵味醇厚、行腔流畅为特色的杨派生腔，徐桂芳创立的以高亢激越、宽厚明亮为特色的徐派老旦腔等。

海派淮剧百余年的历史，见证了上海与苏北的不解情缘。海纳百川的上海滋润了淮剧，为淮剧的发展提供了舞台，淮剧也以它特有的审美气质为海派文化增光添彩。苏北人遗留在上海的淮剧已经成为上海城市文化发展的一段重要历史。淮剧被列为上海市级及国

the history of Huai Opera included LV Bingren, LV Shifeng, LUO Yougui, LUO Baohang, HE Tingyu, HE Kongbiao, WU Xudong, GU Hanzhang, XIE Changyu, SUN Dongsheng, HE Yishan, MA Lintong, HE Jiaotian, XU Guifang and YANG Zhankui, etc. The representative inheritors of Huai Opera included XIAO Wenyan, MA Xiuying, WU Xiaofeng, GU Shaochun, HE Shuanglin and LIANG Weiping, etc.

In the long-term artistic practice, there have formed various schools of Huai Opera, such as the female tune of XIAO School founded by XIAO Wenyan and featured by exquisite, soft, bright and pleasant sounds; the male tune of HE School founded by HE Jiaotian and featured by clear pronunciation and pure rhyme; the free tune of MA School founded by MA Lintong and featured by clear rhythm and stratified ups and downs; the female tune of LI School founded by LI Yuhua and featured by urgent sentence without chaotic pneuma and tight tunes without vague words; male tune of YANG School founded by YANG Zhankui and featured by lingering charm and fluent tunes; and the old female tune of XU School founded by XU Guifang and featured by sonorous and passionate

↗《西楚霸王》

家级非物质文化遗产是淮剧的骄傲。

  在当前新的都市文化环境中,淮剧遇到了新的挑战。应对挑战,发展淮剧,需要社会的支持,需要淮剧艺人坚定的职业信仰,需要淮剧自身的改革创新。相信只要经过方方面面的努力,淮剧剧种的艺术特色和现代观众的审美情趣一定会实现和谐统一,淮剧新的春天必将到来。

2012 年 12 月

sounds and broad and bright tunes, etc.

The 100-year history of Shanghai-style Huai Opera has witnessed the relationship between Shanghai and northern Jiangsu. The inclusive Shanghai has promoted the development of Huai Opera and provided a stage for the development of Huai Opera. Meanwhile, with its unique aesthetic charm, Huai Opera has also added luster to Shanghai-style culture. Huai Opera introduced by the people of north Jiangsu into Shanghai has become an important part of Shanghai's cultural development history. It is the pride for Huai Opera to be listed as Shanghai municipal and national intangible cultural heritage.

In the new urban cultural environment, Huai Opera is facing new challenges. In order to meet the challenges and promote the development of Huai Opera, social support and Huai Opera artists' strong professional belief, as well as the reform and innovation of Huai Opera are indispensable. We believe that with every effort, the artistic features of Huai Opera and the aesthetic taste of modern audiences will achieve harmony and unity, and the new spring of Huai Opera will certainly come.

December 2012

老上海的爵士乐

爵士乐作为世界性的大众音乐传入中国是从上海开始的。回顾老上海爵士乐的历史,对于创新发展我国的传统音乐,丰富城市音乐生活极富意义。

爵士乐于19世纪末20世纪初发祥于美国南部港口城市新奥尔良,至今已有110多年历史。爵士乐音乐的根基来自"拉格泰姆"和"民间蓝调",以后经历了上世纪20年代以集体即兴演奏为主的"迪克西兰",30年代以伴舞为主要职能的"摇摆乐",40年代以和弦演奏为基础做即兴演奏的"比波普",50、60年代风格迥异的"比波普"和"酷"以及随后的"自由"派,70、80年代"摇滚"和爵士乐的融合,90年代的"新经典主义"等。进入新世纪后,虽然爵士乐在不断演变、融合、发展,但每一种爵士风格都依然活跃在今天的舞台上。具有强烈持久生命力的爵士乐经过百年演进,早已突破了地域、种族和国界的局限,成为与古典音乐相提并论的世界性音乐。

爵士乐在上世纪20年代传入上海。1923年,美国人奥斯邦创办了上海第一家也是中国第一家广播电台ECO。奥斯邦带来的爵士乐随着电波飘散在老上海的洋房和里弄,使上海人开始接触这种全新

Jazz of Old Shanghai

Shanghai is the first city in China that introduced the jazz, the worldwide popular music. It is of rich significance for the innovative development of China's traditional music and the enrichment of urban music life to review the jazz history of old Shanghai.

Jazz, originated in the port city of the United States — New Orleans in the turning of the 19th and 20th centuries, has a history of more than 110 years. Jazz music was first based on "ragtime" and "folk blues" and then experienced the "Dixieland" featured by collective extemporize in the 1920s, the "swing music" with dancing accompaniment as the main function in the 1930s, the "Bebop" which conducted extemporization on the basis of chord performance in the 1940s, the different styles of "Bebop" and "Cool" in the 1950s and 1960s, and the subsequent "free style", the integration of "rock" and jazz in the 1970s and 1980s, the "neoclassicism" in the 1990s and so on. After entering the new century, although jazz has experienced constant evolution, integration and development, each jazz style is still alive on the stage today. After a century of evolution, jazz, with its strong and persistent vitality, has already broken through the limitations of regions, races and national boundaries and become a worldwide music in the same breath as classical music.

Jazz was introduced into Shanghai in the 1920s. In 1923, the American Osborn founded ECO, the first radio station in Shanghai and China. The jazz music brought by Osborn was broadcast through the radio waves all over Shanghai, exposing old Shanghai people to this new form of music. The opening of the Paramount in 1933 marked the arrival of the heyday of the urban entertainment industry in Shanghai. Foreign jazz bands and Filipino musicians were active in the Paramount and other ballrooms of Shanghai.

老年爵士乐队

的音乐形式。1933 年，百乐门舞厅开张，标志着上海都市娱乐业鼎盛时代的到来，洋人爵士乐队和菲律宾乐手活跃在百乐门及上海各大舞厅。在爵士音乐的感召下，老上海的爱乐者钟情起这种有着浓郁都市情调的音乐，并开始形成具有上海特色的爵士乐。

上海绍兴路 5 号是幢西班牙风格的房子，主人朱季琳是虔诚的天主教徒。这幢房子里诞生了上海第一支家庭爵士乐队。乐队先由朱家子弟为主，后在上海法租界生活的瑞典、美国、苏联的爵士乐发烧友陆续加入。乐队不仅为家族的教堂和派对演奏爵士乐，还常常外出演奏，倾倒了大批喜欢爵士乐的上海年轻人。一次，上海工部局在金诚大剧院举办音乐会，朱家乐队胜出其它三支洋人专业乐队荣获第一。这支家庭乐队成为上海最早呼应爵士乐的青春之声。金怀祖是当时上海圣约翰大学物理系的中国学生，又名吉米金。他

Under the inspiration of jazz, music lovers in old Shanghai fell in love with this music which has strong urban charm. Therefore, the jazz with Shanghai characteristics began to come into being.

The owner of the Spanish-style house located at No. 5, Shaoxing Road in Shanghai was ZHU Jilin, a devout Roman Catholic. The first family jazz band of Shanghai was founded in this house. The band members first consisted of the children of the ZHU Family, and later the Swedish, American and Soviet jazz enthusiasts living in the French Concession of Shanghai joined it. The band not only played jazz for the family's church and parties, but also for other activities outside, attracting a large number of young people in Shanghai who liked jazz. Once at the concert sponsored by Shanghai Industrial Bureau in Jincheng Theater, the ZHU Family band defeated other foreign bands and won the champion. This family band became the first youth voice to advocate jazz in Shanghai. JIN Huaizu, also known as Jimmy Kim, was then a Chinese student in the Department of Physics at St. John's University in Shanghai. He formed a 16-member jazz band called Jimmy King in 1946. YU Gefei, then owner of the Paramount, appreciated Jimmy King's musical talents very much and invited his band to perform in the Paramount. The instant hit of this all-Chinese jazz band made the Paramount become very famous. Jimmy Kim became the first professional Chinese jazz band in Shanghai.

Just the same as the New Orleans Jazz, the Old Shanghai Jazz was composed of piano, clarinet, saxophone, trumpet, trombone, bass, drum, maracas and percussion. However, the Old Shanghai Jazz mainly involved Shanghai-style mandarin pop songs, such as *Nightlife in Shanghai*, *Rose, Rose, I Love You* and *Shangri-La*, which made the performance and singing style blend in the nostalgic and lyric Chinese style, thus forming the jazz with Shanghai characteristics.

Due to the war and the political environment after the founding of the People's Republic of China, the development of Shanghai jazz had been suspended for more than 30 years. After the reform and opening-up, jazz returned to Shanghai after a long absence. In 1980, ZHOU Wanrong, an old Shanghai jazz musician who once served as the chief trumpet of Shanghai Symphony Orchestra, organized a 6-member senior jazz

于 1946 年组建了 16 人编制的 Jimmy King 爵士乐队。当时百乐门老板郁格菲十分欣赏吉米金的音乐天份，聘请他的乐队到百乐门演奏。这支全部由华人组成的爵士乐队一炮打响，使百乐门名噪一时。吉米金乐队成为上海第一支华人专业爵士乐队。

老上海的爵士与新奥尔良爵士同样由钢琴、单簧管、萨克斯、小号、长号、低音提琴、鼓、沙槌、打击乐合成。但老上海爵士以海派国语流行曲为主，如《夜上海》、《玫瑰玫瑰我爱你》、《香格里拉》等，使演奏和演唱风格融入了怀旧、抒情的中国色彩，形成了具有上海特色的爵士乐。

由于战争和建国后的政治环境，上海爵士乐出现了 30 多年的断层。改革开放后，爵士乐重返阔别已久的上海。1980 年，曾任上海交响乐团首席小号的老上海爵士乐手周万荣组建了一支 6 人老年爵士乐队，活跃在外滩最具老克勒风情的和平饭店一楼爵士吧，使人们重温了老上海的爵士梦。这支乐队在这间散发着古老味道的酒吧里，用热情洋溢的风格、精到娴熟的技艺接待了来自世界各国的嘉宾，英国女王伊丽莎白二世、法国总统密特朗和美国总统克林顿等都曾来这里欣赏过他们的出色表演。1996 年，和平饭店老年爵士酒吧被美国《新闻周刊》评为世界最佳酒吧之一。当年百乐门吉米金乐队的贝司手、年届九旬的郑德仁老先生与上海著名歌手纪晓兰一起组建了上海海邻爵士乐团。乐团以传承和创新海派都市文化为宗旨，专演海派经典爵士，先后参加了上海世博会、上海国际艺术节等重大演出，被誉为"上海顶级爵士乐团"。

当年美国南部种植园黑人奴隶用以表达自己生活和情感的爵士

band, which was active in the jazz bar on the first floor of the Peace Hotel, the most "clerk" style hotel in the bund, making people realizethe jazz dream of old Shanghai. This band, with its ebullient style and consummate skills, performed for guests from all over the world in this venerable bar. Queen Elizabeth II of England, French President Francois Mitterrand and President Clinton of the United States all came here and appreciated their wonderful performances. In 1996, the senior jazz bar of Peace Hotel was named one of the best bars in the world by the American magazine *News Week*. In the same year, Mr. ZHENG Deren (the bassist of Paramount's Jimmy King Band who was 90 years old) and the reputedShanghai singer JI Xiaolan jointly founded the Shanghai Hailin Jazz Orchestra. The band, committed to the inheritance and innovation of Shanghai urban culture and specialized in classic Shanghai-style jazz, has successively participated in Shanghai World Expo, Shanghai International Festival of Arts and other events, being praised as "the top jazz orchestra in Shanghai".

Jazz, once used by the black slaves in plantations of South United States to

↗ 房主姚乃炽（前右一）与伙伴们在"怪屋"客厅里练琴

乐，已成为和当代社会中时代精神相契合的音乐形式。上海作为中国爵士乐活动的发祥地，应该以海纳百川的胸怀接纳多样的音乐元素，并使爵士乐与中国音乐相结合，创建具有东方韵味的爵士音乐体系，给人们以更多更美的音乐享受。

2013 年 1 月

expresstheir lives and emotions, has become a music form in line with the zeitgeist of contemporary society. As the birthplace of jazz activities in China, Shanghai should embrace diverse music elements with an inclusive spirit, combine jazz with Chinese music to create the jazz system with oriental charm and bring more and more aesthetical music for people to enjoy.

January 2013

老上海的唱片

老上海的唱片，记录着中国历史上的艺术音响和珍贵资料。

1877年美国科学家爱迪生的蜡筒式留声机诞生，开启了人类记录和复制声音的先河。1887年德国科学家伯利纳研制成功的圆盘式唱片和留声机，为世界留声事业开创了新纪元。上海是中国最早引进唱片的城市。1889年蜡筒式留声机随大批洋货进入上海口岸，20世纪初唱片开始在上海洋行销售。1908年，法国百代公司在上海成立"东方百代唱片公司"，标志着中国唱片业的正式诞生。此后，大中华、高亭、长城、巨雷、宝芳、心声、百乐等唱片公司纷纷成立。截止1926年末，在上海从事唱片、唱机业务的企业已近30家，规模之盛，冠于全国。经过激烈竞争，到上世纪30年代初，上海形成了以百代、胜利、大中华三大唱片企业为核心的局面。当时中国本土制作的唱片大都由这三家企业出品。在新中国成立前的数十年间，上海是中国名副其实的唱片中心。

老上海的唱片，是那个时代文化特征和社会风貌的真实反映。随着留声机上唱片的缓缓转动，你可以寻觅到往昔岁月的流风余韵。电影演员杨耐梅为影片《良心复活》配唱的《乳娘曲》是中国第一首电影歌曲，由百代公司灌成唱片。电影《野草闲花》插曲《万里

Records of Old Shanghai

The records of old Shanghai have kept the artistic sounds and valuable materials in the history of China.

In 1877, the American scientist Thomas Edison invented the wax cylinder phonograph, opening the history for humans to record and reproduce sounds. In 1887, German scientist Berliner successfully invented the disc and the gramophone, which opened a new era for the world's record industry. Shanghai was the first city in China to introduce records. In 1889, the wax cylinder phonograph entered the port of Shanghai with a large number of foreign goods. In the early 20th century, records began to be sold in foreign firms of Shanghai. In 1908, the French EMI Group founded the "Oriental Emi Record Company" in Shanghai, marking the official birth of China's record industry. Since then, Great China, ODFON, Great Wall, Julei, Baofang, Xinsheng, Baile and other record companies have beensuccessively founded. By the end of 1926, nearly 30 companies had been engaged in record and phonograph business in Shanghai, ranking the state's first prize in the scale. In the early 1930s, the three major record companies — EMI, Victor and Great China stood out from the fierce competition. At that time, these three companies manufactured most of the locally-produced records in China. In the decades before the founding of People's Republic of China, Shanghai was worthy of the name "the record center" in China.

The records of old Shanghai have truly reflected the cultural characteristics and social features of that era. As the phonograph slowly rolls around, you can enjoy the charm of music in the past. The film actress YANG Naimei sang China's first film song *Wet Nurse Song* for the film *Revival of Conscience*, which was recorded by EMI. The film song *Finding Brothers* for the film *Wild Flowers by the Road* was sung by the hero and heroine

寻兄词》由影片男女主角金焰和阮玲玉演唱，当年的唱片有两个版本，一个由大中华唱片公司灌制，另一个由新月唱片公司灌制，这是阮玲玉仅有的一次录音留声。胡蝶在中国第一届电影皇后加冕典礼上献唱的新歌《最后一声》，也由百代公司灌制唱片。唱片除了欣赏娱乐外，也是政治斗争的有力武器。上海《中国晚报》社1924年为孙中山先生录制的《勉励国民》和《告诫同志》的演讲唱片，是孙中山一生仅有的一次录音留声，也是革命先驱利用近代科学发明宣传政治主张，唤起民众的最早尝试。冼星海、聂耳创作的后来成为中华人民共和国国歌的《义勇军进行曲》，在上海徐家汇的一幢小红楼里录制而成。这些唱片今天已成为中国历史文化的珍稀之物。

作为娱乐性的老上海唱片，既有流派纷呈的京剧、典雅婉转的昆曲和独具地方特色的各种梆子戏等50多个戏曲剧种，也有时人所痴迷的流行金曲。清末重要的京剧老生流派之一孙菊仙的唱片由上海胜利唱片公司灌制，他因此成为中国历史上最早灌制唱片的京剧演员。京剧"四大名旦"梅兰芳、程砚秋、尚小云、荀慧生，"四大须生"余叔岩、严菊朋、高庆奎、马连良等京剧名伶名媛都在上海百代、高亭、蓓开、胜利等唱片公司灌制过大量唱片。1927年，中国现代流行音乐教父黎锦晖创作了中国第一首流行歌曲《毛毛雨》，由他18岁的女儿黎明晖演唱。这首令人耳目一新的流行歌曲由百代公司灌制成唱片，通过收音机和留声机迅速传遍大街小巷。上海由此升腾起一股流行歌曲的热潮。从上世纪30年代起，周璇、李香兰、白虹、姚莉、白光、吴莺音等歌坛巨星灌制了大量的流行金曲唱片。这些国语老歌，直至今日仍在全球各地的华人世界中被传唱，

of the film — JIN Yan and RUAN Lingyu. There were two versions of the record, once produced by Great China Record Company and the other by Xinyue Record Company. This was the only phonographic record of RUAN Lingyu. The new song *The Last Sound*, sung by HU Die at China's first "Queen of Film" Coronation Ceremony, was also produced by EMI Record Company. Besides the functions of appreciation and entertainment, record was also a powerful weapon in the political struggle. The speech records of Sun Yat-sen made by *Chinese Evening Newspaper* in 1942 — *Encouraging the People* and *Warning the Comrades* were the only phonographic record of Sun Yat-sen in his life, and also the earliest attempt for the revolutionary pioneers to publicize political views and arouse the public by using modern scientific inventions. The *March of the Volunteers*, later becoming the national anthem of the People's Republic of China, was

↗ 百代唱片公司

人们从中可以重温、感受、领略老上海的韵味风情。

唱片因它特有的功能在近现代上海社会生活中地位独特。而今，随着科学技术的飞速发展，声音存储传播介质发生了巨大变化，唱片的辉煌年代已成为过去。然而作为各种历史声音的收藏品，老上海唱片的价值正日益凸显。

资料表明，老上海留下的唱片母盘有数万张，这是上海宝贵的历史、艺术遗产。如何收集整理这些老唱片，充分发挥老唱片的艺术价值和史料价值，应成为上海文化建设的一项内容。

2013 年春节

created by XIAN Xinghai and NIE Er and recorded in a small red building in Xujiahui, Shanghai. These records have become rarity of Chinese history and culture today.

The records of old Shanghai, as a means of recreation, involved more than 50 kinds of operas, including various schools of Peking Opera, elegant Kun Opera and various Bangzi operas with unique local characteristics, as well as the popular songs sometimes obsessed by people. The record of SUN Juxian, from one of the most important Peking Opera schools of Laosheng-role in the late Qing Dynasty, was produced by Shanghai Victor Record Company, making him the earliest Peking Opera performer who had records in China. The "four famous Dans in Peking Opera" — MEI Lanfang, CHENG Yanqiu, SHANG Xiaoyun and GOU Huisheng, the "four famous elderly male roles in Peking Opera" — YU Shuyan, YAN Jupeng, GAO Qingkui and MA Lianliang and other prestigiousfemale and male Peking Opera artists had also made a large number of records in Shanghai EMI, ODFON, Beka, Victor and other record companies. In 1927, LI Jinhui, godfather of Chinese modern pop music, composed China's first pop song *Drizzling* which was sung by his 18-year-old daughter LI Minghui. This refreshing pop song was recorded by EMI and quickly spread through the streets via radio and phonograph. Therefore, a pop music craze swept through Shanghai. Since the 1930s, ZHOU Xuan, LI Xianglan, BAI Hong, YAO Li, BAI Guang, WU Yingyin and many other famous music stars had made a large number of records of popular songs. These old Chinese songs are still widely sung by Chinese people all over the world, which can make people review, experience and appreciate the charm of old Shanghai.

Due to its specific functions, records play a unique role in the social life of modern Shanghai. Now, with the rapid development of science and technology, the sound storage and transmission medium has undergone tremendous changes while the glorious age of records has become a thing of the past. However, as a collection of historical voices, the value of the records of old Shanghai is becoming increasingly prominent.

The materials show that there are tens of thousands of mother discs of records handed down from old Shanghai, which are valuable historical and artistic heritage for Shanghai.

老上海的昆曲

联合国教科文组织宣布为首批世界"人类口头及非物质遗产代表作"的中国昆曲,在上海地区的活动已延绵了500多年。

昆曲,现称昆剧,相传为元末明初江苏昆山人顾坚初创,明中叶经魏良辅改革形成曲调委婉的"水磨腔"。明万历年间,上海松江地区一带开始传唱昆曲。1578年青浦演出的《浣纱记》,为上海昆剧演出的最早记录。据史料记载,当时上海众多的家庭戏班和民间班社演出的昆曲传奇杂剧有20多部。徐霖、沈采、沈龄、陈继儒等是明代上海地区涌现的剧作家和评论家。由明入清后,上海昆曲极为繁盛,新作不断问世,班社纷纷入沪。大章班、大雅班、全福班、鸿福班等苏州四大昆班相继南下,活跃在上海的舞台茶园。新乐府、仙霓社、赓春曲社、平声曲社、同声曲社、栗社等昆班曲社纷纷在上海创建。1783年即乾隆四十八年,昆曲的戏班组织专门成立"上海局",足见其规模之盛。清末民初,在京剧、徽剧等剧种的竞争下,昆曲日渐衰落。上海的有识之士和工商企业家纷纷资助兴办昆曲传习所,加之上海民间大量的曲社活动始终不断,为昆曲存亡继绝作出了卓越贡献。全国解放后,上海成立戏曲学校和京昆剧团,培养昆曲新人,举办昆剧观摩演出,使得昆曲这一古典艺术得以传

Kun Opera of Old Shanghai

Kun Opera, listed in world's first batch of "Masterpieces of the Oral and Intangible Heritage of Humanity" by UNESCO, has a history of more than 500 years in Shanghai.

According to the legend, Kunqu, now called Kun Opera, was first created by GU Jian from Kunshan of Jiangsu in the turning of the Yuan Dynasty and the Ming Dynasty. In the middle Ming Dynasty, it was reformed by WEI Liangfu, thus forming the euphemistic "Shuimo Tune". During the Wanli period of the Ming Dynasty, Kun Opera started to be sung in the Songjiang area of Shanghai. *A Tale of Hair Washing* performed in Qingpu in 1578 was the earliest record of the performance of Kun Opera in Shanghai. According to historical records, at that time, there were more than 20 legendary plays of Kun Opera performed by numerous family troupes and folk troupes in Shanghai. There also emerged some dramatists and critics in Shanghai in the Ming Dynasty, such as XU Lin, SHEN Cai, SHEN Ning and CHEN Jiru, etc. During the turning of the Ming Dynasty and the Qing Dynasty, Kun Opera was very prosperous in Shanghai and there constantly emerged new works while many troupes entered Shanghai. The four major Kun Opera troupes in Suzhou, including Dazhang Troupe, Daya Troupe, Quanfu Troupe and Hongfu Troupe, came to Shanghai successively and became active on the opera stages in Shanghai. Many Kun Opera societies were founded in Shanghai, such as Xinyuefu, Xianni Society, Gengchunqu Society, Pingshengqu Society, Tongshengqu Society and Li Society, etc. In 1783, the 48th year of Qianlong's reign, the Kun Opera troupes specially established the "Shanghai Bureau", which well demonstrated the prosperity of Kun Opera. In the late Qing Dynasty and the early years of Republic of China, Kun Opera gradually declined due to the competition from Peking Opera and Hui Opera.

承。"文革"期间,昆曲历史被中断。十年动乱结束后,上海组建昆剧团,昆曲进入新的发展时期。

在昆曲的发展历史中,涌现出了一大批优秀剧目和著名演员。清末民初并非昆曲的辉煌时期,但经常上演的剧目仍有800余出。《琵琶行》、《拜月亭》、《西厢记》、《长生殿》、《牡丹亭》、《蔡文姬》等优秀剧目传演至今。1956年,浙江省昆苏剧团演出的《十五贯》轰动全国,毛泽东主席先后两次观看,周恩来总理誉之为昆剧百花

↖ 张静娴、蔡正仁联袂演绎
《长生殿》

People of insight and business entrepreneurs in Shanghai funded the establishment of Kun Opera training institutions, and a large number of folk Kun Opera activities were held in Shanghai, which made remarkable contributions to the survival of Kun Opera. After the national liberation, Shanghai set up traditional opera schools and Kun Opera troupes, cultivated new learners of Kun Opera and held performance activities for people to appreciate Kun Opera, thus developing the classic art — Kun Opera be preserved. During the Cultural Revolution, the history of Kun Opera was suspended. After ten years of unrest, Shanghai organized Kun Opera troupes, thus making the development of Kun Opera enter a new period.

In the development of Kun Opera, there emerged a large number of excellent plays and renownedperformers. The heyday of Kun Opera was not in the late Qing Dynasty and the early years of Republic of China, but there were still more than 800 plays performed at that time. Excellent plays, such as *Song of a Pipa Player*, *Obeisance Moon Cabin*, *Romance of the Western Chamber*, *Palace of Eternal Life*, *Peony Pavilion* and *Cai Wenji*, are still performed today. In 1956, *Fifteen Strings of Cash* performed by Kun Opera troupe in Zhejiang Province made a sensation throughout the country. Chairman MAO Zedong watched it twice. Premier ZHOU Enlai praised it as the "orchid" in the circle of Kun Opera and "a play that saved a kind of opera". *Fifteen Strings of Cash* was performed in Shanghai in 1890. Famous Kun Opera performers in Shanghai in the Ming and Qing Dynasties included GE Zhixiang, JIN Jingfu, LI Zimei, ZHANG Ba, XIA Shuangshou, WU Jinshan, CHEN Lanpo, LI Guiquan, WU Qingshou, TAN Yafang, ZHOU Fenglin, XIAO Guilin, SHEN Xiqing, WU Yisheng, RONG Gui, DING Lansun, JIN Aqing, CHEN Shuiquan, etc. Among them, ZHOU Fenglin was praised as "the best Dan in modern Kun Opera". In the 1920s and 1930s, famous artists of Kun Opera active in Shanghai included YU Zhenfei, ZHANG Mouliang, WU Wozun, ZHU Chuanming, ZHANG Chuanfang, ZHENG Chuanjian, SHEN Chuanzhi, ZHAO Chuanjun, HUA Chuanhao, etc. The first generation Kun Opera artists cultivated by the Republic of China included HUA Wenyi, CAI Zhengren, YUEMeiti, JI Zhenhua, LIANG Guyin, WANG Zhiquan, ZHANG Jingxian, etc. The principal young and

园中的"兰花"、"一出戏救活了一个剧种"。而《十五贯》在上海地区的演出则在 1890 年。明清时期上海著名的昆曲演员有葛芷香、金景福、李子美、张八、夏双寿、吴锦山、陈兰坡、李桂泉、吴庆寿、谈雅芳、周凤林、小桂林、沈锡卿、吴义生、荣桂、丁兰荪、金阿庆、陈水泉等,其中周凤林有"近代昆旦第一"之誉。上世纪 20、30 年代活跃在上海昆坛的著名艺人有俞振飞、张某良、吴我尊、朱传茗、张传芳、郑传鉴、沈传芷、赵传珺、华传浩等。华文漪、蔡正仁、岳美缇、计镇华、梁谷音、王芝泉、张静娴等则是共和国培养起来的第一代昆曲艺术家。张军、谷好好、沈昳丽、倪泓、吴双、黎安等中青年演员是当今上海昆坛的台柱。

昆曲是集文学、舞蹈、音乐、戏剧为一体的艺术表演形式,经历代艺术家的精雕细琢与发展完善,成为中国古典表演艺术的经典。它音乐的主要特征是以曲牌为其声腔的载体,音律要求严格,历史上有着空谷幽兰的雅名。全国解放后,上海昆曲艺人在对传统昆剧音乐进行挖掘整理的基础上,通过灵活运用曲牌联套、改造传统唱腔、发展伴唱形式等,对昆剧音乐进行改革创新,使其进入新的艺术境界。昆曲的表演讲究角色行当分工,综合运用唱、念、做、打、翻等手段和注重人物眼神,载歌载舞,身段优美,声容真实,净、丑戏生活化。上世纪 50 年代以来,在俞振飞等昆曲艺术家的努力下,使上海昆剧表演形成了家门齐备、技艺全面,突破行当、塑造形象,发展武戏、文武兼备的显著特点。梁谷音称昆曲是具有文学美、音乐美、舞姿美、感情美、意境美的典雅艺术。

随着经济发展和社会变革,许多传统和民间文化艺术受到不同

middle-aged performers of Kun Opera in Shanghai today include ZHANG Jun, SHEN Dieli, NI Hong, GU Haohao, WU Shuang and LI An, etc.

Kun opera is a kind of artistic performance form integrating literature, dance, music and drama. Through the elaboration and improvement of generations of artists, it has become a classic of Chinese classical performance art. Its music is mainly featured by Qupai systematic tunes as the carrier and rigid melody requirements, enjoying the reputation of "Soratani Orchids" in the history. After the national liberation, on basis of exploration and sorting of traditional Kun Opera, Kun Opera artists in Shanghai reformed and innovated the music of Kun Opera to enter a new artistic realm by the flexible use of the traditional Qupai series music, transformation of traditional voices for music and development of vocal accompaniment forms. Kun Opera performance is particular about the division of roles and responsibilities and the comprehensive application of singing, reading, doing, beating, turning and other means, and pays attention to the expression of characters in the eyes, which not only involves singing and dancing, but also the beautiful shape of the characters, authentic acoustic capacitance and life-oriented play of Jing and Dan roles. Since the 1950s, Kun Opera artists including YU Zhenfeihave made great effortstoendow the performance form of Kun Opera with prominent features includingdiversified schools, comprehensive skills, artistic breakthrough, image shaping, development of martial scenes, integration of martial arts and cultural arts. Liang Guyin said that Kun Opera was an elegant art with literary beauty, music beauty, beautiful dancing posture, emotional beauty and beauty of artistic conception.

With economic development and social reform, many traditional and folk cultures and arts are suffering different degrees of impact, and Kun Opera is also facing the difficulties of survival and development. Although the protection of Kun Opera has been enhanced over the years, the protection and revitalization of Kun Opera has been seriously affected by the shortage of scriptwriters, the loss of traditional plays, the lack of fund for troupes, the shortage of students, the narrow performance market and the difficulty in forming new audiences. With the prosperous development of socialist culture today, it should be an important subject of cultural construction to establish an effective

程度的冲击，昆曲也面临生存发展的困难。尽管这些年来昆曲保护工作不断加强，但编剧人才缺乏、传统剧目流失、院团经费不足、昆曲生源匮乏、演出市场狭窄、新的观众群难以形成等问题严重影响了昆曲的保护和振兴。在繁荣发展社会主义文化的今天，尽快建立有利于昆曲艺术保护的有效机制，积极抢救一批濒危的经典剧目，挖掘整理珍贵的昆曲文物和历史资料，改变艺术人才匮乏的局面，使昆曲艺术的生存状态与其在世界文化的地位相匹配，理当成为文化建设的重要课题。

曾经为昆曲艺术的传承发展作出过重要历史贡献的上海，应在抢救、继承、革新、发展昆曲这一人类文化遗产中有更大的担当。

2013 年 3 月

mechanism for the protection of Kun Opera as soon as possible, actively rescue a batch of endangered classic plays, dig and sort out precious Kun Opera relics and historical materials and change the situation of lack of artistic talents, thus making the survival state of Kun Opera art match with its status in the world culture.

Shanghai, which has made important historical contributions to the inheritance and development of Kun Opera, should play a greater role in rescuing, inheriting, renovating and developing Kun Opera, the human cultural heritage.

March 2013

老上海的金曲

老上海的金曲即上世纪20至40年代诞生于上海的流行歌曲。这些优美动听的歌曲曾经装饰过一个繁华时代,铸就了中国流行音乐的第一个绚丽高峰。

一股音乐潮流的兴起,总是与其所处时代的政治、经济和文化背景有关。上世纪20至40年代,上海已经具备资本主义商业化都市的特征,经济畸形繁荣,西方特别是美国流行音乐通过舞厅、电影、广播电台等媒介流入申城,加之中国学堂乐歌的开设,市民文化生活和情感世界中已出现对流行音乐的需求。老上海的流行音乐正是在这样的历史背景下应运而生。从音乐家黎锦晖1927年发表中国最早的流行歌曲《毛毛雨》起到1949年,前后20余年时间,约有8000余首流行歌曲在上海诞生。这些歌曲大量的是以爱情和城市生活为主题,其中也包括抗战爆发后上海音乐人创作的流行于民众间的抗日救亡歌曲。这些歌曲借助广播、电影、唱片和舞台等各种传媒产生了极大的社会影响力,许多优秀作品传唱至今,成为华人世界中永恒的怀旧金曲。

老上海的流行音乐造就了中国近代一批著名音乐人。黎锦晖是中国儿童歌舞剧的创始人、中国歌舞学校的创办者,也是中国流行

Golden Oldies of Old Shanghai

The golden oldies of old Shanghai refer to the popular songs born in Shanghaiduringthe period of the 1920s to the 1940s. These beautiful and moving songs once decorated a prosperous era and created the first heyday of Chinese popular music.

The rise of a music trend is always related to the political, economic and cultural background of the era. During the period of the 1920s to the 1940s, Shanghai had already possessed the characteristics of a commercialized capitalist metropolis, where the economy underwent abnormal prosperity and western elements especially the American pop music were introduced into Shanghai through ballrooms, films, broadcasting stations and other media. Moreover, the opening of music classes in Chinese schools promoted the demand for pop music in citizens' cultural life and emotional world. The pop music of old Shanghai came into being in such a historical background. It had been more than 20 years from 1927 when the musician LI Jinhui issued the earliest pop song *Drizzling* to 1949. During this period, there were about 8,000 pop songs born in Shanghai. The majority of these songs were themed by love and city life, among which there were also songs themed by anti-Japanese national salvation created by Shanghai musicians and favored by the masses. These songs had generated great social influences through various media such as radios, films, records and stages. Many excellent songs still widely sung today have become the eternal golden oldies across the Chinese-speaking world.

The pop music of old Shanghai brought up a large number of famous musicians in modern China. LI Jinhui was the founder of China's children music drama, the initiator of China's song and dance school and also the originator of China's pop music. His song *Drizzling* initiated a new category of Chinese music culture, marking the birth of a new

老上海红歌星（左起）白虹、姚莉、周璇、李香兰、白光

音乐的鼻祖。他的《毛毛雨》开创了中国音乐文化的新门类，标志着中国歌坛一个时代的诞生。此后 10 年间，他创作的流行歌曲至少有 400 余首。抗战爆发后，他创作了一批抗日救亡歌曲，当时红军队伍中就流行过他的《中华民族战歌》、《十里送夫》歌。享有"歌王"之誉的黎锦光和"歌仙"之誉的陈歌辛是老上海流行乐坛的杰出代表。黎锦光的《夜来香》、《采槟榔》、《五月的风》，陈歌辛的《玫瑰玫瑰我爱你》、《蔷薇处处开》、《渔家女》至今盛唱不衰。《何日君再来》是作曲家刘雪庵 1932 年在上海国立音专读书期间为同学联欢会写的曲子，1937 年这首曲子成为影片《三星伴月》的插曲，

era in Chinese music history. Over the next 10 years, he created at least 400 pop songs. After the outbreak of the Anti-Japanese War, he wrote a number of songs themed by Anti-Japanese national salvation. His songs *Chinese National Warsong* and *Ten Miles of Send-off for Husbands* were very popular among the Red Army. The outstanding representatives in the pop music circlesof old Shanghai were the "King of Song" LI Jinguang and the "Genius of Song" CHEN Gexin. LI Jinguang's *Night Blossom*, *Picking Betel Nuts* and *Wind of May* and CHEN Gexin's *Rose, Rose, I Love You*, *Roses Spread out Everywhere* and *The Fisher Maiden* are still widely sung today. The composer LIU Xuean wrote the song *When Will You Return?* for the student get-together party during his study in Shanghai National Music College in 1932. In 1937, this song became the interlude to the film *Stars Moving around the Moon*, the lyric of which was composed by HUANG Jiamo. Later, this song was accused as smutty song so that LIU Xuan was blamed for decades of years until he rehabilitated his reputation in 1979. It was unknown to many people that this famous musician had also created the songs including

→ 陈歌辛

由黄嘉谟填词。后来这首歌被扣上黄色歌曲的帽子，刘雪庵因此背了几十年的黑锅，直至1979年才恢复名誉。许多人并不知道，这位著名音乐家创作的《上前线》、《长城谣》等歌曲，是当时中国抗日歌曲的力作。那个时期的著名音乐家还有任光、严个凡、贺绿汀、安娥、严折西、聂耳、黄贻钧、李厚襄、刘如曾等。任光、安娥的《渔光曲》，贺绿汀的《天涯歌女》、《游击队歌》，聂耳的《卖报歌》、《义勇军进行曲》，黄贻钧的《花好月圆》，刘如曾的《明月千里寄相思》已成为中国歌坛的经典作品，《义勇军进行曲》建国后被定为中华人民共和国国歌。

老上海歌坛唱红了中国近代一批著名歌星。周璇、龚秋霞、白光、李香兰、姚莉、白虹、吴莺音被誉为老上海歌坛的七大歌星。陈娟娟、陈云裳、陈燕燕是老上海影坛、歌坛声形辉映的"三陈"。周淑安、黄友葵、喻宜萱、周小燕、郎毓秀、斯义桂、蔡绍序、应尚能、胡然等是老上海学院派出身的著名歌手。姚敏、王人美、李丽华、胡蝶、欧阳飞莺、张露、云云、张伊雯等也都是那个年代的红歌星。"金嗓子"周璇因灌录唱片最多，被称为"华人唱片第一人"，她演唱的《夜上海》被称为上海的"音乐名片"。龚秋霞因歌喉甜润婉转，享有"银嗓子"的美称，凄婉哀怨的《秋水伊人》让人回味不已。白虹曾在1934年上海举办的"播音歌星竞赛"中荣获第一名，是老上海第一个举办个人演唱会的歌星，有"歌唱皇后"的美誉。

老上海金曲诞生的年代距今已近一个世纪。建国后的30多年中，以爱情和城市生活为主题的老上海金曲被认为是"靡靡之音"

Go to the Front and *Great Wall Ballad* , etc. , which were the masterpieces among the songs themed by Anti-Japanese War. Famous musicians during that period also included REN Guang, YAN Gefan, HE Lvting, AN 'E, YAN Zhexi, NIE Er, HUANG Yijun, LI Houxiang and LIU Ruzeng, etc. Most of their songs has become of the classic works in China's song circles, including REN Guang and AN 'E's *Song of Fishing Light*, HE Lvting's *The Wandering Songstress* and *Song of Guerrilla* , NIE Er's *Song of Selling Newspapers* and *March of the Volunteers* , HUANG Yijun's *Blooming Flowers and Full Moon* and LIU Ruzeng's *Miss You Under Moonlight* . After the founding of People's Republic of China, *March of the Volunteers* has been recognized as the national anthem.

There brought up a large number of prestigious singers in the song circles of old Shanghai. ZHOU Xuan, GONG Qiuxia, BAI Guang, LI Xianglan, YAO Li, BAI Hong, WU Yingyin were praised as the seven major singers of old Shanghai. CHEN Juanjuan, CHEN Yunshang and CHEN Yanyan were praised as the "Three CHENs" in the film and song circles of old Shanghai. The reputedacademic singers of old Shanghai included ZHOU Shuan, HUANG Youkui, YU Yixuan, ZHOU Xiaoyan, LANG Yuxiu, SI Yigui, CAI Shaoxu, YING Shangneng and HU Ran, etc. YAO Min, WANG Renmei, LI Lihua, HU Die, OUYANG Feiying, ZHANG Lu, YUN Yun, ZHANG Yiwen, etc., were also popular singers in that era. The "Golden Voice" ZHOU Xuan had made the most records so that she was known as "the first person in Chinese record history". The *Nightlife in Shanghai* sung by her was praised as the "music card" of Shanghai. GONG Qiuxia had sweet and mild voice, so as to enjoy the reputation of "Silver Voice". The sad and beautiful song — *Lovers in Autumn* sung by her was evocative. BAI Hong won the champion in the "Broadcasting Singer Competition" held in Shanghai in 1934. She was the first singer who held the solo concert in old Shanghai and praised as "the Queen of Singing".

It has been nearly one century since the birth of the golden oldies in old Shanghai. In over 30 years since the founding of the People's Republic of China, the golden oldies of old Shanghai themed by love and urban life were banned as "decadent music". After the

而封杀。改革开放后，对老上海金曲有了重新研究和认识。其实在香港和东南亚华人界，在老上海人的心里，这些金曲从来就没有失去过生命力。回眸往昔，老上海的那段音乐历史是值得珍视的。在短短 20 余年时间里，一个城市出现了引领一个时代音乐的潮流，诞生了那么多的金曲、音乐家和歌星，这是这座城市的骄傲。

音乐创作如何反映人类普遍的情感需求，同时又在音乐本体的艺术创造中融合中西、不断创新，引领社会的审美情趣，老上海金曲对我们不无启迪。

2013 年 3 月

reform and opening-up, there was a new research and understanding on the golden oldies of old Shanghai. In fact, for old Shanghai people in Hong Kong and Southeast Asia, these golden oldies have never lost vitality. Looking back at the past, the music history of old Shanghai is worth cherishing. In just over 20 years, there had emerged a music trend leading an era, as well as so many golden oldies, musicians and singers in a city, which is the pride of this city.

The golden oldies of old Shanghai enlighten us to explore how to reflect the universal emotional needs of humans in the creation of music and at the same time, how to integrate the Chinese and the western styles and keep innovating in the art creation of music ontology, thus leading the aesthetic taste of society.

March 2013

老上海的琴行

琴行是老上海繁华街市的一道独特景观。

1843年上海开埠，带来了许多中国之前从未出现过的经济和文化现象，琴行便是其中之一。就在上海开埠的那一年，由英国商人投资经营西乐的谋得利琴行在南京路正式开业。这是中国历史上第一家经营西乐的琴行，专营英国生产的钢琴、风琴和供教堂用的管风琴。"新式八音琴，本行新到大小八音琴，内敲钟鼓，其音甚妙，以及号筒、战鼓、洋笛、洋箫等各色乐器俱全……请至英大马路3号便是。谋得利琴行启"。从这条刊登在1894年《申报》上的广告可以看出，谋得利琴行经营的乐器品种之丰富。1875年，在清朝官吏周孝堂的资助下，英国商人又在南京路开办了罗办臣琴行。此后，葡萄牙籍的印度商人又在南京路开设了来瑞罗琴行。这个琴行不仅经营各种西洋乐器，还经营乐谱。当时全国各地音乐团体、音乐院校都向它采购，可谓是中国第一家西洋乐器和乐谱的专业商行。

19世纪末，除了几家西洋琴行外，上海出现了一批国人自己开设的琴行。这些华人琴行的创始人和谋得利琴行有着不可分割的联系。他们大都是原谋得利琴行的技工，用在谋得利学得的技

Musical Instrument Stores of Old Shanghai

Musical instrument stores werethe unique landscape of the bustling markets in old Shanghai.

The port opening of Shanghai in 1843 brought many economic and cultural phenomena that had never been seen before in China and the musical instrument store was one of these phenomena. In the same year, Moudeli Musical Instrument Store invested by the British businessman and engaged in the western musical instruments was officially opened atNanjing Road. It was China's first musical instrument store specialized in the operation of piano, organ and church pipe organ manufactured in the UK. "We have new-style musical box, the new arrivals of large and small musical boxes and inner-knocking bells and drums with wonderful tunes, as well as horns, war drums, foreign flutes, foreign vertical bamboo flutes and all kinds of other Musical instruments. Please visit Moudeli Musical Instrument Store at No. 3, Yingdama Road." According to this advertisement published on *Shun Pao* in 1894, we could know a rich variety of musical instruments in Moudeli Musical Instrument Store. In 1875, ZHOU Xiaotang, an official in the Qing Dynasty, funded the British businessman to open the Luobanchen Musical Instrument Store at Nanjing Road. Then, Portuguese Indian businessmen opened the Lairuiluo Musical Instrument Store at Nanjing Road. This musical instrument store not only engaged in all kinds of western musical instruments, but also the musical scores. At that time, musical groups and musical colleges all over the country purchased from this store, which was the first professional store of western musical instruments and musical scores in China.

At the end of the 19th century, besides several western musical instrument stores, a

术和经营之道开办自己的琴行。原谋得利工人黄祥兴等人于1890年在现汉口路福建中路开办的祥兴琴行是国人开办的第一家西乐琴行。此后，原祥兴琴行工人程定国在四川北路开办了永兴琴行，原谋得利工人顾之荣等人在闸北开办了精艺琴行，贺春生等人开办了上海琴行。至上世纪30、40年代前后，上海经销西洋乐器的琴行达数十家。

琴行催生了上海近代乐器制造业。谋得利琴行因华工劳动力廉价和"华界"地价便宜，于1870年在闸北太阳庙路宝山路兴建了谋得利钢琴厂，这是中国第一家钢琴厂。上世纪30年代前后，谋得利钢琴厂生意兴隆，全厂有200余工人，月产钢琴超过100架，占上海钢琴市场总量的50%。接着，罗办臣、永兴、精艺等琴行也都纷纷开设钢琴厂，并拥有了自己生产的品牌钢琴。永兴琴行的施特劳斯牌钢琴、精艺琴行的精艺牌钢琴、上海琴行的莫扎特牌钢琴、鸣凤琴行的华格纳牌钢琴、美惠琴行的霍夫曼牌钢琴、罗办臣琴行的鲁滨逊牌钢琴等，都是当时颇受市场青睐的品牌钢琴。由此，使上海始于清乾隆、嘉庆年间小作坊式的传统民族乐器业转向规模化、产业化的现代乐器制造业。建国后成立的上海钢琴厂就是以这些琴行工厂为基础组建的。

琴行助推了近现代上海音乐教育。19世纪末20世纪初，在变法维新思想影响下，创办新式学堂的现代教育潮流开始兴起，代表中国近代新音乐的学堂乐歌应运而生。当时学堂音乐课和教堂所用的西洋乐器及乐谱大多从琴行购得，有些家境较好的学生也到琴行的琴房练琴。现今上海琴行艺校或琴行音乐培训中心与老上海琴行的

batch of musical instrument stores managed by Chinese people emerged in Shanghai. The founders of these Chinese musical instrument stores had an inseparable relation with Moudeli Musical Instrument Store. Most of them were skilled workers of Moudeli Musical Instrument Store, and relied on the skills and business methods acquired at Moudeli to set up their own stores. HUANG Xiangxing and other people who were former workers at Moudeli opened the first Chinese-owned western musical instrument store — Xiangxing Musical Instrument Store betweentoday's Fujian Road (Middle) andHankou Road in 1890. Hereafter, CHENG Dingguo, the former worker of Xiangxing, opened the Yongxing Musical Instrument Store at North Sichuan Road. GU Zhirong and other people who were former workers of Moudeli opened Jingyi Musical Instrument Store in Zhabei. HE Chunsheng and other people opened Shanghai Musical Instrument Store. Until the 1930s and 1940s, there were dozens of musical instrument stores engaged in western musical instruments in Shanghai.

The musical instrument stores spawned the modern musical instrument manufacturing industry in Shanghai. Due to the low cost of Chinese labor and land, Moudeli founded a piano factory betwwen Baoshan Road and Taiyangmiao Road in Zhabei in 1870, which was the first piano factory in China. Around the 1930s, the business of Moudeli Piano Factory was booming. It had more than 200 workers and produced more than 100 pianos every month, accounting for 50% of the total piano market in Shanghai. Later, Luobanchen, Yongxing, Jingyi and other musical instrument stores opened piano factories successively and owned their self-manufactured and branded piano. The Straus piano of Yongxing Musical Instrument Store, the Jingyi piano of Jingyi Musical Instrument Store, the Mozart piano of Shanghai Musical Instrument Store, the Wagner piano of Mingfeng Musical Instrument Store, the Hoffman piano of Meihui Musical Instrument Store and the Robinson piano of Luobanchen Musical Instrument Store, etc., were popular piano brands in the market. Therefore, the traditional Chinese musical instrument industry in Shanghai starting in the periods of Qianlong's and Jiaqing's reign in the Qing Dynasty developed into the large-scale and industrialized modern musical instrument manufacturing industry. After the founding of the People's Republic of China, the piano

音乐教育有着历史的渊源。始建于 1927 年的国立音乐学院即现上海音乐学院开办之初，16 位音乐教师中有 9 位是授钢琴、小提琴等西乐的。创办于 1912 年的上海美专在中国现代著名音乐教育家刘质平的推动下，专设音乐系并开了钢琴课。琴行则为这些院校的新音乐教育提供乐器和乐谱。

老上海的琴行　贺竹元绘

factories in Shanghai were established on basis of these musical instrument stores.

The musical instrument stores had also promoted the musical education in modern Shanghai. At the turning of the 19th century and the 20th century, under the influence of the idea of constitutional reform and modernization, the modern education trend of establishing new-style schools began to rise, marking the birth of the school songs of new music in modern China. At that time, most of the western musical instruments and musical scores used in musical classes of schools and churches were purchased from the musical instrument stores. Some students with good family financial situation also went to the musical instrument stores for practicing piano. The musical institutions and training centers in today's Shanghai still have historical ties with the musical education of instrument stores in old Shanghai. At the beginning of the founding of the National Academy of Music (now Shanghai Conservatory of Music) in 1927, nine of the 16 teachers were responsible for the teaching of piano, violin and other western musical instruments. Promoted by the famous music educator LIU Zhiping in modern China, Shanghai Training School of Fine Arts, founded in 1912, specially established the Faculty of Music and opened the piano classes. The musical instrument stores provided musical instruments and musical scores for the new music education in these institutions.

The musical instrument stores have witnessed the rise and fall of the city. The musical instrument stores in Shanghai have gone through a long and arduous journey of 170 years. In the course of its development, the musical instrument stores were once influenced by the wars and the political movements after the founding of the People's Republic of China. Due to the Pacific War in 1941 and the outbreak of the Anti-Japanese war of the United States and the UK, Moudeli Musical Instrument Store was officially closed. During the Cultural Revolution, the musical instrument stores in Shanghai almost disappeared. After the reform and opening-up, the music industry in Shanghai quickly recovered and increasingly showed an unprecedented prosperity. At present, there are hundreds of musical instrument stores along East Jinling Road and the adjacent Fenyang Road, forming the trend of industrialized development.

The music quality of a city can reflect the quality of the city. We wish that the urban

琴行见证城市兴衰。屈指算来，上海琴行已走过了整整170年艰辛漫长的历程。在琴行的发展过程中，曾受到战争的影响和建国后政治运动的冲击。谋得利琴行就因1941年太平洋战争爆发，美英与日开战而正式关闭。"文革"期间，上海的琴行几乎消失。改革开放后，琴行在申城迅速复苏，日益呈现出前所未有的兴旺景象。目前仅金陵东路乐器一条街及汾阳路附近的琴行就达上百家，形成了产业化发展的趋势。

城市音乐素质反映城市品质。希望今天星罗棋布的都市琴行在提升市民音乐素质、推动音乐文化产业发展、打造高品质的文化大都市中发挥更大的作用。

2013 年 4 月

musical instrument stores spreading all over the city will play a greater role in improving the music quality of citizens, promoting the development of music cultural industry and creating a high-quality cultural metropolis.

April 2013

老上海的滑稽戏

滑稽戏是由曲艺独脚戏演变发展而来的一种独特喜剧艺术样式，可谓是中国剧坛的奇葩。上海对于滑稽戏的形成和发展起着不可替代的历史作用。

清朝末年，江南农村出现了专门"说潮报"的民间艺人，演唱内容以新闻和时事为主，其中穿插滑稽故事和笑话。上世纪20年代，文明戏演员王无能、江笑笑和刘春山将"说潮报"的形式融入新剧，使上海曲艺舞台相继出现了各具特色的独脚戏，从而宣告了一个新的曲艺形式——独脚戏的诞生。这三位演员被誉为"滑稽三大家"。30年代是独脚戏发展的鼎盛时期，当时上海各大游乐场、电台播音和堂会演出的艺人最多时达100多档。40年代初，太平洋战争爆发，日军侵占租界，上海游乐场营业萧条、堂会生意清淡、电台被敌伪封锁，独脚戏艺人谋生困难。于是，出现了独脚戏艺人联合起来演出大型滑稽戏的局面。1942年初，江笑笑发起和组织杨天笑、赵宝山、仲心笑等采用文明戏的体制和滑稽戏的表演手法，演出了有故事情节和人物扮演的正本大戏《一碗饭》。这是由独脚戏演变为滑稽戏的第一部剧目。与此同时，江笑笑、鲍乐乐等在上海组织成立了中国第一个滑稽戏剧团"笑笑剧团"。随后，其他独脚戏艺

Burlesque of Old Shanghai

Burlesque, a miracle in the world of Chinese opera, is a unique style of comedic art developed from the monodrama. Shanghai plays an irreplaceable historical role in the formation and development of burlesque.

In late Qing Dynasty, there appeared folk artisans who specialized in "news telling". The contents of their singings were news and current affairs which were integrated with burlesque stories and jokes. In the 1920s, the actors of modern drama WANG Wuneng, JIANG Xiaoxiao and LIU Chunshan integrated modern drama into the "news telling" and successively formed characteristic monodramas on the stage of opera in Shanghai, thus to mark the birth of a new form of folk art — monodrama. These three actors were known as "the three major burlesquers". The development of burlesque experienced the heyday in the 1930s. At that time, there were more than 100 burlesquers performing in Shanghai's amusement parks, broadcasting radios and entertainment parities. In the early 1940s, with the breakout of the Pacific War, the Japanese invaded the concession, resulting in the depression of amusement park, business decline of entertainment venues, blockade of broadcasting stations and the living difficulties of burlesquers. Therefore, the burlesquers united together to perform large-scale burlesques. In 1942, JIANG Xiaoxiao launched and organized people including YANG Tianxiao, ZHAO Baoshan, ZHONG Xinxiao and so on to adopt the system of modern drama and the performance method of burlesqueand perform the original drama with a storyline and roles *A Blow of Rice* , which was the first play transformed from monodrama into burlesque. Meanwhile, JIANG Xiaoxiao, BAO Lele and other people in Shanghai set up China's first burlesque troupe, "Xiaoxiao Troupe". Subsequently, other monodrama artists and modern opera

人和文明戏演员也纷纷组织滑稽戏剧团。至 40 年代末，上海有大小职业滑稽戏剧团近 50 个。上海解放后，滑稽戏走向成熟，出现了《三毛学生意》、《七十二家房客》、《满意勿满意》等一批经典剧作。在"文革"那个没有笑声的年代，滑稽戏自然消失。改革开放使滑稽戏迎来又一个黄金时代，80、90 年代涌现了一批具有重大影响的优秀剧目。进入新世纪后，受主客观因素影响，滑稽戏出现式微征候。

滑稽戏经过曲折漫长的艺术发展道路，形成了自己独特的艺术

↖ 30 年代的筱快乐剧团的演出

actors also organized burlesque troupes. By the end of the 1940s, there had been nearly 50 professional burlesque troupes in Shanghai. After the liberation of Shanghai, burlesque came to maturity and there emerged a batch of classic plays, such as *Three Hairs Learns Business*, *The House of 72 Tenants* and *Satisfaction or Not Satisfaction*, etc. During the difficult period of the Cultural Revolution, burlesque disappeared. The reform and opening-up made burlesque usher in another golden era. There emerged a large number of excellent plays with great influence in the 1980s and 1990s. After entering the new century, affected by subjective and objective factors, burlesque underwent a decline.

After a long and tortuous path of artistic development, burlesque has formed its own unique artistic characteristics and aesthetic features. In terms of subject matter, it is good at selecting and extracting comedy themes and comedy characters from the daily life of ordinary people in the bottom of society, raising the social issues of concern, conveying the general sentiment of the public, revealing the philosophy of life in the Times and

→ 斗斗滑稽剧团的主要演员

个性和美学特征。在题材上，它善于从底层社会普通人的日常生活中选取和提炼喜剧题材和喜剧人物，提出众所关注的社会问题，传达广大民众的普遍情绪，揭示时代生活哲理，反映市民审美情趣。在表现手法上，既继承民族喜剧艺术传统，又借鉴外国喜剧艺术优长，从民间说唱、杂技、相声、地方戏曲等到中外话剧、电影电视、舞蹈美术，不拘一格、兼收并蓄，方言杂出、众腔并举，融汇百家、自成一体。在演出风格上，注重运用传统写意化的变形夸张手法和"噱头"技巧，生活气息浓郁、地方特色鲜明、喜剧气氛热烈，寓庄于谐，雅俗共赏。滑稽戏的角色行当开始按文明戏旧例，分滑稽、老生、小生、旦、老旦等，以滑稽为主。50年代中期以后，滑稽戏以演现代戏为主，讲究喜剧结构、突出人物性格，要求演员能演各类角色，原有的滑稽戏行当被突破。

一个优秀的滑稽戏演员，不仅要会多种戏曲、各种流派的唱腔，还要口齿伶俐、反应敏捷，能讲一口漂亮的各地方言甚至外语，同时还能做特别夸张的形体动作，表演要求特殊。在滑稽戏发展的各个历史时期都有一批代表性的著名演员。继滑稽戏初创时期的"滑稽三大家"之后，杨华生、张樵侬、笑嘻嘻与沈一乐被誉为滑稽戏"四大天王"。现代著名演员有姚慕双、周柏春、袁一灵、林燕玉、严顺开、吴双艺、童双春、王双庆、翁双杰等。王汝刚、钱程、陈国庆、秦雷、顾竹君、胡晴云、小翁双杰、何赛飞等则是当今上海滑稽戏舞台上的中坚力量。

从历史上看，滑稽戏的剧目大致可分为五类：一是根据独脚戏的"段子"改编而成，二是从文明戏移植而来，三是从话剧、戏曲、

reflecting the aesthetic taste of the public. In terms of expression techniques, it not only inherits the tradition of national comedy art, but also learns from the excellence of foreign comedy art, folk rap, acrobatics, crosstalk, local opera and other Chinese and foreign dramas, the film and television, as well as dance art. It is inclusive and follows no set form, and even integrates with the dialects. It has formed many different tunes and schools, as well as a style of its own. In terms of the performance style, it pays attention to the application of the traditional freehand deformation exaggeration technique and "stunt", which hasstrong life vitality, distinct local characteristics and warm comedy atmosphere, implying sobriety in humor and suiting both refined and popular tastes. According to the former practices of modern drama, the roles of burlesque include the Funny, Laosheng, Xiaosheng, Dan and Laodan, with the Funny as the leading role. After the mid-1950s, burlesque mainly focused on the modern drama and was particular about the structure of comedy and the highlighting of the roles' characteristics. It required the actors be able to play all kinds of roles, which broke through the former role division of burlesque.

An excellent burlesquer should not only be able to sing in a variety of operas and tunes, but also be articulate, responsive and able to speak local dialects and even foreign languages in a beautiful way. At the same time, he/she can also make exaggerated physical movements, the requirements of which are very special. In each historical period of the development of burlesque, there are a number of representative famous burlesquers. After the "three major burlesquers" in the beginning period of burlesque, YANG Huasheng, ZHANG Qiaonong, XIAO Xixi and SHEN Yile were known as the "Four Kings of Burlesque". Famous modern burlesquers include YAO Mushuang, ZHOU Baichun, YUAN Yiling, LIN Yanyu, YAN Shunkai, WU Shuangyi, TONG Shuangchun, WANG Shuangqing and WENG Shuangjie, etc. WANG Rugang, QIAN Cheng, CHEN Guoqing, QIN Lei, GU Zhujun, HU Qingyun, WENG Shuangjie, HE Saifei and so on are the backbone on today's burlesque stage in Shanghai.

Historically, burlesque can be divided into five categories: first, it is adapted from the "cross-talk" of monodrama; second, it is transplanted from a modern drama; third,

电影剧本移植改编,四是根据外国剧本改编,五是新创作。《满园春色》、《笑着向昨天告别》、《一千零一天》、《我是一个兵》、《出色的答案》、《性命交关》、《路灯下的宝贝》、《阿混新传》、《特别的爱》等都是建国后深受观众欢迎的优秀剧目。《满园春色》1965年曾进中南海演出,周恩来、陈毅、李先念等中央领导亲临观看。《阿混新传》被改编成电影并获国际喜剧节"金拐杖"奖。

新世纪是一个笑的时代。只要滑稽戏坚持特有的民间艺术色彩和幽默诙谐、嬉笑怒骂、自由狂欢的喜剧精神,拓宽思路、拥抱现实,深入生活、贴近民生,融汇中西、借鉴古今,就一定会给我们的城市带来更多的欢乐和笑声。

2013年5月

it is transplanted from a play, opera and film script; fourth, it is adapted from a foreign script; fifth, it is a new creation. After the founding of the People's Republic of China, people's favorite burlesque plays include *Spring Garden, Say Goodbye to Yesterday with A Smile, The Thousand and One Days, I Am A Soldier, Excellent Answer, Dangerous Time, Honey Under the Street Lamp, The Story of Ahun* and *Special Love* . *Spring Garden* was once performed in Zhongnanhai and watched by ZHOU Enlai, CHEN Yi, LI Xiannian and other central leaders. *The Story of Ahun* was adapted into a film and won the "Golden Crutch Award" at the international comedy festival.

The new century is an age of laughter. As long as burlesque adheres to its unique folk-art color and the comedy spirit of humor and carnival freedom, expands the way of thinking, embraces the reality, goes deep into life and people's livelihood, integrates the Chinese and Western cultural elements and learns from the past and present experience, it will surely bring more pleasure and laughter to our city.

May 2013

老上海的报业

老上海的报业史，是中国近现代新闻史的缩影。

研究老上海的报业，不能不提到望平街。在中文报刊史上，望平街犹如美国纽约的华尔街、英国伦敦的舰队街一样，有着举足轻重的地位。望平街即今天的上海山东中路，从福州路口至南京东路一段。这条当年的碎石小街是19世纪上海报业的发源地。1872年《申报》在望平街开业后，由于这里地处英租界，具有政治荫庇作用，加上英国的印刷技术和印刷机械又最早在这一带推广普及，因而望平街成了当时上海报人开办报馆的首选地。至上世纪30、40年代，约有四五十家报馆集中于此，连"中国第一流之新闻纸"天津《大公报》也在望平街设立分馆。众多的明星报人集聚望平街，并从这里走向全国走向世界。

研究老上海的报业，又不能不提到当时在全国最具影响的上海新闻界"三巨头"：《申报》、《新闻报》和《时报》。《申报》的创刊打破了创建于1861年的《上海新报》独家经营的格局，呈现出近代报纸比较完备的形态。《申报》自创办到停刊的78年间，见证并记录了清同治、光绪和宣统三个朝代的更替，两次世界大战、俄国十月革命、中法战争、甲午战争、日俄战争以及维新变法、义和团运

Newspaper Industry of Old Shanghai

The history of newspaper industry in old Shanghai is the epitome of China's modern journalism history.

To study the newspaper industry of old Shanghai, we have to mention Wangping Street. In the history of Chinese newspaper, Wangping Street occupies a decisive position, just as the Wall Street for New York and the Fleet Street for London. Wangping Street is the Middle Shandong Road in today's Shanghai, the section from the intersection of Fuzhou Road to Nanjing East Road. This gravel street is the birthplace of Shanghai's newspaper industry in the 19th century. In 1872, *Shun Pao* was officially issued at Wangping Street. Because it belonged to the British concession with political influence and was the first place to popularize the British printing technology and printing machinery, Wangping Street became the first choice for newspapermen to open newspaper offices in Shanghai at that time. By the 1930s and 1940s, about 40 or 50 newspapers had been set up there, and even "China's first-class newspaper" Tianjin *Ta Kung Pao* set up branch at Wangping Street. Lots of famous newspapermen gathered at Wangping Street and sought further development throughout the country and even the world here.

To study the newspaper industry of old Shanghai, we have to mention the most influential "three newspaper giants" in Shanghai: *Shun Pao*, *The News* and *Eastern Times*. The initial issue of *Shun Pao* broke the exclusive dealing of *Shanghai News Times* founded in 1861, thus to present a relatively complete form of modern newspaper. Over the 78 years from its founding to its suspension of publication, *Shun Pao* had witnessed and recorded the replacement of the three dynasties of Tongzhi, Guangxu and Xuantong, two world wars, the October Revolution of Russia, Sino - French War, the First Sino-

大公报

动、八国联军入侵北京等一系列重大历史事件，可谓是"近现代史的百科全书"。1893年，《新闻报》在望平街创刊。虽然它比《申报》创办迟20年，但由于该报注重改革报纸内容和版面，信息量大，又善于经营管理，因而其影响和声誉与《申报》不相上下。1904年，狄楚青在望平街创办《时报》，成为维新变法后改良派在国内创办的第一份报纸。由于该报在评论、编辑、出版等方面大胆革新，聘首创"时评体"的陈景韩等优秀报人专辟时评栏，应时而发、精悍明快，颇受时人欢迎。《时报》很快成为发行范围覆盖全国的报纸。当时上海有影响的报纸还有，于右任的《神州日报》和《民立报》，张竹平的《时事新报》，章太炎主笔的《大共和日报》和

Japanese War, Russo-Japanese War, Constitutional Reform and Modernization, Yihetuan Movement, Eight-Power Allied Forces invading Beijing and other series of major historical events, which may be called "an encyclopedia of modern history". In 1893, the first issue of The News was initiated at Wangping Street. Although it was founded 20 years later than Shun Pao, its influence and reputation were equal to that of Shun Pao due to its emphasis on reforming the content and layout of the newspaper, its large amount of information and good management. In 1904, DI Chuqing founded Eastern Times at Wangping Street, which became the first national newspaper founded by the reformists after the Constitutional Reform and Modernization. Because it conducted bold innovation in commentary, editing, publishing and other aspects, invited CHEN Jinghan and other excellent newspaper writers who had initiated the "commentary style" to set up a special commentary column, and issued news timely and appropriately, Eastern Times was very popular among people at that time. Eastern Times soon became a newspaper distributed throughout the country. Influential newspapers in Shanghai at that time also

→ 申报馆编辑部

《苏报》，戴季陶经理的《民权报》，邵力子主办的《民国日报》，梁启超的《时务报》，蔡元培的《警钟日报》和《国民日报》等。

研究老上海的报业，还不能不提到商业化的报刊发行方式。望平街之所以成为"报馆街"，从某种程度上讲，得益于与近代报刊几乎同时产生的报贩。《申报》创刊后，在利用邮局、书局、会馆等发行渠道的同时，主要利用报贩挨家挨户上门送报，以致逐渐形成了一个强大的报贩群体。后来创办的《新闻报》、《时报》等也都采用这一模式。1911年，报贩在望平街成立了自己的行会组织——捷音公所。当时有人这样描述望平街的盛况：每天清早，报贩云集望平街，成捆的报纸从各报馆运出，有的车拉，有的肩扛，还有很多报童手提，将报纸发往上海和全国各地。一旦出现重大新闻，贩运报纸的人更是把整条望平街挤得水泄不通，煞是热闹。

老上海报业有力推动了历史和革命。曹聚仁曾指出："短短望平街，代表着西风吹动以来的中国文化，从这一街巷的浪潮上，体会着时代的脉搏。从启蒙运动以来，每一个和政治动向有关的人物，没有不在望平街上留下他们的足迹。"毛泽东曾回忆说："当我在长沙的中学读书时，我第一次读到的报纸，报名《民立》，是民族主义派的报纸，里面有反抗满清的广州起义及在一个湖南人领导下的72烈士就难的情形。我读了以后，极为感动，并发现《民立》里面充满了有刺激性的材料，同时我也知道了孙中山的名字和同盟会的会纲。"老上海报业的影响力由此可见一斑。

全国解放后，上海报业历经政治风雨考验，走过了曲折的道路。改革开放后，上海逐步形成了以《解放日报》、《文汇报》、《新民晚

included YU Youren's *Shenzhou Daily* and *People's Independence Journal*, ZHANG Zhuping's *The China Times*, ZHANG Taiyan's *Rebuliean Times* and *Su Bao*, DAI Jitao's *Minquan Bao*, SHAO Lizi's *The Republic of China's Daily*, LIANG Qichao's *The Chinese Progress*, and CAI Yuanpei's *Alarming Bell Daily News* and *People's Daily*, etc.

To study the newspaper industry of old Shanghai, we have to mention the commercialized issuing way of newspapers and magazines. To some extent, Wangping Street became the "street of newspapers" due to the "newspaper hawker" produced almost at the same time as modern newspapers. After its initial issue, besides the publishing channels including post office, publishing house and club house, *Shun Pao* mainly relied on the newspaper hawkers to deliver the newspapers from house to house, thus to gradually form a strong group of newspaper hawkers. *The News*, *Eastern Times* and other newspapers founded later also adopted this mode. In 1911, the newspaper hawkers set up their own industry organization — Jieyin Association at Wangping Street. At that time, people described Wangping Street like this: early in every morning, newspaper hawkers gathered at Wangping Street; bundles of newspapers were shipped out from the newspaper offices; people used all kinds of way to carry the newspapers and then delivered them throughout Shanghai and even the whole country. If there was big news, Wangping Street would be packed like sardines by the newspaper hawkers, which was very bustling.

The newspaper industry of old Shanghai had vigorously pushed forward the history and revolution. CAO Juren once pointed out, "Wangping Street represents the Chinese culture after the introduction of western culture; you can experience the pulse of the Times through the tides of this street. Since the Enlightenment Movement, every person concerned with political developments has left their footprints at Wangping Street." MAO Zedong once said, "When I was studying in the middle school in Changsha, I read the newspaper for the first time. It was a nationalist newspaper named *People's Independence Journal*, in which there was content about Guangzhou Uprising which aimed to fight against the Qing Dynasty and the news about a Hunan people who had led 72 martyrs to

报》三张主流报纸为首，各专业报刊和小报百舸争流的生动局面。进入新世纪后，随着新媒体的迅速发展，传统媒体面临着新的挑战。

如何发扬老上海报业创新竞争精神，使传统媒体与新媒体优势互补，更好地发挥正确的舆论导向作用，这是需要上海报业回答解决的现实课题。

2013 年 6 月

fight and die in the battle. When I read it, I was deeply moved and found that the newspaper was full of stimulating materials. At the same time, I also knew the name of Sun Yat-sen and the outline of Tung Meng Hui." All these have well demonstrated the great influence of the newspaper industry in old Shanghai.

After the national liberation, the newspaper industry of Shanghai experienced political tests and tribulations, and went through tortuous road of development. After the reform and opening up, the newspaper industry of Shanghai gradually formed the competition landscape, where *Jiefang Daily*, *Wenhui Daily* and *Xinmin Evening News* were the three mainstream newspapers and there were also various professional newspapers and small-sized newspapers. With the rapid development of new media in the new century, traditional media are facing new challenges.

It is a realistic subject for the newspaper industry of Shanghai that how to carry forward the innovative and competitive spirit of the old Shanghai newspaper industry, make traditional media and new media complementary to each other and give better play to the correct public opinion guidance.

June 2013

老上海的书业

　　书业的繁荣或凋零，折射社会政治、经济、文化的盛衰变幻。

　　老上海书业历史悠久。古代上海，街坊就有进行图书销售的书肆。宋元时期，时属江浙的松江、金山地区官府、私家和书坊都有刻本流传。明清时期，刻本问世者甚众。维新运动后，新学书籍的需要量大增，木刻业无法适应，铅石印迅速发展。1905年，上海书业公所和上海书业商会成立，标志上海现代书业形成。民国以后，中华书局、大东书局、世界书局、开明书店纷纷开业，大小新书店一时间发展到200家左右，出版的图书品种和数量大大增加，书刊发行业日趋发达。河南中路的棋盘街和福州路一带书店林立，被誉为"文化街"。至上世纪20、30年代，上海书业进入繁盛时期。据统计，1936年上海书籍仅贩卖业就有100多家。

　　上海书业虽不比北京、南京、苏州和浙东地区历史久远，但却能后来居上以至成为中国近代书业的中心，有其独特的原因。就政治环境而言，在战乱的情况下，由于外国租界的存在，使上海成为中国知识分子的避风港和聚居地。前清的遗老遗少、激进的革命人士、学者教授、书家藏家，一时风云际会，聚集一隅，造就了一个极其庞大的图书需求市场。就经济而言，晚清以后，上海凭借独特

Book Industry of Old Shanghai

The rise and fall of the book industry always reflect the vicissitudes of social politics, economy and culture.

The book industry of old Shanghai has a long history. In old Shanghai, there were bookstoresin the streets. In Song and Yuan Dynasties, there were block-printed editions handed down from the regional governments of Songjian and Jinshan (belonged to Jiangzhe at that time), private libraries and bookshops. In Ming and Qing Dynasties, there emerged a large number of block-printed editions. After the Constitutional Reform and Modernization, the demands for books of new learning became larger and larger, but the block-print industry couldn't meet the needs, thus to bring the rapid development of lithographic printing. In 1905, Shanghai Book Industry Association and Shanghai Book Industry Chamber of Commerce were founded, marking the formation of Shanghai's modern book industry. After the Republic of China, Zhonghua Book Company, Dadong Book Company, World Book Company and Kaiming Bookstore opened up successively. There were all kinds of 200 bookstores and the variety and quantity of published books increased greatly. The publishing industry developed increasingly. There were numerous bookstores along the Qipan Street at Henan Middle Road and Fuzhou Road so that it was known as "the cultural street". In the 1920s and 1930s, the book industry in Shanghai began to flourish. According to statistics, there were more than 100 book peddling stores in Shanghai in 1936 alone.

Although the book industry of Shanghai has shorter history of that in Beijing, Nanjing, Suzhou and eastern Zhejiang, it became the center of modern Chinese book industrydue to special reasons. In terms of political environment, due to the war, the

大东书局

的地理位置，开放的人文政策，迅速成为远东地区的金融与商业中心。繁荣的经济催生了书业的迅速发展。据《近现代上海出版业印象记》一书统计，民国时期，上海大大小小的出版机构多达 500 余家，出版的书刊总量占据了中国的大半壁江山。就地理环境而言，毗邻上海的苏州、浙东均是书业发达地区。民国时期，两地有许多旧家的藏书散向上海，如苏州的玉海棠、群璧楼，南浔的嘉业堂、适园，宁波的天一阁、醉经阁等，有力助推了上海书业的发展。

老上海的书业有的是编、印、发三位一体，有的出版兼发行，有的专营发行。商务印书馆、中华书局、大东书局、世界书局、开明书店等为影响最大。1897 年成立于上海的商务印书馆是中国历史最悠久的现代出版机构，创造了中国出版业的诸多第一，走出了陈云、张元济、矛盾、陈叔通、周建人等一大批杰出人物。1924 年 4

existence of foreign concessions made Shanghai a safe haven and settlement for Chinese intellectuals. Theantediluvian survivals of Qing Dynasty, radical revolutionaries, scholars and professors, book collectors gathered in Shanghai and created an extremely large book-demanded market. In terms of economy, after the late Qing Dynasty, Shanghai rapidly became the financial and commercial center of the far east area by virtue of its unique geographical location and open humanistic policy. The booming economy gave rise to the rapid development of the book industry. According to *Impression of Shanghai Publishing Industry in Modern Times*, during the Republic of China, there were more than 500 large and small publishing agencies in Shanghai, accounting for more than half of all books and periodicals publishing in China. In terms of geographical environment, Suzhou and East Zhejiang adjacent to Shanghai were the developed areas of book industry. During the Republic of China, many collections of old families in both places were scattered to Shanghai, such as Yuhaitang and Qunbilou in Suzhou, Jiayetang and Shiyuan in Nanxun, Tianyige and Zuijingge in Ningbo, etc., which strongly promoted the development of Shanghai's book industry.

There were different operation modes in the book industry of old Shanghai where some were an integration of editing, printing and publishing; some were only engaged in editing and publishing and other were only specialized in publishing. The Commercial Press, Zhonghua Book Company, Dadong Book Company, World Book Company and Kaiming Bookstore were the most influential. The Commercial Press founded in 1897 was the oldest modern publishing institution and created the most No. 1 in Chinese publishing industry. It brought up a large number of outstanding figures, including CHEN Yun, ZHANG Yuanji, MAO Dun, CHEN Shutong and ZHOU Jianren, etc. On April 18, 1924, the Ceremony for Shanghai People Welcoming the Indian Poet RabindranathTagorewas held in the Commercial Press. After the founding of the People's Republic of China, the commercial press completed the reform of public-private partnership and moved to Beijing. Founded in Shanghai in 1912 by LU Feikui, Zhonghua Book Company was the best professional publishing house which represented China's publishing level of ancient books and academic works and had rich human resources in

月18日，上海各界欢迎印度诗人泰戈尔大会曾在商务印书馆举行。新中国成立后，商务印书馆完成公私合营改造后迁址北京。由陆费逵于1912年在上海创立的中华书局，是最能代表中国古籍、学术著作出版水准的专业出版社，拥有传统学术和古籍整理的雄厚人才资

← 开明书店

↗ 中华书店

sorting traditional academic and ancient books. *Twenty-Four Histories* and other books were the representative works of Zhonghua Book Company. Dadong Book Company, founded by LV Ziquan, WANG Youtang and WANG Junqing in 1916, had not only published textbooks for premier and middle schools, series of books on law, sinology, Chinese medicine, literature and art and social science, as well as children's books, but also had published a batch of books with academic, historical and documentary value, such as GUO Moruo's *Study on Oracle Bone Scripture* and *Study on Inscriptions of Bronze Wares in Yinzhou*. Dadong Book Company was also responsible for printing the paper money and revenue stamp of the Kuomintang government. The World Book Company, founded by SHEN Zhifang in 1917, first mainly engaged in the publishing novels and then involved in editing and publishing textbooks for premier and middle schools. In the textbook publishing industry, it formed the situation of tripartite confrontation with Commercial Press and Zhonghua Book Company. Kaiming Bookstore, founded by ZHANG Xichen and other people in Shanghai in 1926, was famous for serious publishing and high quality. The "Kaiming staff" and "Kaiming style" with profound knowledge, honest simplicity, upright personality, open mind, sincere

源,《二十四史》等是该书局的代表书籍。由吕子泉、王幼堂、王均卿等于1916年在上海创办的大东书局,除主要出版中小学教科书、法律、国学、中医、文艺、社会科学丛书和儿童读物外,还出版了一批如郭沫若的《甲骨文字研究》、《殷州青铜器铭文研究》等具有学术、史料和文献价值的图书,该书局还承印国民党政府钞票、印花税票等。由沈知方于1917年在上海创办的世界书局,先是以出版小说为主,后编辑出版中小学教科书,在教科书出版业中与商务、中华形成三足鼎立之势。由章锡琛等于1926年在上海创立的开明书店,以出书严肃认真、质量上乘著称,所形成的学识渊博、朴质笃实、为人正派、思想开明、待人真诚、一丝不苟的"开明人"、"开明风",对老上海书业产生了重要影响。

　　全国解放后,上海书业受政治环境影响,经历了50年代至60年代初的公私合营、整合发展,"文革"期间横遭批判、书业凋零,改革开放后重振书业、改革发展和进入新世纪后既逢机遇、又遭挑战几个不同的历史阶段。今天的上海书业,早已告别了"文革"中上海新华书店只可出售200余种社会科学图书的凋零局面,出版市场繁荣活跃,3000余家书店遍布上海的大街小巷。然而,上世纪80年代那种书店为街市最热闹和拥挤之处的状况也已不再,网上购书、电子阅读的流行打破了书业的常规业态。

　　面对网络的冲击和影响,上海书业如何创专业化特色,走综合经营之路,在市场经济的博弈中实现自己的文化理想,这是一道不容回避的历史命题。相信上海书业定会交出合格的答卷。

2013年7月

attitude and meticulous spirit had an important influence to the book industry of old Shanghai.

After the national liberation, influenced by the political environment, the book industry of Shanghai experienced the public-private partnership and integrated development from the 1950s to the early 1960s; during the period of Cultural Revolution, the book industry declined due to the political criticization; after the reform and opening up, the book industry revived; after entering the new century, the book industry faced both opportunities and challenges in different historical stages. The book industry of Shanghai had got rid of the decline situation during the Cultural Revolution when Xinhua Bookstore in Shanghai could only sell more than 200 kinds of social science books and welcomed the prosperity of the publishing industry. More than 3000 bookstores scattered all over Shanghai. However, the prosperous situation in the 1980s when bookstores were the busiest and the most crowded places on the streets had gone. The popularity of online book purchase and e-reading has broken the conventional pattern of the book industry.

In face of the impact and influence of the Internet, it is an unavoidable historical proposition for Shanghai book industry to create professional features, take the road of comprehensive management and realize its cultural ideal in the environment of market economy. We believe that Shanghai book industry will hand over the qualified solution.

July 2013

老上海的京剧

海派京剧是近代上海特有的城市文化哺育下的产物。它为传统戏曲艺术开拓了通俗化、大众化之路,从而促进了京剧艺术乃至中国传统戏曲的创新发展。

早在徽班进京的乾隆时期,里下河徽班来上海演出,这是形成上海京剧的源头。1867 年,英籍华人罗逸卿建成仿京式戏园"满庭芳",天津和北京京班名角纷纷来沪演出,京剧正式传入上海。一时间"京剧风行,戏园斯盛"。至同治、光绪年间,上海开设的京班戏园不下 50 个,京剧成为沪上影响最大的剧种。沪上京剧艺人适应本埠地域环境,吸收接纳徽班、梆子、昆曲等地方剧种之长,使初入上海的京剧开始了海化的进程。19 世纪末,随着讲究故事情节的连台本戏的传入、灯彩戏的兴起、时事京剧的上演,使上海京剧显现出不同于京城京剧的新的艺术特征:戏剧题材由历史转向关注现实;美学心态由传统保守转向追求新奇和感官刺激;戏剧审美意识由以听觉欣赏为主转向追求视觉听觉的全面审美需要;欣赏态度由以诗兴、韵味品评为尚转向注重故事情节。《铁公鸡》、《左公平西》、《湘军平逆传》三部剧作的上演是海派京剧形成的标志。

20 世纪上半叶,国内政治、社会剧烈动荡,中西文化碰撞交流,

Peking Opera of Old Shanghai

Shanghai-style Peking Opera is the product of the unique urban culture of modern Shanghai. It has opened up a path for the popularization of traditional opera art, thus promoting the innovative development of Peking Opera art and even Chinese traditional opera.

As early as the Qianlong period when Huiban came to Beijing, Huiban from Lixiahe area came to Shanghai and performed here, which was the origin of Shanghai-style Peking Opera. In 1867, British Chinese LUO Yiqing built the imitation Beijing-style drama garden "Mantingfang". Therefore, the famous Peking Opera artists in Beijing and Tianjin successively came to Shanghai and performed here, so that Peking Opera was officially introduced into Shanghai. At that time, Peking Opera was very popular so that the opera theaters were booming. In Tongzhi and Guangxu periods, there were more than 50 Peking Opera theaters in Shanghai and Peking Opera became the most influential opera in Shanghai. Peking Opera artists in Shanghai adapted to the local regional environment and absorbed the essence of Huiban, Bangzi, Kun Opera and other operas, thus to start the Shanghai-style evolution of Peking Opera. In the late 19th century, with the introduction of series drama, the rise of Dengcai opera and the performance of current-affair Peking Opera, Shanghai-style Peking Opera began to present new artistic features different from Peking Opera: the opera theme transformed from history to reality; aesthetic mentality shifted from traditional conservatism to the pursuit of novelty and sensory stimulation; the aesthetic consciousness of opera changed from hearing appreciation to pursuing the comprehensive aesthetic needs of visual hearing; the appreciation attitude shifted from the poetic inspiration and lingering charm to the focus on the plots. The debut performances

19世纪晚期上海京剧戏班演出照

使海派京剧进入不同寻常的发展时期。海派京剧开拓者汪笑侬演出的新编京剧《党人碑》，预示着戏曲改良运动的到来。从那个时候起，海派京剧进一步显示出自觉为社会政治服务，反对封建专制，追求改革创新的鲜明特征。上海京剧舞台出现了一大批关注现实人生、宣传新思想、高歌爱国主义、鼓吹社会和文化革命的新剧目。1908年，一批开明绅商和京剧艺人受西方文明影响，在上海南市建成了中国第一家新式剧场—新舞台。新舞台不仅在剧场建筑结构上大大改变了茶园式剧场的做法，在管理方式上也有重大改进，成为京剧改良运动的艺术实践基地，使海派京剧真正具有了不同于传统京剧的近代化性质。此后，上海的新式剧场和戏院纷纷落成开业。从新舞台建立到1917年上海最后一家茶园式剧场"贵仙茶园"歇业，前后只经历了约10年时间。民国后，作为海派京剧艺术标志之

of Iron Cock, Zuogong Pacified the West and Legend of Hunan Army Pacifying Renegades marked the formation of Shanghai-style Peking Opera.

In the first half of the 20th century, the political and social turmoil in China and the collision and exchange between Chinese and western cultures brought Shanghai-style Peking Opera into an unusual period of development. The new Peking Opera *Partisan Stele* performed by WANG Xiaonong, a pioneer of Shanghai-style Peking Opera, portended the coming of opera reform movement. From then on, Shanghai-style Peking Opera further displayed the distinct characteristics of self-consciously serving social politics, opposing feudal autocracy and pursuing reform and innovation. A large number of new operas which focused on real life, publicized new ideas, carried forward patriotism and advocated social and cultural revolution appeared on the stage of Peking Opera in Shanghai. In 1908, a group of enlightened gentry merchants and Peking Opera artists, influenced by western civilization, built China's first new-type theatre — the New Stage in Nanshi of Shanghai. The New Stage not only greatly changed the practice of the tea-garden style theater in terms of its architectural structure, but also greatly improved its management mode, becoming an art practice base for the reform movement of Peking Opera, which made Shanghai-style Peking Opera really possessed modern nature different from the traditional one. Since then, new-type playhouses and theaters opened up in Shanghai successively. It had been only about 10 years since the establishment of the New Stage to the closing of "Guixian Tea Garden" — the last tea garden theatre in Shanghai in 1917. After the Republic of China, machine-operated stage scenery series drama, as one of the artistic symbols of Shanghai-style Peking Opera, was further developed. In 1921, the performance of the series drama *YAN Ruisheng* at New Stage marked that Shanghai-style Peking Opera began to dominate the Peking Opera stage in Shanghai. The formation and development of ZHOU Xinfang's QI School and GAI Jiaotian's GAI school brought Shanghai-style Peking Opera into its heyday.

Shanghai-style Peking Opera was a model of the modernization and transformation of traditional opera. In terms of the relationship between art and life, Shanghai-style Peking Opera broke the shackles of pursuing refinement, departing from the realities of life and

一的机关布景连台本戏得到进一步发展。1921年连台本戏《阎瑞生》在新舞台的演出，标志海派京剧开始主导上海京剧舞台。周信芳麒派艺术和盖叫天盖派艺术的形成与发展，使海派京剧艺术进入鼎盛时期。

海派京剧是传统戏曲近代化转型的典范。在艺术与生活的关系上，海派京剧突破了京剧入宫演出后追求精致、脱离生活、丧失活力的桎梏，使京剧贴近现实、关注民生。海派京剧不仅有大量时事剧的创作，而且在历史题材剧目创作演出中也无不彰显着鲜明的时代特征。在继承与创新的关系上，海派京剧既遵循京剧的艺术规范，同时又追求艺术风格的发展变化，容纳中西，开拓了京剧艺术表演的新领域。在演员与观众的关系上，海派京剧立足上海的商业化城市特征和文化生态，适应市民偏重"看戏"、注重情节、追求新奇的需求，着力开拓艺术市场，使得京剧艺术从高雅殿堂走向通俗化、大众化之路。

海派京剧大大突破了传统戏曲总是围绕帝王将相打转的局限，涌现了一大批优秀剧目。如表达爱国主义思想的《徽钦二帝》、《学拳打金刚》，弘扬民族民主精神的《鉴湖女侠》、《宋教仁》，歌颂社会正义的《狸猫换太子》、《火烧红莲寺》，演绎历史事件的《汉刘邦》、《明末遗恨》，劝戒世道人心的《黑籍冤魂》、《斗牛宫》等。海派京剧诞生了常春恒、赵嵩绶、王鸿寿、李春来、冯志奎、夏月珊、潘月樵、夏月润、赵如泉、冯子和、欧阳予倩等一批早期代表性艺人和童芷苓、李玉茹、言慧珠、沈金波、童祥苓、尚长荣、李炳淑等著名艺术家。

全国解放后，京派、海派互相交流，好戏连台。国家为京派、海派京剧代表人物梅兰芳、周信芳共同举办舞台生活50年纪念活

losing vigor after Peking Opera entered the imperial palace, became closer to the reality and paid more attention to people's livelihood. Shanghai-style Peking Opera not only had a large number of plays themed by current affairs, but also displayed the distinctive characteristics of the Times in the creation of plays themed by historical subjects. In terms of the relationship between inheritance and innovation, Shanghai-style Peking Opera not only followed the artistic norms of Peking Opera, but also pursued the development and change of artistic style, accommodated the Chinese and western cultures, and explored the new fields of Peking Opera art performance. In terms of the relationship between the actors and the audience, Shanghai-style Peking Opera focused on Shanghai's commercial urban features and cultural ecology, adapted to the public's demands for emphasizing "watching drama", highlighting the plots and pursuing novelty, and vigorously developed the art market, thus to make the Peking Opera transform from high art to popular art.

Shanghai-style Peking Opera greatly broke through the limitations of traditional opera that always centered on emperors and generals, and there emerged a large number of excellent plays, such as *Empro Hui and Qin* and *Learn Boxing to Fight King Kong* which expressed the patriotic thoughts, *QIU Jin* and *SONG Jiaoren* which carried forward the national democratic spirit, *Racoon for a Prince* and *The Burning of the Red Lotus Temple* which eulogized social justice, *LIU Bang of Han Dynasty* and *Eternal Regret for Late Ming Dynasty* which was themed by historical events, *Victims of Opium* and *Big Dipper Palace* which expostulated the manners and morals of the time, etc. Shanghai-style Peking Opera had brought up a batch of representative artists in the early period, such as CHANG Chunheng, ZHAO Songshou, WANG Hongshou, LI Chunlai, FENG Zhikui, XIA Yueshan, PAN Yueqiao, XIA Yuelun, ZHAO Ruquan, FENG Zihe, OUYANG Yuqian, etc., and a large number of famous artists, including TONG Zhiling, LI Yuru, YAN Huizhu, SHEN Jinbo, TONG Xiangling, SHANG Changrong, LI Bingshu, etc.

After the national liberation, Peking Opera and Shanghai-style Peking Opera exchanged from each other and presented wonderful performances one by one. The state held the Joint 50-Year Anniversary of Stage Life for the representatives of Peking Opera

动,为盖叫天举办舞台生活60年纪念活动,使京剧舞台出现了京海交融、欣欣向荣的景象。"文革"时期文艺倍受摧残,京剧舞台只剩"样板戏"。改革开放使海派京剧复苏,新世纪又为海派京剧创造了广阔的发展前景。《曹操与杨修》等一批新剧目和史依弘、王珮瑜等优秀青年演员的出现,使海派京剧焕发新的光彩。

  历史启示我们,只要坚持改革创新,坚持适应时代,坚持开拓市场,坚持贴近观众,海派京剧就一定会走向新的繁荣!

2013 年 8 月

梅兰芳(《贵妃醉酒》饰杨玉环)

and Shanghai-style Peking Opera — MEI Lanfang and ZHOU Xinfang, and held the 60-Year Anniversary of Stage Life for GAI Jiaotian, which made the stage of Peking Opera display the landscape of "prosperity and integration of Peking Opera and Shanghai-style Peking Opera". During the period of the Cultural Revolution, the literature and art circles underwent destroy and only the "model opera" was preserved on the stage of Peking Opera. The reform and opening-up revived Shanghai-style Peking Opera while the new century created broad prospects for the development of Shanghai-style Peking Opera. A batch of new plays such as *CAO Cao and YANG Xiu* and excellent young actors such as SHI Yihong appeared, thus to make Shanghai-style Peking Opera generate new glories.

History enlightens us that as long as we persist in reform and innovation, adapt to the Times, open up the market, and keep close to the audience, Shanghai-style Peking Opera will surely welcome new prosperity!

August 2013

老上海的装帧

上海是中国现代装帧艺术的发源地。

上海现代书籍装帧设计始于清末民初。19世纪末20世纪初，西方先进的石印、金属活字、照相制版、三色版、珂罗版等先进技术传入上海。当时除一些特殊印本仍然保留部分传统的凸版木刻水印和短版印刷工艺外，传统的雕版印刷逐渐淡出历史舞台，书籍装帧也逐渐脱离线装形式，趋向现代的铅印平装。《申报》《点石斋画报》等当时均运用了西方的先进印刷技术。"五四运动"后，新文化运动迅速兴起，新旧思想强烈冲突，中西文化激烈碰撞，新式书籍日渐增多，使上海书籍的出版印刷方式和设计形态逐渐脱离传统样式，形成了现代书籍装帧设计。上世纪20至40年代，随着上海经济的畸形发展、商业文化的传播普及，以及国外现代艺术设计理念的传入，上海书籍装帧出现了杰作纷呈、百花争艳的繁荣局面。

提及老上海的现代书籍装帧，就不能不提到鲁迅。鲁迅不仅是一个伟大的革命文艺家，而且也是中国现代装帧艺术的开拓者。他特别重视对古今中外书籍装帧艺术的研究，提倡向外来艺术包括西方设计艺术学习。他非常注重书籍装帧艺术的整体风貌，主张将封面、版式编排、字形纸张、印刷装订等结合在一起整体进行设计。

Bookbinding Industry of Old Shanghai

Shanghai is the birthplace of China's modern bookbinding art.

The modern bookbinding design of Shanghai dated from the late Qing Dynasty and the early Republic of China. In the turning of the 19th century and the 20th century, the advanced western technologies including lithographic printing, metal movable type printing, photoengraving, three-color halftone, collotype and so on were introduced into Shanghai. At that times, except that some special printed books still retained part of the traditional woodblock printing and short-run printing process, traditional block printing gradually faded out of history. The bookbinding also gradually transformed from the traditional thread binding to modern letterpress printing paperback. *Shun Pao, Tian-Shi-Zhai Pictorial* and others all used the advanced western printing techniques. After the May 4th Movement, the New Culture Movement rose rapidly. The intense conflict between old and new ideas, the violent collision between Chinese and western cultures and the increasing number of new books, gradually separated the publishing and printing methods and design forms of Shanghai books from the traditional styles, thus to form the modern bookbinding design. From the 1920s to the 1940s, with the abnormal development of Shanghai's economy, the spread and popularization of commercial culture and the introduction of modern art design ideas from abroad, the bookbinding in Shanghai saw a flourishing situation.

When it comes to the modern bookbinding in old Shanghai, we cannot but mention LU Xun. LU Xun is not only a great revolutionary writer and artist, but also the pioneer of Chinese modern bookbinding art. He paid special attention to the study of bookbinding art at home and abroad and advocated learning from foreign art including western design

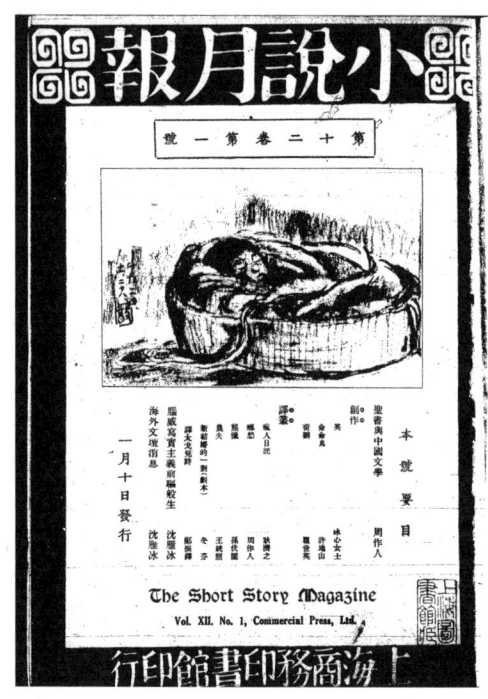

《小说月报》

他提出了"天地要阔、插图要精、纸张要好"的书籍设计基本要求。他主张版面要有设计概念,版面设计与书籍内容应整体一致,并对版式、版权页都做过细心研究。他重视作家、编辑和美编的合作关系。他还亲自设计了《呐喊》、《海上述林》、《引玉集》、《华盖集》、《野草》等数十种书籍的封面。

在鲁迅的影响和倡导下,一批优秀设计艺术大师和优秀书籍装帧作品应运而生。陶元庆是中国现代书籍装帧史上采用新颖的图案装帧作为书籍封面设计的第一人,他设计的《苦闷的象征》、《彷徨》、《中国小

art. He paid great attention to the overall style of bookbinding art, and advocated the integrated design of cover, layout, zigzag paper, printing and binding, etc. He put forward the basic requirements for book design — "broad layout, exquisite illustration and quality paper". He advocated the layout with design concept, the global uniform of the layout and book content, and the careful study on the format and the copyright page. He valued the partnerships between writers, editors and art editors. He also designed the covers of dozens of books, including *Scream, Hai Shang Shu Lin, Collection of Foreign Masterpieces, Huagui Collection* and *Wild Grass*, etc.

Under LU Xun's influence and advocacy, a number of excellent design art masters and excellent bookbinding works emerged. TAO Yuanqing was the first person in the history of China's modern bookbinding industry who adopted novel pattern bookbinding as book cover design. The excellent bookbinding works designed by him, such as *Symbolism of Depress, Wandering, A Brief History of Chinese Fiction, Homeland*, etc., had made great influence. QIAN Junxuan played a major role in promoting modern book art design and designed more than 4000 bookbinding works in his life. Most of the works of new-literature writers during the May 4th Movement period were designed by him, such as BA Jin's *Home*, YE Shengtao's *Ancient Heroes' Stone Images* and MAO Dun's *Midnight*, etc. He was known as "the master of book cover". FENG Zikai was a cartoonist and essayist, as well as a master of bookbinding. He was good at the cartoon-themed design of book covers which had strong artistic appeal, such as *Drunk, Literary Talk, Diary of A Soldier* and so on. The famous bookbinding design artists in old Shanghai also included CHEN Zhifo, SITU Qiao, PANG Xunqin, CAO Xinzhi and so on. In addition, writers and artists such as WEN Yiduo, YE Lingfeng, HU Feng, BA Jin, ZHANG Guangyu, SHEN Congwen, LIN Fengmian, HUANG Miaozi, AI Qing, BIAN Zhilin and XIAO Hong also actively participated in the book cover design at that time. It can be said that Shanghai has set a precedent for China's modern bookbinding art.

The great changes of Shanghai book binding and design were closely related to the economic, political and social environment of Shanghai at that time. The introduction of

说史略》、《故乡》等优秀装帧作品影响巨大。钱君匋对现代书籍艺术设计起过重大推动作用，一生设计的书籍装帧作品多达 4000 多件，巴金的《家》、叶圣陶的《古代英雄的石像》、茅盾的《子夜》等五四时期新文学作家的作品大多由他设计，享有"钱封面"的雅称。丰子恺既是一位漫画家和散文家，也是书籍装帧大师。他设计的封面以漫画见长，如《醉里》、《文坛逸话》、《从军日记》等，具有很强的艺术感染力。老上海著名的装帧设计艺术家还有陈之佛、司徒乔、庞薰琹、曹辛之等。此外，闻一多、叶灵凤、胡风、巴金、张光宇、沈从文、林风眠、黄苗子、艾青、卞之琳、萧红等作家和艺术家也都积极参与了当时书籍的封面设计。可以说，上海为中国现代装帧艺术开了先河。

上海书籍装帧设计所发生的巨变，与当时上海经济、政治和社会环境有着紧密联系。西方先进印刷技术入沪是上海书籍装帧进入现代化的重要背景，外国美术运动的传入促进了上海书籍装帧的变革，五四新文化运动则是上海现代书籍装帧得以兴起和发展的直接动因，上海商业城市的形成也为书籍装帧提供了经济支撑。正是在多种因素的作用下，上海书籍装帧逐步走出古籍装帧的形式结构，开始向现代化方向迈进。

上海的解放开创了装帧艺术新的纪元。上世纪 50 年代到 60 年代初，上海的装帧艺术摒弃了复古和崇洋等不健康倾向，进入发展提高的新阶段。1959 年中国在莱比锡国际书籍艺术展览会上争得了重大荣誉，其中上海的获奖作品占全国获奖总数的三分之一。"文革"使得装帧艺术停滞和倒退。改革开放又使上海装帧艺术获得新生。新世纪以来，上海的书籍装帧出现了生气勃勃的新景象。

advanced western printing technology was an important background for the modernization of bookbinding in Shanghai. The introduction of foreign fine arts movement promoted the reform of bookbinding in Shanghai. The May 4th New Culture Movement was the direct cause for the rise and development of modern bookbinding in Shanghai. The formation of Shanghai as a commercial city also provided economic support for bookbinding. It was under the effect of a variety of factors that the bookbinding of Shanghai had gradually stepped out of the formal structure of ancient bookbinding and started to move towards modernization.

The liberation of Shanghai ushered in a new era for bookbinding art. From the 1950s to the early 1960s, the bookbinding art in Shanghai abandoned the unhealthy tendency of returning to the ancients and worshiping everything foreign and entered a new stage of

→《小说月报》

随着数码技术的介入与数码设计的出现，为书籍装帧艺术的发展既带来机遇也带来挑战。如何保持中国书籍装帧设计的独特艺术语言，同时又充分运用好丰富的现代技术表现手段，不断推动书籍装帧设计艺术的创新发展，这是需要出版和装帧界回答解决的新课题。开中国现代书籍装帧设计之先河的上海，应当交出更加完满的答卷。

2013 年 8 月　　↖ 柔石《为奴隶的母亲》

development and improvement. In 1959, China won great honors at the international book art exhibition held in Leipzig and Shanghai won a third of the total honors. The "Cultural Revolution" made the bookbinding art stagnate and retrograde. The reform and opening-up brought new life to Shanghai's bookbinding art. Since the new century, the bookbinding in Shanghai had appeared a new dynamic scene.

With the introduction of digital technology and the emergence of digital design, the development of bookbinding art faces both opportunities and challenges. It has been the new subjects for the publishing and bookbinding industries that how to maintain the unique artistic language of book binding design in China, and at the same time make full use of rich modern technological expression means to constantly promote the innovative development of bookbinding design art. Shanghai, the pioneer of China's modern bookbinding design, should deliver a more comprehensive solution.

August 2013

老上海的服饰

海派服饰的兴起，是近现代上海都市化进程中一个重要的文化现象。可以说，老上海的服饰是近现代海派文化变迁史的外在写照。

海派服饰风格的形成始于 19 世纪中叶，即上海开埠之初。清代中期，中国南方的消费中心在苏州、杭州及广州等处。自 1860 年清政府在上海派驻"南洋通商大臣"起，上海很快成为中国最大的对外商业中心。随着西方文化和外国资本的涌入，随着民族工商业的壮大和市政交通的发展，上海成了百年间中国近代化程度最高的城市。清末民初，上海五方杂居、华洋共处，西装革履与中装绣鞋并存，崇尚生活享受的商业化社会风气开始形成，以奢华、精致、优雅、时髦为特点的海派服饰逐渐风靡。

上世纪 20 至 40 年代，是海派服饰的辉煌时期。当时，巴黎当季的时装仅 3 个月左右就会输入到上海，经过上海人的巧手改良，使上海服饰既与巴黎同步又具独特的海派风格。中国各地都以上海的服饰流行趋向为楷模，一衣一扣、一鞋一袜，四方仿效。"人人都学上海样，学来学去学不像，等到学到三分像，上海已经变了样。"这首流行歌谣，生动形象地反映了当时上海在中国服装界的显赫地位。

海派服饰有自己独特的风格特征。相比固守陈规、含蓄质朴且

Costume of Old Shanghai

The rise of Shanghai-style costume is an important cultural phenomenon in the urbanization process of modern Shanghai. It can be said that the costume of old Shanghai is an external portrayal of Shanghai-style cultural change history in modern times.

The formation of Shanghai-style costume began in the mid-19th century, namely atthe beginning of Shanghai's port opening. In the mid-Qing Dynasty, the consumption center in south China was located in Suzhou, Hangzhou and Guangzhou. Since 1860 when the Qing Dynasty government stationed the "Nanyang Commercial Exchange Minister" in Shanghai, Shanghai had soon become the largest foreign commercial center in China. With the influx of western culture and foreign capital, the growth of national industry and commerce and the development of municipal transportation, Shanghai became the most modern city in China in the past 100 years. In the late Qing Dynasty and the early Republic of China, Chinese people from different cities and foreign people from different countries came to live in Shanghai. The commercial social atmosphere of advocating life enjoyment began to take shape. Western dress and leather shoes and Chinese traditional tunic suit and embroidery shoes coexisted in Shanghai. The commercial social ethos of worshipping amenity of life began to come into being. The Shanghai-style costume featured by luxury, exquisiteness, elegance and fashion became more and more popular.

During the 1920s and the 1940s, Shanghai-style costume welcomed its gloriousperiod. At that time, it took only 3 months or so for the new-arrival costume in Paris to be imported to Shanghai. After the innovative improvement of Shanghai people, it would make the new-arrival costume not only be as fashionable as that in Paris, but also enjoydistinctive Shanghai style. The fashion trend of Shanghai-style costume was regarded

具有官派特征的京派服饰而言，海派服饰则是标新立异、西化程度高且具有浓厚的商业气息。传统服饰当时以丝、棉织物、软缎等为常用面料，而海派服饰则以物美价廉的洋布为常用面料。资料显示，1845年上海进口欧美纺织品就达144万匹。与传统服饰在面料、纹样和图案上追求繁丽、体现地位标识的特点相比，海派服饰显现出注重简洁实用的西式风格。传统服饰在造型上采用繁杂细致的方式，不追求人体的表现。而海派服饰受西服影响，趋于窄瘦合身、显露体形。上海当时专事男子西服的"红帮裁缝"与专事女子服饰的

↖ 20世纪40年代的上海名媛

as a model by people in other Chinese cities and people began to imitate the fashion of Shanghai-style costume. There was a popular ballad which vividly reflected the prominent position of Shanghai in China's costume industry at that time, "All people imitate the Shanghai-style costume, but they always fail; when they work hard and get one third essence of the Shanghai-style costume, there are new arrivals in Shanghai."

Shanghai-style costume had its unique style characteristics. Compared with the traditional, reserved and simple Beijing-style costume with the characteristics of official costume, Shanghai-style costume were novel and westernized with strong commercial elements. At that time, silk, cotton fabric, soft satin and other common fabrics were used in traditional costume while Shanghai-style costume were always made of foreign cloth which was attractive in price and quality. Data shows that in 1845, Shanghai imported 1.44 million bolts of European and American textiles. Compared with the characteristics of traditional costume which pursued luxury in fabrics, texture and pattern to show the social status, Shanghai-style costume showed a western style that emphasized simplicity and practicality. Traditional costume used multifarious and meticulous way on modelling and never pursued the expression of human body. However, Shanghai-style costume was influenced by western costume and tended to be well-fitting for showing the shape of human body. At that time, the "red-school tailor" specialized in men's costume and the "white-school tailor" specialized in women's costume both adopted the western three-dimensional cutting structure, and used this structure to influence and transform the traditional Chinese costume. The birth of Shanghai-style cheongsam which showed exquisite female curve and beautiful figure was the typical example of Shanghai-style fashion. In terms of the way of wearing, Shanghai-style costume was the combination of Chinese and western style. For example, the cheongsam was matched with fur coats, silk stockings, high heels, necklaces and watches, and men's costume were matched with duck caps, handbags, gloves and sunglasses, which subverted the traditional way of wearing long gowns and mandarin coats. At that time, the magazines in Shanghai, such as *Exquisite* and *Yongan Monthly* introduced a large number of articles about the way of wearing and matching suits, which had a profound impact on transforming Chinese

"白帮裁缝",均采用西式立体裁剪结构,并用这种结构影响和改造中国的传统服饰。刻意展示女性玲珑精致的曲线和美妙身材的海派旗袍的诞生,则是海派时尚的典型。在穿着方式上,海派服饰走的是中西合璧之路。如旗袍与裘皮大衣、丝袜、高跟鞋、项链、手表等搭配,男装与鸭舌帽、手提包、手套、墨镜搭配等,颠覆了时人长袍马褂的传统穿着方式。当时上海的《玲珑》、《永安月刊》等杂志介绍了大量关于西服穿着与搭配方式的文章,对促成国人穿着方式由中向西变革产生了深远影响。

海派服饰的兴起除其特殊的时代和文化背景外,明清时期上海及周边地区的纺织业基础和新兴的上海服装制作业也是推动海派服饰迅速兴起的重要原因。当时,上海及周边地区每年棉布的输出量均在100万匹以上,加之这里又是全国主要的产丝区,为海派服饰的形成提供了坚实的物质基础。原先上海只有专做中式服装的苏广成衣铺,时称"本帮裁缝"。随着上海洋人的不断增多,逐渐分离出一支专为洋人缝制西式服装的"红帮裁缝"。开设在四川北路8号的"和昌洋服店"是上海第一家成规模的洋服店。此后,荣昌祥、培罗门、王兴昌等洋服店纷纷开业。上世纪30年代,仅宁波人在上海开设的洋服店就达90多家。40年代末,上海裁缝师傅达4万之余。上海裁缝广泛吸取罗宋派、英美派、日本派、犹太派等各派服饰特点,形成了面料高档、款式新颖、做工精细的海派西服。随着西方大工业生产方式和造型工艺渐入上海,上海诞生了近代中国第一家缫丝厂、第一家棉纺厂、第一家针织厂。规模庞大的服装制作业,有力助推了海派服饰的兴盛。

people's way of dressing from the traditional Chinese style to the western style.

In addition to the special Time and cultural background, the basis of textile industry appearing in Shanghai and surrounding areas during the Ming and Qing Dynasties and the emerging costume manufacturing industry in Shanghai were also the important reasons for the rapid rise of Shanghai-style costume. At that time, the annual output of cotton cloth in Shanghai and surrounding areas was above 1 million bolts. Moreover, Shanghai was the main silk producing area in China, which provided a solid material foundation for the formation of Shanghai-style costume. Originally, there were only Suzhou and Guangzhou ready-to-wear shops specialized in traditional Chinese costume in Shanghai, which were called "local-school tailor". With the increasing number of foreigners in Shanghai, there

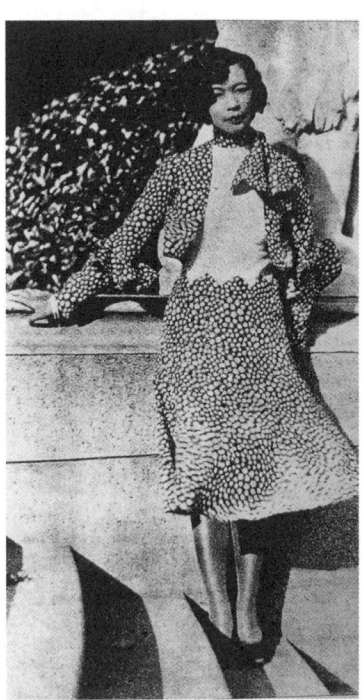

→ 穿着西式服装的名媛

全国解放后至60年代初，上海服饰由缤纷多彩转向简朴平实的时髦。60年代中期，上海流行军绿色。70年代，上海流行西装领便服和百褶裙。改革开放后，西式服装再度流行。进入新世纪以来，海派服饰呈现多种时尚并存的新局面。但无论时代如何变迁，精致优雅、时髦灵巧、讲究做工、注重搭配的海派服饰传统始终没有变。

海派服饰作为上海这座城市的流动景观，经过了160多年的历史演进。今天的上海正处在国际化大都市建设进程中，海派服饰能否融入并引领国际流行服饰潮流，向多样化、个性化、时装化方向发展，彰显新的魅力，这是摆在上海服装业面前一道新的命题。

2013 年 10 月

gradually emerged the "red-school tailor" specialized in designing western-style costume for foreigners. Hechang Western Costume Company located at No. 8, North Sichuan Road was the first large-scale western costume store in Shanghai. Since then, Rongchangxiang, Peiluomen, Wangxingchang and other western-style costume stores opened successively. In the 1930s, there were more than 90 western-style costume stores opened alone by Ningbo people in Shanghai. In the late 1940s, there were more than 40,000 tailors in Shanghai. The tailors in Shanghai had extensively absorbed the characteristics of costumes of various schools, such as Luosong School, Anglo-American School, Japanese School and Jewish School, thus t have formed the Shanghai-style suit with high-grade fabrics, novel styles and fine workmanship. With the introduction of western industrial production methods and molding techniques into Shanghai, China's first silk reeling factory, first cotton spinning factory and knitting factory were born in Shanghai. The large-scale costume manufacturing industry greatly promoted the prosperity of Shanghai-style costume.

From the national liberation to the early 1960s, costume in Shanghai had transformed from colorful fashion to simple and plain fashion. In the mid-1960s, military green was popular in Shanghai. In the 1970s, tailored-collar casual wear and pleated skirt were popular in Shanghai. After the reform and opening up, wester-style costume became popular again. Since entering the new century, Shanghai-style costume presented the new situation that a variety of fashions coexist. However, no matter how the Times change, the traditions of Shanghai-style costume — exquisite and elegant, fashionable and dexterous, exquisite craftsmanship and paying attention to costume matching, have never changed.

Shanghai-style costume, as the running landscape of Shanghai, has gone through more than 160 years of historical evolution. Today, Shanghai is in the process of building an international metropolis. It has been the new proposition for Shanghai's costume industry that whether Shanghai-style costume can integrate into and lead the international fashion trend, develop towards the directions of diversification, individualization and fashion, and reveal new charm.

October 2013

老上海的广告

上海是近代中国广告的发源地。回眸老上海广告演进的历史，不仅可以使我们重温老上海的历史和风情，而且可以汲取蕴含其中的文化内涵。

19世纪中叶上海开埠后，上海逐渐成为中国工业和商业的中心。在外国资本和文化的双重影响下，随着食品、纺织、服装、建材、制药、烟酒等领域民族工业企业的兴办和商店、旅馆、银行、饭店、理发、修理、浴室、游乐等社会服务性第三产业的形成，上海近代广告业应运而生。1872年《申报》创办，标志着上海近代广告开始进入发展繁荣期。20世纪20、30年代，上海广告业出现繁华多姿的景象。1919年中国广告业界最早的行业组织"中国广告公会"在上海成立。1927年旧中国规模最大的广告行业组织"中华广告公会"在上海组建。至30年代，上海的中外广告社和广告公司已达100多家。

广告是一种借助某种媒介物传递商品信息的经济文化形态。近代上海广告彻底改变了中国古代以酒旗、幌子、招牌等为形式的零星促销手段，从广告制作技术和广告设计两方面完成了广告媒体的历史性变革。在近代技术和城市市场的影响下，上海创造了一系列

Advertising of Old Shanghai

Shanghai is the birthplace of modern China's advertising. To review the evolution history of Old Shanghai's advertising can not only make us relive the history and customs of old Shanghai, but also absorb its cultural connotation.

After the opening of Shanghai port in the middle 19th century, Shanghai had gradually become the center of Chinese industry and commerce. Under the dual influence of foreign capital and culture, modern advertising industry in Shanghai emerged with the establishment of national industrial enterprises in the fields of food, textile, clothing, building materials, pharmacy, tobacco and wine, and the formation of social service tertiary industries such as shops, hotels, banks, restaurants, hairdressing, repair, bathrooms and recreation. The establishment of *Shun Pao* in 1872 marked that the modern advertising in Shanghai entered the period of prosperity. In the 1920s and 1930s, Shanghai's advertising industry became more prosperous and colorful. In 1919, China Advertising Association, China's earliest advertising industry organization, was founded in Shanghai. In 1927, Great China Advertising Association, China's largest advertising industry organization, was established in Shanghai. By the 1930s, there had been more than 100 advertising companies and agencies in Shanghai.

Advertising is an economic and cultural form that conveys information of commodities through a certain medium. Modern Shanghai's advertising had completely changed the sporadic promotion means in the form of wine flag, mask and signboard in ancient China, and completed the historic transformation of advertising media inthe aspects of the advertising production technology and advertising design. Under the influence of modern technology and urban market, Shanghai created a series of novel

20 世纪 40 年代大世界门口密集的广告牌

新颖的广告媒体。如印刷广告。国内外的广告史学将报刊广告的出现视作近代广告史的开端。19 世纪 60、70 年代《上海新报》、《申报》、《汇报》等报刊的创办，使近代上海印刷广告腾飞。《申报》一度广告面积占全张报纸版面近 60%。由中国特有的民间传统美术形式年画演变而成的月份牌广告，也是风靡老上海的印刷广告。又如橱窗广告。这是由近代城市商店敞开售货经营方式培育出来的新式广告媒体。1920 年诞生于上海的"勒吐精"奶粉橱窗是中国最早的

advertising media, such as printing advertisement. The domestic and foreign history of advertising regarded the emergence of newspaper advertising as the beginning of modern advertising history. In the 1960s and 1970s, the establishment of *Shanghai New Newspaper*, *Shun Pao* and *Report* , etc., enabled modern Shanghai's printing advertising to rise rapidly. At one time, the advertisements accounted for nearly 60% of the layout of *Shun Pao* . The calendar-poster advertising, evolved from the unique Chinese folk-art form — traditional New Year pictures, was also a popular print advertisement in old Shanghai. For example, window advertisement was a new advertising medium cultivated by the open selling way of modern urban stores. The milk powder window of "Lactogen", born in Shanghai in 1920, was the earliest window advertisement in China. Subsequently, large department stores in Shanghai, such as Xianshi, Yong'An, Xinxin had set up shop window advertising in front of the store. This advertising medium, which conveyed information of goods by the sales place, not only vividly presented the goods, but also beautified the appearance of the store. Another example was the outdoor advertisement. Besides the forms of road signs, signboard and advertising column, the most mentionable outdoor advertisement in old Shanghai was neon-light advertisement, which was the product of the technological change of advertisement production brought by industrial revolution. The English typewriter advertisement at the window of Evans Books Company at EastNanjing Road in 1926, was the earliest neon-light advertisement in Shanghai. Shanghai Far East Chemical Factory was China's first neon light factory. The advertisement signboard of "Hostel Central" at Hubei Road was Shanghai's first neon-light advertisement signboard. In the 1930s, almost all the major commercial facilities in Shanghai, especially the entertainment facilities, were equipped with all kinds of neon-light advertisement signboards. The neon-light advertisement raised modern Shanghai's advertising to a new historical level, and made the advertisement truly an integral part of the modern Shanghai's city culture. The thirdexample was the radio advertisement. In 1922, China's first radio station "Ausbond" was founded in Shanghai. In 1931, "Tianling" radio station, specialized in operating advertisement business, was founded in Shanghai. In the 1930s, there were more than 50 radio stations and more than 3,000

橱窗广告。随后，先施、永安、新新等上海大型百货公司先后在商店门前设立橱窗广告。这种以销售地点传递商品信息的广告媒体，不仅生动形象地展示了商品，而且美化了商店的外观。再如户外广告。老上海的户外广告除路牌、招牌、广告栏等形式外，最值得一提的是霓虹灯广告。霓虹灯广告是工业革命带来的广告制作技术变革的产物。1926年南京东路伊文思图书公司橱窗内的打字机英文广告是上海最早的霓虹灯广告，上海远东化学制造厂是中国最早的霓虹灯制造厂，湖北路"中央旅社"广告招牌是上海第一具霓虹灯广告招牌。30年代，上海各大商业设施尤其是娱乐设施几乎都装有各种样式的霓虹灯招牌广告。霓虹灯广告将上海近代广告提高到一个崭新的历史水平，使广告真正成为近代上海城市文化不可分割的组成部分。还如电波广告。1923年中国第一家广播电台"奥斯邦"在上海创办。1931年，上海诞生了一座以经营广告业务为主的"天灵"无线电台。30年代上海广播电台多达50多家，有收音机3000多台。电波广告成为近代无线电技术革命条件下的新型广告媒体。除上述四大广告媒体外，近代上海还有银幕广告、商标广告、邮政广告、空中广告等其他广告媒体。

近代上海广告媒体形式和制作技术上的变革都呈现为广告设计上的艺术化趋势。如广告表现手法的生动化、通俗化，广告语言的简明化、音律化，视听效果的形象化、情感化。琳琅满目的橱窗广告，醒目生动的印刷广告，五光十色的霓虹广告，美妙悦耳的电台广告，设计师们利用色彩、图案、光影、文字、音响等材料充分表现广告的感染力和视觉冲击力，使单调的商品裹上了一种丰富多彩

sets of radios in Shanghai. The radio advertisement became the new advertisement media under the condition of modern radio technology revolution. In addition to the above four advertising media, other advertising media in modern Shanghai also included screen advertising, trademark advertising, postal advertising and aerial advertising, etc.

The changes of the form and production technology of modern Shanghai's advertising media showed the artistic trend in advertising design, such as the vivid and popular way of advertising expression, the simplicity and melody of advertising language, and the visualization and emotionalization of audio-visual effects. There were diverse window ads, vivid printing ads, colorful neon-night ads and beautiful radio ads. The designers used colors, patterns, light and shadow, characters, acoustics and other

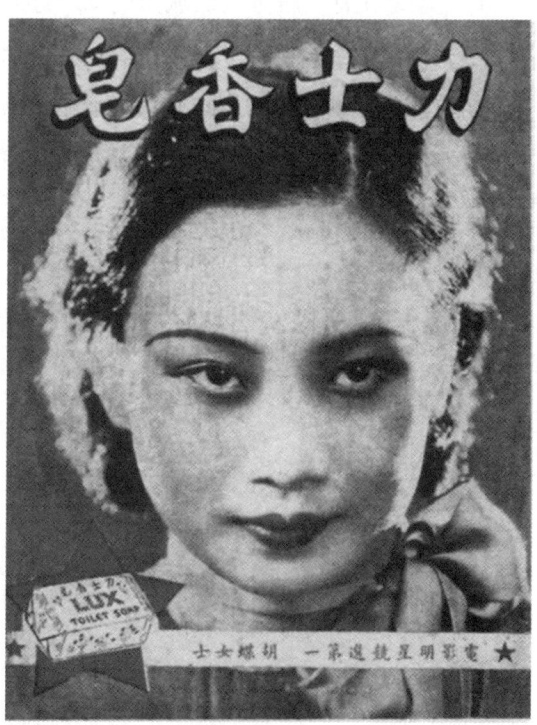

→ 胡蝶为力士香皂做的广告

的艺术氛围，使产品信息染上了一层情感的文化色调。这种富于艺术性、民族性的广告设计是老上海广告的特色。

时尚与欲望，是近代上海广告带给这座城市的特殊文化效应。老上海广告不只是消费内容的引导，而且具有社会文化特质。人们在满足消费欲望、追求消费时尚的同时，为广告的形式所倾倒，为广告的魅力所吸引，为广告散发出来的知识的、情感的文化信息所神往。上海市民逛马路兜商店习惯的形成，一个重要原因是广告给了他们视觉、听觉和心理上的满足。近代上海市民大众从千姿百态的广告媒体中获得了自己的文化。

广告总是在有广告感觉的城市萌动。进入新世纪以来，注重广告业的传统在上海新一轮建设发展中得到了弘扬广大，国际 4A 广告公司纷纷落户上海，再一次彰显了上海作为中国广告先行者的强势地位。我们有理由相信，上海广告业在四个中心建设进程中必将越来越走向国际化道路。

2013 年 11 月

materials to fully demonstrate the appeal and visual impact of the advertisement, thus making drab commodity possess a kind of rich and colorful art atmosphere and making the product information have cultural tinge of emotion. This kind of artistic and national advertising design was the feature of old Shanghai's advertising.

Fashion and desire were the special cultural effects that modern Shanghai's advertising had brought to the city. Advertising in old Shanghai was not only the guide of consumption contents, but also had social and cultural characteristics. While the consumption desire and pursuing consumption fashion were satisfied, people were attracted by the form and charm of advertisements, and fascinated by the intellectual and emotional cultural information in advertisements. One of the important reasons for the formation of Shanghai citizens' habit of "sauntering about the street" is that advertisements give them visual, auditory and psychological satisfaction. In modern times, Shanghai citizens usually gain their own culture from various advertising media.

Advertising always stirs up in the city with advertising feeling. Since the new century, paying attention to the traditions of advertising has been carried forward in Shanghai's new round of construction and development. The international 4A advertising companies have stationed in Shanghai successively, which again demonstrates Shanghai's strong position as a pioneer of China's advertising. We firmly believe that Shanghai's advertising industry is bound to be increasingly international in the building process of "four centers".

November 2013

老上海的旗袍

老上海的旗袍，是近代中国女性时装的典型代表。它以其流动的旋律和浓郁的诗情，展现近代中国女性的典雅、温婉、柔美、含蓄。其深厚的人文底蕴和审美特质酿造了令人神往的东方风韵。

旗袍最初为清代女性旗人所穿之袍。由于受封建礼教的影响，当时的旗袍装饰繁琐、形制传统，女性身体的曲线毫不外露。1911年辛亥革命爆发，使中国社会风俗发生了划时代变革。上海是妇女寻求解放的重镇。在新文化运动和五四运动的影响下，寻求解放的社会大气候荡涤着服饰妆扮上的陈规陋习，海派旗袍应运而生。

上世纪20年代，上海旗袍开始卸去繁琐的传统负担，制作工艺逐渐西化，款式趋于简洁，重视曲线对女性特征的衬托，肩、胸乃至腰部呈合身之趋势。1929年国民政府首次颁布的《服制条例》确定了旗袍的国服地位。30年代，中西服饰文化进一步交融，上海出现了"别裁法"和"改良旗袍"，旗袍改变了整个袍身呈"倒大"的形状，结构、款式、风格都发生了根本性变化。旗袍的开襟有如意襟、琵琶襟、斜襟、双襟、圆襟等；领有高领、低领、无领、荷叶领、西式翻领等；袖有长袖、短袖、无袖、荷叶袖等；开衩有高开衩、低开衩；还有长旗袍、短旗袍、夹旗袍、单旗袍等分类。富贵

Cheongsam of Old Shanghai

The cheongsam of old Shanghai is the typical representative of the female dresses in modern China. It well demonstrates the elegance, gentility, softness and implicit beauty of women in modern China through its flowing melody and strong poetry. Its profound cultural heritage and aesthetic characteristics have brewed the fascinating oriental charm.

Cheongsam was originally the dress worn by Banner women in the Qing Dynasty. Due to the influence of feudal ethics, at that time, the traditional cheongsam had tedious ornaments and traditional structures, and never exposed the curve of the female body. The outbreak of the Revolution of 1911 brought about an epoch-making change in Chinese social customs. Shanghai became an important city for women to seek liberation. Under the influence of the new Culture Movement and the May 4th Movement, the social trend of seeking liberation cleansed the bad customs and stereotype of costumes and ornaments. Therefore, the Shanghai-style cheongsam came into being.

In the 1920s, Shanghai cheongsam began to get rid of the heavy traditional burdens. The production process was gradually westernized, the style tended to be simple, the emphasis was placed on the foil of female features, and the well-fitting design of shoulder, chest and waist was the trend. In 1929, the national government first issued the *Regulations on Apparel*, which defined the national apparel status of cheongsam. In the 1930s, the Chinese costume culture and western costume culture werefurther integrated, and the "special tailoring method" and "improved cheongsam" appeared in Shanghai. Cheongsam changed the strange shape of the robe, and the structure, pattern and style had all undergone fundamental changes. The top fly of the cheongsam included cloud opening, lute opening, slant opening, double breasted, round opening and so on;

20世纪30年代，穿旗袍的三姐妹

典雅、曲线起伏、风韵柔美的海派旗袍经过报刊、电影、绘画等的宣传推动很快风靡全国，由此引领中国女装进入近代最灿烂的时期。40年代是海派旗袍走向经典的时期。受西方晚礼服等时装的影响，旗袍由平面裁剪变为立体裁剪，加之西方面料的大量入沪和拉链的出现，旗袍的款式、图案和色彩更加丰富多姿，袍身更加舒适合体。尽显东方女性娴静妖娆的海派旗袍，成为近代中国真正融入世界服饰潮流的女性时装。国际时装界一直以来所推崇的现代中国旗袍，实际上就是海派旗袍。

海派旗袍与传统旗袍相比特征鲜明。传统旗袍宽大平直，不显

the collar included the high collar, low collar, collarless, lotus-leaf collar, western turn-down collar and so on; the sleeves included long sleeves, short sleeves, sleeveless, lotus-leaf sleeves and so on; the slit included high vented and low vented; and there were also categories of long cheongsam, short cheongsam, interlining cheongsam and single cheongsam. The Shanghai-style cheongsam with fashionable elegance, undulating curves and gentle charm was promoted by newspapers, films and paintings, and soon swept the country, thus leading Chinese women's costume to enter the heyday in modern times. In the 1940s, Shanghai-style cheongsamtrended to be classic. Influenced by western fashion such as evening dresses, cheongsam has been changed from planar cutting to three-dimensional cutting. In addition, a lot of western fabrics had been imported into Shanghai and zippers had appeared, which made the cheongsam more colorful in design, pattern and color and more comfortable and well-fitting. The Shanghai-style cheongsam, which well demonstrated oriental women's quiet and enchanting charm, had become the female costume in modern China that truly integrated into the world's fashion. The modern Chinese cheongsam praised highly by the international fashion circle actually refers to the Shanghai-style cheongsam.

Compared with traditional cheongsam, Shanghai-style cheongsam had its distinct characteristics. The traditional cheongsam was broad and straight, without revealing the curve of the body; Shanghai-style cheongsam adopted three-dimensional modeling and pursued well-fitting waist and breast design to show the curve of the female body. The traditional cheongsam matched with long pants and embroidered trouser legs could be seen at the open vents; Shanghai-style cheongsam matched with underwear and silk stockings and had barelegged design. The traditional cheongsam was made of heavy brocade or other jacquard fabrics, and the ornaments were tedious; Shanghai-style cheongsam was made of light fabric with more printed fabrics and simple ornaments. While boldly absorbing the western cutting method, the tailors in old Shanghai also applied the traditional Chinese costume-making process of inlaying, embedding, rolling, breaking, coiling, embroidering, pasting, painting, drawing and nailing into it, thus making Shanghai-style cheongsam become more enchanting, elegant and exquisite.

露形体；海派旗袍立体造型，开省收腰，展现女性体态之美。传统旗袍内着长裤，开衩处可见绣花的裤脚；海派旗袍内着内裤和丝袜，开衩处露腿。传统旗袍以厚重的织锦或其他提花织物为面料，装饰繁琐；海派旗袍面料轻盈，印花织物增多，装饰简约。老上海裁缝在大胆吸纳西式裁剪法的同时，把中国传统的镶、嵌、滚、宕、盘、绣、贴、绘、钉的服饰制作工艺应用其中，使得海派旗袍既流光溢彩，又典雅精致。

上世纪 30、40 年代，上海女性十之八九穿着旗袍，旗袍成为当时女性衣橱中不可或缺的服饰。时人根据不同的穿着风格将旗袍女子分为公馆太太派、女生职业派、明星舞女派。宋氏三姐妹等政坛名媛，中国第一位大学女校长吴贻芳、中国的居里夫人吴健雄、传奇新女性张幼仪等海上才女，杨耐梅、胡蝶、阮玲玉、周璇等影星歌星都是当时海派旗袍的形象大使。

上海女性善穿着搭配。披肩、披风、西式外套、毛衣、背心与旗袍配伍；发型与旗袍配伍；鞋袜与旗袍配伍；围巾、丝巾、项链等不同的颈饰与旗袍配伍；手包、眼镜、戒指、耳环、扇子、伞等与旗袍配伍。海上女子通过各种不同的旗袍配伍，塑造出端庄优雅、妩媚俏丽、干练大方、清纯简洁等不同的衣着形象。旗袍推动了老上海的服装业。茂名南路是海上著名的旗袍街，鸿翔、云裳、丽古龙等是海上知名的旗袍店。

全国解放后，旗袍经历了 50 年代逐渐淡出，60、70 年代被批判、受冷落，80、90 年代重返女装舞台，新世纪作为奥运会、世博会等大型国际活动礼仪服饰的曲折历史过程。以旗袍元素为代表的

In the 1930s and 1940s, more than 80% of women in Shanghai wore cheongsam, which became an indispensable part of their wardrobes. According to different dressing styles, the women who wore cheongsam were divided into the official madam style, female profession style and celebrity& dance-hostess style. Young ladies of note in the political circles such as "The Soong Sisters", China's first female university President WU Yifang, "Madame Curie of China" WU Jianxiong, the "legendary new woman" ZHANG Youyi and other talented women, the film stars and famous singers such as YANG Naimei, HU Die, RUAN Lingyu, ZHOU Xuan and so on were the image ambassadors of Shanghai-style cheongsam.

Shanghai women were versed in costume matching. Cheongsam was matched with the cape, mantle, western coat, sweater, vest; the hairstyle was also compatible with the cheongsam, so were the footgear, neck scarves, silk scarves, necklaces and other neck ornaments, as well as the handbags, glasses, rings, earrings, fans, umbrellas and so on. Through different matchings with the cheongsam, Shanghai women shaped different dressing images, such as dignified and elegant, charming and pretty, capable and generous, pure and simple, etc. Cheongsam had promoted the development of old Shanghai's costume industry. South Maoming Road was the most famous cheongsam street while Hongxiang, Yunshang and Ligulong were the most famous cheongsam stores in Shanghai.

After the national liberation, cheongsam experienced tortuous historical processes, including the gradual fading in the 1950s, the criticizing and ignoring in the 1960s and 1970s, the returning in the 1980s and 1990s, and being the etiquette dress of major international events such as Olympic Games and World Expo in the new century. In recent years, the "Chinese style", represented by cheongsam elements, has been blowing up in the fashion industry again. The cheongsam show on the T stage fully demonstrates the beauty and charm of contemporary Chinese women.

Cheongsam has weathered a hundred years of history. In face of the highlyinternationalized fashion trend, people expect Shanghai, which once has promoted cheongsam to transform fromthe traditional costume into the representative of modern

"中国风"近些年再度在时尚界刮起，T台旗袍秀将当代中华女性的风姿绰约展示得淋漓尽致。

旗袍在风风雨雨中走过了百年历史。面对服饰流行高度国际化，曾经促使旗袍由传统服饰衍变为现代中华女性衣饰文化代表的上海，能不能在保持海派旗袍工艺灵魂的同时，演绎与国际时尚相融的新的经典，使旗袍再铸辉煌，这是人们所期待的。

2013 年 11 月

Chinese women's costume culture, will continue to preserve the soul of Shanghai-style cheongsam technology and at the same time display new classicswhich can be integrated into the international fashion, thus makingcheongsam revive again.

November 2013

老上海的广播

上海是开中国境内广播电台播音历史先河的城市。以传递声音为特性而风靡一时的大众广播，对于上海在 20 世纪前半叶逐渐成为全国的经济中心、政治新闻中心和文化中心起了积极作用。

广播的传播活动，来自于都市社会对信息的大量需求。上海开埠后，国内外物质、人口、文化资源聚集，催生了近代广播电台在上海的兴起。1923 年 1 月 23 日晚 8 点整，美国人开办的奥斯邦广播电台在上海开播。这是中国领土上出现的第一座广播电台，比世界上第一家广播电台即美国匹兹堡市广播电台只晚了两年三个月时间。其后，美商新孚洋行、开洛公司、日商新昌公司办的广播电台先后在上海开播。这 4 座广播电台是中国境内最早的一批广播电台，虽然他们的开播都未经中国政府许可批准，侵犯了中国电信主权，但毕竟把 20 世纪初重大的广播电台技术引进了上海，打开了中国人学习无线电技术的窗户。

外商广播电台的开播在上海引起轰动。奥斯邦电台开播之前，广播从业人员四处宣传广播穿越时空的神奇价值，时人称之为"空中传声法"。首播当日就引起听众的轰动，当时的娱乐场所如大来洋行楼顶、礼查饭店、卡尔顿大剧院、中华基督教青年会大楼礼堂、

Broadcasting of old Shanghai

Shanghai was China's first city to pioneer the history of broadcasting stations. The public broadcasting featured by transmitting voices became popular for a time, which played an active role in gradually promoting Shanghai to become the national economic, political and cultural center in the first half of the 20th century.

　　Broadcasting activities were based on the huge information demand of urban society. After the opening of Shanghai port, material, population and cultural resources at home and abroad gathered, which gave birth to the rise of modern broadcasting stations in Shanghai. At 8:00 PM on January 23, 1923, the American-run broadcasting station Osborn was launched in Shanghai. It was the first broadcasting station in China, which was launched two years and three months later than the world's first broadcasting station, the Pittsburgh Broadcasting Station of the United States. After that, the broadcasting stations of Xinfu Foreign Firm run by the American businessmen, Kailuo Firm and Xinchang Firm run by the Japanese businessman successively started broadcasting in Shanghai. These four broadcasting stations were the first batch of broadcasting stations in China. Although they didn't get licenses and approvals from the Chinese government and violated China telecom's sovereignty, the introduction of major broadcasting technologies into Shanghai in the early 20th century opened the window for Chinese to learn radio technologies.

　　The debut of foreign broadcasting stations made a stir in Shanghai. Before the launch of Osborn Broadcasting Station, broadcasting practitioners began to spread the magic of broadcasting across time and space, which was known as "aerial sound transmission method". On the day of debut, it made a stir among the audience. Hundreds of people

老上海电台演播室内现场录制节目的场景

杜美路俱乐部等聚集的听众都达数百人。奥斯邦电台播音的第三天便播出了孙中山的《和平统一宣言》，孙中山亲自祝贺电台开播成功并发表了简短讲话。

外商广播电台在上海的开播，激发了国人对无线电技术的浓厚兴趣和模仿效应。1927年3月18日，新新公司在南京路开设的广播电台首次播音，这是中国人自己开设的首家民营广播电台。随后，亚美、大中华、亚声、李树德堂、东方、鹤鸣等一批广播电台在上海诞生，呈现出民营电台异军突起的繁荣景象。至1930年代中期，上海广播电台迅速发展至40多家，形成了一个广播电台群落，其中民营电台超过了外商电台数量，成为上海电台广播的主力军。其后官方电台相继开办，形成了上海电台广播的多元属性。

gathered together at the entertainment venues such as the roof of Dalai Foreign Firm, Astor House, Carlton Theatre, the auditorium of Chinese Young Men's Christian Association and Route Doumer Club, etc. On the third day of its broadcast, Osborn broadcast Sun Yat-sen's *Declaration of Peaceful Reunification* . Sun Yat-sen personally congratulated the station for its successful debut and delivereda short speech.

  The launch of foreign broadcasting stations in Shanghaistimulated the Chinese people's keen interest in radio technologies and the imitation effect. On March 18, 1927, Xinxin Company opened its first broadcasting station at Nanjing Road, which was the first private broadcasting station opened by the Chinese. Subsequently, a number of radio stations such as Asian America, Greater China, Voice of Asia, Lishude's Radio Station, the Oriental, and Heming were born in Shanghai, showing the prosperity of private broadcasting stations. By the middle 1930s, the broadcasting stations in Shanghai rapidly had grown to more than 40 ones, forming a community of broadcasting stations, among which private broadcasting stations exceeded the number of foreign broadcasting stations and became the main force of Shanghai's radio broadcasting. Since then, the official broadcasting stations had been launched, forming the diversified nature of Shanghai's radio broadcasting.

  The prosperously developing broadcasting in old Shanghai was involved in all fields of social life. Each radio station had its characteristic programs. The broadcasting had become a medium for Shanghai to radiate outwards and communicate frequently inwards, which had become a new link in the social network structure. At that time, the broadcasting programs were divided into more than ten categories, including current politics, news, economy, health and hygiene, common sense, education, language, family life, entertainment& leisure, and religion, etc. The sources of the programs were the integration of the Chinese and western elements, the northern and southern elements, and the ancient and modern elements. The radio, known as "magic box" at that time, also went from the garden houses in the concession to the homes of ordinary people. At its debut, Osborn Broadcasting Station had only a few thousand listeners and there were about 500 radios in the city. By 1940, there were nearly 200,000 radios and nearly one

繁荣发展的老上海广播强劲介入社会生活各个领域。多种性质的电台分期开播，每个电台都有自己的节目特点，广播成为上海向外辐射、向内频繁交流的媒介，成为社会网络结构中一个新的连接环节。当时的广播节目分为时政类、新闻类、经济类、健康卫生类、常识类、教育类、语言类、家庭生活类、娱乐休闲类、宗教类等十多个类别。节目来源兼中西于一体，汇南北于一堂，融古今为一炉。被时人称之为"神奇魔匣"的收音机也从租界的花园洋房进入寻常弄堂间，来到平民百姓家。奥斯邦电台首播时全市收音机数量约 500 台、听众只有数千人，至 1940 年前后，全市收音机数量近 20 万台、听众近百万人。广播给上海这座城市带来了从思想观念、价值取向到生活方式等一系列重大变化。

老上海广播在淞沪抗战中发挥了巨大作用。"9·18"后，上海逐渐成为全国抗日救亡运动宣传的中心。"1·28"淞沪抗战至"8·13"战争爆发期间，上海的广播电台主动融入战时社会总动员行列，几乎所有的电台都坚持播音，充分发挥广播自身的新闻动员、物质动员和精神动员功能，即时报道战况、发布募捐信息、播放救亡歌曲，成为战时最具社会影响力的传播媒介和武器，产生了战时动员的强大效果，为中国广播史谱写了辉煌的一页。

上海沦陷后，在日伪广播电台活动猖獗的情况下，一些民营电台和亲华外国电台坚持把世界反法西斯战场的真实情况传递给听众，坚定上海民众救亡图存的信念。抗战胜利后，由中共上海地下党组织创办的中联广播电台及一些民营电台在揭露国民政府腐败，配合上海解放中发挥了积极作用。上海解放后，人民政府全面接管了 22

million listeners in the city. The broadcasting had brought a series of major changes to Shanghai, including the ideology, value orientation and lifestyle.

The broadcasting in old Shanghai played a vitalrole in the Songhu Anti-Japanese War. After "9. 18 Mukden Incident", Shanghai had gradually became the center of the national campaign of resistance against Japanese aggression and national salvation. During the "1. 28" Songhu Anti-Japanese War to the "8. 13" Shanghai Resistance War, broadcasting stations in Shanghai actively integrated themselves into the society during wartime. Almost all of them insisted on broadcasting and giving full play to the functions of news mobilization, material mobilization and spiritual mobilization to report the war situation immediately, release the fund-raising information and play national salvation songs, thus becoming the most socially influential medium and weapon in wartime, producing a powerful effect of wartime mobilization and writing a brilliant page for the history of Chinese broadcasting.

After Shanghai was occupied by the enemy, some private broadcasting stations and pro-China foreign broadcasting stations insisted on passing on the real situation of the world anti-fascist battlefield to the audience under the circumstance of the rampant activities of Japanesebroadcasting stations, and confirmed the belief ofShanghai people to save the country. After the victory of the Anti-Japanese War, Zoomlion Broadcasting Station and some private broadcasting stations founded by Shanghai underground communist party organization played an active role in exposing the corruption of the national government and cooperating in the liberation of Shanghai. After the liberation of Shanghai, the people's government took over all 22 public broadcasting stations run by the Kuomintang, united to transform private broadcasting stations, and set up Shanghai People's Broadcasting Station, which gave new life to Shanghai's broadcasting stations.

Shanghai broadcasting stations have experienced more than 90 years of history since its birth, witnessed and promoted the great changes and development of Shanghai in the past century. Nowadays, with the rapid development of new media, broadcasting, as one of the important traditional media, is facing the challenges of how to cooperate with new

家国民党办的公营电台,团结改造私营电台,成立上海人民广播电台,使上海的广播电台获得了新生。

上海广播电台诞生至今已经历了 90 多个寒暑春秋,见证并助推了近百年来上海这座城市的巨大变化和发展。在新媒体迅速发展的今天,广播作为重要的传统媒体之一,如何联手新媒体,针对特定的听众群,不断创新节目内容和形式,谋求新的生存空间和发展机遇,这是需要新广播人加以努力的。

2013 年 12 月

media to constantly innovate the contents and form of programs and seek for new living space and development opportunities for specific audience groups, which requires the efforts of new broadcasting practitioners.

December 2013

老上海的期刊

期刊作为一种大众传媒形态，在中国已有近 200 年的历史。20 世纪中叶之前，上海是我国现代期刊出版发行的中心。回顾老上海期刊的历史，对于繁荣发展今天的上海期刊市场不无意义。

1815 年 6 月，英国传教士马礼逊与米怜共同主编的第一份中文期刊《察世俗每月统计传》创刊，使中国期刊进入初创期。1857 年 1 月，由英国传教士主编的《六合丛谈》在上海创刊，标志着上海第一份中文期刊的问世；1868 年 9 月，由英美传教士主编的《中国教会新报》（后改为《万国公报》）在上海创刊。这一时期的中文期刊主要由西方传教士创办，其本质是思想文化渗透侵略，但他们的办刊活动也为在中国传播西方新的科学知识和新的政治学说，促进中国近代期刊的创建产生了积极作用。1896 年 8 月，以维新派代表人物梁启超为总撰述的《时务报》在上海创刊，开始了中国人书写我国近代期刊史的历史。接着，《集成报》、《蒙学报》、《工商学报》、《点石斋画报》、《农学报》等纷纷在上海创刊，期刊数量种类之多、影响之广，为我国其他城市所不及。辛亥革命时期，《东方杂志》、《国粹学报》、《小说月报》、《中华教育界》、《女学报》等期刊先后在上海创办，对于宣传爱国反帝，冲破封建禁锢，传播先进思想，普

Periodicals of Old Shanghai

As a form of mass media, periodical has a history of nearly 200 years in China. Before the middle 20th century, Shanghai was the center of the publishing and distribution of China's modern periodicals. To review the periodical history of old Shanghai is of great significance for the prosperity and development of today's Shanghai periodical market.

In June 1815, the first Chinese periodical — *Chinese Monthly Magazine*, jointly edited by British missionary Morrison and Milne, was launched, thus bringing Chinese periodicals into the initial stage. In January 1857, *Shanghae Seria*, edited by British missionaries, was first published in Shanghai, marking the launch of the first Chinese periodical in Shanghai; in September 1868, the *Newspaper of Chinese Church* (later changed to *A Review of the Times*), edited by British and American missionaries, was first published in Shanghai. The Chinese periodicals in this period were mainly founded by western missionaries, which aimed at the invasion of ideology and culture. However, their activities of founding periodicals also played a positive role in spreading western scientific knowledge and political theories in China, as well as promoting the establishment of modern Chinese periodicals. In August 1896, LIANG Qichao, a representative of the reformists, acted as the editor-in-chief and founded *The Chinese Progress*, which was first published in Shanghai, thus starting the history of Chinese people writing our own periodical history in modern times. Then, *Collections of Various Journals*, *Journal of Enlightening Education*, *Journal of Industry and Commerce*, *Tian-Shi-Zhai Pictorial*, *Journal of Agriculture* and so on were successively initiated in Shanghai, the quantity, variety and influence of which were greater than that of other cities in China. During the Revolution of 1911, *Eastern Miscellany*, *Academic Journal of the Quintessence of*

及科学知识产生了重大影响。1915年，陈独秀在上海创办《青年杂志》即《新青年》，使中国的思想学术文化发生了巨大变化。此后，《劳动界》、《共产党》、《新妇女》等新型期刊先后在上海创办。这些期刊宣传马克思列宁主义，推动新文化运动，为中国共产党的创建作了重要的思想准备。

上世纪20至30年代，中国出现了被时人称之为"期刊热"、"杂志年"的新一轮办刊热潮。至30年代中期，上海期刊品种达400

↖《良友》

Chinese Culture, *Novel Monthly*, *China Educational Review*, *Journal of Women's Education* and other periodicals were successively initiated in Shanghai, which exerted a great influence on propagating patriotic anti-imperialist, breaking through feudalism, spreading advanced thoughts and popularizing scientific knowledge. In 1915, CHEN Duxiu founded the *Youth Magazine* (namely, *New Youth*) in Shanghai, which greatly changed China's ideological and academic culture. Subsequently, *Labor's Circle*, *The Communist Party*, *New Women* and other new periodicals were initiated in Shanghai. These periodicals made important mental preparations for publicizing Marxism-Leninism, promoting the New Cultural Movement and founding the Communist Party of China.

In the 1920s and 1930s, China witnessed a new round of climax to initiate periodicals, known as "periodical craze" and "magazine year". By the mid-1930s, there were more than 400 kinds of periodicals and magazines in Shanghai, accounting for more than 70% of the total magazines in major regions in China, and it became an unshakable publishing center of Chinese periodicals. The influential periodicals established in Shanghai during this period included *Guide*, *Chinese Youth*, *Bolshevik*, *Creation Quarterly*, *Torrente*, *Popular Literature*, *Mengya*, *Literature*, *Life*, *Middle School Students*, etc. After the "9.18" Mukden Incident, the propaganda of anti-Japanese and national salvation became the editorial direction of the progressive periodicals. From the eve of the Anti-Japanese War to the victory of the Anti-Japanese War, more than 230 kinds of anti-Japanese progressive periodicals, such as *Resistance Against Japan*, *Salvation*, *Scream* and *World Affairs*, etc., were initiated in Shanghai, including a large number of anti-Japanese literary periodicals. After the outbreak of the civil war, in face of the white terror of the Kuomintang dictatorship and the persecution of progressive publications, Shanghai's publishing circle followed the instruction of comrade ZHOU Enlai to divide the periodical magazines into tier-I, tier-II and tier-III and take a variety of open, legal and covert means to struggle and deal with the enemy, which made important contributions to the liberation of Shanghai and the whole country.

In the tortuous development history of old Shanghai's periodical, there appeared such famous publishing organizations as Commercial Press, Zhonghua Book Company,

余种，占全国主要地区杂志总数的 70% 以上，成为不可撼动的中国期刊出版中心。这一时期在上海创办的有影响的期刊有《向导》、《中国青年》、《布尔什维克》、《创造季刊》、《奔流》、《大众文艺》、《萌芽》、《文学》、《生活》、《中学生》等。"9·18"事变后，抗日救亡宣传成为进步期刊的编辑方向。从抗战前夕到抗战胜利，上海创办了《抗战》、《救亡》、《呐喊》、《世界知识》等 230 多种抗日进步期刊，其中包括大量的抗日文学期刊。内战爆发后，面对国民党独裁政权的白色恐怖和对进步刊物的迫害，上海出版界按照周恩来同志的指示，将期刊分为一、二、三线，采取多种公开、合法和隐蔽的手段，与敌人进行斗争和周旋，为上海和全国的解放做出了重要贡献。

在老上海期刊曲折的发展历程中，出现了商务印书馆、中华书局、大东书局、世界书局、开明书店等著名出版机构。成立于 1897 年的商务印书馆把办期刊作为传播先进思想文化，推动社会发展的经营方针。该馆"五四"前出版的期刊就达 19 种，不仅品种多样、内容丰富、覆盖面广、影响力大，而且为我国期刊事业积累了许多宝贵的经验。在老上海期刊的各个历史时期，涌现了一批有抱负、有思想、有眼光的编辑家。其中最为著名的有梁启超、陈独秀、鲁迅、茅盾、邹韬奋、叶圣陶、胡愈之等。

全国解放后至 50 年代中期，上海期刊进入恢复、发展、繁荣期。以后受政治运动干扰，期刊发展艰难。"文革"时期，期刊受到摧残和破坏。改革开放使期刊进入新的发展时期，至 20 世纪 90 年代，上海期刊总数近 600 种。进入新世纪后，上海期刊呈现出异彩

Dadong Book Company, World Book Company and Kaiming Bookstore. Founded in 1897, Commercial Press regarded the establishment of periodicals as the business policy of spreading advanced ideology& culture and promoting social development. Commercial Press published 19 kinds of periodicals before the May 4th Movement, which was not only diverse in variety, rich in content, wide in coverage and great in influence, but also accumulated a lot of valuable experience for Chinese periodical industry. In each historical period of the development of old Shanghai's periodical, there emerged a group of ambitious, thoughtful and insightful editors and the most reputedones included LIANG Qichao, CHEN Duxiu, LU Xun, MAO Dun, ZOU Taofen, YE Shengtao, HU

→《新青年》劳动节纪念号

纷呈、繁荣发展的崭新景象。

在中国期刊漫长的发展进程中,上海为中国期刊的发展做出了历史性贡献。面对市场经济和新兴媒体带来的机遇和挑战,上海期刊应该发扬老上海办刊人坚持导向、兼容并包、勇于开拓、力创品牌的优良传统,提高运用现代科技手段进行自我更新的能力,利用期刊特有的功能和优势,在建设国际化文化大都市中发挥更大的作用。

2014 年 2 月

Yuzhi, etc.

From the national liberation to the middle 1950s, periodicals of Shanghai experienced the periods of recovery, development and prosperity. Later, the political movements interfered with the development of periodicals. During the Cultural Revolution, periodicals were destroyed and damaged. The reform and opening-up has brought the periodical into a new development period. By the 1990s, there were nearly 600 periodicals in Shanghai. After entering the new century, periodicals of Shanghai presented a new scene of colorful and prosperous development.

In the long development history of Chinese periodicals, Shanghai has made historic contributions to it. In face of the opportunities and challenges brought by market economy and emerging media, Shanghai periodicals should carry forward the excellent traditions of adhering to orientation and compatibility, daring to blaze new trails and strengthening brand influences, improve the ability to use modern technological means for self-renewal and utilize the distinct features and advantages of periodicals, thus playing a greater role in building an international cultural metropolis.

February 2014

老上海的跑马场

上海是中国最早开辟跑马场的城市。

1850年前后，英国侨民霍格、吉勃等5人组织跑马总会，在现南京东路、河南中路交界，以每亩不足10两银子的价格"永租"土地81年，开辟了近代中国第一个跑马场。这距上海开埠不到10年。当时跑马场跑道直径不到800米，骑手经常把马骑到外面的泥石路上，时人把这些路称作马路。这便是后人称城市街道为马路的缘由。这个跑马场1851年开始娱乐性赛马，前后共赛了7次。因地价飞涨，跑马总会于1854年将第一跑马场的土地高价卖出，又从浙江中路南京路两侧圈地170亩建造了第二个跑马场。第二跑马场仅使用到1861年前后又被高价出售。翌年，跑马总会在英国驻沪领事的支持下又圈占今上海人民公园、人民广场一带400多亩土地辟筑第三个跑马场，时人称"上海跑马厅"。跑马厅除跑道外，还建有欧式风格的跑马总会大楼、看台、钟楼和上海地区第一个游泳池，堪称远东第一。

跑马总会成员均为洋人，年满21岁的任何国籍外国人均可申请入会，只有华人除外。自1863年至1919年，跑马厅每年春秋两季举行跑马博彩大赛，1920年后赛事增加。赛马之日，各领事衙门、

Racecourses of Old Shanghai

Shanghai was China's first city to open the racecourse.

Around 1850, the British Chinese Hogg, Gibb and other three people organized the Horse Race Club located at today's junction of East Nanjing Road and Middle Henan Road and obtained the 81-year "perpetual lease" of the land with the price of less than 10 taels of silver per mu (1 mu≈666.6666667 m^2), thus opening the first racecourse in modern China, which was less than 10 years since the opening of Shanghai port. The racetrack at that time was less than 800 meters in diameter, and riders often took their horses out onto the mud and stone roads, known as "horse roads". This racecourse had held recreational horse races for seven times since its first horse race in 1851. Due to the soaring land price, the Horse Race Club sold the land of the first racecourse at a high price in 1854 and obtained enclosure of 170-mu land along Middle Zhejiang Road and Nanjing Road to establish the second racecourse. In 1861, the second racecourse was sold at a high price. In the following year, with the support of the British consul general in Shanghai, the Horse Race Club captured and built the third racecourse in the area of today's Shanghai People's Park and People's Square, covering more than 400 mu of land, known as "Shanghai Horse Race Hall". Besides the running track, there was also the European-style building of the Horse Race Club, spectators stand, bell tower and the first swimming pool in Shanghai, which was the best in the Far East.

Members of the Horse Race Club were foreigners. Foreign nationals of any nationality aged 21 or above can apply for membership except for the Chinese. From 1863 to 1919, horse race gambling contests would be held in the horse race hall in spring and autumn every year for twice and after 1920, the horse race gambling contests

银行商贾或半日或全日停止办公和营业,海关也于午时闭关,租界达马场之各路人满为患。1909年起,中国人被允许购票进跑马厅博彩,赌博的名目因此日益繁多。西人巧取豪夺,聚敛搜刮中国市民百姓的钱财,牟取惊人暴利。当时跑马厅年佣金收入1000万银元上下,而当地大银行的资本在200万银元以上的也是凤毛麟角。

"独赢"、"连位"、"摇彩"等众多的博彩名目和暗箱操作,使绝大多数赌马市民百姓血本无归。当时上海因赌马倾家荡产、跳黄浦、喝毒药的惨剧时有发生。一个名叫阎瑞生的职员因赌马输钱,便杀死一名富裕妓女,抢得金银首饰逃走,后被捕处死。这一事件被编成京戏、文明戏和各种地方戏、拍成故事片,成为赌马害人的血证。

1909年,江南富贾叶贻铨因忍受不了洋人的侮辱,决心在华界建造中国人自己的跑马场。他在今武川路、武东路处以高价从农民手中征得1200亩土地,仿照"上海跑马厅"的式样,建起了江湾跑马场,又称"万国体育会"。为使参加赛马游客有赏景休憩的场所,

↖ 1908年的跑马厅马厩外景

increased. On the day of the horse race, consul-generals and bankers closed their offices and business for half or full day, and the customs closed at noon. The racecourse was filled with people. Since 1909, Chinese people had been allowed to buy tickets and participated in the horse race gambling, hence resulting in the growing number of gambling titles. Westerners seized the opportunity to plunder Chinese people's money and acquired amazing profits. At that time, the annual commission revenue of the horse race hall reached about10 million silver yuan while that of few large local banks couldreach 2 million silver yuan.

Various gambling items and darkroom operations such as "capot", "winning streak" and "policy racket" made most of the citizens participating in the gambling lose everything. At that time, due to the horse gambling, tragic events such as jumping in Huangpu River and drinking poison happened frequently in Shanghai. A clerk named YAN Ruisheng was arrested and executed after killing a rich prostitute, stealing gold and silver jewelry and fleeing for money on a horse bet. The incident was adapted into Beijing Opera, modern drama and a variety of local operas, which had become the solid evidence that horse gambling would harm and destroy a person.

In 1909, YE Yiquan, a wealthy man from the south of the Yangtze River, was determined to build his own racecourse in China because he could not stand the insults of foreigners. He purchased 1,200 mu of land from farmers at a high price betweentoday's Wuchuan Road and Wudong Road, and imitated the style of the "Shanghai Horse Race Hall" to have built Jiangwan Racecourse, also known as the "international recreation club". In order to give the racegoers a place to enjoy the scenery, he built a garden featured by landscape of rockery, lake and waterfall on the northeast side of the racetrack, known as YE Family's Garden. After the opening of Jiangwan Racecourse in May 1911, it not only attracted many wealthy businessmen, but also some foreigners who had unrestrained gambling in "Shanghai Horse Race Hall" came here for gambling. Jiangwan Racecourse paid the government tax of more than one million yuan every year, and pledged the civilian's education funds. In 1924, a group of gang leaders in Shanghai set up the Yinxiangxiang Racecourse in the area of today's Shuangyang Road

他又在马场东北面征地建造了一座以假山湖泊瀑布取胜的花园，即叶家花园。江湾跑马场1911年5月开业后，不但吸引了众多富商巨贾，就连一些原在"上海跑马厅"豪赌的外国人，也改换门庭来这里参赛。江湾跑马场每年交纳政府库税高达百万元，并认捐平民教育款项。1924年，上海一批帮会头目在今双阳路、长阳路一带建起了引翔乡跑马场，同泰钱庄的老板谭竹馨为第一任董事长，后由杜月笙接任。时人称该跑马场为上海第五跑马场。

盛行于老上海的赛马博彩，使得骑术学校、马房、马妆专卖店、马匹租赁、马厩等以马为主题的服务性行业盛极一时。当去骑术学校在外侨圈成为时尚后，有钱的华人男女便开始效仿这种贵族运动。到西郊骑马娱乐社交成为时尚，虹桥路上一度出现了浩浩荡荡的华洋杂处的骑马者队伍。骑马成了老上海上流社会的标志。

赛马也成为老上海报刊宣传的重要内容，当时上海最有影响的《申报》在创刊号上刊登的第一则新闻就是《驰马角胜》，第一篇文艺作品竟也是《观西人斗驰马歌》。

赛马这一怡情悦性的运动，在近代上海特殊的历史背景下被扭曲了。跑马厅由开始的休闲娱乐逐渐演变为赌博销金的魔窟、歧视华人的场所、殖民主义权力的象征、帝国主义炫耀武力的地方。上海解放后，人民政府收回了跑马厅。1951年9月，"上海跑马厅"改建成人民公园和人民广场，跑马总会大楼改为上海图书馆。江湾跑马场建国后新建起了一批工厂学校，叶家花园由叶贻铨慷慨捐出，为上海市第一肺科医院。引翔乡跑马场盖起了幸福公寓，成为市民

and Changyang Road, known as the fifth racecourse in Shanghai. TAN Zhuxin, the boss of Tongtai Money Shop, was the first chairman of the racecourse and was later replaced by DU Yuesheng.

↗ 老上海的跑马场 贺竹元绘

The prevailing horse-racing gambling in old Shanghai had led to the flourishing of

居住区。

老上海的跑马场，是近代上海政治、经济、文化畸形发展的产物。这页历史虽然早已翻过，但它给上海这座城市所留下的荣辱沧桑我们不该忘却。

2014 年 2 月

equestrian schools, stable houses, horse makeup stores, horse rental, stable and other horse-themed service industries. When riding school became fashionable in the foreign settlers' circle, wealthy Chinese men and women began to follow suit. It became the fashion of recreation and social contacts to ride horses in the western suburb. There even appeared the phenomenon that a large number of Chinese and foreignerswere riding horses atHongqiao Road. Horse riding became the symbol of the select society in old Shanghai.

Horse racing also became an important part of the publicity contentsin old Shanghai newspapers. The first news published on the first issue of *Shun Pao*, the most influential newspaper in Shanghai at that time, was *The Champion of the Horse Racing* while its first literary and artistic work was also *Song of Watching Westerners Horse Racing*.

Horse racing, a pleasant sport, was distorted in the special historical background of modern Shanghai. The Horse Race Hall had gradually evolved from a place for leisure and entertainment into a gambling den, a place of discrimination against the Chinese, a symbol of colonial power, and a place for imperialist to show off force. After the liberation of Shanghai, the people's government took back the Horse Race Hall. In September 1951, "Shanghai Horse Race Hall" was transformed into People's Park and People's Square and the building of the Horse Race Club was transformed into Shanghai Library. After the founding of People's Republic of China, a number of new factories and schools were built in Jiangwan Racecourse. YE Yixuan generously donated the YE Family's Garden to build Shanghai First Pulmonary Hospital. The happiness apartment was built in Yinxiangxiang Racecourse and it became a residential area for citizens.

The racecourses of old Shanghai are the products of the abnormal development of politics, economy and culture in modern Shanghai. Although this page of history has already been turned, the honors or disgraces it has brought to Shanghai would never be forgotten.

February 2014

老上海的教堂

富于历史厚重感和沧桑感的老上海教堂，是西方文化在上海交汇融合的产物。它不仅是异国建筑风格和宗教文化的充分体现，而且也是我们了解海派文化的重要窗口。

早在 16 世纪，基督教就开始传入上海。徐光启对基督教在上海的传播起了极大的推动作用。1640 年其子孙助建于梧桐路 137 号的敬一堂是上海最早的天主教堂。这座庙宇式的西式教堂是天主教在上海扎根的标志。上海开埠初期，外国宣教士大多在本国领事馆中兼任职务，因而出现了天主堂与领事馆共处一地的特殊现象。19 世纪中后叶，随着上海逐渐成为宣教的重镇，进入上海的西方各差会纷纷兴建教会建筑。至 19 世纪末，上海共有大小教堂 300 余所。其中比较知名的有：位于江西路九江路的圣三一教堂，老北门第一浸会堂，苏州河以北最早的教堂救主堂，南苏州路的天安堂，北京西路的圣彼得堂，虹桥石皮弄的天恩堂，上海租界最早的教堂洋泾浜天主堂，董家渡天主堂，徐家汇天主堂（圣·依纳爵堂）等。

进入 20 世纪后，随着租界的进一步扩大，上海城市中心区域迅速扩展。至 1920 年，上海已有马路 370 余条，里坊 2130 余处，学校 500 余所，旅馆 30 余家，银行钱庄 230 余家，医院 60 余所，工

Church of Old Shanghai

The historical and ancient churches of old Shanghai were the products of the convergence of western culture in Shanghai. They are not only the full reflection of the exotic architectural style and religious culture, but also the important window for us to understand Shanghai-style culture.

As early as the 16th century, Christianity began to be introduced into Shanghai. XU Guangqi played a vitalrole in promoting the spread of Christianity in Shanghai. In 1640, his descendants helped build the first Catholic church at No. 137, Wutong Road in Shanghai. The temple-style western church was a sign of Catholicism in Shanghai. In the early days of Shanghai's opening port, most foreign missionaries held concurrent posts in their own country's consulate, thus emerging the special phenomenon that the Catholic church and the consulate were located at the same place. In the middle tolate 19th century, as Shanghai became an important place for promoting religion, the missionary societies successively established church buildings after entering Shanghai. By the end of the 19th century, Shanghai had more than 300 large and small churches. The well-knownones included Church of the Holy Trinity betweenJiujiang Road andJiangxi Road, First Baptist Church at Old North Gate, the earliest Church of Our Saviour in the north of Suzhou River, Church of Heavenly Peace at SouthSuzhou Road, St. Peter's Church at West Beijing Road, Church of the Emperor's Kindness Shipi Nong of Hongqiao, the earliest church in Shanghai concession Pidgin Catholic Church, Dongjiadu Catholic Church, Xujiahui Catholic Church (St. Ignatius Church), etc.

After entering the 20th century, with the further expansion of the concession, the central area of Shanghai expanded rapidly. By 1920, Shanghai had more than 370 roads,

1854 年始建的虹口美国礼拜堂（在百老汇路）

厂 500 余家，影戏院 30 余家，近代上海城市的格局基本形成。此后，上海城市建设进入一个迅猛发展时期，为教会建筑的建造提供了更广阔的空间。教堂经历了模仿西式教堂的移植期，开始形成与上海狭小的城市用地相适应的海派西式教堂建筑样式。天主教堂、基督教堂、东正教堂、犹太教堂等各种类型、各等规模的教会建筑拔地而起，出现了上海教堂建筑艺术的高峰。20 世纪初的 30 多年时间里，西方传教士在上海建造的教会建筑比整个 19 世纪建造的还要多。教会建造活动大致可分为三类：一是对初期建造的简陋建筑进行翻新、改建、扩建；二是为一批早期成立却没有独立建筑的教会机构建造新建筑；三是建造新创办机构的教会建筑。徐家汇天主堂

over 2, 130 li-fang, 500-plus schools, over 30 hotels, 230-plus banks and money shops, more than 60 hospitals, over 500 factories and more than 30 cinemas and theaters, basically forming the pattern of modern Shanghai. Since then, Shanghai's urban construction had entered a period of rapid development, providing a broader space for the construction of church buildings. The church experienced the transplant period of imitating the western church, and began to form the Shanghai-style church adapting to the narrow urban land of Shanghai. Catholic churches, Christian churches, Eastern Orthodox churches, Jewish synagogues and other church buildings of various types and sizes had been built, showing the peak of church architectural art in Shanghai. For more than 30 years in the early 20th century, western missionaries built more church buildings in Shanghai than in the entire 19th century. Church building activities could be divided into three categories: first, it was the renovation, reconstruction and expansion of the primitive buildings; second, they were the new buildings for a group of churches that had been established in the early days but had no independent buildings. Third, it was the church building of the new institution. After expansion, Xujiahui Catholic Church could housenearly 3, 000 people to worship at the same time, becoming the largest Catholic Church in Shanghai. The First Baptist Church at Old North Gate was also demolished and rebuilt. At the same time, Shanghai Community Church, Allen Memorial Church, All Saints Church, Hong-de Tang Church, Moore Memorial Church, Mu-En Church, New Gospel of Grace Church and many other new churches were built. After 1937, due to the war, the church construction activities in Shanghai almost stopped.

The old Shanghai churches, with unique modeling and distinct style, was a wonderful combination of the world's architectural design trend, aesthetic orientation, engineering technology and traditional Chinese culture at that time. The Baroque-style embossed Dongjiadu Catholic Church with an integration of the Chinese and western elements, the Medieval Gothic Xujiahui Catholic Church with sharp-arch window frames and lead colorful ikon glass windows, the Sheshan Catholic Church with an integration of the Greek, Roman and Gothic architectural art, the Church of the Holy Trinity with tall and gorgeous modeling and red-brick wall space which was known as "red church", the

经过扩建后可容纳近 3000 人同时礼拜，成为上海最大的天主教堂。老北门第一浸会堂也将老堂拆除进行了重建。同时，国际礼拜堂、景林堂、诸圣堂、鸿德堂、慕尔堂、沐恩堂、新福音堂等一大批教堂新建而成。1937 年后，由于战争的原因，上海的教堂建筑活动几乎全部停止。

造型别致、风格迥异的老上海教堂，是当时世界建筑设计潮流、审美取向、工程技术与中国传统文化的美妙结合。巴洛克式风格、浮雕中西杂糅的董家渡天主堂，中世纪哥特式建筑、尖拱门窗楹、铅条彩色圣像玻璃窗的徐家汇天主堂，融希腊、罗马、哥特式建筑艺术于一炉、中西合璧的佘山天主教堂，造型挺拔秀丽，墙面用红砖砌筑，俗称"红礼拜堂"的圣三一教堂，捷克著名建筑师邬达克设计的哥特复兴式建筑慕尔堂，带有西亚古朴的拜占庭风格的息焉公墓堂等都是老上海著名的教堂建筑。

教堂，使上海城市建设迈入西化的历程。最初上海县城的建设，基本是按照中国古代传统方式建造。开埠后，各国开始在租界建造各种类型的西式建筑，特别是各具风格和特色的教堂，带来了与中国传统建筑完全不同的景象，从城市格局和空间上西化着这个城市，改变着人们对城市空间中心的认知。圣三一教堂高高耸立的塔楼，徐家汇天主堂哥特式双尖顶，苏州河畔新天安堂的钟塔等，打破了旧城肌理，以一种绝对强势的视觉语言出现，并占据着城市至高点，成为当时上海城市新的地标。随着教堂和教堂区的建设，近代教育模式和教会学校、现代医疗护理机构和教会医院、期刊社、印书馆、博物馆、天文台、育婴堂、孤儿院等现代文明也都逐渐进入上海，

Gothic revival Moore Memorial Church designed by the famous Czech designer Ladislav Hudec, the Xiyan Cemetery Church with simple Byzantine style and other churches were the famous church buildings in old Shanghai.

Church made the construction of Shanghai enter the course of westernization. Initially, the construction of Shanghai basically followed the traditional way in ancient China. After the opening of the port, other countries began to build various types of western architectures in the concession, especially churches with different styles and characteristics, bringing a completely different scene from the traditional Chinese architecture, thus westernizing the city inthe aspects of urban patterns and space and changing people's understanding of the urban space center. The high tower of Church of the Holy Trinity, the Gothic double pinnacles of Xujiahui Catholic Church, the bell tower of the Church of Heavenly Peace along Suzhou River and others broke the texture of the old city, appeared in an absolutely powerful visual language and occupied the high points of the city, becoming the new landmarks of Shanghai at that time. With the

→ 1906 年建造，1910 年完成的
徐家汇大教堂

使这座传统城市开始变为一个带有较多西方近代城市性质的新兴城市。

上海解放后，在战争中毁坏的教堂得到修复，基督教、天主教走上了自立、自传、自养的道路。十年动乱中，教堂遭到浩劫。改革开放后，宗教组织、宗教活动得到恢复，被占用的教堂得以归还，遭破坏的部分教堂得以修复。

老上海的教堂，是历史留给这座城市的一份珍贵的建筑文化遗产，是城市发展和历史文化积淀的重要载体，是中西文化交流融汇的见证。如何对待这些遗产，充分运用其具有的宗教、历史、科学和艺术价值，则是需要我们今天加以重视的问题。

2014 年 3 月

construction of the church and the church area, modern education mode and the church school, modern medical care institutions and hospitals, the journal office, press, museum, observatory, foundling homes, orphanages and modern civilizations were also gradually introduced into Shanghai, making the traditional city transform into a new city with more modern western urban natures.

After the liberation of Shanghai, the churches destroyed in the war were restored, and the Christian and Catholic churches began to be self-supporting, self-preaching and self-cultivating. The churches were destroyed during the decade of unrest in the Cultural Revolution. After the reform and opening-up, the religious organizations and religious activities were restored, the occupied churches were returned and some of the damaged churches were restored.

The churches of old Shanghai are precious architectural cultural heritage of the city, important carriers of urban development and historical and cultural accumulation, as well as the witness of the integration of Chinese and western culture. The issue that we should pay great attention to today is how to treat these heritages and make full use of their religious, historical, scientific and artistic values.

March 2014

老上海的西餐

上海是中国西餐业发展最早最快的城市。作为立体展现西方物质与精神综合形象的西餐,是近代上海市民了解和接收西方文化的重要载体。西餐对于近代上海城市文化空间的拓展功不可没。

明万历年间,徐光启在把意大利传教士郭居静等人引入上海时,就同时引进了西菜,当时叫做"番菜"。中国人一直自以为是世界中心,因而将别的国家都称之"番邦"。上海开埠后,西方饮食文化通过各种途径输入上海。19世纪60至70年代,上海有了由外国人经营,以外国大班和买办官员等为主要服务对象的西餐馆,其中以开设在今延安东路上的"密菜里"西餐馆最为有名。1882年,由中国人开的"海天春番菜馆"在上海诞生,开始了中国人经营西餐的历史。到上世纪初,上海的西餐馆已达几十家。这些西餐馆大多集中在今福州路一带,名气比较大的有一品香、一家春、吉祥春、江南村、万年春等。上世纪30年代前后,上海西餐的重心转移到今淮海路一带。康斯坦丁劳勃里、飞亚克、茜顿、华盛顿、卡夫卡斯、檀香山等西餐馆盛极一时。与此同时,老大昌、沙利文、康生、麦瑞、凯司令、哈尔滨、起士林等西点铺、西饼屋相继开张。至上世纪40年代,上海西餐业出现畸形繁荣的局面,各类西餐馆、面包房、西

Western Food of Old Shanghai

Shanghai is a city which boasts China's earliest and fastest development of Western-food industry. Western food, as a three-dimensional representation of Western material and spirit, is an important carrier for Shanghai citizens to understand and receive Western culture in modern times. Western food has made great contributions to the expansion of modern Shanghai's urban space of culture.

During the Wanli's Reign of the Ming Dynasty, while the Italian missionary GUO Jujing and other people were brought to Shanghai by XU Guangqi, the Western food, then called "foreign food", was also introduced into Shanghai. The Chinese had always thought of themselves as the center of the world, so they call other countries "foreign nations". After the opening of Shanghai port, Western food culture was imported into Shanghai in various ways. From the 1960s to the 1970s, Shanghai had a Western restaurantoperated by the foreigner and mainly serving foreign top classes and comprador officials, among which the Western restaurant "Micaili" opened at today's Yan'An East Road was the most famous. In 1882, "Haitian Chunfan Restaurant" opened by Chinese people was opened in Shanghai, starting the history of Chinese people running Western food. By the beginning of last century, there were dozens of Western restaurants in Shanghai. Most of these Western restaurants were located in the area of today's Fuzhou Road, and the famous ones included Yixiang, Yijiachun, Jixiangchun, Jiangnancun and Wannianchun, etc. Around the 1930s, the center of Western food in Shanghai shifted to today's Huaihai Road. Western restaurants such as Constantine Laubury, Fiaker, Dasey's, Washington, Kafkas, Honolulu and many other restaurants flourished. At the same time, Chang Restaurant, Sullivan, Kang Sheng, Micrel, Kay Commander,

▶ 一品香西菜馆

饼屋达百余家。

　　西餐改变了上海市民传统的饮食习惯和食品构成。随着西餐馆的出现,葡萄酒、啤酒、汽水、咖啡、奶茶等酒品饮料登上了上海人的餐桌,酒吧、咖啡馆、啤酒屋、汽水店等出现在上海租界的街头。19世纪80年代埃凡洋行在上海首开啤酒制造厂,生产的啤酒除供应本埠外还大量运销香港及其它口岸。以面包、牛奶、肉类为主的西餐,改变了国人常食五谷,不注重饮食中蛋白质和脂肪肉类摄取量的习惯,罐头、蛋糕、面包、饼干等西式食品成为畅销食品。肉类加工厂、罐头厂、蛋粉厂、面粉厂等西式食品制造业在上海迅速发展,成为上海近代工业的重要组成部分。

Ha'erbin, Kissling and many other bakeries and pastry stores were successively opened. In the 1940s, the Western-food industry in Shanghai experienced an abnormal prosperity, with over 100 restaurants, bakeries and pastry stores.

Western food had changed Shanghai citizens' traditional eating habits and food composition. With the emergence of Western restaurants, wine, beer, soda, coffee, milk tea and other alcoholic beverages had been served on the table of Shanghai people while bars, cafes, beer houses and soda shops appeared on the streets of Shanghai concessions. In the 1880s, Evan Foreign Firm opened its first beer factory in Shanghai, producing beer which was not only supplied to the local people, but also exported to Hong Kong and other ports. Western food, mainly bread, milk and meat, changed the Chinese people's habit of eating five cereals without paying attention to the consumption of protein and fat meat in the diet. Western food such as canned food, cakes, bread and biscuits had become the popular food. Meat processing factory, canning factory, egg flour factory, flourmill and other western food manufacturing industries rapidly developed in Shanghai and became an important part of Shanghai's modern industry.

The introduction of Western food also brought the typical Western etiquette culture — Western dining etiquette to Shanghai. Western dining etiquette paid attention to the concept of dining environment, dining atmosphere, table order, tableware use and butler service, as well as the principle of politeness, temperance and appropriateness in the process of sitting, dining and talking, which profoundly affected the lifestyle of Shanghai citizens. Western food became an important part for people to understand the Western daily lifestyle and western culture.

The Western food-cooking method and dining form promoted the conflict and integration of the Chinese and Western food culture. In order to attract the Chinese people, the first Western restaurant opened by the foreigner in Shanghai started to implement the localization strategy in the very beginning, adding Shanghai elements like sweet, greasy, heavy and other elements to the Western food, so as to adapt to the local eating habits. The Shanghai chef also organically combined the Western cooking method in the book of *Making Foreign Food* with the practice of local cuisines, hence to produce

西餐的引入也为上海带来了西方礼仪文化的典型——西餐礼仪。西餐讲究用餐环境、进餐氛围、餐桌秩序、餐具使用、贴身服务的理念,以及入座、就餐、交谈过程中注重礼貌、节制、适宜的原则,深刻影响着上海市民的生活方式。西餐成为时人了解西方人日常生活方式和西方文化的重要环节。

西餐的烹调方法和就餐形式,催发了中西饮食文化的冲突和交融。最早在上海开西餐馆的外国人为了吸引华人消费,一开始就实施本土化战略,在西餐中融入了喜甜腻、偏浓郁等上海元素,以适应本埠人的饮食习惯。上海大厨也将《造洋饭书》中做西餐的方法与本帮菜肴的做法有机结合,因此有了海派西餐的说法。"法国人不知拿破仑蛋糕,俄罗斯人不识罗宋汤"的笑话,便是改良西餐的佐证。同时,西餐选料精细、坚持标准、注重营养以及讲究卫生的分餐制形式被中餐所吸纳,从而在上海形成了西餐中吃与中菜西吃的中西饮食文化交融的局面。

上海解放后,在"左"的思想影响下,吃西餐被视为追求资产阶级生活方式,西餐逐渐淡出。至上世纪 70 年代末,上海只剩下红房子、天鹅阁、蓝村等十来家西餐馆。改革开放的春风使西餐业复苏。进入新世纪后,上海西餐业迅速发展。目前上海的西餐馆、蛋糕房、西饼屋和各种西式快餐店数以万计。

在上海城市建设日趋国际化的今天,西餐扮演着越来越重要的角色。洋溢着异国情调、又融合了海派风味的西餐,赢得了上海市民和中外游客的普遍青睐。衷心地希望西餐成为我们这座城市永远靓丽的风情景观。

2014 年 4 月

the saying of "Shanghai-style Western food". It was the evidence of the reform of Western food that "the French do not know Napoleon Cake and the Russians do not know borscht". At the same time, the advantages of Western food including fine materials, adhering to standards, paying attention to nutrition and hygiene were absorbed by traditional Chinese food, thus forming a situation of integration of Chinese and Western food culture — Western-style Chinese food and Chinese-style Western food.

After the liberation of Shanghai, under the influence of "left-wing" thought, eating Western food was regarded as the pursuit of bourgeois lifestyles, and Western food gradually faded out. In the late 1970s, there were only about a dozen of Western restaurants in Shanghai, including Red House, Swan Pavilion and Blue Village, etc. The spring breeze of reform and opening-up made Western-food industry revive. After entering the new century, the Western restaurant industry in Shanghai developed rapidly. According to incomplete statistics, there are tens of thousands of Western restaurants, bakeries, pastry stores and various western fast-food restaurants in Shanghai at present.

Today, with the internationalization of Shanghai's urban construction, Western food plays a more and more important role. The Western food, which is full of exotic charm and integrated with Shanghai styles, has been generally favored by Shanghai people and tourists from home and abroad. We sincerely hope that Western food will become the beautiful scenery of our city forever.

April 2014

老上海的女校

上海是开中国女子教育先河的重要城市。

在传统的中国社会,"女子无才便是德"的偏见根深蒂固,妇女没有权力享受学校教育。上海开埠后,这一现象开始改变。1850年,美国圣公会传教士裨治文夫人格兰德感慨于中国妇女教育程度之低,在上海创立裨文女塾。这是上海第一所女子学校,标志着基督教在上海开办女子学校教育的开始。次年,美国传教士琼司女士在虹口创办文纪女塾。其后,上海的教会女子学校纷纷创办。至19世纪末,上海教会女子学校已有10余所,约占全国教会女子学校总数的三分之一。其中比较知名的有,创办于1861年的清心女子中学、创办于1881年的圣玛利亚女中、创办于1892年的中西女子中学、创办于1897年的晏摩氏女中等。基督教在上海创办女校的初衷是传教、发展教徒,其本质是一种文化侵略,但客观上却起到了改变中国社会观念,促进上海近代女子教育发展和妇女解放的积极作用。

基督教会女校在上海的创办,刺激了国人自己开办女校的热情,同时也为上海士绅和进步人士自办女校提供了模本。在梁启超、经元善等人的倡议和筹办下,中国近代史上第一所国人自办的女子学

Girls' School of Old Shanghai

Shanghai is an important city to first pioneer Chinese women education.

In traditional Chinese society, the prejudice that "lack of talents in a woman is a virtue." has been deeply rooted, and women have no right to enjoy schooling. After the opening of Shanghai port, this phenomenon began to change. In 1850, Eliza Gillette, the wife of an American episcopal missionary Elijah Coleman Bridgman, was impressed by the low education level of Chinese women, and founded Bridgman Memorial School in Shanghai. It was the first girls' school in Shanghai, marking the start of the education of girls' school opened by Christianity in Shanghai. In the following year, the American missionary Emma Jones founded Wenji Girls' School in Hongkou. Afterwards, church girls' schools were founded one after another in Shanghai. By the end of the 19th century, Shanghai had more than 10 church girls' schools, accounting for about onethird of the total number of church girls' schools in China. The famous ones included Qingxin Girls' Middle School founded in 1861, St. Mary's Girls' Middle School founded in 1881, Zhongxi Girls' Middle School founded in 1892 and Yanmoshi Girls' Middle School founded in 1897, etc. The original intention for Christianity to establish a girls' school in Shanghai was to proselytize and develop churchgoers, actually a kind of cultural invasion, but it objectively played a positive role in changing Chinese social concepts and promoting the development of women education and women's liberation in modern Shanghai.

The establishment of the girls' Christian church school in Shanghai stimulated the enthusiasm of Chinese people to start their own girls' schools, and also provided a model for the gentry and progressives in Shanghai to start their own girls' schools.

校上海女学堂（又称经正女学）于1898年成立。其后，务本女塾、爱国女学、城东女学社、宗孟女学堂等华人女校纷纷创办。1906年被视为上海华人女学成立之大年。这一年里，相继有民立女中学堂、三育女学堂、祝群女校、萃秀女学堂、辅强女学堂、南州女校、润鸿女学堂等8所女子学校成立。至1920年代初期，上海已有40余所华人私立女校，呈现华人女校与教会女校并驾齐驱、共同发展之势。

辛亥革命的爆发，使上海女子教育进入新的发展期。许多女校在小学基础上发展出中学部，部分教会女校还开设了高等教育。随着女校学制的逐步完善，上海的华人大学与教会大学相继向女学生放开入学限制，使得女子开始享受高等教育。同时，平

← 中西女塾五年级学生合影

Under the initiative and organization of LIANG Qichao, JING Yuanshan and other people, Shanghai Girls' School (also known as Jing Zheng Girls' School) was established in 1898, China's first self-run girls' school in modern history. After that, girls' schools including Wuben Girls' School, Aiguo Girls' School, Chengdong Girls' School and Zongmeng Girls' School were successively founded. In 1906, it was regarded as the major year for the founding of Shanghai's Chinese girls' schools. In this year, there were 8 girls' schools successively established, including Minli Girls' School, Sanyu Girls' School, Zhuqun Girls' School, Cuixiu Girls' School, Fuqiang Girls' School, Nanzhou Girls' School and Runhong Girls' School, etc. By the early 1920s, there were more than 40 private Chinese girls' schools in Shanghai, showing the trendthat Chinese girls' schools and missionary girls' schools are developing side by side.

With the outbreak of the Revolution of 1911, Shanghai women's education entered a new period of development. Many girls' schools developed secondary school departments on the basis of primary schools, and some of them set up higher education. With the gradual improvement of the girls' school system, Chinese universities and missionary universities in Shanghai liberalized their enrollment to female students, enabling women to enjoy higher education. At the same time, civilian girls' schoolswere also gradually established. In the civilian girls' school founded by LI Da in 1921, he specially invited CHEN Duxiu, CHEN Wangdao, SHAO Lizi, SHEN Yanbing, LIU Shaoqi, ZHANG Tailei and DENG Zhongxia to serve as teachers, make theme lectures, spread Marxism, and guide female students to develop themselves and step into society.

Around the 1930s and 1940s, Shanghai women education presented a diversified development trend. Shanghai not only had the best women's basic education in China, but also had its own women's university founded by Chinese people. At the same time, the female vocational education developed rapidly. Compared with other female vocational schools in other cities in China, the emerging major of female vocational education — business accounted for the largest proportion in Shanghai female vocational education

民女校也逐步创建。李达于1921年开办的平民女校特邀陈独秀、陈望道、邵力子、沈雁冰、刘少奇、张太雷、邓中夏等出任学校教员，为学生作专题讲座，传播马克思主义，引导女学生发展自身、走向社会。

至上世纪30、40年代前后，上海女子教育呈多样化发展趋势。上海不仅女子基础教育位居全国之首，而且还出现了国人自办的女子大学。同时，女子职业教育发展迅速。与全国其他城市女子职业学校相比，上海女子职业教育中所占比重最大的并非是蚕桑、纺织、缝纫、刺绣、家事、助产等传统专业，而是女子职业教育的新兴学科——商科。1935年，周振韶在上海创设上海妇女教育馆。这个类似女子教育俱乐部的机构既帮助女性提高文化水平，也有与女子职业教育衔接紧密的妇女职业指导所、妇女工艺传习所，为上海女子教育做出了许多有益的尝试。

随着上海女子教育的不断发展，沪上女学生成为一个特殊的女性群体活跃在社会生活各个领域。女生们开始从校园步入外面的世界，在婚姻、服饰、社交等方面最早突破传统的限制，将男女平等、女性独立等现代观念和新的社会风尚传播于都市之中。毕业女生开始告别固守闺房的传统生活，踏上社会，成为职业女性。老上海女校走出了近代中国首批女教育家、女科学家、女实业家、女医生、女护士、女报人。随着女学生走向社会，参加爱国活动，女学生联合会等女生社会团体在上海应运而生，女学生成为一个独立的群体站在了历史舞台上。

新中国成立后，人民政府以法律形式确定了妇女在政治、经

instead of the traditional majors such as silkworm mulberry, textile, sewing, embroidery, family affairs, midwifery, etc. In 1935, ZHOU Zhenshao established Shanghai Women Education Center in Shanghai. This organization, similar to women education clubs, not only helped the women to improve the level of culture, but also had women's vocational guidance institute and women's craft teaching institute which connected closely with female vocational education. It had made many beneficial attempts for the women education in Shanghai.

With the continuous development of Shanghai women education, female students in Shanghai had become a special group of women active in all fields of social life. Girls began to step out of the campus and step into the outside world, break through the traditional restrictions in marriage, clothing, social and other aspects of the first, spread modern concepts and new social fashion such as gender equality and women's independence in the city. The graduation girl began to bid farewell to the traditional life of staying at home as housewives. Instead, they stepped into society and became the professional women. The girls' schools in old Shanghai had brought up the first batch of female educators, female scientists, female industrialists, female doctors, female nurses and female reporters in modern China. With female students stepping into society and participating in patriotic activities, female student associations and other female social groups emerged in Shanghai, and female students became an independent group in the history.

After the founding of the People's Republic of China in 1949, the people's government determined in legal form that women should enjoy equal rights with men in political, economic, education and other aspects, and women's social status was greatly improved. Women education in Shanghai was developing in a good social environment and atmosphere. At present, besides the girls' middle schools and girls' colleges, more than 60 institutions of higher education and nearly 1,500 primary and secondary schools are open to girls in Shanghai. Nowadays, the extensive popularization and high level of women education in Shanghai is unprecedented.

Today, women education is no longer a problem. But we cannot forget that the girls'

济、教育等各个方面享有与男子同等的权力，妇女的社会地位大大提高。上海的女子教育在良好的社会环境和氛围下得以不断发展。目前，上海除女子中学、女子学院外，60余所高等院校和近1500所中小学向女生开放，女子教育的普及面之广、教育程度之高都是前所未有的。

在女子教育不再是问题的今天，我们不能忘却老上海女校对推动近代上海社会进步所作的重要贡献。

2014年5月

schools of old Shanghai have made important contributions to promoting the social progress of modern Shanghai.

May 2014

老上海的小吃

小吃是饮食文化的重要组成部分，最能展示一个城市的市井风情。老上海的小吃以其广博的风味、琳琅的品种、精美的造型、绝佳的口感赢得了中外食客的青睐，为上海这座城市平添了一份魅力。

明清以来，随着上海商业日趋繁荣，人口不断增加，从上海本地食摊起家的小吃日益发展。据《嘉定县续志》、《松江府志》、《上海县志》等史书记载，开埠前的上海，"春玺"、"糖团"、"花糕"、"纱帽"（即烧卖）等各种民间小吃已达百余种。上海开埠后，银行、钱庄、交易所、商行、旅馆纷纷开张，海内外商贾纷至沓来，催生了小吃摊担的迅速发展。当时饭店还不多，许多流动职业者、海关人员、洋行跑街、交易所职员等一日三餐不能定时的人员，常在摊上就食，许多市民除正常用餐外，也需要食用点心，造就了"吃食摊担举目皆是，八方美食里弄飘香"的繁荣景象。至上世纪40年代末，全市已有几万家小吃摊担、上千个小吃品种。

在小吃摊担成群发展的同时，各种小吃店和糕团店也迅速发展起来，并成为上海小吃市场的主体。创建于1875年的沈大成糕团店，集南北风味小吃之大成，注重选料，讲究制作，善于创新，因而一举成名。于明嘉靖年间开业的绿波廊，其点心小巧玲珑、色调

Snacks of Old Shanghai

Snacks, as an important part of the diet culture, can best show local customs of a city. Old Shanghai snacks, with a wide range of flavors, varieties, exquisite shapes, excellent tastes, were favored by Chinese and foreign diners, thus adding a kind of charm to the city.

Since the Ming and Qing Dynasties, with the increasing prosperity of Shanghai's business and population, snacks which originated from the local food stalls had developed increasingly. According to *Sequels of Jiading County Annals*, *Songjiang Prefecture Annals*, *Shanghai County Annals* and other records in historical documents, before the opening of Shanghai port, there were more than 100 species of folk snacks in Shanghai, such as "chunxi", "tangtuan", "huagao", "maosha" (namely, shaomai). After the opening of Shanghai port, banks, money shops, stock exchanges, commercial firms and hotels were opened successively and business people from home and abroad came to Shanghai, which promoted the rapid development of snack stalls. At that time, the number of restaurants was so small that many itinerant workers, customs officers, workers of foreign firms, staff of stock exchanges, and other people whose three meals could not be scheduled often dinedat the stalls while many citizens also needed to eat snacks in addition to normal meals, thus resulting in the booming scene that "food stalls are everywhere and delicious food are everywhere". In the late 1940s, there were tens of thousands of snack stalls and thousands of snack varieties in the city.

Along with the cluster development of snack stalls, various snack shops and cake shops also developed rapidly and became the main part of Shanghai's snack market. Founded in 1875, the Shendacheng Rice Cake Shop was famous for integrating the

高雅、造型精美、口味独特,堪称沪上一绝。创始于1909年的乔家栅云集了众多点心名师高手,所做的糕团点心在沪上也是独树一帜。始建于1945年的王家沙点心店,以上海点心为本,结合江南点心风味变化出新,兼收并蓄,自成一格,所做的虾肉馄饨、蟹粉生煎、豆沙酥饼、两面黄四款特色点心,被誉为老上海点心的"四大名旦",有"上海点心状元"之称。杏花楼、南翔小笼、小常州、小绍兴、萝春阁、老半斋、松月楼等都是老上海有名的小吃店。

在众多的上海小吃中,有不少是创于上海本地的经典小吃,穿越世纪,驰名中外。已有百余年历史的南翔小笼,小巧玲珑,晶莹透黄,以皮薄、馅多、卤重、味鲜而久负盛名。蟹壳黄因其

20世纪初上海穿街走巷的小吃流动摊贩

essence of the northern and southern snacks, focusing on material selection and paying attention to the production and innovation. Due to its small and exquisite desserts, elegant tinge, beautiful modeling and unique taste, Lvbolang, opened in the period underEmperor Jiaqing'sreign of the Ming Dynasty, could be called a distinct restaurant in Shanghai. Founded in 1909, Qiaojiazha gathered a number of prestigious pastry masters, and its rice cakes and deserts were also unique in Shanghai. Established in 1945, Wangjiasha took Shanghai desserts as the basis to make combination with Jiangnan desserts, thus developing characteristic new desserts. The shrimp huntun, pan fried crabmeat paste, sweet mashed bean crisp cake and noodle pancake were its four characteristic desserts, known as "the four most famous desserts" of old shanghai and "the best Shanghai desserts". Famous snack bars in old Shanghai also included

→ 街头小吃摊

形圆色黄似蟹壳而得名,咸甜适口,皮酥香脆,有人写诗赞它:
"未见饼家先闻香,入口酥皮纷纷下"。糟田螺是用个大肥美、肉
头厚实的田螺为原料,烧好后加陈年香糟制成,肉质鲜嫩,汁卤
醇厚,入口鲜美,是上海五味斋和鲜得来两家点心店的特色风味
小吃。擂沙团是乔家栅的风味名点,色香俱全,软糯爽口,携带
方便,深受游客欢迎。老上海著名的小吃还有小常州的排骨年糕、
小绍兴的鸡粥、城隍庙的开洋葱油拌面、春风松月楼的素菜包、
沈大成的桂花条头糕、绿波廊的枣泥酥、杏花楼的月饼、老半斋
的千层油糕等。

　　老上海的小吃也是海纳百川,除本地名点外,荟萃了全国各地
的著名小吃。扬州的翡翠烧卖、淮阴的汤包、黄桥的烧饼、广州的
云吞、宁波的猪油汤团、嘉兴的粽子、山东的水饺、天津的狗不理
包子等等,凡是外地的名点都在上海的小吃市场占有一席之地。同
时,来自英国、美国、法国、德国、日本、意大利、丹麦、俄罗斯
等国的西点也都随着上海的开埠云集沪上,上海成为当时全国风味
小吃品种最多的一个城市。

　　上海解放后,受政治、经济、社会诸因素的影响,上海小吃在
曲折中发展,但一些传统名点在民间保留了下来。改革开放使上海
小吃业焕发了青春。进入新世纪以来,随着国际化大都市建设的加
速推进和人民生活水平的不断提高,上海小吃市场呈现空前繁荣的
景象,小吃门店数以万计,小吃种类无以计数。

　　在餐饮业日益繁荣的今天,如何继承和发扬本帮传统小吃的技
术精华,融传统、创新、引进于一炉,使上海的传统小吃工艺焕发

Xinghualou, Nanxiang Xiaolong, Xiaochangzhou, Xiaoshaoxing, Luochunge, Laobanzhai and Songyuelou, etc.

Among the numerous Shanghai snacks, many are the classic snacks created in Shanghai and well-known at home and abroad. The small, exquisite, glittering and translucent Nanxiang Xiaolong, with a history of more than one hundred year, is famous for its thin skin, rich stuffing, thick gravy and delicious taste. Crab shell cake, named for its round yellow crab shell, is famous for appropriate sweetness and salinity and crispy skin and delicious taste. Someone wrote a poem to praise it, "Feel the enchanting smell of the cake before you can see the cake shop, fall in love with the delicious taste after you have it." Caotianluo is made of large and fat escargots with thick meat and integrated with ancient pot-ale after it is cooked well. It is the special local snack for Wuweizhai and Xiandelai in Shanghai. Leishatuan is the special local snack for Qiaojiazha with wonderful color and taste, soft and waxy flavor, and easy to take, thus being well favored by the tourists. The famous snacks in old Shanghai also included the "spare ribs with rice cakes" of Xiaochangzhou, the "chicken porridge" of Xiaochangzhou, the "noodles mixed with scallion, oil and soy sauce" of Chenghuangmiao, the "vegetarian bun" of Chunfeng Songyuelou, the "Osmanthus bar cakes" of Shendacheng, the "date mash cake" of Lvbolang, the "moon cake" of Xinghualou, and the "multiple layer oil cake" of Laobanzhai.

The snacks of old Shanghai were diverse and gathered the famous snacks from all over the country. Famous snacks of other places could all win a place in the snack market, such as the jadeite shaomai of Yangzhou, the soup dumpling of Huaiyin, the Chinese style baked roll of Huangqiao, the wonton of Guangzhou, the stuffed lard and sesame dumplings of Ningbo, the zongzi of Jiaxing, the boiled dumplings of Shandong, the Goubuli steamedstuffed bun of Tianjin, etc. At the same time, western desserts from Britain, America, France, Germany, Japan, Italy, Denmark, Russia and other countries also gathered in Shanghai with the opening of Shanghai port, thus making Shanghai become a city with the largest variety of local snacks.

After the liberation of Shanghai, influenced by political, economic and social

新的活力,形成以本帮传统小吃为特色,各种中西小吃荟萃的小吃市场,则是需要上海餐饮业关注的问题。

2014 年 6 月

factors, Shanghai snacks experienced tortuous development, but some famous traditional desserts were preserved in folk. The reform and opening-up made Shanghai's snack industry revive. Since the beginning of the new century, with the acceleration of the construction of international metropolis and the continuous improvement of people's living standards, Shanghai snack market has witnessed an unprecedented prosperity, with tens of thousands of snack stores and countless snack varieties.

Today, as the catering industry is booming, it has been the inevasible problem for Shanghai catering industry that how to inherit and carry forward the technical essence of traditional snacks, integrate the tradition, innovation and introduction into one and make Shanghai's traditional snack craft revitalize, thus forming the snacks market featured by local traditional snacks and the integration of the Chinse and Western snacks.

June 2014

老上海的银楼

上海是我国银楼业的发祥地。它的兴衰荣枯是上海滩百年风云变幻的真实写照。

1644年，日升金铺在上海华亭（今松江）创立，这是老上海第一家银楼。1773年，杨庆和银楼在今南市地区的庙前大街开设。10年后，老庆云银楼在城隍庙方浜中路开市营业。上海开埠后，由于经济的迅速发展，原先比上海历史悠久的苏州、扬州、南京一带的银楼业日渐式微，这一带的银楼业主就将这一行的中心逐渐转移到上海。至1852年，凤祥裕记银楼（今老凤祥）、东来升银楼、景福银楼几乎在同一时期位于南市小东门方滨路上开办。1828年创建于苏州的恒孚银楼，也于这一期间将分店开设到了上海的方滨路。1901年，麒派创始人周信芳的岳父裘氏开办的裘天宝礼记银楼在山东路开业。此后，方九霞、宝成、费文元、庆福星等银楼也相继开张。当时上海的银楼主要经营妇女金银饰品、金银器皿和黄金销售。至20世纪20、30年代，上海银楼林立，极盛时达400多家，可谓一派繁华景象。

为了建立和规范上海银楼行业的信誉，杨庆和、老庆云、凤祥、裘天宝、景福、宝成、方九霞、费文元、庆福星等9家在上海滩信

Jewelry Stores of Old Shanghai

Shanghai is the birthplace of China's jewelry industry. Its rise and fall has testified to Shanghai's vicissitudes in a century.

In 1644, Risheng Gold Shop was founded in Huating (today's Songjiang), Shanghai, which was the first jewelry store in old Shanghai. In 1773, Yagqinghe Jewelry Store was founded in the area of today's Miaoqian Street of Nanshi. Ten years later, Laoqingyun Jewelry Store was opened at Middle Fangbang Road of Town's God Temple. After the opening of Shanghai port, due to the rapid economic development, the jewelry stores in Suzhou, Yangzhou and Nanjing, which originally had a long history in Shanghai, gradually declined, and the owners in this area moved the center of this industry to Shanghai. By 1852, Fengxiangyuji Jewelry Store (now called Lao Feng Xiang), Donglaisheng Jewelry Store and Jingfu Jewelry Store were established almost at the same time at Fangbin Road of Small East Gate in Nanshi. Established in Suzhou in 1828, Hengfu Jewelry Store also opened branches at Fangbin Road in Shanghai during this period. In 1901, Mr. QIU, the father-in-law of the founder of Qi School ZHOU Xinfang, opened Qiutianbaoli Jewelry Store at Shandong Road. Since then, Fangjiuxia, Baocheng, Feiwenyuan, Qingfuxing and other jewelry stores had also been opened successively. At that time, Shanghai's jewelry stores mainly engaged in women gold and silver jewelries, gold and silver utensils and gold sales. By the 1920s and 1930s, there were more than 400 jewelry stores in Shanghai in the peak period, presenting a scene of prosperity.

In order to establish and standardize the reputation of Shanghai's jewelry

誉较好的银楼，于1896年在南市大东门花团街建造银楼公所，时人称其为"大同行"。这是老上海最早的银楼同业公会，也是当时上海唯一的银楼团体。银楼公所积极联络和协调各银楼间的关系，逐步建立起了一套服务规范，既大大提高了上海银楼的声誉，也促进了金银工艺技术水平的提高。与此同时，银楼公所内部金银通兑的措施促进了区域内贵金属的融通交易和定价机制的

→ 老上海的银楼　贺竹元绘

industry, Yangqinghe, Laoqingyun, Fengxiang, Qiutianbao, Jingfu, Baocheng, Fangjiuxia, Feiwenyuan, Qingfuxing and other 9 jewelry stores with good reputation established the Trade Association of Jewelry Industry at Huatuan Street of Large East Gate in Nanshi, known as "great industry association" at that time. It was the earliest trade association of jewelry industry in old Shanghai and the only jewelry industry group in Shanghai at that time. The Trade Association of Jewelry Industry actively maintained and coordinated the relationship among the jewelry stores and gradually established a set of service specifications, which not only greatly improved the reputation of Shanghai's jewelry stores, but also promoted the improvement of gold and silver processing technologies. At the same time, the internal exchange of gold and silver within the Trade Association of Jewelry Industry promoted the perfection of the trading and pricing mechanism of precious metals in the region, laying the foundation for Shanghai to become the gold trading and financial center of China and even Asia at that time.

In terms of the jewelry stores of old Shanghai, we cannot but mention Lao Feng Xiang. The predecessor of Lao Feng Xiang is the "Fengxiangyuji Jewelry Store" founded at Large East Gate Street of Shanghai in 1848. In 1886, it moved to the intersection between today's East Nanjing Road and Shandong Road. In 1908, it was relocated to today's No. 432, East Nanjing Road and has headquartered here until now. Lao Feng Xiang is famous for producing gold & silver jewelries, pearls, jades and diamonds. Its silverware and silver gifts are well-crafted, elegant and luxurious, thus being popular with customers. In the first half of the 20th century, FEI Zushou, chairman of Lao Feng Xiang, actively advocated the idea of "being skilled in products and sincere in services", and made Lao Feng Xiang stand out among the jewelry industry with its unique management thoughts and service characteristics. It is precisely such historical origins and the inheritance and development of later generations that has made Lao Feng Xiang become China's only time-honored shop developing from more than a century and a half ago until today and become the century brand of Chinese

完善，为上海成为当时中国乃至亚洲黄金交易和金融中心奠定了基础。

说老上海的银楼，就不能不提老凤祥。老凤祥银楼的前身是1848年在上海大东门大街创建的"凤祥裕记银楼"，1886年迁址今南京东路山东路口，1908年迁址今南京东路432号延续至今，现为老凤祥总店。老凤祥银楼以制作金银首饰、珠翠钻石闻名遐迩。其银器和银制礼品精雕细刻、高雅华贵、口彩吉利，深受顾客青睐。20世纪前半叶，老凤祥的掌门人费祖寿先生积极倡导精于产品、诚于服务的理念，以独到的经营思想和服务特色，使老凤祥银楼傲视群雄。正是这样的历史渊源和后人的继承发展，使得老凤祥成为全国唯一由一个半多世纪前相传至今的百年老店，成为中国首饰业的世纪品牌。

抗战爆发前后至上海解放前的10多年间，上海银楼受时政和战争的影响，几经起落、经营惨淡、风雨飘摇。1948年，国民政府实行"币制改革"，再次废止黄金买卖。银楼所有金条，均需遵令上交国家银行，违者以黑市买卖按律论处。上海乃至全国的银楼业再次遭到空前的打击，被迫停业。

上海解放后，人民政府加强了对金银的控制，颁布了金银管理暂行办法，规定银楼只准按规定价格出售，不得再行收进。上海银楼恢复经营后因存货售完收盘歇业，老凤祥等银楼转为国营。改革开放后，尤其是进入新世纪以来，上海银楼业得到了健康快速的发展。1982年，豫园商场城隍庙大殿内开出的黄金饰品专柜，是国务院批准国内恢复销售黄金饰品后上海开设的第一家黄金饰品零售店。

jewelry industry.

Influenced by the political environment and war at that time, Shanghai's jewelry stores experienced ebb and flow several times during the 10 years from the outbreak of the Anti-Japanese War to the liberation of Shanghai. In 1948, the national government implemented the "currency system reform" and abolished the gold trade again. All gold bars in the jewelry stores should be handed over to the state bank according to the national regulation and violators would be punished according to law for committing the crime of black market trading. Jewelry stores in Shanghai and even the whole country again suffered an unprecedented blow and were forced to close.

After the liberation of Shanghai, the people's government strengthened its control over gold and silver, and promulgated interim measures for the control of gold and silver, stipulating that the jewelry stores should only sell gold and silver at the prescribed price and can't purchasegold and silver. After the recovery of operation, Shanghai's jewelry stores sold out the inventory and closed the business. Lao Feng Xiang and other jewelry stores became state-owned ones. After the reform and opening up, especially after entering the new century, Shanghai's jewelry industry experienced healthy and rapid development. In 1982, the gold jewelry counter set up at the main hall of Town's God Temple in Yuyuan Shopping Mall was the first retail store opened in Shanghai after the State Council approved the resumption of domestic sales of gold jewelry. In 1993, Yayi Gold Jewelry Shop was opened. At present, "Town's God Temple Gold Jewelry Shop" and "Yayi Gold Jewelry Shop" have become China's leading enterprises of gold jewelry industry. Yuyuan district has become the largest gold and jewelry sales center in China, named as "the first city of gold and jewelry in China" by the China Gold Association.

Today, with the economic development and the continuous improvement of people's living standards, Shanghai's jewelry industry has ushered in a rare opportunity for development. As long as the people in jewelry industry adhere to the fine tradition of being cautious and conscientious, making every effort and being good at operation, and

1993年，亚一金店开张。目前，"老庙黄金"、"亚一金店"已成为中国黄金珠宝业的龙头企业。豫园地区已成为中国最大的黄金珠宝销售中心，被中国黄金协会命名为"中国黄金珠宝第一城"。

今天，随着经济的发展和人民生活水平的不断提高，上海银楼业迎来了难得的发展机遇。只要银楼人始终秉承兢兢业业、励精图治、善于经营的优良传统，不断提高产品品质和服务水平，上海银楼业就一定能在国际金融中心建设和为民服务中发挥更大的作用。

2014 年 7 月

constantly improve the product quality and service level, Shanghai's jewelry industry will surely play a greater role in building the international financial center and serving the people.

July 2014

老上海的花园洋房

　　风格迥异、各呈姿色的老上海花园洋房，是我们这座城市极为宝贵的文化遗产。

　　1843年上海开埠后，外国传教士和侨商纷纷来上海，在外滩建起了一批砖木结构的以二层楼为主的西式房屋，供居住和经商之用，时人称之为"券廊式"洋房。19世纪末，专供居住的花园住宅开始在上海出现，建造和居住者都为外国人。第一次世界大战结束后，随着世界经济的复苏、上海工商业的日益繁荣，加之建筑材料的发展和工程技术的进步，西方各种建筑风格的独立式花园洋房不断被引入上海租界，中国的富有阶层也争相效仿，使得上海花园洋房的建设进入高峰期。目前上海的老花园洋房，大都建于上世纪20、30年代。抗战爆发后，以巨资建造花园洋房者甚少，只有少数巨贾豪富鉴于市场通货膨胀，转向投资兴建花园洋房，使上海近代花园洋房的建设进入尾声。

　　老上海花园住宅的分布与租界的扩展有着密切的关联，呈由东向西发展的趋势。就区域而言，徐汇、长宁、卢湾、静安是花园洋房最为集中的区域，虹口、黄浦次之。就路段而言，衡山路、武康路、复兴西路、岳阳路、湖南路、永嘉路、思南路、华山路、新华

Garden House of old Shanghai

The garden houses with different styles and different shapes in old Shanghai are the most precious cultural heritage of our city.

After the opening of Shanghai port in 1843, foreign missionaries and overseas Chinese merchants came to Shanghai and built a number of post and panel structure Western-style houses in the Bund, mainly two-storey buildings for living and business purposes, known as "coupon gallery garden house". In the late 19th century, the garden houses began to appear in Shanghai, built and occupied by foreigners. After the end of the First World War, with the recovery of the world economy and the increasing prosperity of Shanghai's industry and commerce, as well as thedevelopment of building materials and the progress of engineering technologies, the western independent garden houses of various architectural styles were constantly introduced into the Shanghai concession. China's wealthy classeswere also eager to follow the trend, thus bringing the construction of garden houses in Shanghai to the peak. The old garden houses in Shanghai now were mostly built in the 1920s and 1930s. After the outbreak of the Anti-Japanese War, there were very few people who built garden houses with a considerable amount of money. Only a few wealthy tycoons turned to invest in garden houses in view of the market inflation, thus bringing the construction of modern garden houses in Shanghai to an end.

The distribution of old Shanghai garden houses was closely related to the expansion of the concession, developing from east to west. In terms of region, Xuhui, Changning, Luwan and Jing'An are the most concentrated areas of garden houses, followed by Hongkou and Huangpu. In terms of road sections, Hengshan Road, Wukang Road,

路、愚园路、虹桥路、延安西路、陕西北路、铜仁路等都是花园洋房分布比较密集的路段。据不完全统计,从上海开埠到 1949 年上海解放止,全市各式花园洋房达 5000 多栋。

上海之所以被誉为近代"万国建筑博览",花园洋房的建造功不可没。最初建造的老上海花园洋房受西欧文艺复兴思潮的影响,多为欧洲古典主义建筑风格。1919 年后,上海花园住宅的建筑形式大多为英国乡村别墅式。到上世纪 30 年代,西班牙式住宅流行。40 年代前后,受国外现代建筑思潮的影响,上海开始出现现代式花园住宅。位于延安西路 64 号的嘉道理住宅、愚园路 1136 弄 31 号的王伯群住宅和淮海中路 1547 号的盛宣怀住

→ 邬达克旧居

West Fuxing Road, Yueyang Road, Hunan Road, Yongjia Road, Sinan Road, Huashan Road, Xinhua Road, Yuyuan Road, Hongqiao Road, West Yan'An Road, North Shaanxi Road, Tongren Road, etc. are the sections with where garden houses are densely distributed. According to incomplete statistics, from the opening of Shanghai port to the liberation of Shanghai in 1949, there were more than 5,000 garden houses with various styles in Shanghai.

The construction of garden houses has made great contributions to Shanghai's being praised as the modern "World Architecture Expo". The original old Shanghai garden houses were influenced by the Renaissance trend in Western Europe and were mostly European classical architecture style. After 1919, the architectural form of most garden houses in Shanghai followed the style of English country villas. By the 1930s, Spanish-style housing was in vogue. Around the 1940s, under the influence of foreign modern architectural trends, modern garden houses began to appear in Shanghai. The Kadoorie Residence located at No. 64, West Yan'an Road, the Wangboqun Residence located at No. 31, Lane 1136, Yuyuan Road and the Shengxuanhuai Residence located at No. 1547, Middle Huaihai Road were the representative buildings of Shanghai's archaistic garden houses. The Sassoon Villa located at No. 2419, Hongqiao Road and the Lilac Garden located at No. 849, Huashan Road were the classic representatives of country villas in Shanghai. The Zhou Residance located at No. 73, Sinan Road and the Dingguitang Residence located at No. 45, Fenyang Road were the models of the Spanish-style garden houses in Shanghai. The Wutongwen Residence located at No. 333, Tongreng Road and the Yao Family Residence located at No. 200, Huaiyin Road were examples of modern garden houses in Shanghai. In addition, the garden houses of old Shanghai also included the northern European style, Mediterranean style, Italian style, American colonial style, mixed style, Southeast Asian colonial style, Chinese traditional style and many other architectural styles.

The garden houses of old Shanghai have experienced the vicissitudes of Shanghai since modern times, and witnessed ebb and flow of this colorful world. Each garden

宅，是上海仿古典式花园住宅的代表性建筑。位于虹桥路 2419 号的沙逊别墅和华山路 849 号的丁香花园，则是上海乡村别墅式建筑的经典代表。位于思南路 73 号的周公馆和汾阳路 45 号的丁贵堂住宅，堪称上海西班牙式花园住宅的典范。位于铜仁路 333 号的吴同文住宅和淮阴路 200 号的姚氏住宅，则又是上海现代式花园住宅的范例。除此以外，老上海的花园住宅还有北欧式、地中海式、意大利式、美国殖民地式、混合式、东南亚殖民地式、中国传统式等多种不同的建筑风格。

　　老上海的花园洋房，历经过上海近代以来的风云际会，见证了十里洋场、花花世界的荣辱兴衰。每一栋花园洋房都是老上海历史的一个片段，都有属于自己的故事。位于香山路 7 号的孙中山故居，曾经是酝酿国共合作之地。位于皋兰路上的张学良寓所，是当年谋划"西安事变"的地方。思南路周公馆，是当年周恩来与国民党军警特务进行"公开的地下斗争"的场所。思南路 87 号，是京剧大师梅兰芳在上海定居长达 25 年之处。东平路 9 号，是蒋介石与宋美龄的"爱庐"。虹桥路 1140 号，则是美国飞虎将军陈纳德和陈香梅的寓所。还有依照当年马勒最宠爱的小女儿一个梦境设计的马勒别墅，民国第一任内阁总理唐绍仪旧居，老上海帮会大亨黄金荣、杜月笙的公馆，国民党将领白崇禧和著名作家白先勇父子住过的白公馆等等，无不承载着当年上海滩的传奇故事。正如雨果面对塞纳河边的巴黎圣母院所发出的感慨一样，建筑是石头写成的史书。

　　建国后，老上海花园洋房的保护和再利用走过了曲折发展的

house is a fragment of old Shanghai's history and has its own story. The Sun Yat-sen's Former Residence, located at No. 7, Xiangshan Road, was once the place that contributed to Kuomintang-Communist cooperation. ZHANG Xueliang's Former Residence, located at Gaolan Road, was the place where "the Xi'an Incident" was planned. Zhou Residence at Sinan Road was the place that Zhou Enlai and Kuomintang military and police spices proceeded "open underground conflicts". The residence at No. 87, Sinan Road was the place in Shanghai that MEI Lanfang, the Peking Opera master, had lived for 25 years. The place at No. 9, Dongping Road was the "sweet home" of Chiang Kai-shek and Song Meiling. The place at No. 1140, Hongqiao Road was the residence of American general Chennault and CHEN Xiangmei. There were also other places which also boasted legendary stories of old Shanghai, such as Moller Villa established by Moller according to his favorite daughter's dream, the former residence of TANG Shaoyi (the first cabinet premier of Republic of China), the residences of old Shanghai's gang leaders such as HUAG Jinrong's and DU Yuesheng's residences and the White Residence where the father and son — the Kuomintang general BAI Chongxi and the famous writer BAI Xianyong had lived, etc. Architecture is the history written by stone, as Hugo remarked when he confronted Notre Dame de Paris along the bank of the Seine.

After the founding of the People's Republic of China, the protection and reuse of old Shanghai's garden houses experienced a tortuous process of development. Since Shanghai was approved by the State Council as a national historic and cultural city in 1986, the protection of excellent modern buildings had been put on the agenda. Over the past 20 years, Shanghai has issued a series of policies and regulations to standardize the protection measures of excellent modern buildings and ensure the protection and reuse of old Shanghai's garden houses.

The garden houses of old Shanghai have rich historical, artistic, social, economic and ecological values, and their historical connotation is built more than by a single brick and tile. After a hundred years of historical precipitation, they have become the buildings bearing both properties of historical relics and natures of urban culture. In

历程。自1986年上海被国务院批准为国家历史文化名城开始，优秀近代建筑保护才真正提到议事日程。20多年来，上海市出台了一系列政策法规，规范了优秀近代建筑的保护措施，使得老上海花园洋房的保护和再利用有了法规保障。

老上海花园洋房具有丰富的历史、艺术、社会、经济和生态价值，它内藏的底蕴绝非一砖一瓦所能砌成。经过百年沉淀，它已成为历史文物与城市文化双重性质的建筑。保护和再利用好这批历史建筑，是传承历史文脉，塑造城市特色的一项重要任务，我们应当努力。

2014年8月

order to inherit the historical civilization and shape the characteristics of the city, it has been an important task for us to make every effort to protect and reuse these historic buildings well.

August 2014

老上海的石库门

兴起于19世纪60年代的石库门里弄，是一个多世纪以来上海最普遍的民居样式，承载了海上多少家族的兴衰荣辱、悲欢离合。今天重新阅读这一最具海派特征的居住建筑，可以引发对历史的追忆和文化的思索。

上海开埠后，英、美、法等列强为保护自己本国的利益，相继在上海划定自己的势力范围即租界。后由于太平天国和小刀会的起义，上海县城和江浙等地的地主、富绅及大量难民涌入上海租界避难，"华洋分居"的局面被打破。一些洋商抓住难民租房这一商机，采用伦敦联排式布局，并以"里"作为名称，大量营建两至三层的木制联排房屋出租给中国人，这成为上海石库门里弄的雏形。1870年后，这种简易的木制房因存有安全隐患被取缔。当时的设计师把江南地区对称、规整、以天井为核心的厅堂式传统民居与欧洲联排布局相结合，将木制房改造成砖木结构，形成了石库门里弄最初的形式，史称老式石库门。20世纪20年代后，虹口北四川路一带开始出现一批以青红砖和清水墙为外墙，设有阳台的新式里弄住宅，并很快在租界普及开来。发展到后期，有的还安装卫生设备，少数的有汽车间，史称新式石库门。这种更能体现西洋建筑本质的里弄住

Shikumen of Old Shanghai

Shikumen Lilong, which originated in the 1860s, had been the most common residential style in Shanghai for more than a century, bearing the ebb and flow as well asvicissitudes of life of many families in Shanghai. Rereading the most Shanghai-style residential building today can make us recall the history and think about the culture.

After the opening of Shanghai port, the British, American, French and other foreign powers delimited their own sphere of influences in Shanghai, namely, the concession, thus protecting their own interests. Later, due to the uprising of Taiping Rebellion and Small Swords Society, landlords, rich gentry and large numbers of refugees from Shanghai County, Jiangsu and Zhejiang provinces flocked in Shanghai concessions for refuge, thus breaking the situation of "Chinese and foreigners living apart". Some foreign businessmen seized the opportunity of renting houses to refugees, adopted the London townhouse layout and named it as "Li'. They built a large number of wooden townhouses with two or three storeys and rented them to Chinese people, which became the prototype of Shikumen Lilong in Shanghai. After 1870, these simple wooden houses were banned because of security risks. At that time, the designers combined the "European townhouse layout" with the traditional "hall-style residence" which was featured by symmetry and orderliness and regarded the courtyard as the core, and transformed the wooden house into brick and wood structures, thus having formed the original form of Shikumen, known as the Old Shikumen in the history. After the 1920s, a batch of new Lilong houses which regarded the green red bricks and plain brick wall as the outer wall and had balconies began to appear along the North Sichuan Road in Hongkou and soon became popular in the concessions. In the later period, some of the

↖ 20 世纪 30 年代石库门房子鸟瞰

宅，与原有的中西折衷形式的里弄一起，成为上海里弄住宅的两大主流。到上世纪 40 年代末，石库门里弄占上海市区全部住宅面积的 60% 以上。

红瓦屋顶、清水砖墙、石料门框、黑漆木门、铜质门环、欧洲贵族族徽浮雕或中国传统砖雕图案装饰的半圆形门楣、狭小局促的天井，是石库门建筑最具代表性的视觉元素。无论是三楼三底还是两楼两底，无论是单开间还是双开间，无论是新式石库门还是老式石库门，他们共同的特征，是把中国传统民居的封闭式院落住宅样式和欧洲联排式住宅样式巧妙融合在一起。石库门群体布局，相互毗连，一座接一座，一排连一排，从街面向纵深延展形成弄堂。由于每条里弄相对封闭，因而给居住者以强烈的地域感、认同感和安

houses were even equipped with the sanitary and a few of them had the automobile room, which was known as the Modern Shikumen. The modern Lilong house and the traditional Lilong house became two major mainstreams of Shanghai's Lilong buildings. By the late 1940s, Shikumen Lilong accounted for more than 60 percent of all residential areas in downtown Shanghai.

The most representative visual elements of Shikumen buildings included the red-tile roof, plain brick wall, stone door frame, black-painted wooden door, brass knocker, semicircular door lintel decorated by European aristocratic family crest relievo or Chinese traditional tile carving and cramped courtyard. No matter the house with three storeys and three foundations or the house with two storeys and two foundations, the house with single standard width or double standard width, and the house with modern Shikumen style or the Old Shikumen style, their common feature is to have combined the traditional Chinese closed courtyard residential style with the European townhouse style. The layout of Shikumen building groups is to keep adjacent to each other with one by one and row by row, thus extending from the street front to the deep street and form the Longtang. Because each Lilong is relatively closed, it gives the occupants a strong sense of place, identity and security. Just as Hutong is the characteristic of Beijing, Lilong is the scenery of Shanghai. Xingrenli, established at today's Ningbo Road in 1872, is now recognized as the earliest Shikumen Lilong. The famous Shikumen Lilong of old Shanghai also included Xinxinli at Dapuqiao, Dakangli at Shunchang Road, Ronghuali in Caojiadu, Yaoshuilong, Renanli, Yugu Village, Bugaoli and Fuxingfang, etc.

Shikumen has witnessed the changes of life and time since the 19th century, and spawned unique Shikumen Lilong folk culture. Money shops, firms, workshops, itinerant peddlers, hawkers, children play, fluffing cotton, repairing brown shed, tailor shops, rouge shops, food stalls, tiger cooking ranges, integration and friction between residents, harmony and conflict among the neighborhood, the war among the "72 tenants", the warm salutations including Muma, Adie, Yeshu, Niangniang, A'po and A'sao, the fold slangs and the Longtang games are the unique scenery of Longtang in modern Shanghai and the most natural and sweet memory Shikumen has left to Shanghai

全感。正如胡同是北京的特色，弄堂则是上海的风景。1872年建于今宁波路的兴仁里是目前公认的最早的石库门里弄，打浦桥新新里、顺昌路大康里、曹家渡荣华里，以及药水弄、人安里、愚谷村、步高里、复兴坊等都是老上海著名的石库门里弄。

石库门见证了19世纪以来上海人的生活百态和岁月变迁，孕育了独特的石库门里弄民俗文化。钱庄、商号、作坊、货郎、叫卖、婴戏、弹棉花、修棕棚、裁缝铺、胭脂店、吃食摊、老虎灶，居民间的融合与摩擦，邻里间的其乐融融与唇枪舌剑，"72家房客"的相互争斗，姆妈、阿爹、爷叔、娘娘、阿婆、阿嫂的热络称呼，世俗俚语，弄堂游戏，这些都是上海近代城市里弄的独特风景，是石库门留给上海人的最淳朴最温馨的记忆。

老上海的石库门也是中国近现代政治史和文化史的缩影。陈独秀的《新青年》创办于吉谊里，陈望道翻译的《共产党宣言》在渔阳里，党的一大在兴业里76号召开，上海工人第三次武装起义在西成里密划，五卅运动指挥部设在新新里。石库门里弄还走出了鲁迅、蔡元培、郭沫若、茅盾、巴金、丁玲、沈钧儒、邹韬奋、徐悲鸿、张大千、黄宾虹、周璇、赵丹、阮玲玉、胡蝶、上官云珠、盖叫天等一大批文化巨匠和艺术名家，产生了中国现代文学史上特殊的文学派别——亭子间文学。

曾经哺育了几代上海人的石库门里弄，如今已成为上海的"文化符号"。这是百年沧桑铭刻在上海和上海人心中的符号。在上海步入国际大都市建设，人们逐步告别多家混居、几代同住的里弄住宅的今天，如何保护好一些典型的石库门里弄，研究它的文化内涵及

people.

　　Shikumen of old Shanghai is also the epitome of the political and cultural history of modern China. CHEN Duxiu's *New Youth* was founded in Jiyili; CHEN Wangdao interpreted *The Communist Manifesto* in Yuyangli; the First National Congress of the CPC was held at No. 76, Xingyeli; the Shanghai Labor's Third Armed Uprising was planned in Xichengli; the headquarters of the May Thirtieth Movement was located at Xinxinli. A large number of great cultural masters and art master had lived in Shikumen Lilong, such as LU Xun, CAI Yuanpei, GUO Moruo, MAO Dun, BA Jin, DING Ling, SHEN Junru, ZOUTaofen, XUBeihong, ZHANG Daqian, HUANG Binhong, ZHOU Xuan, ZHAO Dan, RUAN Lingyu, HU Die, SHANGGUAN Yunzhu, GAI

→ 余庆里 典型的上海石库门弄堂

其历史、社会和艺术价值，传承弘扬和谐、温馨、融洽的邻里风气，使城市生活更加美好，这是需要各方加以努力的。

2014 年 9 月

Jiaotian, thus having produced the special literature school in the history of modern Chinese literature — Tingzijian Literature.

Shikumen Lilong, which has nurtured generations of Shanghainese, has become a "cultural symbol" of Shanghai. For Shanghai and Shanghainese, this is a symbol engraved by the hundred years of history. Today, Shanghai has began the construction of international metropolis and people have gradually abandoned the Lilong residence. It requires the efforts of all parties to well protect some typical Shikumen Linong buildings, study their cultural connotations and their historical, social and artistic values, inherit and carry forward the warm, cordial and harmonious neighborhood atmosphere, thus creatinga better urban life.

September 2014

老上海的电信

1871年大北电报公司在上海开办电报业务，拉开了中国近代电信历史的帷幕。一部老上海的电信史，也是一部老上海的城市发展史。

18世纪中叶，当电报、电话在西方世界日益盛行时，上海还在延续着邮驿传递和民营信局车船运传等传统的通信方式。当时传递公文最快的驿站马匹从上海到北京快者一周，慢者需半月以上。而电信传递信息的速度已达每秒环绕地球7次半。上海开埠后，随着经济和城市建设的快速发展，迫切需要新的通信技术与之相适应。当时西方一些国家提出要在上海开设电信，但遭到了清政府的一概拒绝。西方列强见提出的要求难以获准，便采取先斩后奏的策略造成既定事实。1871年4月18日，丹麦商人蒂根创立的大北公司正式开通上海至香港的电报水线，成为中国大陆地区开通的第一条电报水线。同年8月，大北公司又将沪崎水线从大戢山岛接至上海。由此，上海的电报通信北经日本与俄国相通，南经香港与欧美相连。中国与世界的电信联络正式开启，上海成为中国大陆地区国际电报的唯一出入口局。大北公司虽然侵犯了中国的电信主权，但客观上打开了中国近代电信的大门。

Telecom of Old Shanghai

In 1871, Great North Telegraph Company launched telegraph business in Shanghai, unveiling the curtain of China's modern telecom history. The telecom history of old Shanghai is also the urban development history of old Shanghai.

In the middle 18th century, when telegraph and telephone became more and more popular in the Western world, Shanghai continued its traditional communication methods, such as postal delivery, private letter service and car or shipping delivery. At that time, it took at least one week or even more than half a month for the fastest post horse to deliver official documents from Shanghai to Beijing. The speed at which telecom transmitted information could reach "going around the earth 7.5 times in a second". With the rapid development of economy and urban construction after the opening of Shanghai port, new corresponding communication technology was urgently needed. At that time, some Western countries proposed to open telecommunications in Shanghai, but the Qing Government refused them all. When Western powers found it difficult to get their demands approved, they adopted a strategy of acting first and reporting afterwards, thus creating the established fact. On April 18, 1871, the Great North Company founded by a Danish businessman named Teagan officially launched the telegraph waterline from Shanghai to Hong Kong, becoming the first telegraph waterline in Mainland China. In August of the same year, Great North Company brought Hu-Qi waterline from Dajishan Island to Shanghai. Since then, telegraphic communication in Shanghai had been linked north through Japan to Russia and south through Hong Kong to Europe and America. China's telecommunication contact with the world was officially opened, and Shanghai became the only import and export bureau of international telegram in Mainland

↖ 大北电报公司接线生

　　囿于传统的观念，从 19 世纪 60 年代到 70 年代，清政府既不准洋人在中国架设电报线，也不准备自己开设电报。洋务派官员和维新派思想家面对严峻的国际形势，纷纷向朝廷提议自办电报。1877 年 6 月 15 日，李鸿章建成自上海行辕到江南机器制造局的电报专线，拉开了晚清自办电报的序幕。1881 年 3 月，上海电报局成立。同年，中国大陆地区第一条长途公众电报电路——津沪电报线全线开放使用。随后，电话进入上海。1882 年 3 月 1 日，大北电话交换所正式开放通话、对外营业，成为中国第一个人工电话交换所。同年，英国电气工程师别晓泼主持的上海电话互助协会对外开办电话业务。1900 年 8 月，华洋公司编制发行的中国电信史上第一张《用户电话号码表》在上海诞生。清末电信在内外竞争中艰难发展，至

China. Although Great North Company violated China's telecommunications sovereignty, but it objectively unveiled the history of China's modern telecommunications.

Constrained by conventional wisdom, from the 1860s to the 1870s, the Qing Government neither permitted foreigners to set up telegraph lines in China nor prepared to open a telegraph of its own. In face of the severe international situation, officials of Westernization Group and the reformists proposed to the imperial court to establish telegrams by themselves. On June 15, 1877, LI Hongzhang established a special telegraph line from Shanghai Xingyuan to Jiangnan Machinery Manufacturing Bureau, which unveiled the prelude of self-operated telegraph in the late Qing Dynasty. In March 1881, Shanghai Telegraph Bureau was established. In the same year, the first long-distance public telegraph circuit in Mainland China – Tianjin-Shanghai telegraph line was fully open for use. Soon after that, telephone was introduced into Shanghai. On March 1, 1882, the Great North Telephone Exchange Center was officially open to the public and became the first manual telephone exchange center in China. In the same year, the Mutual Telephone Exchange Association of Shanghai, chaired by British electrical engineer Bishop, launched the telephone business. In August 1900, the first *User Phone Number List* in the history of Chinese telecommunications compiled and issued by Huayang Company was launched in Shanghai. In the late Qing Dynasty, telecom experienced struggled and tortuous development in internal and external competition. By the 1890s, the China telecom network with Shanghai as the center in the late Qing Dynasty had basically covered the main provinces and districts in China. Shanghai became the center of China's telegraph and commercial telephone bureau.

Around the Revolution of 1911, Shanghai became the focus city for all parties to fight for the right of telecommunications management. From the 1920s to the Comprehensive Anti-Japanese War, Shanghai telecom network continued to be improved and expanded with the abnormal prosperity of Shanghai's economy. In 1924, the telephone user number in the eastern district of Shanghai had reached five figures. In the same year, Shanghai began using short-wave communications. In 1930, International Great Radio Station was set up in Shanghai, ending more than half a century of humiliating

19世纪90年代，以上海为中心的晚清中国电信网络已基本覆盖全国的主要省区。上海成为中国的电报中心和商电局中心。

辛亥革命前后，上海成为各方争夺电信经营权的焦点城市。从20世纪20年代到全面抗战前，上海电信网随着上海经济的畸形繁荣不断完善拓展。1923年，上海开始创办长途电话业务。1924年，上海东区电话用户号码已至5位数。同年，上海开始使用短波通信。1930年，国际大电台在上海建成，结束了外商垄断中国国际通信主权半个多世纪的屈辱历史。1933年，外商电报水线登陆专利权被取消，标志着外商电报水线公司在上海、在中国电报收发权的彻底结束。到全面抗战前夕，上海的电话用户已达数万户之众，市内电信网、国内长途电信网、国际电信网基本形成。上海成为当时世界上为数不多的拥有多种先进通信方式和新型通信网络的城市。

"8·13"淞沪抗战爆发，上海的通信设备和网络在战火中遭到毁灭性破坏。至抗战胜利前夕，上海仅存6条有线电报电路、17条无线电报电路。抗战胜利后，上海电信有所恢复，但随着内战的爆发，上海电信的损毁程度也在不断加深。电信战线的广大职工在中共上海地下党的领导下，积极开展护局保台运动，对保护通信设施设备、维护上海的通信畅通起到了重要作用，为新中国成立后上海城市建设发展打下了坚实的基础。

说起老上海的电信史，有几个人是断然不能忘记的。如最早改变观念、先后几次上书清廷提出自办电报主张、并在上海建成中国第一条专用电报线的洋务派首领李鸿章，中国电报总局第一任总办盛宣怀，上海电报局第一任总办郑观应，以及经元善、谢家福等。

history that foreign companies monopolized China's international communications sovereignty. In 1933, the landing right of foreign telegraph waterline was cancelled, which marked the complete end of the telegraph transmission rights of the foreign telegraph waterline companies in Shanghai and China. By the eve of the Comprehensive Anti-Japanese War, the number of telephone users in Shanghai had reached tens of thousands of households and the city telecommunications network, the domestic long-distance telecommunications network and the international telecommunications network were basically formed. Shanghai became one of the world's few cities that had advanced communication methods and new communication networks.

With the outbreak of the "8.13" Shong-hu Anti-Japanese War, communications equipment and networks in Shanghai were destroyed in the war. By the eve of the victory

↗ 上海较早出现的公用电话亭

上海解放后,人民政府接管了上海电信,使电信步入全面发展轨道。改革开放后,上海电信迅速恢复"文革"造成的巨大伤害,建设步入快车道,成为中国最大国际通信出口局。进入新世纪后,上海电信走在转型发展的前列,跨入全业务经营时代。

今天,电信迎来了新的历史性巨变。面对互联网的蓬勃兴起,面对电信市场的激烈竞争,面对产业环境的急剧变化,开中国电信先河的上海如何继承优良传统,融合时代精神,以变革求发展,为上海智慧城市的建设再创新业,这是值得期盼的。

2014 年 10 月

of the Anti-Japanese War, there were only 6 wire telegraph circuits and 17 wireless telegraph circuits in Shanghai. After the victory of the Anti-Japanese War, to some extent all telecommunications in Shanghai were recovered. But with the outbreak of the Civil War, the extent of damage to Shanghai's telecommunications was also deepened. Under the leadership of Shanghai underground party of the communist party of China (CPC), the vast number of workers in the telecom industry actively carried out the campaign of protecting the telecom bureaus and stations, which played an important role in protecting communication facilities and equipment and maintaining smooth communication in Shanghai, thus laying a solid foundation for the urban construction and development of Shanghai after the founding of People's Republic of China.

When talking about the telecom history of old Shanghai, we cannot forget these people, such as LI Hongzhang, the leader of the Westernization Group who first changed his mind, submitted several written statements to the Qing Court to propose the idea of self-service telegraph and built China's first special telegraph line in Shanghai; SHENG Xuanhuai, the first executive supervisor of Imperial Chinese Telegraph Bureau; ZHENG Guanying, the first executive supervisor of Shanghai Telegraph Bureau; and JING Yuanshan and XIE Jiafu, etc.

After the liberation of Shanghai, the people's government took over Shanghai's telecom, leadingit on the track ofcomprehensive development. After the reform and opening-up, Shanghai telecom quickly recovered from the great damage caused by the "Cultural Revolution", and became China's largest international telecommunication export bureau. After entering the new century, Shanghai's telecom has been at the forefront of transformation and development, and stepping into the era of full-service operations.

Today, telecommunications has ushered in a new historic change. In face of the booming Internet, the fierce competition in the telecommunications market and the drastic changes of industrial environment, it is worth expecting that how Shanghai, the pioneer of China's telecom, inherits the fine tradition, integrates the spirit of The times and strives for development through reform, thus making new contributions to Shanghai's construction of a smart city.

October 2014

老上海的旅馆业

上海是中国近代旅馆业最为发达的城市。

旅馆业作为社会经济链条中不可或缺的部分，是社会发展到一定阶段的产物。上海旅馆业的前身是客栈、旅社，大都分布在车站、码头和交通要道附近，是迎来送往，行旅憩息之处。上海开埠后，随着经济、文化和交通的发展，上海的社会经济形态由传统向近代化转变，催生了上海的新式旅馆业。1846年英商礼查在今金陵东路外滩创办了上海第一家西式旅社——礼查饭店（今浦江饭店）。1875年英商帕克沃在南京路外滩建成汇中饭店（今和平饭店南楼）。这种由外商投资兴建并主要为外国人服务的饭店，从建筑外观到经营服务理念都与传统的中国客栈有着很大不同，时人称之为新式旅馆或西式旅馆。进入20世纪后，上海逐渐成为中国的贸易中心、金融中心、工业中心和文化中心，城市人口快速增长，商业活动日趋频繁，旅馆业进入鼎盛时期。由于旅馆获利丰厚，上海的民族资本在外国资本投资西式旅馆的刺激以及西式旅馆的新技术和新观念的影响下，也纷纷投资兴建起了一批中西式旅馆。至上世纪30年代，上海已经涌现了东亚饭店、大东旅社、金门饭店、华懋饭店、国际饭店、百老汇大厦、扬子饭店等一批著名旅馆。这些新式旅馆与旧式旅馆并

Hotel Industry of Old Shanghai

The hotel industry of Shanghai has been the most developed one in modern China.

As an indispensable part of social economic chain, hotel industry is the product of a certain stage of social development. The predecessors of Shanghai's hotel industry were the inns and hostels mainly distributed nearby the train stations, wharfs and vital communication lines for people to have a rest. After the opening of Shanghai port, with the development of economy, culture and transportation, the social and economic form of Shanghai changed from tradition to modernization, which spawned the new hotel industry in Shanghai. In 1846, a British businessman Richards established the first western style hotel in Shanghai — the Astor House Hotel (today's Pujiang Hotel) at today's Jinling East Road in the Bund. In 1875, a British businessman Parker built Palace Hotel (the south building of today's Peace Hotel) at Nanjing Road of the Bund. This kind of hotel built by foreign businessmen mainly served for the foreigner and was very different from the traditional Chinese inns in the aspects of the building appearance and the management service concept, which was known as the new-type hotel or western-style hotel by people at that time. Since the 20th century, Shanghai had gradually become China's trade center, financial center, industrial center and cultural center. With rapid urban population growth and increasingly frequent commercial activities, the hotel industry had entered its heyday. Because the hotel industry was profitable, stimulated by the foreign capital investment in western-style hotels and influenced by new technologies and new concepts of western-style hotels, Shanghai's national capitals were also used in the investment into a batch of traditional Chinese and western-style hotels. In the 1930s, a number of famous hotels appeared in Shanghai, including East Asia Hotel, Great Eastern Hotel, Golden Gate

存经营，使得上海成为银行钱庄多、电影院多和旅馆多的"三多"城市。据上海市旅店同业公会 1947 年的档案记载，当时全市旅馆数量达 404 家，其中新式旅馆为中国开埠通商城市之最。

新式旅馆为上海带来了国外先进的建筑装饰文化和管理模式，给时人开启了一扇观察了解西方世界的窗口，加速了中西文化交流。如礼查饭店的欧式家具、各式油画、门厅钢琴，给人以现代舒适的感觉。汇中饭店的石膏花纹顶饰、柚木旋转门以及雕工精细的扶手

老上海的旅馆　贺竹元绘

Hotel, Cathay Hotel, International Hotel, Broadway Mansions and Yangtze Hotel, etc. These new-type hotels co-existed with the old ones, making Shanghai become the city with "three mores" — more banks, more cinemas and more hotels. According to the archives of Shanghai Hotel Trade Association in 1947, there were 404 hotels in the city at that time, the most among China's cities which had opened commercial port and trade relations.

The new-type hotel brought the foreign advanced architectural decoration culture and management mode to Shanghai, opened a window for people to observe and understand the Western world, and accelerated the cultural exchanges between China and the West. For example, the European-style furniture of Astor House Hotel, all sorts of oil paintings and vestibular pianos showed a sense of contemporary comfortable feeling. The gypsum decorative pattern crest, teak revolving door and elaborate handrails of Palace Hotel presented the style of English Renaissance period. Cathay Hotel divided the rooms into various styles, such as the German, French, Italian and Spanish styles. Invested by four savings associations including Gold City, Salt Industry, Mainland and Central South, the International Hotel imitated the architectural appearance of the American skyscrapers and had 24 storeys. It was the tallest building in China at that time, known as the tallest building in the Far East. A considerable part of the new-type hotels adopted the corporate system which realized the reasonable separation of ownership and management rights through the board system and manager responsibility system. Compared with the "one shopkeeper, one cashier and one waiter" system of the old hostels, this management system and organization structure were more scientific and reasonable, and the professional degree of service was obviously improved.

The new-type hotel was the gathering place for fashionable liberalists in Shanghai. Shanghai's oldest rooftop garden, tallest building, earliest use of electric lights and first elevator all appeared in new-type hotels. All new-type hotels had facilities such as the dance hall, western restaurant, cafe, bar, ice room, swimming pool and theatre, etc. which represented a fashionable social life style. The new-type hotels were gorgeous places with a collection of social contact, entertainment, conference, business and banquet,

栏杆，呈现英国文艺复兴时期的风格。华懋饭店客房分有德、英、法、意、印和西班牙等各式住房。由金城、盐业、大陆和中南四家储蓄会投资建造的国际饭店，建筑外形模仿美国摩天大楼式，共24层，为当时中国的最高建筑，被称为远东第一高楼。新式饭店相当一部分采用了公司制，通过董事会制和经理负责制实现所有权与经营权的合理分置。较之于旧式旅馆的店主——掌柜——账房、茶房而言，管理体制和组织结构更为科学合理，服务的专业化程度明显提高。

新式旅馆是昔日上海时尚新派的聚集场所。上海最早的屋顶花园、最高的建筑、电灯的最早使用、第一部升降电梯都出现在新式旅馆。代表时尚社会生活方式的舞厅、西餐厅、咖啡厅、酒吧、饮冰室、游泳池、剧场等都在新式旅馆有设。新式旅馆是当时集社交、娱乐、会议、商务、宴请等于一体的华丽场所，承载了那个时代的梦想和渴望，是权力、地位、金钱与上流社会的象征。

旅馆业的兴起，促进了近代上海的现代化城市进程，推进了社会文明。作为社会经济中重要组成部分的旅馆业，同旅游业、餐饮业、娱乐业等其他行业有着密切联系，共同组成了丰富多彩的城市服务体系，有力推动了城市的发展。新式旅馆在食宿方面一改传统旧式旅馆环境恶劣、不讲卫生的现象，客观上促进了传统旧式旅馆环境的改善，同时也促使人们的生活方式和卫生观念朝着健康文明的方向改变。新式旅馆大都采用自来水、电灯、电话等先进的设施设备，这也在一定程度上加速了上海公用事业的发展。当然，老上海旅馆中也存在着种种社会病态行为，这是上海处在社会剧变时期

which conveyed the dreams and aspirations of the era and was a symbol of power, status, money and select society.

The rise of hotel industry promoted the modernization process of Shanghai and also advanced the social civilization. As an important part of the social economy, the hotel industry was closely related to tourism, catering industry, entertainment industry and other industries, which together formed a rich and colorful urban service system, thus strongly promoting the development of the city. In terms of accommodation, new-type hotels changed the bad and unhygienic environment of traditional hotels and objectively promoted the improvement of the environment in traditional hotels, and also promoted people's lifestyle and hygiene concepts to be healthier and more civilized. Amajority of the new-type hotels provided tap water, electric light, telephone and other advanced facilities, which to some extent accelerated the development of Shanghai public utilities.

→ 礼查饭店

产生的问题,也是旧社会丑陋面的必然反映。

全国解放后,上海旅馆业经历了商业改造,公私合营,逐步发展的阶段。改革开放给上海旅馆业带来了空前的发展机遇,使旅馆业进入繁荣发展的新时期。目前上海各类宾馆饭店、快捷酒店、招待所无以计数,五星以上酒店达 130 多家。在旅馆业日益发达的今天,我们不能忘却近代上海旅馆业走过的这段历史。

2014 年 11 月

Of course, there also existed all sorts of social morbid behaviors in old Shanghai's hotels, which was the problem of Shanghai in period of social upheaval and also the inevitable reflection of ugliness in the old society.

After the national liberation, Shanghai's hotel industry experienced the commercial transformation, public-private partnership and the stage of gradual development. The reform and opening-up brought unprecedented development opportunities to Shanghai's hotel industry and made it enter a new period of prosperity and development. At present, there are countless hotels in Shanghai, including big hotels, budge hotels and guesthouses and more than 130 five-star or better hotels. Although the development of hotel industry is increasingly growing today, we can't forget the history of Shanghai's hotel industry in modern times.

November 2014

老上海的慈善业

上海是中国近现代慈善事业发展最快、影响力最大的城市。

上海地区的慈善事业可以追溯到明代以前，但那时参与慈善的人数少，没有形成社会规模。鸦片战争后，天灾人祸频仍，由于清政府的社会影响力降低，官方慈善救济无济于事，民间慈善事业在上海发展起来。19世纪末20世纪初，上海已有善会、善堂等传统慈善机构60余家，同仁辅元堂、普育堂、果育堂等是当时上海具有代表性的善堂。1910年后，由于当时中国社会局势动荡，战事不断，灾荒连年，大量难民从周边各省涌入上海，上海人口中外来的灾民、流民、贫民比重大大上升。止1915年，上海总人口超过200万，为开埠之初上海人口的数倍。城市人口问题的凸显，推动了上海慈善业的快速发展。从1912年开始，上海各类慈善组织尤其是民间慈善组织呈快速增长势头，止1936年达200多家，占当时全国各类慈善组织的三分之一。

上海慈善业快速兴起的另一个重要原因，是民初上海经济的快速发展。上海开埠后租界的设立，20世纪初的"实业救国"思潮和辛亥革命后对民族工业的鼓励，使上海成为中国民族资本最集中的地方，成为当时中国的经济、贸易和金融中心。巨大的社会财富，

Philanthropy of Old Shanghai

Philanthropy of Shanghai enjoys the fastest development and the greatest influence in modern China.

Philanthropy of Shanghai can date back to the Ming Dynasty, but the number of people involved in charity was small and did not form a social scale at that time. After the Opium War, natural disasters and man-made disasters were frequent. As the social influence of the Qing Government declined, official charity relief was useless and private philanthropy began to develop in Shanghai. At the turning of the 19th century and the 20th century, there were more than 60 traditional charitable institutions in Shanghai, such as sodalities and charity centers. Tongren Fuyuan Charity Center, Puyu Charity Center and Guoyu Charity Center, etc., were the most representative charitable institutions in Shanghai. After 1910, due to the social unrest, continuous wars and successive disasters in China, a large number of refugees flocked in Shanghai from the surrounding provinces. The proportion of displaced people, refugees and poor people in Shanghai increased greatly. By 1915, the total population of Shanghai was more than 2 million, several times that of Shanghai at the beginning of Shanghai's opening port. The highlight of urban population problem promoted the rapid development of Shanghai's philanthropy. Since 1912, the number of Shanghai's various charitable institutions, especially the non-governmental ones, had been growing rapidly. By 1936, there were more than 200 charitable institutions, accounting for onethird of all charitable institutions in the country.

Another important reason for the rapid rise of Shanghai's philanthropy was the rapid economic development of Shanghai in the early Republic of China. The establishment of the concession areas after the opening of Shanghai port, the ideological trend of "saving

天主教会孤儿院收养的孤儿合影

为上海慈善事业的发展提供了坚实的物质基础。民国时期在上海举办慈善事业的慈善家，几乎都是具有相当经济实力的资本家和商人。他们大多有感于民族多难、民众百无聊赖，以救济民生为己任，积极呼吁、倡导、策划、推动各种社会慈善事业。

上海是西学在近代中国的传播中心。开埠后的上海在"欧风美雨"的浸染下，西方慈善思想通过教会慈善事业、西学报刊等渠道传入，使上海慈善业从理念、组织形式到内容由传统向近代转变。西方"教养并重"的慈善理念对于中国传统的施衣、施米、施材、

the nation by engaging in industry" in the early 20th century and the encouragement of national industry after the Revolution of 1911 made Shanghai the most concentrated place of Chinese national capitals and became the economic, trade and financial center of China at that time. The great social wealth provided a solid material foundation for the development of Shanghai's philanthropy. The philanthropists who hosted the philanthropy in Shanghai during the Republic of China were nearly all capitalists and businessmen with considerable economic strength. Most of them were committed to saving the nation and the people, improving people's livelihood, and actively advocating, planning and promoting various social charities.

Shanghai was the communication center of Western learning in modern China. Influenced by the "European and American cultures", the Western charity thoughts were introduced into Shanghai through such channels as church charity, Western newspapers and periodicals, etc., thus making the traditional concept, organizational form and contents of Shanghai's philanthropy transform into those appearing in modern times. The Western charity concept of "balance between education and cultivation" had a positive impact on the traditional Chinese charity concept of "donating clothes, rice, materials and porridge, etc." The core of charity concept transformed from the traditional "benevolence" and "love" into "rights" and "responsibilities" and the charity measures also transformed from the traditional "donation" and "feeding" into "cultivation of self-reliance" and "education instead of feeding". Along with the traditional "blood-transfusion" material relief, the charity industry in Shanghai began to develop "blood-production" culture and skills training. At that time, there were education charities for poor children in Shanghai, such as Shanghai Orphanage, Guangci Children's Home, Shanghai Benevolent Industrial Institution and New Puyutang Orphanage, which were all influential children's charitable institutions. There were also charity vocational education organizations for adults, which enabled the underprivileged to acquire the knowledge and skills necessary for modern society. Moreover, there were also charitable education institutions for the problematic groups in the society, such as workhouses for the poor, rehabilitation centers for disabled and homeless people and beggars, and workhouses for

施粥等消极治标的救济慈善发生了积极影响。慈善救济观的核心由传统的"仁"、"爱"转为"权利"和"责任",救济手段由"施"、"养"转为"培养自立","以教代养"。上海慈善业在传统的"输血式"物质救济的同时,开始出现"造血式"的文化和技能培训。当时上海既有针对贫苦儿童的慈善教育,如上海孤儿院、广慈苦儿院、上海贫儿教养院、新普育堂孤儿院等都是有影响的儿童慈善教养机构。又有针对成年人的慈善职业教育,使贫苦的社会下层人掌握近代化社会所必须的知识和技能。还有针对社会问题群体的慈善教育,如贫民习艺所、淞沪残废乞丐游民教养院、乞丐教养院等。

在上海近现代慈善业的发展过程中,涌现了一大批著名的慈善机构和有影响的慈善家。实业家、书画家王一亭,是近代上海许多重要慈善团体的发起人和组织者。他从19世纪80年代起就开始组织书画助赈,惠及上海及周边各省。他参与组织创办的著名慈善组织有上海慈善团、普济善会、中国救济妇孺总会、中国济生会、中国红十字会等。上海著名绅商、慈善家朱葆三不仅积极为全国的水旱灾害举办义赈,同时也是沪上很多慈善组织的创办者,著名的有佛教慈悲义赈会、中华慈善团全国联合会、浦东医院、上海时疫医院、商界难民收容所等。经元善、李平书、聂云台、虞洽卿、陆伯鸿、曾铸、沈缦云、沈敦和等都是近代以来上海有影响的慈善家。他们为上海民间慈善事业的发展,维护当时社会稳定,推进上海慈善公益事业的近代化进程,作出了历史性的贡献。

今天的中国,综合国力迅速增长,人民生活水平不断提高。但由于整个社会处于转型时期,区域经济发展不平衡,贫富差异依然

beggars, etc.

During the development of Shanghai's modern philanthropy, a large number of famous charities and influential philanthropists emerged. WANG Yiting, an industrialist and painter, was the initiator and organizer of many important charitable organizations in modern Shanghai. Since the 1880s, he had begun to organize painting and calligraphy relief to benefit Shanghai and neighboring provinces. He participated in the organization and establishment of the famous charitable organizations such as Shanghai Charity Society, General Charity Relief Association, China Women and Children Relief Association, China Philanthropic Institution, the Red Cross Society of China and so on. ZHU Baosan, a famous squire and philanthropist in Shanghai, not only actively organized relief activities for the national flood and drought disasters, but also founded many charitable organizations in Shanghai, including the Buddhist Charity Relief Commission, the

→ 当年土山湾孤儿院里的学生正在学习西洋画

存在。如何发扬上海近代以来慈善业的光荣传统，有效利用社会资源，壮大社会慈善事业，为促进社会稳定作出更大的贡献，是我们这座城市义不容辞的责任。

2015 年 1 月

National Federation of Chinese Charity Groups, Pudong Hospital, Shanghai Epidemic Hospital, and Refugee Shelters for Business People, etc. Since modern times, the influential philanthropists in Shanghai included JING Yuanshan, LI Pingshu, NIE Yuntai, YU Qiaqing, LU Bohong, ZENG Zhu, SHEN Manyun, SHEN Dun and so on. They had made historic contributions to the development of Shanghai folk charity, the maintenance of social stability and the modernization of Shanghai's philanthropy.

In today's China, the overall national strength has grown rapidly and the people's living standards have been continuously improved. However, as the whole society is in a transitional period and regional economic development is unbalanced, the gap between the rich and poor still exists. It is our city's bounden responsibility to carry forward the glorious traditions of Shanghai's philanthropy since modern times, effectively make use of social resources, strengthen social philanthropy, and make greater contributions to promoting social stability.

January 2015

老上海的邮政

在中国邮政现代化进程中,上海邮政的地位举足轻重。近代以来上海邮政曲折发展的历史,无疑是中国邮政的一个缩影。

在近代新式邮政创办前,中国的信递主要通过驿站和民信局两种途径,前者主要传递官方书信文件,后者为民间邮递组织。上海开埠后,代表近代物质文明的邮政设施被引入租界。1861年初,英国政府香港邮政总局与英驻沪领事达成协议,在南京路领事署内设立邮政代办所即大英书信馆,成为近代第一个在上海成立的客邮机构。此后,法国书信馆、美国书信馆、日本书信馆、德国书信馆、海关邮政所等纷纷在上海设立。1863年公共租界工部局创办工部书信馆,成为租界当局公用事业建设之端倪。当时,上海正处在中西文明交汇的初期,既存在着大量传统民间邮政机构,又有实行西方邮政制度的客邮机构,体制不一。这一时期,以工部书信馆为代表的客邮机构,未获中国政府赋予的邮政职权,侵犯了中国的邮政主权。但客观上,客邮机构对于推动以上海为中心的中国邮政系统、邮政网络的建设,拓展邮政服务种类起到了一定的积极作用。

1896年3月,大清邮政开办。1897年2月,以上海海关拔驷达局为基础组建成立了大清上海邮政局。面对当时邮递机构混乱,竞

Postal Industry of Old Shanghai

The postal industry of Shanghai plays a vital role in the modernization of China's postal industry. The tortuous development history of Shanghai's postal industry since modern times is undoubtedly an epitome of the history of China's postal industry.

Before the initiative of modern postal industry, the message passing in China mainly relied on two ways — courier station and civil postal office. The former one was mainly used to deliver the official letters and documents while the latter one was the civil postal organization. After the opening of Shanghai port, the postal facilities representing modern material civilization were introduced into the concession. In early 1861, the Hong Kong General Post Office of the United Kingdom and the British consul stationed in Shanghai reached an agreement to establish a postal agency, namely, the British Post Office in the consular office of Nanjing Road, which became the first postal agency established in Shanghai in modern times. Since then, the French Post Office, the American Post Office, the Japanese Post Office, the German Post Office, the Customs Post Office and so on had beenestablished in Shanghai. In 1863, the Municipal Council of Shanghai International Settlement set up the Post Office of Municipal Council, which became the start of public utilities construction in the concession. At that time, Shanghai was during the early period of the integration of Chinese and Western civilizations. There were a large number of traditional private postal agencies and Western private postal service institutions, which adopted different postal systems. During this period, the postal agencies represented by the Post Office of Municipal Council did not have the postal rights approved by the Chinese government, which violated China's postal sovereignty. But objectively, the Western private postal agencies played a positive role in promoting the

↖ 20 世纪初上海公共租界里的马拉邮政车

争激烈的局面,大清上海邮政局通过增办业务,提高运速,改善员工待遇等举措,努力发展邮政业务,借以与其他邮局相抗衡。辛亥革命后,大清邮政被中华邮政所取代,上海邮政局改称为上海邮务管理局。1914 年,中国加入万国邮政联盟,上海邮务管理局被定为国际邮件互换局,成为国内最大的国际邮件进出口中心。1931 年 9 月,上海邮务管理局改称为上海邮政管理局。这一时期虽然社会动荡,战乱不断,但中华邮政发展迅速,驿站、民信局、客邮先后被裁撤、取缔、废除,邮权实现了统一。至抗战爆发前,上海邮政管理局已下设 25 个二等局,25 个三等局,34 个支局,共计 85 个局和 117 个邮政代办所。村镇信柜、邮站、邮票代售处、邮亭近 1300 个。做到了租界、华界、市区、城郊及上海周边地区全部通邮。

上海邮政的迅速发展,得益于上海作为当时中国最大的国际性

construction of China's postal systems and postal networks with Shanghai as the center, and expanding the types of postal services.

In March 1896, the Post Office of the Qing Dynasty was opened. In February 1897, the Shanghai Post Office of the Qing Dynasty was established on the basis of the Post Office of Shanghai Customs. In face of the chaos and fierce competition in the postal industry, the Shanghai Post Office of the Qing Dynasty tried to develop postal business by increasing its business, improving its speed and enhancing the treatment of its employees, so as to compete with other post offices. After the Revolution of 1911, the Post Office of the Qing Dynasty was replaced by the Post Office of China and the Shanghai Post Office was renamed the Shanghai Mail Administration Bureau. In 1914, China joined the Universal Postal Union, and the Shanghai Mail Administration Bureau was designated as the international mail exchange bureau, becoming the largest international mail import and export center in China. In September 1931, Shanghai Mail Administration Bureau changed its name to Shanghai Postal Administration Bureau. Despite the social unrest and

↗ 上海邮局的邮递员

大都市经济文化的有力推动。开埠后的上海工商经济发展旺盛，吸引了大量外地移民流入上海。人口聚集的城市迫切需要交往和信息交流，邮政则成为公众交往的重要纽带。随着西学的入沪，上海逐渐成为近代中国的文化中心、教育重镇。教材、书刊、报纸等的发行流通离不开邮政。文教事业的繁荣推动着邮政事业的发展，而邮政事业的发展又进一步促进了文教事业的繁荣。上海作为当时中国的贸易中心、工业与制造中心、银行金融中心，也极大促进了邮政业的发展。以上海为中心的信息物流网，网络了全国各主要大中城市，并与海外相连接，这一张大网主要由邮政来编织。

抗日战争时期，上海邮工面对劫难坚持通邮，利用工作之便积极宣传抗日救国思想，并组建邮工义勇军和邮工医疗队，亲赴战场救死扶伤，不少邮工为抗日救国献出了宝贵的生命。解放战争时期，上海邮工坚持邮路不断，并积极保护邮政通信设施，迎接黎明的到来。

在中国近代邮政史上，上海创造了许多第一。1878年6月中国第一套国家邮票——大龙邮票在上海印制，上海由此成为中国国家邮票的诞生地。1929年7月，带运邮件的飞机由上海首飞南京，由此开通了中国第一条定期航空邮路。1922年12月动工新建，1924年12月正式启用的上海邮政大楼是我国目前建造最早、规模最大、仍在使用的邮政标志性建筑之一，堪为中国百年邮政的历史见证。

上海解放后，邮政获得了新生。上海邮政随着时代的变革经历了曲折发展的过程。进入新世纪以来，面对邮政业务多元、经营主

constant wars, China's postal industry developed rapidly. Courier station, civil post office and western private post office were successively dissolved, banned and abolished, and the postal rights were unified. Before the outbreak of the Anti-Japanese War, Shanghai Postal Administration Bureau had set up 25 second-class, 25 third-class and 34 sub-bureaus, thus forming a total of 85 bureaus and 117 post offices. There were nearly 1300 mail counters, post offices, stamp sales offices and postal kiosks in villages and towns. Postal communication was accessible in the Shanghai concession, the downtown of Shanghai, the urban areas, the suburbs and the surrounding areas of Shanghai.

The rapid development of Shanghai postal industry benefited from the powerful promotion of Shanghai as the largest international metropolis in China at that time. After the opening of the port, Shanghai's industrial and commercial economy developed vigorously, which attracted a large number of immigrants into Shanghai. Cities with a large population urgently needed communication and information exchange, and the postal service became an important link for public communication. With the introduction of Western learning, Shanghai gradually became the cultural center of modern China and the important city of education. The distribution and circulation of teaching materials, books and periodicals, newspapers, etc. cannot be separated from postal services. The prosperity of cultural and educational undertakings promoted the development of postal services while the development of postal services further promoted the prosperity of cultural and educational undertakings. Shanghai, as China's trade center, industrial and manufacturing center, and banking and financial center, also greatly promoted the development of the postal industry. The information logistics network with Shanghai as the center covered major cities across the country and connected with overseas network. This large network was mainly operated by postal industry.

During the Anti-Japanese War, the postal workers in Shanghai insisted on postal delivery, made use of their work to actively publicize the idea of resisting Japan and saving the nation, and organized the postal volunteers and postal medical team to go to the battlefield and rescue the wounded in the war. Many postal workers sacrificed their precious lives for the Anti-Japanese War. During the War of Liberation, the postal

体多元的复杂局面,上海邮政在转型中发展,在创新中前行。但如何进一步深化改革,真正走开邮政市场化的路子,实现新的跨越,则需要上海邮政人作更大的努力。

2015 年 3 月

workers of Shanghai insisted on postal delivery and actively protected postal and communications facilities to welcome the incoming victory of the war.

In the postal history of modern China, Shanghai created many first places. In June 1878, China's first set of national stamps — the Large Dragon Stamps were printed in Shanghai, thus making Shanghai become the birthplace of China's national stamps. In July 1929, the first plane carrying mails arrived in Nanjing from Shanghai, opening China's first regular air mail route. The Shanghai Post Building, which started construction in December 1922 and officially opened in December 1924, is one of the earliest, largest and still in-use postal landmark buildings in China, being the historical witness of China's century-old postal industry.

After the liberation of Shanghai, the postal industry began to revive. With the change of times, Shanghai's postal industry has experienced tortuous development. After entering the new century, in face of the complex situation of diversified postal services and operating entities, Shanghai's postal industry has been developing in transformation and advancing in innovation. However, we should make greater efforts to further deepen the reform and truly open the marketization of postal industry, thus realizing the new great-leap-forward development.

March 2015

老上海的钱庄

被誉为老上海"百业之枢"的钱庄，曾经在社会经济生活中发挥过巨大作用。

钱庄是中国封建社会后期出现的一种传统金融机构，起源于银钱兑换。上海的钱庄历史悠久，据钱庄业较为普遍的传说，上海钱庄是由浙江绍兴商人在南市所开设的煤炭店兼营货币的存放款而起。1685年康熙开海禁，上海因地处南北航运的中心，商业繁荣贸易兴盛，钱庄业发展迅速。乾隆年间，钱庄在上海已经成为一个具有相当规模的独立行业。上海钱业公所的内园碑记有这样的记载：从1776年到1796年时期内，历年承办的钱庄共有106家之多。

上海开埠后，随着外国洋行和外资银行纷纷涌入上海，随着城市商贸的不断发展，上海钱庄的功能发生了蜕变，主要业务由银钱兑换向汇兑、存放款、发行庄票等多元发展。随后逐渐形成了以上海为中心，其他口岸城市为主干的、以钱庄为主体的包括货币汇兑、资金拆借、国内汇兑、金银买卖等内容的金融市场体系。当时华资银行尚未兴起，上海金融业中形成了外国银行和钱庄两强称雄的局面。19世纪末，华资银行创办，其最初10多年的经营者中，钱业出身者占极重要的地位，为华资银行起到了一种人才奠基石的作用。

Money Shops of Old Shanghai

The money shop, known as the "hub of all industries" of old Shanghai, once had played a huge role in social and economic life.

The money shop, originated from the exchange of silver money, was a kind of traditional financial institution in the late feudal society of China. The money shop of Shanghai had a long history. According to the most common legendary, Shanghai's money shop was originated from the coal store which concurrently engaged in the deposit and loan of money. The coal store was located in Nanshi and founded by a businessman from Shaoxing of Zhejiang. In 1685, Emperor Kangxi opened the country to foreign trade. As Shanghai was located in the center of south-north shipping, its commerce and trade flourished, and the money-shop industry developed rapidly. During the reign of Emperor Qianlong, the money-shop industry in Shanghai became an independent industry with considerable scale. There is such record in the inscription of the inner garden of Shanghai Banking Industry Association that: During 1776 to 1796, there were 106 money shops in Shanghai.

After the opening of Shanghai port, foreign banks and foreign-invested banks flocked in Shanghai. With the continuous development of the city's commerce and trade, the functions of Shanghai's money shops changed. The main business of Shanghai's money shops developed from exchange of silver money to the exchange, deposit and loan of money and the issue of bank notes. Soon afterwards, there formed the financial market system with Shanghai as the center, other port cities as the trunk, money shop as the economic subject and currency exchange, capital lending, domestic exchange and gold& silver transaction as the contents. At that time, Chinese-invested banks had not yet

与此同时，钱庄还为华资银行提供了大量的初创资金。从 19 世纪末到 20 世纪 20 年代，银行和钱庄始终作为一个共同利益体存在，使得当时一度形成了外国银行、华资银行和钱庄三足鼎立的局面。这一时期可谓是上海钱庄业的黄金时代。

老上海的钱庄多为江浙财阀所把持，他们的一举一动都会影响到当时全国的金融市场。从 19 世纪后半期到 20 世纪初，上海拥有 4 家钱庄以上的 9 个钱庄资本家族集团都是江苏和浙江籍的。这些钱

老上海的钱庄　贺竹元绘

emerged, thus forming the dominated situation by the most powerful strength in the financial industry of Shanghai — foreign banks and money shops. In the late 19th century, the China-owned bank was founded. Among its operators for more than 10 years, those in money industry occupied an extremely important position, which laid solid talent foundation for China-owned banks. At the same time, the money shops provided a lot of start-up capitals for Chinese-owned banks. From the late 19th century to the 1920s, the money shops and Chinese-owned banks always existed as a common interest, which led to the situation of tripartite confrontation of foreign banks, Chinese-owned banks and the money shops. This was the golden period of Shanghai's money-shop industry.

The money shops in old Shanghai were dominated by the Jiangsu and Zhejiang chaebols, and their every move would affect the financial market of the whole country at that time. From the second half of the 19th century to the beginning of the 20th century, the chaebol families which had more than four money shops in Shanghai were all from Jiangsu and Zhejiang. The managers of these banks were mostly from Ningbo, Shaoxing and Zhenjiang and Jiangsu, thus making the manager in these banks form the "Ningshao School" and "Zhenjiang School". When the northern exchange shops were in vogue, the power of the Shanghai banks could prevent the northern exchange shops from crossing the Yangtze River, which well demonstrated the strong influence of the Jiangsu and Zhejiang chaebols.

From the late Qing Dynasty to the early days of the Nanjing National Government, the central government was weak, with neither a central bank nor a regulatory body. Therefore, the credit of the money shops was mainly realized by the self-management of peer organizations. Shanghai had long been rich in money industry association and other trade organizations. Shanghai Money Industry Association was established in 1917. The money industry association had its own rules, a strict access system and a prudent exit system. The association not only supervised the members, but also paid attention to protect their interests. A major responsibility of Shanghai Money Industry Association was to guard against financial risks and financial fluctuations. At that time, when the government did nothing and the central bank system was not set up, Shanghai Money

庄的经理则多数为浙江宁波、绍兴和江苏镇江等地人,因而又形成了钱庄经理的"宁绍"和"镇江"等帮别。当北方票号盛行时,上海钱庄的力量能阻止北方票号势力越过长江,江浙财阀的势力由此可见一斑。

从清末直至南京国民政府初期,中央政府很弱,既没有中央银行,也没有监管机构,因此钱庄的信用主要靠同业组织的自我管理实现。上海很早就有钱业总公所等同业组织,1917年成立了上海钱业公会。钱业公会有自己的行业规则,有严格的准入制度和审慎的退出制度。公会既对会员进行督导,同时也注重维护会员的利益。上海钱业公会的一项重大职责就是防范金融风险和金融波动。在当时政府无作为又缺乏中央银行制度设置的情况下,上海钱业公会参与了部分救济市面的融资活动,一定程度上维护了社会的稳定。

1933年南京国民政府实行"废两改元"方案,即废用银两、改用银元,建立"四行二局一库"(中央银行、中国银行、交通银行、中国农民银行;中央信托局、邮政储金汇业局;合作金库)的金融垄断体系。在行政性的金融垄断之下,上海钱庄的生存空间越缩越小,到抗战时期已经奄奄一息。以后随着内战的爆发,由于国民党军事上的失败导致经济崩溃,钱庄更是每况愈下,仅能苟延残喘。上海解放后,1952年底尚在营业的28家钱庄被并入公私合营银行,钱庄的历史宣告结束。

综观近代以来上海钱庄走过的历史,我们应该辩证地看待钱庄的性质与作用。鸦片战争后,西方金融势力开始利用中国本土原有的金融组织,来构建一种有别于西方的中国通商口岸的金融组织。

Industry Association participated in some financing activities to relieve the market, and to some extent maintained social stability.

In 1933, the Nanjing National Government implemented the plan of "discarding the taels of silver and unifying the currency system by silver dollar", namely, to replace silver tael with silver dollar, and established the financial monopoly system of "four banks, two bureaus and one exchequer" (namely, Central Bank, Bank of China, Bank of Communications, Farmer's Bank of China; Central Trust of China, Postal Saving and Remittance Bureau; Cooperation Exchequer). Under the administrative financial monopoly, the living space of Shanghai's money shops was shrinking, and it was dying in the Anti-Japanese War. Later, with the outbreak of the Civil War, the economy collapsed due to the military failure of the Kuomintang, and the situation of money shops became worse and worse, only lingering out a feeble existence. After the liberation of Shanghai, 28 banks which were still in operation at the end of 1952 were merged into the public and private joint-venture bank, marking the end of history of the money shops.

Reviewing the history of Shanghai's money shops since modern times, weshould dialectically think about the nature and functions of money shops. After the Opium War, Western financial forces began to use the original financial organizations in China to build a kind of financial organization of China's treaty ports which was different from Western ones. In this context, the money shops were used by foreign invaders to serve the goods and capital export and the plunder of the Chinese economy by Western powers, which had the nature of feudal comprador. But at the same time, the prosperity of the money shops played a positive role in modern Shanghai's import and export trade, the disintegration of the hinterland's natural economy, the activation of domestic exchange market at that time, and the rise and development of the Chinese-owned banks. A set of capitalist allocation and settlement system initially established by the money shops further played the role of modern financial industry and promoted the development of China's capitalist economy.

So far, the money shops of old Shanghai have disappeared for more than 60 years. In the reform of the market-oriented financial system today, it should be the subject for

在这一背景下，钱庄被外国入侵者所利用，服务于西方列强的商品输出、资本输出和对中国经济的掠夺，具有封建买办性。但同时，钱庄对近代上海进出口贸易的繁荣，对腹地自然经济的解体，对活跃当时的内汇市场，对华资银行的兴起和发展发挥了积极作用。钱庄初步建立的一套资本主义的划拨清算制度，进一步发挥了近代金融业的作用，促进了中国资本主义经济的发展。

上海钱庄告结迄今已一个多甲子。在市场化金融体制改革的今天，如何深化对钱庄这一近代私营金融形态的研究，历史的客观的评价近代上海钱庄的性质和作用，借鉴其在长期发展过程中所形成的制度体系和运作机制，推进民间金融改革，应是上海金融中心建设的一道课题。

2015 年 4 月

the construction of Shanghai financial center that how to deepen the research on the modern private financial form of the money shops, historically and objectively evaluate the nature and function of modern Shanghai's money shops, draw lessons from the institutional system and operation mechanism formed in its long-term development process and promote the reform of private finance.

April 2015

老上海的租界

存时近一个世纪的上海租界，对中国政治、经济、文化等诸方面都曾产生过重大影响。

上海开埠后，西方列强为了扩张在华特权，建立起独立于中国行政体系之外的政治区域和管理体系，1845 年 11 月 29 日，英方与上海道签订了《上海土地章程》，设立了中国近代第一个租界——英租界。此后，美租界于 1848 年、法租界于 1849 年相继在上海辟设。1863 年，英美两租界合并，称公共租界，1899 年改称"上海国际公共租界"。经历次扩张，到 1915 年上海租界总面积已达 48653 亩，是 1845 年的 57 倍多。至 1936 年，上海租界总人口已超过 160 万，形成了公共租界、法租界和华界三分天下的奇特格局。

开埠前的上海虽已立县 500 年，但当时的上海只是东南海滨的一个县城。上海城仍是中国传统的小县城模式，整个城厢位于苏州河以南，占地不足 2 平方公里。由于租界的建立和扩张，上海城市的性质、结构和形态等都发生了巨大的转型。随着港口建设加快，上海从一个封闭型的县城转换为外向型通商港城，城市功能发生了质的变化。由于租界的畸形繁荣发展，使得租界由原来的荒地成为城市的重心，城市中心跨过苏州河北移，沿黄浦江发展，拓展了城

Concession of Old Shanghai

The Shanghai concession, which had existed for nearly a century, hadexerted great influences on China's politics, economy and culture.

After the opening of Shanghai port, Western powers established political regions and management systems independent of China's administrative system in order to expand their privileges in China. On November 29, 1845, the British signed *The Shanghai Land Regulations* with Shanghai Government at that time and established the first concession in modern China — the British Concession. Since then, the American Concession was set up in 1848 and the French Concession was set up in 1849. In 1863, the British and American concessions were merged, known as the Public Concession. In 1899, it was renamed as "Shanghai International Settlement". After several rounds of expansion, by 1915, the total area of Shanghai concessions had reached 48653 mu (1 mu $\approx$ 666. 6666667 m^2), more than 57 times that of 1845. By 1936, the total population of Shanghai concession had exceeded 1. 6 million, forming the unique pattern of coexistence of International Settlement, French Concession and Chinese territory.

Although Shanghai had been a county for 500 years before the opening of its port, it was just a small county on the southeast coast. Shanghai still followed the model of traditional smalltown in China, entirely located at south of Suzhou River with an area of less than 2 square kilometers. Due to the establishment and expansion of concessions, the nature, structure and form of Shanghai city had undergone tremendous transformation. With the acceleration of port construction, Shanghai changed from a closed county to an export-oriented trading port city, and the city's function changed qualitatively. Due to the abnormally prosperous development of the concession, it transformed from the original

市中心区域，改变了城市空间结构。城市道路也由封建城市结构转化成与资本主义经济相适应的现代工商业城市道路结构。到1911年，租界内外道路总长度已达110英里，形成了现代城市道路网络。与此同时，高耸的西式建筑、先进的有轨电车、电灯、电报、电话、汽车、自来水等西式事物纷纷在上海出现，租界内呈现出"十里洋场"的繁荣景致。上海的政治、经济和文化地位迅速提升，至20世纪30年代，上海已成为远东最大的城市。

上海是中国最早植入西方城市管理理念和制度的城市。1854年

↖ 拓宽后的南京路

wasteland into the center of the city. The city center moved across Suzhou and Hebei and developed along the Huangpu River, thus having expanded the central area of the city and changed the urban spatial structure. The urban road structure also transformed from the feudal urban structure into the modern industrial and commercial urban road structure appropriate for the capitalist economy. By 1911, the total length of roads inside and outside the concession had reached 110 miles, forming a modern urban road network. At the same time, towering western-style buildings, advanced trams, electric lights, telegrams, telephones, cars, tap water and other western things appeared in Shanghai, and a flourishing scene of "ten-mile foreign market" emerged in the concession. Shanghai's political, economic and cultural status rose rapidly, and by the 1930s it had become the largest city in the Far East.

Shanghai was the first city in China to incorporate Western urban management concepts and systems. The establishment of the Municipal Council on July 17, 1854 kicked off the institutionalized management of the concession. As a municipal administrative body with real local autonomy in the concession, the Municipal Council, by virtue of the rights conferred by *The Shanghai Land Regulations* and the *Supplementary Articles*, exercised overall control over public affairs throughout the concession. Its earliest administrative management system had been continuously developed and improved and always maintained the unity and continuity in the 100-year history of the Shanghai concession. Shanghai concession was also the first place in China to transplant the modern rule of law. As "a state within a state", the concession had its own legislative body and legislative power. The legal system, legal structure, trial system, lawyer system, prison system and other systems which reflected the modern legal system were all the first to appear in the Shanghai concession.

The Shanghai concession, as the foremost region influenced by the Western culture and civilization, formed the concession culture with distinct coloniality, miscibility and modernity during its development. The foreigners in the concession introduced advanced western material culture, system culture, lifestyle and values into the concession, forming the process that Western culture was gradually understood, accepted, imitated and

7月17日工部局的设立，拉开了租界制度化管理的序幕。工部局作为租界真正意义上带有地方自治色彩的市政管理机构，凭借《上海土地章程》及其《附则》所赋予的权利，全面统辖整个租界内的公共事宜。其最初确立的行政管理制度在上海租界百年间不断发展完善并始终保持着统一性和连贯性。上海租界也是中国最早移植现代法治的地方。租界作为实际上的"国中之国"，拥有自己的立法主体和立法权。体现现代法制的法规体系、法规结构、审判制度、律师制度和监狱制度等都最早出现在上海租界。

上海租界作为被欧风美雨吹打的前沿地域，在其发展过程中，形成了具有鲜明的殖民性、混合性、近代性的租界文化。租界里的外国人把不乏先进的西方物质文化、制度文化、生活方式和价值观念带入租界，形成了西方文化在上海被逐渐理解、接受、模仿、采用的过程。1853年小刀会起义前后，大批华人涌入租界避难，打破了"华洋分居"的格局，形成了"华洋杂处"、"五方杂处"的局面。不同文化背景的移民聚集租界，为培育新型文化提供了土壤。租界文化就是租界历史上逐渐发展出的移民之间彼此认同的共同文化。以开放、宽容、求新、进取为主流特征的近代移民文化，100多年来深刻影响着上海的城市精神风貌。

1943年8月，上海租界的历史结束。客观地看，上海租界具有两重性。它既是近代中国遭受列强欺凌的耻辱标志，同时又是近代文明的窗口。第一幢高楼、第一盏电灯、第一辆电车、第一座欧式剧场、第一家广播电台等，中国的许多第一都产生在这里。它既是西方列强经济掠夺的基地，同时又加速了中国自然经济的解体，创

adopted in Shanghai. Around the time of the uprising of the Small Swords Society in 1853, a large number of Chinese people rushed to seek refuge in the concession, breaking the pattern of "the Chinese and foreigners living apart" and forming the situation of "the Chinese and foreigners living together" and "people throughout the countries living together". Immigrants from different cultural backgrounds gathered in the concession, which provided the soil for cultivating new culture. The concession culture was the common culture of immigrants in the history of concession. The modern immigrant culture, featured by openness, inclusiveness, innovation and progress, had exerted a profound influence on Shanghai's urban spirit over the past 100 years.

The history of Shanghai concession ended in August 1943. Objectively speaking, Shanghai concession had duality. It is not only the stigma of the bullying of the great powers in modern China, but also the window of modern civilization. Many of China's

→ 法国总会前的迈尔西爱路

造了近代工商业发展的环境，使得上海逐渐成为中国近代的经济和贸易中心。它既有为殖民主义政治扩张、经济侵略服务的文化渗透，同时也促进了新学的传播，创造了比较适合文化发展的环境，形成了具有明显的开放性、灵活性、创新性特点的海派文化，使上海成为当时中国的文化中心。另外，由于租界的特殊性，使其成为中国封建、军阀统治下的一个权利薄弱点，充当了保护革命进步势力的不自觉的工具。

今天的上海，已是一个繁荣发展的社会主义国际化大都市。租界这样的耻辱，在上海将一去不返。但如何运用历史唯物主义的原理，客观评判上海租界这一中国近代史上复杂的历史现象，则需要史学界认真加以研究。

2015 年 6 月

first places, such as the first tall building, the first electric lamp, the first tram, the first European-style theater, the first radio station, etc., all happened here. It was not only the base of economic plunder of Western powers, but also accelerated the disintegration of China's natural economy and created the environment for modern industrial and commercial development, making Shanghai gradually become modern China's economic and trade center. It not only served the cultural penetration of colonial political expansion and economic aggression, but also promoted the dissemination of new learning, created a more suitable environment for cultural development, and formed the Shanghai-style culture featured by obvious openness, flexibility and innovation, making Shanghai the cultural center of China at that time. In addition, due to the particularity of concessions, it became a weak point of right under the rule of Chinese feudalism and warlords, and acted as an involuntary tool to protect the revolutionary progressive forces.

Today, Shanghai is a socialist international metropolis with prosperous development. Such a humiliation as the concession will never return in Shanghai. However, it requires the historians to study seriously that how to apply the principle of historical materialism to objectively judge the Shanghai concession, a complex historical phenomenon in modern Chinese history.

June 2015

老上海的体育

上海是中国最早开展近代体育的城市。

开埠前,上海只是一个三级县城,体育活动仅局限在武术、射箭、龙舟、棋类等中国传统体育活动领域。开埠后,带有西方文化内涵的近代体育随着一批批侨民入沪进入上海。在西方体育的冲击下,在中国社会转型的大背景下,上海近代体育逐渐发展起来,大致经历了1843年上海开埠至1911年的萌芽期,1911年至1927年的发展期,1927年至1937年的繁荣期,1937年至1949年的萎缩期。

1848年,英国人在今南京东路和河南中路交界兴建了占地81.7亩的跑马场,拉开了西方体育在上海传播的序幕。赛马、体操、田径、足球、篮球、排球、网球、棒球、游泳、帆船等西方体育运动成为租界侨民生活的重要部分。18世纪50年代后,英国总会、德国总会、法国总会等综合性的西人俱乐部和跑马总会、板球总会、棒球总会、划船总会等西人专业体育组织纷纷在上海成立。至清末,当时欧美流行的各种体育项目几乎都显身上海。由于西方的排华行为,加上中西体育文化差异造成的隔阂,最初西人组织的体育竞赛和活动华人只能作"看客",不能参与。"西人比赛,国人观看",就是当时的写照。但客观上,却给上海输入了西方体育观念、体育运

Sports of Old Shanghai

Shanghai is the earliest city in China to develop modern sports.

Before the opening of the port, Shanghai was only a third-tier county and its sports activities were only limited in the field of traditional Chinese sports such as martial arts, archery, dragon boat and chess, etc. After the opening of the port, modern sports with Western cultural connotation entered Shanghai with groups of emigrants. Under the impact of Western sports and against the background of China's social transformation, Shanghai's modern sports had gradually developed. The modern sports of Shanghai experienced the germination period from the opening of Shanghai port in 1843 to 1911, the development period from 1911 to 1927, the booming period from 1927 to 1937 and the shrinking period from 1937 to 1949.

In 1848, the British built an 81.7-mu(1 mu$\approx$666.6666667 m^2) racecourse at the junction of today's East Nanjing Road and Middle Henan Road, which marked the beginning of the spread of Western sports in Shanghai. The Western sports such as horse racing, gymnastics, track and field, football, basketball, volleyball, tennis, baseball, swimming and sailing became an important part of life for emigrants in the concession. After the 1750s, comprehensive Western clubs such as the British Club, the German Club and the French Club, as well as professional western sports organizations such as the jockey club, the cricket club, the baseball club and the boating club were set up in Shanghai. By the end of the Qing Dynasty, almost all kinds of sports popular in Europe and America appeared in Shanghai. Due to the anti-Chinese behavior in the West and the estrangement caused by the differences between Chinese and Western sports culture, the Chinese could only be spectators and could not participate in the sports competitions and

动项目、体育组织的管理方式和体育运动规则，对上海近代体育起到了引导和示范作用。

19世纪后叶至20世纪初，在教会学校的传播、基督教青年会的推动下，学校体育制度开始建立，学校与社会的体育互动逐步展开，原本盛行于西方侨民生活中的体育运动项目，开始在上海大中学校师生和中上层华人圈中出现。形式多样的西方体育活动给上海人带来了全新的生活观念和生活方式，广大市民对西方体育由开始的惊诧到接受，由模仿到吸纳，由共处到竞争。随着各种运动会的举办、体育场馆的纷纷建立，激发了时人参加体育运动的兴趣，比赛和竞争的观念逐渐在上海市民中确立起来。

20世纪20、30年代，上海近代体育进入兴盛时期。近代10届远东运动会由中国举办的3届，即第2、第5和第8届全都由上海承办。上海选手在历届远东运动会上先后20人次获得金牌、44人次获得银牌、6人次获得铜牌，雪耻了"东亚病夫"的形象。1921年上海举办的第5届远东运动会上，国际奥委会的正式代表加纳治五郎出席开幕式并发表讲话，使中国第一次聆听"奥运之声"。近代中国举办的7届全国运动会，上海承办了2届。在第1、4、5、6届全运会上，上海的比赛成绩均居全国之首。

华人体育社团的兴起、体育专业教育的推进、体育人才的集聚、体育经济的发展等，也是上海近代体育兴盛的标志。1924年在上海成立的"中华全国体育协进会"，实际上是中国近代的"国家奥委会"组织。上海中华足球、篮球、网球、棒球、排球联合会等5个单项体育组织和上海中华运动裁判会等当时都具有全国影响。近代

activities organized by Western people. "The Western race while the Chinese watch" is the portrayal of that time. But objectively, it has introduced Western sports concept, sports project, sports organization management mode and sports rules into Shanghai, which played a guiding and demonstration role in the development of Shanghai's modern sports.

From the late 19th century to the early 20th century, driven by the spread of missionary schools and the Young Men's Christian Association, the school sports system began to be established, and the sports interaction between schools and societieshad been gradually developed. The sports activities that were originally popular in the life of the Western emigrants began to appear in the circles of high-school teachers and students and the upper-middle Chinese circles. Various forms of Western sports activities brought new life concepts and lifestyles to Shanghainese. The majority of citizens were surprised to accept Western sports, from imitation to absorption, from coexistence to competition. As various games were held and stadiums were set up, people's interest in sports was aroused. The concept of contests and competitions was gradually established among Shanghai citizens.

In the 1920s and 1930s, modern sports in Shanghai entered a prosperous period. Among all the 10 sessions of the Far Eastern Games in modern times, Shanghai organized all the 3 sessions of Far Eastern Games held in China, namely, the Second Far Eastern Games, the Fifth Far Eastern Games and the Eighth Far Eastern Games. Shanghai athletes had won 20 gold medals, 44 silver medals and 6 bronze medals in the games, abandoning the image of "Sick Man of East Asia". At the 5th Far Eastern Games held in Shanghai in 1921, Mr. Kano Jigoro, the official representative of the International Olympic Committee, attended the opening ceremony and delivered a speech, making China listen to the "Voices of the Olympic Games" for the first time. Shanghai hosted two of the seven national games held in modern China. At the 1st, 4th, 5th and 6th national games, Shanghai's competition performance ranked first in the country.

The rise of Chinese sports associations, the promotion of sports major education, the gathering of sports talents and the development of sports economy were also the

↑ 上海精武体育会的会员正在练习拳术

中国共有体育专门学校30余所，上海就有18所，占据半壁江山。近代上海培养了马约翰、凌希陶、周家骐等优秀运动员和著名体育活动家；引进了梁扶初、余衡之、林宝华等海内外体育精英；汇聚了霍元甲、吴鉴泉、陈子正等国术高手。于此同时，体育用品的生产销售，体育场馆的建造经营，体育书刊的出版发行，使上海出现了体育产业的现代雏形。近代上海大型体育场馆达30多个，出版的体育报刊40多种、体育书籍600余种。

symbols of the prosperity of modern sports in Shanghai. The "China National Amateur Athletic Federation", founded in Shanghai in 1924, was actually an organization of "National Olympic Committee" in China. At that time, Shanghai China Football Joint Association, Basketball Joint Association, Tennis Joint Association, Baseball Joint Association, Volleyball Joint Association and other five individual sports organizations, as well as the Shanghai China Sports Referee Association all had national influences. In modern China, 18 of China's more than 30 specialized sports schools were in Shanghai, accounting for half of the total. In modern times, Shanghai appeared lots of excellent athletes and famous sports activists, for example, MA Yuehan, LING Xitao and ZHOU Jiaqi had introduced LIANG Fuchu, YU Hengzhi, LIN Baohua and other sports elites at home and abroad, and gathered HUO Yuanjia, WU Jianquan, CHEN Zizheng and other masters of Chinese martial arts. At the same time, the production and sales of sports supplies, the construction and operation of sports stadiums and the publication and distribution of sports books and periodicals gave rise to the modern prototype of the sports industry in Shanghai. In modern times, there were more than 30 large stadiums in Shanghai, with more than 40 sports newspapers and magazines and over 600 varieties of sports books.

Shanghai's modern sports is the product of modern Shanghai's politics, economy, culture, education and social environment. The opening of the port and the formation of typical immigrant city forced by the great powers had promoted the sports exchanges between the East and the West, and made Shanghai a gathering place for various competitive sports talents. The formation and prosperity of the national economic center provided the economic foundation for the development of Shanghai's modern sports. The earlier development of new education in Shanghai promoted the popularization and spread of modern sports. The formation of the national cultural center and the open news media made Shanghai become the main place where Western modern sports were introduced into China and then spread to the whole country.

Shanghai's modern sports has shortened the distance between Chinese sports and world sports and promoted the revival of Chinese traditional sports culture. Today,

近代上海体育，是近代上海政治、经济、文化、教育和社会环境的产物。强权下的对外开埠、典型移民城市的形成，促进了东西方体育交流，也使上海成为各路竞技体育人才的汇聚地。全国经济中心的形成、繁荣的工商业文明，为近代上海体育的发展提供了经济基础。上海新式教育的率先开展，使近代体育得到普及和传播。全国文化中心的形成、开放的新闻媒介，使上海成为西方近代体育传入中国的主要扩散地，继而辐射全国。

上海近代体育缩短了我国体育与世界体育之间的距离，促进了中国传统体育文化的复兴。今天，上海现代体育正面临新的发展机遇。在实现"国际体育知名城市"目标的进程中，上海近代体育走过的路或许能为我们提供一些有益的借鉴。

2015 年 8 月

Shanghai's modern sports is facing new development opportunities. In the process of realizing the goal of "famous international sports city", the history of Shanghai's modern sports may provide us some useful references.

August 2015

老上海的路名

　　路名,是城市历史文化的标识。近代以来上海路名的发展演绎,是上海城市变迁的佐证。

　　19世纪40年代前的上海,道路没有管理机构和命名法则,路名都是根据当地习惯叫起来的。如附近有教堂就叫"教堂路",有庙就叫"庙街"。老城厢的道路大多使用"街"、"巷"、"弄"等。上海开埠后,随着租界的不断扩张,道路建设迅速发展,取路名摆到了当局的议事日程。1846年英租界成立了"道路码头委员会",曾给租界内的道路取名。19世纪60年代后,租界当局对租界内的路名作了调整和重新取名。在英租界内,通常以中国行政省名命名南北向道路,以中国城市名命名东西向道路。如南北向的四川路、江西路、河南路、山东路等,东西向的南京路、九江路、汉口路、福州路等,这些路名一直沿用至今。美租界内的路一般以上海周边城镇命名。至今仍在使用的有吴淞路、昆山路、乍浦路、南浔路等。法租界的路开始以中国的山川命名,后改用殖民主义者心目中的杰出人物命名,如辣斐德路(今复兴中路)、霞飞路(今淮海中路)、福熙路(今延安中路)等。此外,租界内的路也有以天主教的主教和神父、基督教的教士名字命名的,有以外国驻华公使和驻沪总领事名字命

Road Names of Old Shanghai

Road names are symbols of the city's history and culture. The development of Shanghai's road names since modern times are the evidences of Shanghai's urban changes.

In Shanghai before the 1840s, there were no administrative organizations or nomenclature rules, and road names were called according to local customs. For example, if there was a church nearby, the road would be named "Church Road"; and if there was a temple nearby, the road would be named "Temple Road". Most of the roads in the old downtown areas were called "street", "lane" or "alley", etc. After the opening of Shanghai port, with the continuous expansion of the concession, road construction developed rapidly so that naming the roads was put on the agenda by the authorities. In 1846, the "Road and Wharf Committee" was founded by the British concession, which was responsible for naming the roads in the concession. After the 1860s, the concession authorities adjusted and renamed the road names within the concession. Within the British Concession, the north-south extending roads were usually named after the Chinese administrative province, and the east-west extending roads were named after the Chinese city. For example, the south-north extending Sichuan Road, Jiangxi Road, Henan Road, Shandong Road and so on, the east-west extending Nanjing Road, Jiujiang Road, Hankou Road, Fuzhou Road and so on, have been used up to now. The roads in the American Concession were generally named after the towns around Shanghai. Wusong Road, Kunshan Road, Zhapu Road, Nanxun Road and so on are still in use. The roads in the French Concession were first named after the mountains and rivers in China, and later were named after the prominent figures in the hearts of the colonialists, such as Route Lafayette (now Middle Fuxing Road), Avenue Joffre (now

名的，还有以工部局和公董局总董名字命名等。而华界的路名，尤其是郊区，基本保留了江南水乡特色，一般以"泾"、"浦"、"塘"、"浜"、"行"等命名。如新泾路、彭浦路、蒲江塘路、肇家浜路、闵行路等。上世纪30年代，为发展华界，在五角场一带以"国"、"政"、"民"字打头，命名了一批路名。如国定路、国权路、政本路、政通路、民京路、民庆路等。从上海开埠到20世纪40年代初的百年间，上海共有400多条马路命名、更名。这是近代以来上海路名的第一次重大变更。

太平洋战争爆发后，上海租界被日军占领。1943年，汪伪政权

← 光启路

Middle Huaihai Road), Avenue Foch (now Middle Yan'An Road), etc. In addition, the roads within the concession were also named after Catholic bishops and priests, Christian priests, foreign ministers in China and consul-generals in Shanghai, as well as general members of the ministry of industry and the general board of trustees, etc. The road names in Chinese downtown of Shanghai, especially the suburbs, retained the characteristics of Jiangnan watertown, which were generally named "jing", "pu", "tang", "bang", "xing" etc., such as Xinjing Road, Pengpu Road, Pujiangtang Road, Zhaojiabang Road, Minhang Road, etc. In the 1930s, in order to develop the Chinese community, a number of road names in Chinese downtown of Shanghai were named after the characters of "guo", "zheng" and "min", such as Guoding Road, Guoquan Road, Zhengben Road, Zhengtong Road, Minjing Road, Minqing Road and so on. From the opening of Shanghai port to the beginning of the 1940s, more than 400 roads in Shanghai were named and renamed. This was the first major change for the road names of Shanghai in modern times.

After the outbreak of the Pacific War, Shanghai concessionswereoccupied by Japanese troops. In 1943, in order to get rid of the reputation of the traitors and try to win the popular support, Wang Puppet Regime banned more than 200 roads named after Western people and regions, and then these roads were renamed after Chinese provinces, cities and some county-level administrative regions. For example, Route Ferguson in the center of the French Concession was renamed Wukang Road. Therefore, the second large-scale change of road names in Shanghai since modern times had emerged. After the victory of the Anti-Japanese War in 1945, when the Kuomintang government took over Shanghai, it basically acknowledged that Wang Puppet Regime changed the road names in the concession, but changed some of the road names and used "fuxing", "jianguo", "zhognzheng" and so on as the road names. This had been the third change of the road names in Shanghai road since modern times.

After the founding of the People's Republic of China, Shanghai's urban construction entered a new stage of development, and some road names with the color of colonization, feudalism and rule were replaced by memorable ones. For Example, Route

为了摆脱汉奸的骂名，争取民心，将租界内 200 多条以西方人名、地名命名的马路，全部改成以中国各省、市及部分县级行政区域名命名。如把当时法租界的中心福开森路更名为武康路等，形成了近代以来上海第二次大规模的更改路名。1945 年抗战胜利，国民党政府接管上海后，基本承认汪伪政权对租界路名的更改，但对其中一部分路名作了变动，把复兴、建国、中正等用以路名。这是近代以来上海路名的第三次变更。

新中国成立后，上海城市建设进入全新的发展阶段，一些带有殖民、封建和统治色彩的路名被具有纪念意义的路名替代。如兴国路替代了雷上达路，瑞金路替代了中正南路，淮海路替代了林森路等。而新修筑的道路路名则基本沿用了传统做法，以不重复为原则，将全国各地行政区划名称用作道路名称，其中名城、圣地、胜地首选。同时，将上海道路位置与全国相关省市位置相对应。如沪北的闸北区、虹口区北部，多见华北地名；沪东北的杨浦区，常见东北地名；沪西北的普陀区，频现西北地名；处于上海东部的浦东，则以东入黄海的山东省地名命名。在中国各大城市中，上海是运用地名命名道路最多的城市。改革开放后，上海的道路建设突飞猛进。一些新建新辟的道路名更具时代特色和国际化，如世纪大道、五洲大道、美盛路、英伦路等。

如果城市是一部书，路名就是书的索引。近代以来上海的地理变迁、政治事件、经济发展、文化传承，都深深印记在这座城市的大街小巷里。上海的许多道路历史上几易其名。如现在的延安东路开始叫"爱多亚路"，1943 年改为"大上海路"，1945 年又改为"中

↑ 20世纪30年代的百老汇路
（今大名路）

Remi was replaced by Xingguo Road; South Chungcheng Road was replaced by Ruijin Road and Linsen Road was replaced by Huaihai Road, etc. However, the new road names basically followed the traditional practice. On the principle of non-repetition, the administrative division names throughout the country were used as the road names, among which famous cities, holy places and tourist attractions were the first choice. Meanwhile, the location of roads in Shanghai were corresponding to the location of the provinces and cities in the country. For example, the road names in Zhabei District of north Shanghai and in the north of Hongkou District mainly use the place names in North China; the road names in Yangpu District of northeast Shanghai mainly use the place names in Northeast China; roads names in Putuo Distric of northwest Shanghai mainly use the place names in Northwest China; road names in Pudong of east Shanghai mainly use the place names in Shandong Province. Among China's big cities, Shanghai was the city that has used the most place names for road names. After the reform and opening-up, the road construction in Shanghai has made great progress. Some new road names are more characteristic and international, such as Century Avenue, Wuzhou Avenue, Meisheng Road, Yinglun Road, etc.

If a city is a book, the road name is the index. Shanghai's geographical changes,

正东路",解放后才改用现名。路名,可以牵出许许多多往事如烟、柔肠百转的故事。路名后面,其实隐藏着整整一部城市的发展史。

路名是城市历史文化的记忆。上海数以几千计的路名,承载着这座城市的屈辱与抗争,建设与发展,光荣与梦想。把路名文化作为城市发展史研究的重要内容,使路名成为一部生动的城市历史文化教科书,增强人们对这座城市的自豪感和责任感,应是有关方面当下要做的一件事情。

2015 年 11 月

political events, economic development and cultural inheritance since modern times are deeply imprinted in the streets and alleys of this city. Many of Shanghai's roads have changed their names for several times in history. For example, today's East Yan'an Road was named "Avenue Eduard", then renamed "Great Shanghai Road" in 1943 and "East Chungcheng Road" in 1945; after the liberation of Shanghai, it was renamed East Yan'an Road. Road names contained various stories and history. The road names actually imply the whole development history of the city.

Road names are the memory of the city's history and culture. Thousands of road names of Shanghai have carried the city's humiliation and struggle, construction and development, glory and dreams. It has been an urgent task to take the road name culture as an important content for the study on urban development history, thus making the road names become a vivid textbook of urban history and culture and strengthening people's sense of pride and responsibility for this city.

November 2015

老上海的中医

上海是我国近代中医医学的中心。清末民初，上海出现了名医荟萃、流派纷华、学术争鸣、中西汇通的繁荣景象。"中医史，元之前看北方，元之后看江南，近代看上海。"学界的这一评价，足以说明近代上海在我国中医史上的地位。

早在元明清时期，伴随着上海地区农业、贸易和工商业的发展，就出现过大批医家。著名的有青浦何氏世医、龙华张氏世医、江湾徐氏世医和蔡氏世医、浦东顾氏世医等。据资料记载，上海本土传承三代以上的中医各科流派不下数十家。上海开埠后，随着城市建设的快速发展，加之租界的特殊政治地位，上海成为移民城市。全国各地的医家纷纷移居上海发展，如江苏孟河的费氏、巢氏、丁氏三大家，新安的王仲奇，川中的祝味菊、江阴的曹颖甫、宁波的吴涵秋，以及无锡石氏、山东魏氏、河北王氏等。在当时西方医学冲击，疾病谱不断变化的情况下，外来与本土的医家包容进取、承古融今、勇于创新，使上海出现了我国近代第一个中医药团体、第一张中医药报纸、第一所中医学校、第一部中医大辞典和中药大辞典等许多中医史上的第一，引领了当时中医发展的潮流。

近代上海中医教育鼎盛。自1904年李平书、张竹君等开办上海

Traditional Chinese Medicine of Old Shanghai

Shanghai has been the center of Traditional Chinese Medicine (TCM) in modern China. During the late Qing Dynasty and the early Republic of China, Shanghai appeared a flourishing scene, where the famous physicians gathered and there were various medical schoolsand the integration of Chinese and Western medical science. "In terms of the history of TCM, it flourished in north of China before the Yuan Dynasty and flourished in Jiangnan after the Yuan Dynasty. For modern TCM, it flourished in Shanghai." This evaluation in the academic world has well demonstrated the status of modern Shanghai in the history of TCM.

As early as the Yuan, Ming and Qing Dynasties, along with the development of agriculture, trade and industry and commerce in Shanghai, a large number of physicians appeared. Reputedones included physicians of HE Family in Qingpu, physicians of ZHANG Family in Longhua, physicians of XU Family and CAI Family in Jiangwan, physicians of GU Family in Pudong and so on. According to the data record, there were more than a dozen of TCM schools that had been inherited for three generations. After the opening of Shanghai port, due to the rapid development of urban construction and the special political status of concessions, Shanghai became a city of immigrants. Physicians from all over the country moved to Shanghai for development, such as the three major families from Menghe of Jiangsu — FEI Family, CHAO Family and DING Family, WANG Zhongqi form Xinan, ZHU Weiju form middle Sichuan, CAO Yingpu from Jiangyin, WU Hanqiu from Ningbo, SHI Family from Wuxi, WEI Family from Shandong and WANG Family form Hebei, etc. Under the impact of the Western medicine and the situation of constantly changing of spectrum of diseases, the foreign and local physicians joined hand, integrated TCM into modern medicine and made innovations,

第一所中医学校—女子中西医学堂始到解放前，上海开办的各类中医教育机构 40 多家，是近代中国开办中医教育持续时间最长、规模最大、办学形式最广、培养人才最多的。著名的有 1918 年由丁甘仁创办的上海中医学院，1927 年由秦伯未创办的上海中国医学院，1935 年由朱南山创办的新中国医学院等。据不完全统计，这些中医教育机构共培养各类中医药人才 5000 余人，为上海乃至全国输送了可贵的中医力量。

↖ 老上海的中医　贺竹元绘

thus establishing the first TCM group, the first TCM newspaper, the first TCM school, the first TCM dictionary, the first Chinese material medical dictionary and many other first places in the history of TCM, which led the trend of TCM development at that time.

The education of TCM was flourishing in modern Shanghai. From 1904 when LI Pingshu, ZHANG Zhujun and other people opened Shanghai's first TCM school — Women's Chinese and Western Medicine School to the year of liberation, Shanghai has more than 40 TCM education institutions, with the longest duration, the largest scale, the widest form of education and the largest number of talents. The renowned ones included Shanghai TCM College founded by DING Ganren in 1918, China Medical College of Shanghai founded by QIN Bowei in 1927 and New China Medical College founded by ZHU Nanshan in 1935, etc. According to incomplete statistics, these TCM education institutions have cultivated over 5,000 TCM talents, providing valuable TCM strength for Shanghai and even the whole country.

In face of the major impact of Western medicine and the policies of the ruling authorities to suppress TCM, the TCM community in Shanghai set up TCM groups to protect and consolidate the position of TCM. Founded in 1903, Shanghai Medical Association was the first Chinese medical group in modern times. In the 1920s and 1930s, there were dozens of TCM groups in Shanghai, among which there were 8 national TCM groups headquartered in Shanghai, such as the China Pharmaceutical Federation, General Medical Association of China and Chinese Medical Association, etc. In addition, private TCM groups, such as "Huchun", "Mingshe", "Heshe", "Jishe" and "Jingshe" were established in Shanghai, aiming to "conduct academic study on TCM and enter into friendship with physicians in the field of TCM". These groups played the leading and pivotal role in the struggle for rights of TCM in modern China. In 1929, the national government issued the "Abolishment of Chinese Traditional Medicine". More than 240 TCM groups from across the country rallied in Shanghai, sparking a wave of anti-abolition protest, thus stopping the government to back down. After the outbreak of the Anti-Japanese War, the TCM communities in Shanghai quickly established an anti-Japanese and national salvation group to fulfill the duty of the Chinese people and the instinct of physicians.

面对西方医学的重大冲击，以及执政当局压制中医中药的政策，上海中医界为了保护和巩固中医的地位，纷纷成立中医药团体。创办于1903年的上海医会是我国近代第一个中医团体。上世纪20至30年代，上海各类中医药团体数十个，其中总部设在上海的全国性中医药团体如中华医药联合会、神州医药总会、中国医学会等就有8个。另外，"壶春""鸣社""鹤社""济社""经社"等以"研究中医学术，联络同门情谊"为宗旨的中医私人团体也在沪成立。这些团体在近代我国中医争取权利的多次抗争中，发挥了组织领导和中流砥柱的作用。1929年国民政府出台"废止中医案"，上海中医界团结全国240多个中医团体集会上海，掀起了一场声势浩大的反废止风潮，迫使政府让步。抗战爆发后，上海中医药界迅速成立抗日救亡团体，尽国民天职、医师本能，救亡图存。

我国新型中医医疗机构也发端于上海。1904年创办的上海医院是近代中国最早的中医院。1906年宁波同乡会创办的四明医院一直延续至今，是今曙光医院的前身。民国时期，上海先后出现近50家中医院。这些医院多为沪上名医发起或出资创办，其中既有综合性医院，也有专科医院。许多医院如广益中医院、华隆中医院、谦益伤科医院等施诊与慈善并重，施医给药、救护伤残，对特别贫困的病人，住院实行免费，深受广大市民的欢迎。

上海也是我国近代中医药报刊和书籍的出版发行中心。为了交流学术经验，吸取西方医药的有益成分，普及医药知识，中医界人士创办中医药报刊，出版各类中医药书籍。我国第一张中医报纸《医学报》诞生在上海。民国时期上海出版的与中医药有关的报刊近

China's new TCM institutions also originated in Shanghai. Shanghai Hospital, founded in 1904, was the earliest TCM hospital in modern China. The Siming Hospital, founded by Ningbo Townsmen Association in 1906, has existed until now and is the predecessor of today's Shuguang Hospital. During the period of the Republic of China, nearly 50 hospitals were established in Shanghai. These hospitals were mostly initiated or funded by famous physicians in Shanghai, among which there were general hospitals as well as specialized hospitals. Many hospitals, such as Guangyi Hospital of Traditional Chinese Medicine, Hualong Hospital of Traditional Chinese Medicine and Qianyi Hospital of Traumatology, emphasized both treatment and charity and provided free hospitalization

→ 上海中医学院校门

170 种。商务印书馆、世界书局、中华书局等上海著名书局出版了大量中医书籍，仅千顷堂一家书局就先后出版中医书籍 17 类 500 余种。这些报刊书籍发行全国，远销欧美和东南亚，提升了上海中医的名望，扩大了中华医药的影响力。

近代上海在中成药制作和销售方面也处全国领先地位。上世纪 30 年代，全市有新亚、信宜等大型民族药厂 60 多家，医疗器械厂 20 多家，中药店铺 700 多家，药材批发商 600 多家，参店 100 多家，有"沪市药铺林立"之说。蔡同德堂、胡庆余堂、童涵春堂、雷允上药业等中药老字号在上海百年不衰，经营至今。

今天，中医药正处在重要的发展转型期。传承弘扬老上海中医适应时代、包容进取、勇于创新、自我发展的精神，对于提升中医学术水平，提高中医临床诊疗能力，促进中医药的现代化、国际化进程不无意义。

2016 年 3 月

for especially poor patients, thus receiving wide acclaim from the general public.

Shanghai is also the publishing and distribution center of modern Chinese medical newspapers, periodicals and books. In order to exchange academic experience, absorb the beneficial ingredients of Western medicine and popularize medical knowledge, TCM practitioners established TCM newspapers and periodicals and published various TCM books. China's first TCM newspaper *Monthly of Medicine* was initiated in Shanghai. During the Republic of China, Shanghai published nearly 170 kinds of newspapers related to TCM. The Commercial Press, World Book Company, Zhonghua Book Company and many other famous book companies published a large number of TCM books, among which only Qianqingtang Publishing House published more than 17 categories of 500 kinds of TCM books. These newspapers and books were distributed throughout the country and exported to Europe, America and Southeast Asia, which enhanced the reputation of Shanghai's TCM and expanded the influence of China's TCM.

Modern Shanghai also took the leading position in China in the aspect of production and sales of Chinese traditional patent medicine. In the 1930s, there were more than 60 large-scale national pharmaceutical factories including Xinya and Xinyi, etc., and 20-odd medical apparatus factories, 700-plus TCM stores, over 600 pharmaceutical wholesalers and more than 100 ginseng stores in the whole city, known as "herbal medicine stores everywhere in Shanghai". The time-honored TCM brands such as Caitongde Pharmacy, Huyuqing Pharmacy, Tonghanchun Pharmacy and Leiyunshang Pharmacy have existed in Shanghai for more than one hundred years and still opened as usual up to now.

Today, TCM is undergoing an important development transition period. Inheriting and carrying forward the spirit of "adapting to the times, being inclusive and enterprising, daring to innovate and maintaining self-development" of old Shanghai's TCM is of great significance for improving the academic level of TCM, improving the ability of clinical diagnosis and treatment of TCM and promoting the modernization and internationalization of TCM.

March 2016

老上海的公园

公园是城市发展到具有一定文明程度和承载能力时的产物。在近代中国整个城市公园发展史上,上海是最为重要的城市。老上海城市公园的变迁,某种程度上代表了近代中国城市公园的发展。

上海开埠后,在上海的西方人为满足自己的生活需要,把西方的公园文化带到了上海,开始在上海建造公园。1868 年(清同治七年)建成的英美租界公共花园(今黄浦公园),是上海也是中国的第一座城市公园。此后租界当局先后在上海辟建各类公园,其中包括休闲公园、体育公园、儿童公园等 20 多座。今天的中山公园(时称积司非而公园)、复兴公园(时称顾家宅公园)、鲁迅公园(时称虹口公园)、襄阳公园(时称兰维纳公园)等都是富有特色的租界公园。租界公园纯粹是为外国人服务的,拒华人于园门外长达半个多世纪。公共花园当时甚至规定"华人与狗不得入内",激起了中国人民极大愤慨。经过 60 多年坚持不懈的斗争,上世纪 20 年代,租界公园才被迫向中国人开放。租界公园的兴建,当时虽然对中国人民是一种精神戕害,但客观上使上海近代城市公园建设进入最初阶段。

1882 年,受租界公园的影响,上海一些开明商人以股份公司的形式集资建造了兼具公园、游乐场、餐饮等多种功能的申园。申园

Parks of Old Shanghai

Park is the product of the city's developing to a certain degree of civilization and bearing capacity. Shanghai is the most important city in the whole development history of urban parks in modern China. The changes of old Shanghai's parks, to a certain extent, represent the development of urban parks in modern China.

After the opening of Shanghai port, the Westerners in Shanghai introduced the Western park culture into Shanghai for meeting their living needs and began to build parks in Shanghai. The public park of the American and British Concessions (now Huangpu Park) founded in 1868 (the 7th year of Tongzhi's reign in the Qing Dynasty) was the first urban park in Shanghai and China. Since then, the authorities of the concession had established more than 20 various parks in Shanghai, including the leisure park, the sports park and the children's park and so on. Jessfield Park (now Zhongshan Park), GU Family Park (now Fuxing Park), Hongkou Park (now Luxun Park), Lanvina Park (now Xiangyang Park) were the most distinctive parks in the concession at that time. The parks in the concession were only open to the foreigners, and had been closed to Chinese for more than half a century. At that time, the public parks even stipulated that "Chinese people and dogs are not allowed to enter", which aroused Chinese people's great indignation. After more than 60 years of unremitting struggle, the parks in the concession were forced to be open to the Chinese in the 1920s. Although the construction of the parks in the concession was a kind of spiritual persecution to the Chinese people at that time, it objectively brought the construction of modern urban parks in Shanghai into its initial stage.

In 1882, under the influence of the parks in the concession, some enlightened

开放不久即门庭若市，获利丰厚，于是群相效仿。此后，张园、徐园、愚园、大花园、西园等纷纷建成开张，使上海城市公园建设进入"营业性私园"的鼎盛时期。这些私人集资修建的园林花木扶疏，山水相映，楼堂耸立，游乐餐饮设施及服务都达到了当时的最高水平。营业性私园面向大众开放，不分种族、性别、地域和职业，人人皆可入内，使中国人终于有了自己建造的"公园"。

民国时期，随着上海华界统一、行政区域逐渐扩大和近代市政

↖ 上海最早的外滩公园

businessmen raised money in the form of joint-stock companies and built Shenyuan Park with a collection of various functions such as garden, amusement park and catering, etc. Shortly after its opening, Shenyuan Park attracted a lot of visitors and gained lucrative profits, thus making many people follow suit. Since then, many parks such as Zhangyuan Park, Xuyuan Park, Yuyuan Park, Great Garden and West Park were established and open to the public one after another, bringing the construction of urban parks in Shanghai into the heyday of "private commercial parks". These private parks exhibited the highest levelin the aspects of landscape engineering, architectural design, entertainment and catering facilities, as well as services, etc. The private commercial parks were open to the public, regardless of race, gender, region and occupation, which meant that everyone could enter the parks, marking that the Chinese finally had their own "park".

During the period of the Republic of China, with the unification of Chinese downtown of Shanghai, the gradual expansion of administrative regions and the initial establishment of modern municipal management system, the construction of municipal parks in Chinese downtown of Shanghai, under the government's auspices, entered the high-speed development period. Dozens of parks with diverse styles and functions had been built and open to the public, including Shanghai Municipal Garden Landscape Park, Shanghai First Park, Shanghai Municipal Public-School Park, Shanghai Municipal Zoo and Shanghai Municipal Botanical Garden, etc. At the same time, a group of squires and wealthy businessmen, influenced by the modern garden consciousness, also invested in the construction of parks and opened them to the public for free, such as Jungong Road Memorial Park, Gaoqiao Park, Zhongshanlin Park and so on. In 1929, the *Opinions on the Opening and Construction of Downtown Areas in Shanghai* was approved by Municipal Joint Conference of Shanghai Special City, which incorporated the allocation of open spaces, such as parks into the construction plan of the downtown area. It was the earliest embodiment of world urban park system thought in China, and had important historical value in modern urban planning and garden development in China. Meanwhile, Shanghai's public greening activities and the development of park, flower and wood industry also entered a new stage. The national government designated the anniversary of

管理制度的开始建立，上海华界市政公园建设在政府的主持下进入高速发展期。上海市立园林场风景园、上海市立第一公园、上海市立公共学校园、上海市立动物园、上海市立植物园等数十座风格多样、功能多元的公园先后建成开放。同时，一批乡绅、富商受近代园林意识的影响也纷纷出资修建公园，免费向公众开放。如军工路纪念公园、高桥公园、中山林公园等。1929年上海特别市市政联席会议通过的《关于开辟和建设上海市市中心区域的意见》中，将园林等空地的配置纳入到了市中心区域建设规划中。这是世界城市公园系统思想在中国的最早体现，在中国近代城市规划和园林发展史上具有重要的历史价值。与此同时，上海群众绿化活动和园林花木业的发展也进入一个新的阶段。国民政府确定每年孙中山逝世纪念日（3月12日）为植树节。上海市政府举行的第一届植树仪式，市长和各界代表2000多人参加。市政府规定植树节前后一周为"造林宣传周"。在日军侵占上海前，历年均举行此类仪式和活动。

老上海的公园不但继承与拓展了传统园林文化，而且有益吸收了西方近代园林文化，造园风格呈现中西合璧的海派特征。租界公园整体风格主要为西式，但也融入了中国风味，如中山公园、复兴公园内多有中国园。营业性私园以中式传统风格为主，同时也运用了西方园林要素。民国后所建的市政公园，进一步吸纳融合了西方园林的特点，大都为西方规则式、自然风景园和中国传统园林的综合体。

"八·一三事变"后，上海市政府辖区公园及私有园林大多被毁，租界公园部分受损。上海市政公园绿地建设遭到毁灭性破坏，

Sun Yat-Sen's death (March 12) as Tree-Planting Day every year. More than 2,000 people from all walks of life including the mayor attended the ceremony of the first Tree-Planting Day held by the Shanghai Municipal Government. The municipal government stipulated that the weeks before and after the Tree-Planting Day were the "forestation publicity weeks". Before the Japanese invasion into Shanghai, such ceremonies and activities were held every year.

The parks in old Shanghai not only inherited and expanded the traditional garden culture, but also absorbed the Western modern garden culture, thus having formed the Shanghai-style features in the integration of the Chinese and Western culture. The overall style of parks in the concession was mainly Western style, but it was also infused with Chinese style, for example, Zhongshan Park and Fuxing Park and so on were mostly Chinese gardens. The private commercial parks focused on traditional Chinese styles and also adopted the Western garden elements. The municipal parks built after the Republic of China further incorporated the characteristics of Western gardens, most of which were a combination of Western landscape architecture, natural sceneries and traditional Chinese gardens.

After the "August 13th Incident", most of the parks and private gardens under the jurisdiction of the Shanghai Municipal Government were destroyed, while some of the parks in the concession were damaged. The construction of Shanghai municipal parks and green space was destroyed and underwent decline. By 1949, there were only more than 10 well-preserved parks in the outskirts of Shanghai.

After the liberation of Shanghai, the landscape architecture of Shanghai ushered in a new spring. By the late 1950s and early 1960s, more than 50 parks had been built, rebuilt and restored in Shanghai. During the Cultural Revolution, the landscape architecture of Shanghai was seriously damaged. The reform and opening-up have brought new life to Shanghai's parks. Since the 1990s, Shanghai had seen extraordinary development in the construction of park and greenbelt. At present, there are nearly 200 parks in Shanghai, and the urban forest coverage rate reaches 15%. The general public can enjoy more public rest and recreation places and wider green space.

进入衰落期。至 1949 年，上海市郊保留比较完好的公园只有 10 多座。

上海解放后，上海城市园林绿地建设迎来了新的春天。至上世纪 50 年代末 60 年代初，上海新建、改建和修复的公园增至 50 多座。"文革"中，上海园林绿化建设遭到严重破坏。改革开放使上海园林得到新生。上世纪 90 年代后，上海的公园绿地建设得到超常规发展。目前上海已有各类公园近 200 座，城市森林覆盖率达到 15%。广大市民有了更多的休闲娱乐场所和更广阔的绿色空间。

回顾上海公园的历史变迁，对于我们全面了解上海城市发展的历史，珍视今天的城市生态，进一步拓展城市公园绿地的建设不无意义。

2016 年 7 月

Reviewing the historical changes of Shanghai's parks is of great significance for us to fully understand the history of Shanghai's urban development, cherish the urban ecology today, and further expand the construction of urban park and greenbelt.

July 2016

老上海的城厢

老上海的城厢即上海老城厢，它是今天上海城市形成的基础和策源地。

晚清以来，人们对上海县治所习惯称之为上海老城厢（城，指县城；厢，指县城附近的地区）。上海老城厢是与上海租界新城区相对而言的。其区域范围，包括明嘉靖年间在上海南市修筑、1912年拆除的周长九华里城墙以内的行政区和商务区，以及东门、南门外沿黄浦江一带的商业码头区。

公元1292年，元政府设立上海县。明代以后，政府鼓励种植棉花。上海因发达的棉花种植业、纺织手工业，以及便利的水上交通，县城商业开始繁荣，街巷逐渐增多。至嘉庆二十一年（1816年），上海县城有街巷60多条，人口10余万，并成为北洋、南洋、长江、内河、外洋五条航线交汇的港口城市。至上海开埠前，上海城厢内已有沙船业、土布业、豆饼业、米业、酒业、纸业、药业、茶业、丝绸业、钱庄业、铜锡业、煤炭业、典当业、染坊业等各类行业数十个，行业性公馆会所20多个。十六铺地区一带，形成了咸瓜街、豆市街、花衣街、会馆街等专业街市。陆家石桥、红栏杆桥、松雪街等处，成为城厢内的商业闹市。上海当时享有"江海通津，东南

Urban Area of Old Shanghai

The urban area of old Shanghai, namely, Shanghai Old City Area, is the foundation and source for the formation of Shanghai Municipality today.

Since the late Qing Dynasty, people had used to call Shanghai County as "Shanghai Old City Area" ("city" refers to county; "area" refers to the surrounding area of the county). Shanghai Old City Area was corresponding to the new city area of Shanghai concessions. It covered the administrative and business districts within the nine-li-perimeter city wall built in Nanshi of Shanghai during the reign of Emperor Jiajing in the Ming Dynasty and demolished in 1912, as well as the commercial port area along the Huangpu River at the East Gate and South Gate.

In 1292 A. D., the Yuan Government established Shanghai County. After the Ming Dynasty, the government encouraged the planting of cotton. Due to the advanced cotton planting industry, textile handicraft industry, as well as convenient water transportation, business in Shanghai began to flourish with the gradual increase of streets and lanes. By the 21st year of Emperor Jiaqing's reign in the Ming Dynasty (1816), there were more than 60 streets and lanes in Shanghai County with a population of more than 100, 000 people. And it had become a port city where five ship routes of Beiyang, Nanyang, Yangtze River, inland waterway and foreign waterway. Before the opening of Shanghai port, there were dozens of various industries such as largejunk industry, native cloth industry, soybean cake industry, rice industry, wine industry, paper industry, pharmaceutical industry, tea industry, silk industry, money-shop industry, copper and tin industry, coal industry, pawnbroking industry, dyeing industry and other industries, as well as more than 20 industry associations and clubs in Shanghai Old City Area. Lujiashi Bridge,

城厢内百业兴旺

都会"的美誉。

上海开埠后,受小刀会起义、太平天国战争的影响,老城厢的商业遭到重大打击。小东门至大东门一带的街市被清军烧毁。但随着中外贸易的兴起,以及战争期间各地人口向上海的大量聚集,战后老城厢的商业很快得到恢复,有些行业甚至比战前更盛。当时,上海重要的货物码头、钱庄、零售商店和有经验的南北货、洋货商人仍然集中在老城厢。中外商人采购丝、茶、瓷器、鸦片、棉布等都在县城里成交。许多商务、报关事宜也需在县衙中办理。因此,开埠之初十余年间,老城厢仍是上海的经济中心。

1870年代后,世界资本主义空前发展,欧美各主要资本主义国家相继完成了工业革命,极大冲击了中国的自然经济。老城厢与租

Honglangan Bridge, Songxue Street and other places had been the commercialdowntown in Shanghai Old City Area. At that time, Shanghai enjoyed the reputation of "having shipping routes connecting Tianjin, and being the metropolis of southeast China".

After the opening of Shanghai port, influenced by the Small Swords Society Uprising and the War of Taiping Heavenly Kingdom, the business in Shanghai Old City Area suffered a major blow. The markets along the Small East Gate and Large East Gate were burnt down by the troops of the Qing Dynasty. But with the rise of Sino-foreign trade and the mass migration of people to Shanghai during the war, the business in Shanghai Old City Area quickly recovered, and some industries were even more prosperous than before the war. At that time, Shanghai's important cargo wharfs, money shops, retail stores and experienced north-south and foreign businessmen still concentrated in Shanghai Old City Area. Chinese and foreign merchants purchased silk, tea, porcelain, opium, cotton, etc. in the county town. Many business and customs clearance affairs also needed to be handled in the county government. Therefore, in the early ten years of the opening of Shanghai port, the old city area was still the economic center of Shanghai.

After the 1870s, world capitalism developed unprecedentedly, and the major capitalist countries in Europe and America successively completed the industrial revolution, which greatly impacted China's natural economy. The gap between Shanghai Old City Area and Shanghai concessions began to widen. In the urban economy of Shanghai Old City Area, largejunk industry occupied a very important position, known as "Largejunk is the fundamental in Shanghai market". The boom in the largejunk industry led to the prosperity of the city. It was the portrayal of Shanghai Old City Area that sails and masts stood forest-like, merchants flocked here, various goods were accumulated here, and it was crowded with people and horses. However, with the rise of modern shipping industry, Shanghai's largejunk industry gradually declined. In 1890, foreign ships accounted for 86.9 percent of the ships in Shanghai port. By the end of the 19th century, there were less than 50 largejunks in Shanghai, and foreign ships had defeated Chinese civilian ships. At the same time, increasing dumping of foreign cloth made the market of native cloth smaller and smaller. After the introduction of foreign banks, they

界各方面的差距开始拉大。在老城厢的城市经济中，沙船航运业占据着非常重要的地位，"上海市面以沙船为根本"。沙船业的繁荣带动了城市的繁荣，帆樯林立，万商云集，百货山积，人马喧阗，是当时上海老城厢的写照。但随着近代轮船航运业的兴起，上海的沙船业逐步衰落。1890年，外国轮船占上海港船只86.9%。到19世纪末，上海的沙船已不满50只，外国的轮船击垮了中国的民船。与此同时，洋布的大量倾销，使得土布市场越来越小。外国银行进入上海后，很快取得了经营国际汇兑的垄断地位，还吸收了巨额存款，使居老城厢"百业之枢"地位的钱庄成了外国资本、特别是银行资本的附庸。老城厢沙船业、土布业、钱庄业等主要行业的衰落，以及近代工业和一些新兴行业在租界的兴起，使城市经济中心北移至租界地区，老城厢逐渐丧失了原本的商贸中心地位。时人这样形容：当机器的轰鸣在租界最早响起的时候，除了手摇织布机发生的声音以外，老城厢还是一片沉寂。当拔地而起的大烟囱成为租界的象征以后，老城厢地区除了偶尔的金属撞击的声音外，仍然以商贩的叫卖声为主旋律。

在城市管理上，租界工部局（公董局）成立后，引进越来越多的西方近代城市经营、管理理念，建立了租界社会管理体制，制定了包括交通、卫生、食品安全等一系列租界社会管理规范。同时，租界当局运用近代西方城市建设模式，大规模修建道路、码头、学校、医院、剧场、菜场等市政公共设施。自来水、电灯、电话、电报、有轨电车等西方先进科技成果也纷纷进入租界。租界地区逐渐成为一个与前近代中国城市迥异的、具有浓厚西方近代城市特征的

soon gained the monopoly of operating international exchange and also absorbed a great deal of deposits, making the money shop that occupied the position of "the pivot of all industries" in Shanghai Old City Area become the tributaries of foreign capitals, especially bank capitals. The decline of major industries such as the largejunk industry, native cloth industry and money-shop industry, as well as the rise of modern industry and some emerging industries in the concession, the urban economic center moved to the north of the concession, and Shanghai Old City Area gradually lost its original position as a commercial and trade center. At that time, people gave such evaluation as: when the roar of the machine was first begun in the concession, the old city area was silent except for the sound of hand-looms. When the soaring chimneys became the symbol of the concession, the old city area was still dominated by the vendors' hawking, except for the occasional metal crash.

In terms of city management, after the founding of the Municipal Council of Shanghai Concession (Public Board of Directors), more and more Western modern city

→ 老城厢内的商业街

"飞地"。而老城厢仍然承袭中国传统城市的管理模式,虽然在租界的影响下有一定的发展,但上海的城市中心区域已在租界,老城厢只是租界的附庸。

老上海城厢变迁的历史,是一部外国资本主义削弱、打败中国封建主义的历史。老城厢从一个封建的商业城市变成租界附庸的过程,是中国由封建社会沦为半殖民地半封建社会的一个历史缩影。

今天,上海经济社会空前繁荣发展。上海已成为世界一流的国际化大都市。但老上海城厢的那段历史,是不该忘却的。

2017 年 2 月

operation and management concepts were introduced, the social management system of the concession was established and a series of social regulations including transportation, health and food safety were formulated. At the same time, the concession authorities used the modern Western urban construction mode to build roads, wharfs, schools, hospitals, theaters, vegetable farms and other municipal public facilities on a large scale. Tap water, electric light, telephone, telegraph, tram and other advanced Western scientific and technological achievements were also introduced into the concession. The concession area had gradually become an "enclave" different from the cities in pre-modern China, but with distinctive characteristics of modern Western cities. However, the old city area still inherited the management mode of traditional Chinese city. Although it had certain development under the influence of the concession, the central area of Shanghai had already been located in the concession, and the old city area was just a subsidiary of the concession.

The history of the vicissitude of Shanghai Old City Area is a history of foreign capitalism weakening and defeating Chinese feudalism. The process of the old city area's transformation from a feudal commercial city into a subsidiary of the concession is a historical epitome of China's transformation from a feudal society to a semi-colonial and semi-feudal society.

Today, Shanghai enjoys unprecedented economic and social prosperity and development. Shanghai has become a world-class international metropolis. But the history of Shanghai Old City Area should not be forgotten.

February 2017

老上海的车

城市交通工具的嬗变，是城市发展进步的一个重要标志。近代以来上海城市车的变化，不能不说是上海城市变迁的一个佐证。

上海开埠后，最早出现在上海街头的代步工具是马车。上世纪50、60年代，随着西人在上海开设跑马场，马车作为一种日常交通工具在上海流行起来。当时跑马总会特设带有博彩性质的中国马赛马比赛，于是有许多蒙古马被源源不断地运抵上海。运入上海的蒙古马中，大部分未入选为赛马，入选的每年也有淘汰，这些马便成了马车的驭马。当时上海街头的马车不是中国传统样式的马车，而是充满了西洋的情调。车有单马双轮、双马四轮，车身敞开，遮篷漂亮，车厢分前后两厢，宽大舒适。时人称之为西洋马车。乘马车兜风成为当时上海滩上的一大时尚。1867年，西班牙人帕兰特创办了龙飞马车行。不久，曾在跑马厅当过调马师的名叫陶善钟的上海人开设"善钟车行"。这两家车行控制着当时上海80%以上的马车。陶善钟以后成了上海最大的房地产商之一。今天的常熟路当年叫善钟路，就是以陶善钟的名字命名的。

1873年，法国商人米拉看到上海租界市面日趋繁荣，交通工具不敷运用，便向法租界公董局申请在租界设立手拉小车客运服务机

Vehicle of Old Shanghai

The evolution of urban transportation tools is an important symbol of urban development and progress. The changes of Shanghai's vehicles in modern times is also the evidence of the urban changes of Shanghai.

After the opening of Shanghai port, the earliest vehicle to appear on the streets of Shanghai was the carriage. In the 1950s and 1960s, with the establishment of racecourses in the city by the Westerners, horse-drawn carriages became popular as a daily means of transportation in Shanghai. At that time, Shanghai Race Club launched the horserace gambling in Shanghai so that many Mongolian horses were transported to Shanghai. Most of these Mongolian horses were not selected for horse racing and some of the selected horses may be eliminated every year so that these parts of horses would become the riding horses of horse-drawn carriages. At that time, the carriage in Shanghai was not traditional Chinese carriage, but full of Western styles. The carriage included one horse with two wheels or two horse with four wheels, which was wide and comfortable with open carriage body, beautiful awning and two carriage cents, known as the "Western-style carriage". Taking the carriage for a ride became a big fashion in Shanghai at that time. In 1867, the Spanish B · Pallant founded Shanghai Horse Bagaar. Soon afterwards, TAO Shanzhong, who once acted as horse trainer in Shanghai Race Club, founded Shanzhong Carriage Company in Shanghai. The two companies controlled more than 80 percent of the carriages in Shanghai at the time. Later, TAO Shanzhong became one of the largest real estate developers in Shanghai. Shanzhong Road (now Changshu Road) was once named after him.

In 1873, the French businessman Mira saw that the market of Shanghai concession

构。次年，首批 300 辆黄包车从日本引进，作为营业性载人交通工具在租界正式运营。19 世纪末 20 世纪初，黄包车又逐渐由上海传入中国的其他城市。至抗战前，上海正式发照的黄包车已达 8 万多辆，成为当时人们代步的主要交通工具。黄包车夫一般是生活在社会最底层的穷苦人，他们没钱买车，只好到车行租用。当时上海人力车行数千家，依靠拉车谋生的人力车夫达数万人。黄包车夫与贫穷几乎成了同义词。

　　老上海最早出现的现代公共交通工具是有轨电车。1881 年 7 月，上海英商怡和洋行向法租界公董局正式提议开办电车事业。1907 年 4 月 24 日，公共租界有轨电车工程开工。1908 年 3 月 5

↖ 银色汽车公司

was becoming more and more prosperous but the transportation tool was insufficient, so that he applied to the Public Board of Directors of French Concession and set up a handcart passenger service agency in the concession. In the following year, the first batch of 300 rickshaws was introduced from Japan and officially launched ascommercial manned vehicles in the concession. In the late 19th century and early 20th century, rickshaws were gradually introduced from Shanghai to other cities in China. By the eve of the Anti-Japanese War, more than 80,000 rickshaws had been officially launched in Shanghai, becoming the main means of transportation for people at that time. The rickshaw men were poor people living at the bottom of society. They had no money to buy a rickshaw, so they had to rent a rickshaw. At that time, there were thousands of maned vehicle companies with tens of thousands of rickshaw men in Shanghai. Rickshaw man and poverty were almost synonymous.

  The earliest modern public transportation means in old Shanghai was the tram. In July 1881, Shanghai British Jardine Matheson Holdings formally proposed to the Council of the French Concession to open the tram business. On April 24, 1907, the construction of the tram in the International Settlement commenced. On March 5, 1908, the first tramway line in Shanghai was officially opened to traffic, starting from Jing'An Temple to Shanghai General Assembly (today's Guangdong Road Bund) with a total length of 6.04 kilometers. On May 6, 1908, the first tram in the French Concession was put into operation, starting from Shiliupu and extending to Xujiahui with a total length of 8.5 kilometers. In the beginning, the trams in the International Settlement and the French Concession were not connected to each other. At the call of all parties, the tramsin the British and French Concessions began to open to each other in August 1912. In August 1913, the first tramway line invested by the Chinese businessmen was officially open to the public, starting from Small East Gate to Gaochang Temple with a total length of 4.97 kilometers. By the end of 1927, there were 22 tram lines in Shanghai, including 11 ones invested by British businessmen, 7 ones invested by French businessmen and 4 ones invested by Chinese businessmen, which totally carried nearly 500,000 passengers per day. The tram had not only brought convenience to

日，上海第一条有轨电车线路正式通车运营，自静安寺始发至上海总会（今广东路外滩），全程 6.04 公里。1908 年 5 月 6 日，法租界第一条有轨电车正式运营，起始站十六铺，后延伸至徐家汇，全长 8.5 公里。开始，公共租界与法租界的电车互不相通。在各方的呼吁下，1912 年 8 月英法电车公司开始相互通车。1913 年 8 月，华商第一条有轨电车线路正式通车营业，从小东门至高昌庙，全长 4.97 公里。到 1927 年底，上海市区有轨电车线路达 22 条，其中英商 11 条，法商 7 条，华商 4 条，日均运客近 50 万人次。有轨电车不仅给上海市民带来了行路之便，也加快了城市的生活节奏。

1901 年，匈牙利人李恩把第一辆现代通用汽车引进上海，让中国人第一次看到了一种不用人力或畜力就能飞奔的车子。此后几年间，上海街头行驶的汽车逐渐多了起来。1908 年 9 月，美商环球供应公司在四川路 97 号设立汽车出租部。这是上海出现的第一家汽车出租公司。到 1929 年，上海全市的公用出租汽车公司达 100 多家，各类汽车一万多辆。当时世界各大品牌的汽车在上海滩几乎都有。

上海解放后，尤其是改革开放以来，上海的城市交通工具与解放前相比不可同日而语。西洋马车、黄包车在上海早已成为历史。有轨电车的现代化水平已大大提高。汽车更是迅速发展，目前仅登记在册的私家车就有近百万辆。轻轨、地铁、磁悬浮列车等现代交通工具一应俱全。上海城市交通的水平已跻身世界一流城市的行列。

Shanghai citizens, but also accelerated the pace of life in the city.

In 1901, the Hungarian Rinn introduced the first modern general automobile into Shanghai, making the Chinese, for the first time, see a vehicle that could run without human or animal power. Over the following few years, the number of cars on the streets of Shanghai grew. In September 1908, the American company Universal Supply Company established a car rental department at No. 97, Sichuan Road. This was the first car rental company in Shanghai. By 1929, there were more than 100 public car rental companies in Shanghai, with more than 10,000 cars of various types. At that time, cars of almost all world's major car brands could be seen in Shanghai.

After the liberation of Shanghai, especially since the reform and opening-up, Shanghai's urban transportation tools have been not comparable with those before the liberation. Western carriages and rickshaws have already become history in Shanghai. The modernization of trams has been greatly improved. Automobiles are developing rapidly. At

→ 20世纪初的双人两轮马车

上海自开埠至今的 170 多年间，城市交通工具发生了如此巨大的变化，这是我们这个时代和这座城市的骄傲。

2017 年 5 月

present, there are nearly one million registered private cars. Modern transportation means such as light rails, subways and maglev trains are available. Shanghai has become one of the world's top cities in terms of urban transportation.

It has been more than 170 years since the opening of Shanghai port. It is the pride of our time and city that so much has changed in urban transportation.

May 2017

老上海的寺庙

上海的寺庙文化是海派文化的一个组成部分。

上海最早的寺庙龙华寺和静安寺，创建于三国吴赤乌年间。以后随着上海地区经济的发展，人口的增加，以及历代统治者对佛教的扶持，上海的寺庙不断新建，佛教不断发展。

上海的寺庙建筑风格各异，是上海一道别有特色的景观，其中许多建筑被列为优秀历史建筑和文物保护单位。龙华寺、静安寺、玉佛寺是上海三座最负盛名的寺庙。龙华寺是上海地区历史最久、规模最大的古刹，距今已有1700多年历史，按佛经上弥勒菩萨在龙华树下成佛的记载而定名为龙华寺。现今龙华寺的殿宇大部分属清同治、光绪年间的建筑，并保持了宋代伽蓝七堂制的格式。玉佛寺原为清代名宦盛宣怀在江湾的家庵。1882年普陀山僧人慧根在缅甸请得白玉雕释迦牟尼佛像5座，途经上海时，留下坐、卧佛像各1座于寺内，遂更名为玉佛寺。后寺庙毁于战火。1918年僧可成迁寺于今址安远路江宁路口，历经10年，于1928年建成。殿宇仿宋代建筑，黄粉墙垣，飞檐耸脊，照壁高大。静安寺原名"沪渎重元寺"，唐代改名"就泰禅寺"，宋真宗大中祥符元年（1008年）开始称静安寺，一直延续至今。静安寺在元明两代已有相当规模，后屡

Temples of Old Shanghai

The temple culture of Shanghai is an integral part of Shanghai-style culture.

The earliest temples in Shanghai — Longhua Temple and Jing'an Temple, werefounded duringthe Chiwu'sreign of the Wu State of the Three Kingdoms. Later, with the development of regional economy, the increase of population and the support of the rulers of past dynasties to Buddhism, new temples continued to be built in Shanghai and Buddhism continued to develop.

The different styles of temple architecture in Shanghai is a unique landscape for Shanghai, many of which are listed as outstanding historical buildings and cultural relicprotection sites. Longhua Temple, Jing'An Temple and the Jade Buddha Temple are the three most famous temples in Shanghai. Longhua Temple, the oldest and largest ancient temple in Shanghai, has a history of more than 1,700 years. It was named according to the record on the Buddhist sutra that Maitreya Bodhisattva became Buddha under the Longhua Tree. The palace buildings in today's Longhua Temple were mostly established in Emperor Tongzhi's and Emperor Guangxu's reign of the Qing Dynasty and maintained the pattern of sangha-arama seven-hall system of the Song Dynasty. The Jade Buddha Temple was originally the family temple of SHENG Xuanhuai — the famous official in the Qing Dynasty in Jiangwan. In 1882, Huigen, a monk from Mount Putuo, received five whitejade Buddha statues in Myanmar and left one sitting Buddha statue and one reclining one in the temple while he went back by way of Shanghai, thus getting the name the Jade Buddha Temple. The temple was destroyed in the war later. In 1918, it was moved to the junction of Jiangning Road and Anyuan Road and rebuilt in 1928, which took more than ten years. The palace building followed

遭战乱毁坏。今静安寺是在人民政府的支持下,于上世纪90年代初修复的。其建筑风格为明代以前的建筑风格,典型的代表就是斗拱的形制,殿堂巍峨,法像庄严,是汉族地区佛教全国重点寺院之一,也是上海市真言宗古刹之一。

除以上三大寺庙外,老上海知名的寺庙还有黄浦区的沉香阁、法藏讲寺,虹口区的下海庙,长宁区的福缘禅院,杨浦区的法善庵,静安区的居士林、宝华寺,普陀区的真如寺,宝山区的梵王宫(今

↖ 静安寺正门

the style in the Song Dynasty with yellow walls, overhanging eaves and towering image walls. Jing'an Temple was originally named "Hudu Chongyuan Temple" and renamed "Jiutai Zen Temple" in the Tang Dynasty. In 1008, it was named Jing'an Temple and has kept the name up to now. Jing'an Temple had a considerable scale in the Yuan and Ming Dynasties, but later was damaged in the war for several times. Today's Jing'an Temple was restored in the early 1990s with the support of the people's government. It follows the architectural style before the Ming Dynasty. Its typical features include the bracket system, towering palace building and solemn statue. It is one of the key Buddhist temples in the Han nationality and one of the ancient temples of Shingon Buddhism in Shanghai.

In additional to the above three major temples, the reputedtemples in old Shanghai also included Chenxiang Pavillion and Fazangjiang Temple in Huangpu District, Xiahai Temple in Hongkou District, Fuyuan Zen Temple in Changning District, Fashan Nunnery in Yangpu District, Jushi Temple and Baohua Temple in Jing'an District, Zhenru Temple in Putuo District, Chaoyin Nunnery and Biyun Temple in Yangpu District, Wuxing Zen Temple in Jiading District, Songyin Zen Temple in Jinshan District, Xilin Zen Temple in Songjiang District, Qinglong Ancient Temple in Qingpu District, Hongfu Zen Temple in Fengxian District and Shou'an Temple in Chongmign District, etc. Among them, the existing girder, pillar, square-bracket and other main structures and the majority of components in the main hall of Zhenru Temple were original materials in the Yuan Dynasty. It is one of the few well-preserved Yuan Dynasty architectures among the Chinese Buddhist temples.

There have preserved precious cultural treasures in the temples of old Shanghai. There are various versions of Tripitaka, Buddhism classics and many precious cultural relics preserved in the upstairs of Longhua Temple, including the "three treasures of the temple" — 718 letters of Tripitaka granted by the emperor inWanli'sreign of the Ming Dynasty, a golden lotus Vairocana statue and a gold seal granted by the emperor. The sitting and reclining Buddha statues in the Jade Buddha Temple were made of whole white jades, which were rarities. There also preserved more than 7000 volumes of

宝山寺)，闵行区的七宝教寺，浦东新区的潮音庵、碧云净院，嘉定区的吴兴禅寺，金山区的松隐禅寺，松江区的西林禅寺，青浦区的青龙古寺，奉贤区的洪福禅寺，崇明区的寿安寺等。其中真如寺正殿现存的梁、柱、枋斗拱等主体结构以及大部分构件皆为元代原物，是我国佛教寺院中保存下来为数很少的元代建筑。

老上海的寺庙里存有极其珍贵的文化典藏。龙华寺藏经楼上收藏着各种版本的大藏经，佛教经籍及许多珍贵文物。其中包括被称为龙华寺"镇寺三宝"的明万历年间的敕赐大藏经718函，范金千叶宝莲毗卢遮那佛一尊，御赐金印一枚。玉佛寺玉佛坐像和卧像都是用整块白玉雕成，堪为稀世珍品。寺内还藏有清雍正年间雕刻版大藏经7000余卷。静安寺有文物数百种，如光绪九年（1883年）所记的《重修静安寺记碑》、《云汉昭回元阁碑》，另有明洪武大钟、历代名人字画以及石刻的佛像等。法藏讲寺藏有明刻《西藏》、清刻《龙藏》、日本《续藏》等珍贵经典。

老上海的寺庙也是推动佛教与时俱进的平台。开埠后的上海逐步成为中国经济、文化的重镇和中西文化交流的中心，因而上海佛教出现了带有明显时代特点的新景象。寺庙成为佛教居士讲经说法，著书立说，创办佛教院校、佛教团体和佛教出版机构，设立佛学图书馆，举办社会慈善事业等佛事活动的重要场所。今上海佛学院就设在玉佛寺内。

老上海寺庙中举行的各种节庆活动，也是独特的文化景观。春节烧头香、除夕撞钟、佛诞节、盂兰盆会、观音诞辰、成道节、方丈升座等宗教活动，都会引来广大信教者参加。一年一度的迎新年

carved-version Tripitaka of Emperor Yongzheng'sreign in the Qing Dynasty in the temple. Jing'an Temple has hundreds of cultural relics, such as the *Monument of Rebuilding Jing'an Temple* and *Monument of Yuange about Emperor Zhao of Han* recorded in the 9th year of Emperor Guangxu'sreign in the Qing Dynasty (1883), as well as large bell of Emperopr Hongwu's reign in the Ming Dynasty, famous ancient paintings and calligraphy, Buddha statues in stone, etc. Fazangjiang Temple has preserved the *West Buddhist Sutra* carved in the Ming Dynasty, the *Dragon Buddhist Sutra* carved in the Qing Dynasty, the Japanese *Continuous Buddhist Sutra* and other precious classics.

The temples of old Shanghai are also the platform to promote the Buddhism to keep up with the times. Since the opening of the port, Shanghai has gradually become an important economic and cultural city in China and the center of cultural exchange between China and the West so that the Buddhism of Shanghai appeared a new scene with the characteristics of the times. The temples have become the important places for Buddhist scholars to give lectures, write books, establish Buddhist colleges, Buddhist groups and Buddhist publishing institutions, set up Buddhist libraries, and hold Buddhist activities such as social charity. Today's Shanghai Buddhist College is located in the Jade Buddha Temple.

Various festivals held in the temples of old Shanghai are also unique cultural landscapes. Activities such as burning headspace volatile in Spring Festival, striking the bell on Lunar New Year's Eve, Buddha's Birthday, Ullambana Festival, Kuan Yin's Birthday, Buddhahood Festival, Promotion of the Buddhist Abbot and other religious activities usually attract the believers. The annual bell-striking activity of Longhua Temple, Lantern Festival of Town's God Temple and the annual Longhua Temple Fair on lunar Double Third Day have been inherited from the Ming and Qing Dynasties to now, which have become the regular tourist festivals in Shanghai.

Since the reform and opening-up, especially in the new century, the CPC's religious policy has been further implemented. At present, there are nearly 120 temples open to the public in Shanghai, and nearly 6 million people attend various religious activities there

龙华撞钟活动，城隍庙元宵灯会，每年农历三月三的龙华庙会，从明清时期开始一直延续至今，现已成为上海市固定的旅游节庆活动。

改革开放以来，尤其是进入新世纪后，党的宗教政策得到进一步落实。目前，上海有开放寺庙近 120 座（所），每年到寺庙参加各类宗教活动的近 600 万人次。我们有理由相信，在上海国际化文化大都市建设的进程中，上海的寺庙一定会在弘扬佛法，爱国爱教中发挥更大的作用。

2017 年 7 月

every year. We have reason to believe that the temples of Shanghai will play a greater role in promoting Buddhism and patriotism in Shanghai's construction of international cultural metropolis.

July 2017

老上海的商会

商会是中国近代社会政治、经济、文化相互作用下的产物。上海是我国商会成立最早影响最大的城市。这段历史，值得回顾与借鉴。

近代工商业在清代问世后的约 30 年间，维系工商界人士的组织仍然是旧式的以同乡人为主的会馆，和以同业者为主的公所，其作用在于用封建行会的方式保护同业利益。资料显示，商船会馆是上海最早的会馆。1715 年，船业同仁为了处理海难善后事宜，设商船会馆于沪上。此后，徽宁会馆、浙绍公所、泉漳会馆等纷纷在上海设立。至辛亥革命前夕，上海有案可查的会馆公所达 120 多个，其中大多集聚在南市。由于清代长期未立商法，官吏与外商肆意欺凌华商，各行各业的交易各行其是，因此，会馆、公所在保护同业利益方面起了重要作用。

19 世纪 90 年代，清政府出于对列强"商战"的需要开始整饬商务，筹议设立商会。1902 年 2 月，沪上巨商严信厚创办的上海商业会议公所在南京路五昌里正式成立。1904 年 5 月，上海商业会议公所改名为上海商务总会。这是我国诞生的第一个商会。此后，国内工商业较为发达的城市以上海商务总会为楷模，纷纷建立起类似组

Chamber of Commerce of Old Shanghai

Chamber of commerce is the product of the interaction of social politics, economy and culture in modern China. Shanghai is China's first and most influential city for the establishment of chamber of commerce. This phase of history is worthy of review and reference.

Over about 30 years after the emergence of modern industry and commerce in the Qing Dynasty, the organization that maintained the relationship among the industrial and commercial circles was still the old-style provincial or country guilds and the fellow societies, the function of which was to protect the industry interests in the way of feudal guilds. According to the data, Native Shipping Guild was the earliest guild in Shanghai. In 1715, the shipping industry set up the Native Shipping Guild in Shanghai to handle matters relating to problems arising from perils of the sea. Since then, Huining Guild, Zheshao Guild, Quanzhang Guild and other guilds were successively set up in Shanghai. By the Revolution of 1911, there were more than 120 registered guilds in Shanghai, most of which gathered in Nanshi. As there was no commercial law for a long time in the Qing Dynasty, officials and foreign businessmen arbitrarily bullied Chinese businessmen, and all trades in various industries went their own way. Therefore, the guilds and fellow societies had played an important role in protecting the industry interests.

In the 1890s, the Qing Government began to strengthen the commerce and set up the chamber of commerce for the need of "commercial war" against foreign powers. In February 1902, Shanghai Chamber of Business Conference was founded at Wuchangli of Nanjing Road by YAN Xinhou, a prominent businessman in Shanghai. In May 1904, Shanghai Chamber of Business Conference was renamed Shanghai Chamber of Commerce, which was the first chamber of commerce in China. Since then, more

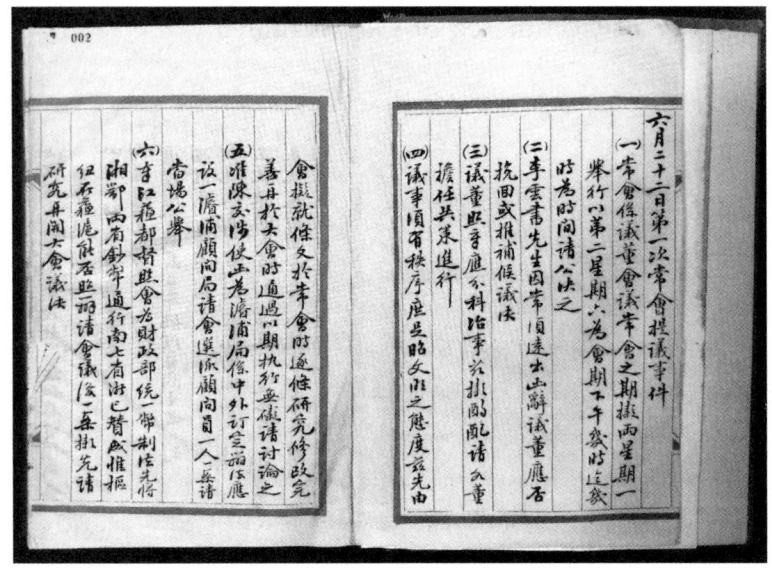

上海总商会办事报告

织。由此，中国新兴的资产阶级开始有了现代意义上的社会团体。上海另一个商会组织沪南商务分所成立于 1905 年，是以南市各业为基础的商人团体。该分所名义上为上海商务总会的分会，实际上是一个独立的商会组织，与上海商务总会并无隶属关系。沪南商务分所先后改称沪南商务分会、南市商会、上海县商会。除成立于晚清的上海商务总会、沪南商会外，民国时期在上海成立的商会组织还有闸北商会、吴淞商会、上海马路商界联合会等。1912 年 5 月，上海商务总会改称上海总商会。1929 年又改为上海特别市总商会，翌年改为上海市商会。上海解放后，改组为上海市工商业联合会。

上海商务总会以"在商言商，振兴实业"为宗旨，设立财政、

developed cities in China had set up similar organizations with Shanghai Chamber of Commerce as a model. Therefore, China's emerging bourgeoisie began to have the social groups with modern features. Another chamber of commerce in Shanghai, Chamber of Commerce North Shanghai Branch, was established in 1905, which was a group of businessmen based on various industries in Nanshi. Chamber of Commerce North Shanghai Branch, nominally the branch of Shanghai Chamber of Commerce, was actually an independent organization of chamber of commerce which has no affiliation with Shanghai Chamber of Commerce. Chamber of Commerce North Shanghai Branch was once renamed South Shanghai Branch Chamber of Commerce, Nanshi Chamber of Commerce and Shanghai County Chamber of Commerce. In addition to Shanghai Chamber of Commerce and Chamber of Commerce North Shanghai Branch founded in the late Qing Dynasty, there were Zhabei Chamber of Commerce, Wusong Chamber of Commerce and Shanghai Road Commercial Joint Association, etc. In May 1912, Shanghai Chamber of Commerce was renamed Shanghai General Chamber of Commerce. In 1929, it was renamed Chamber of Commerce of Shanghai Special City, and in the following year, it was renamed Shanghai Municipal Chamber of Commerce. After the liberation of Shanghai, it was reorganized into Shanghai Federation of Industry and Commerce.

Shanghai Chamber of Commerce adhered to the mission of "business is business and vigorously developing industry" and set up 8 specialized committees including finance, communication, notarization, investigation, publishing, books, display and China business contract to promote the business of the chamber. It had successively initiated the establishment of the Chinese Merchants' Association; set up Chinese Mercantile Bank; opened business schools; established goods exhibition halls and China-made goods shopping malls; organized Chinese goods to participate in world expo; initiated *The Business Monthly*; and built commercial library and so on. Its functions and influences were far more than those of the guilds and fellow societies. Meanwhile, the chamber of commerce took an active part in social and political activities. The great anti-American Movement of 1905 was spearheaded by ZENG Shaoqing, the board director of Shanghai Chamber of Commerce. Shanghai General Chamber of Commerce denounced the warlords' infighting, called for

交际、公证、调查、出版、图书、陈列、华商道契8个专门委员会，推进商会业务。先后发起成立华商联合会；筹设华商银行；开办商业学校；创设商品陈列馆和国货商场；组织国货参加世博会；创刊《商业月报》；建立商业图书馆等，其作用和影响远非会馆公所可比。同时，商会积极参加社会政治活动。1905年声势浩大的抵制美货运动，就由上海商务总会议董曾少卿领衔发起。上海总商会谴责军阀混战，呼吁裁军制宪，反对专制，抨击政府挟官凌商的做法，倡言收回租界权益，保护民族工商业。五·卅运动期间，上海总商会还筹款援助工人的反帝爱国运动。

上海总商会的会长都是当时具有重要影响力的民族资本家。总商会的创始人严信厚是中国近代企业的开拓者，被称为"宁波帮第一人"。他致力实业救国，做了大量的慈善公益事业，曾捐巨资助建塘沽铁路、宁波铁路，在上海办仁济、广益、元济诸善堂。会长朱葆三是当时上海的"商界泰斗，实业领袖"。他兴办实业，创办多家慈善机构，复兴公园门口"华人与狗不准入内"的牌子，是在他的精心策划下迫使法国人摘掉的。会长聂云台是我国纺织机械制造业的先驱。他废除包工制，率先将蒸汽引擎改为电动机，筹建上海纱布交易所，是我国民族实业家的突出代表。会长宋汉章是中国近代银行业的奠基人之一。1931年他创立了中国保险公司，被誉为"中国近代保险业之父"。会长虞洽卿是著名银行家和慈善家。抗战爆发后，他拒绝出任上海伪政府市长，经营滇缅公路运输，支持抗战。他还在家乡宁波做了大量公益事业。

老上海的商会，打破了过去界限分明、壁垒森严的血缘、行业、

↑ 上海总商会会长虞洽卿

disarmament and constitutional reform, opposed autocracy, attacked the government's practice of holding officials to bullying the businessmen, advocated the recovery of concession rights and interests, and protected national industry and commerce. During the May 4th Movement, Shanghai General Chamber of Commerce also raised funds to aid workers' anti-imperialist patriotic movement.

  The chairmen of the Shanghai General Chamber of Commerce were all national capitalists of great influence at that time. YAN Xinhou, founder of Shanghai General Chamber of Commerce, was a pioneer of modern Chinese enterprises, known as "the first person in Ningbo Gang". He devoted himself to saving the country through industry and made a large number of charitable and public welfare undertakings. He donated a large sum of money to help build Tanggu Railway and Ningbo Railway, and established Renji, Guangyi, Yuanji and other charitable organizations in Shanghai. The chairman of the chamber of commerce ZHU Baosan was a "leading businessman and industry leader" in Shanghai. He vigorously developed industries and set up a number of charities. Hemade

→ 上海总商会会议厅正门

帮派、地域等限制，成为跨行业和不限籍贯的商业组织，这是历史的一大进步。在老上海商会的发展过程中，由于受历史的局限性，也有过失，但它对早期上海社会经济发展，对促进我国工商业现代化进程所起的重要作用不可低估。

如今，上海已成为世界一流的工商业城市。目前上海共有商会160多家，其中异地商会102家。在工商业日益繁荣发展的今天，老上海商会心系国家民族命运，勇于改革开拓创新，注重振兴发展实业，力助社会慈善公益的传统，值得我们传承弘扬。

2017 年 10 月

well-planned scenarios to force the French to pick off the indicator drop "Chinese and dogs are not allowed in" at the entrance of Fuxing Park. The chairman of the chamber of commerce NIE Yuntai was the pioneer of textile machinery manufacturing in China. He abolished the piece work system, took the lead in changing the steam engine into the electric motor, and set up Shanghai CottonExchange. He was the outstanding representative of Chinese national industrialists. The chairman of the chamber of commerce SONG Hanzhang was one of the founders of modern banking industry in China. In 1931, he founded the China Insurance Company, known as "the Father of China's Modern Insurance Industry". The chairman of the chamber of commerce YU Qiaqing was a famous banker and philanthropist. After the outbreak of the Anti-Japanese War, he refused to serve as mayor of Shanghai's Puppet Government. He operated Burma road transportation and supported the Chinese People's War of Resistance against Japanese Aggression. He had also made a lot of public welfare undertakingsin his hometown Ningbo.

The chamber of commerce in old Shanghai broke the restrictions of blood, industry, gang and region with clear boundaries and strict barriers in the past, and became a cross-industry and non-limited business organization, which is great progress in history. In the development process of the chamber of commerce in old Shanghai, due to the limitations of history, there are also mistakes. But it has played an important role in accelerating Shanghai's social and economic development in the early stage and promoting the modernization of our industry and commerce.

Today, Shanghai has become a world-class city of industry and commerce. At present, there are more than 160 chambersof commerce in Shanghai, including 102 non-local ones. Today, with the increasingly prosperous development of industry and commerce, it is worth inheriting and carrying forward the traditions of the chambers of commerce in old Shanghai — being dedicated to the destiny of the country and the nation, being brave in reform, pioneering and innovation, paying attention to revitalization and development of industries, and contributing to social charity and public welfare.

October 2017

写在后面

朱争平

《上海年轮》结集出版了，心中甚慰。

2011年，《中共中央关于深化文化体制改革、推动社会主义文化大发展大繁荣若干重大问题的决定》出台前后，我在上海市委组织的讨论会上作过两次发言。时任上海市委书记俞正声听了我的发言后，交待我多多关心上海的文化建设。由此，我便在工作之余，开始涉足上海近现代人文历史的研究。

1843年上海开埠以后逐渐形成的海派文化，是中国近现代最具代表性的文化。1845年11月，中国近代第一个租界——英租界在上海设立。此后，美租界、法租界相继在上海辟设。租界，既是近代中国遭受列强欺凌的耻辱标志，同时又是近代文明的窗口。上海城市的性质、结构和形态等都是因为租界的设立而发生了巨大的转型。在短短数十年的时间内，上海由中国传统的小县城演变为远东最大的城市，成为近代中国经济、金融和文化中心。上海租界作为被欧风美雨吹打的前沿地域，自然不乏为殖民主义政治扩张、经济侵略服务的文化渗透，但"华洋杂处"、新学传播，创造了比较适合文化发展的环境。以开放性、灵活性、创造性为主流特征的海派文化就是在这样的背景下形成的，100多年来深刻影响着上海的城市精神风

Afterword

ZHU Zhengping

Much to my relief, the Growth Ring of Shanghai collection has been published.

In 2011, I delivered two speeches at two symposia organized by Shanghai Municipal CPC Committee near the promulgation of the Decisions of the CPC Central Committee on Import Issues for Deepening the Reform of the Cultural System and Promoting the Great Development and Prosperity of Socialist Culture. YU Zhengsheng, then Secretary of the Municipal CPC Committee in Shanghai, listened to my speeches and told me to pay more attention to cultural development in Shanghai. Therefore, I began to get involved in the studies of Shanghai's modern and contemporary human history in my spare time.

The Shanghai-style culture that gradually formed after the port opening of Shanghai in 1843 is the most representative of modern China. In November, 1845, the first concession in modern China, the British Concession, was set up in Shanghai, followed by the successive establishment of the US and the French Concessions in Shanghai. The concession was not only a symbol of humiliation for modern China to be bullied by foreign powers, but also a window into modern civilization, thus having brought about tremendous transformation to the nature, structure and form of Shanghai. In just a few decades, Shanghai has evolved from a traditional Chinese small county to the largest city in the Far East and the economic, financial and cultural center in modern China. Cultural infiltration is inevitable for the Shanghai concession — the front that witnessed the invasion of America and European countries — for the service of colonial political expansion and economic aggression. However, an environment more suitable for cultural development has been created thanks to the "mixed living of Chinese and foreigners" and the dissemination of new thoughts. The Shanghai-style culture, mainly characterized by

貌。回顾近代以来中国文化的发展史，许多第一都诞生在上海：1843年中国历史上第一家经营西乐的琴行诞生在上海，1850年中国近代第一个跑马场诞生在上海，1867年中国最早的欧式剧场《兰心大戏院》诞生在上海，1868年中国第一座城市花园（黄浦公园）诞生在上海，1907年中国第一部话剧《黑奴吁天录》诞生在上海，1908年中国第一家唱片公司《东方百代唱片公司》诞生在上海，1913年中国第一部电影故事片《难夫难妻》诞生在上海，1923年中国第一家广播电台奥斯邦电台诞生在上海，1927年中国最早的流行歌曲《毛毛雨》诞生在上海。这样的"第一"，还可以列数很多。总之，在中国近现代文化发展过程中，上海始终是领跑者。

城市文化的演进是城市发展的灵魂。如果想要深入解读一座城市，城市文化无疑是最好的入口。从2012年到2017年的6年间，我利用业余时间，查阅了2000多万字的资料，从人文历史的层面解读上海，研究领域涉及戏曲、电影、音乐、报业、书业、出版、影楼、茶楼、戏院、建筑、美食、娱乐、教育、体育、慈善等。研究过程中，我先后撰写老上海人文历史系列随感共50篇。这些文章，先后发表在新民晚报《夜光杯》副刊。几乎每篇文章刊发后，我都会收到一些读者的来信来电，反映文章虽然精短，但信息量很大，每一篇文章都堪称是一部简史。文章中提出的一些文化命题也是需要在今天的城市文化建设中加以研究解决的。许多读者建议将这些文章结集出版，让更多的新老上海人对自己生活的这座城市有更全面的了解。于是，就有了这本《上海年轮》。本书的篇目顺序，就是以文章发表的时间先后排列的。

openness, flexibility and creativity, has been formed against such a background, with a profound influence on the looks and spirits of urban Shanghai in more than 100 years. Looking back at the history of Chinese culture in modern times, Shanghai is the birthplace of multiple first places, including: the first musical instruments shop with western instruments in the history of China in 1843; the first racetrack in modern China in 1850; the earliest European-style theater Lyceum Theatre in 1867; China's first city garden (Huangpu Park) in 1868; China's first drama Uncle Tom's Cabin in 1907; the first record company Oriental EMI in 1908; China's first feature film Die For Marriage in 1913; China's first radio station, the Osborn Radio Station in 1923; the earliest popular song Drizzle in China in 1927, and the list of such firsts can still go on. In short, Shanghai has always been the leader in the development of modern Chinese culture.

Urban culture, whose evolution is viewed as the soul of urban development, is undoubtedly the best entrance to a deep interpretation of a city, if in need. During the 6 years from 2012 to 2017, I made use of my spare time to refer to more than 20 million words of information and interpret Shanghai from the perspective of human history, covering a range of research fields like dramas, films, music, newspapers, book industry, publishing, photo studio, tea houses, theaters, architecture, food, entertainment, education, sports, charity, etc. In course of the research, I wrote a total series of 50 articles on the history of the old Shanghai humanities, which have been successively published in Yeguang Bei, the supplement of Xinmin Evening News. After the publication of every article, I would receive some letters or calls from readers with feedbacks that each article was very informative despite the limited length and could be dubbed as a brief history. Some cultural issues proposed in the articles are also in need of studies and solutions for today's urban cultural development. Many readers suggested that these articles be published together, so that more new and old Shanghainese can have a more comprehensive understanding of the city in which they live. Therefore, the Growth Ring of Shanghai collection is born, with the articles arranged in the order in line with their publishing time.

The publication of the Growth Ring of Shanghai collection is not only a summary of

《上海年轮》的出版,既是对自己前一段研究的小结,同时也想以此来求教于专家学者和广大读者,以使自己今后的学习研究有更深的开掘。

感谢上海文艺出版社为我结集出书。感谢孙晓云先生题写书名。感谢何菲女士作序。感谢贺竹元先生插图。感谢费名瑶先生为书名治印。感谢所有为本书的出版提供过帮助的同志。

2018 年 9 月于上海

my own previous researches, but also a tool to seek for advice from experts, scholars and readers in order to further my own future studies and researches.

Shanghai Literature and Art Publishing House deserves my gratitude for publishing the collection for me. Besides, I owe a debt of thanks to Mr. SUN Xiaoyun for the title-inscription, to HE Fei for her preface, to Mr. HE Zhuyuan for the illustrations, to Mr. Fei Mingyao for imprinting the title of the book and to all the comrades who are of help for the publication of the book.

September 2018, Shanghai

图书在版编目（CIP）数据

上海年轮/朱争平著. -- 上海：上海文艺出版社,2019
ISBN 978-7-5321-7057-9
Ⅰ.①上… Ⅱ.①朱… Ⅲ.①随笔—作品集—中国—当代 Ⅳ.①I267.1
中国版本图书馆CIP数据核字(2019)第152227号

发 行 人：陈　徵
责任编辑：乔　亮
装帧设计：胡　斌

书　　名：上海年轮
作　　者：朱争平
出　　版：上海世纪出版集团　上海文艺出版社
地　　址：上海绍兴路7号　200020
发　　行：上海文艺出版社发行中心发行
　　　　　上海市绍兴路50号　200020　www.ewen.co
印　　刷：上海盛通时代印刷有限公司
开　　本：787×1092　1/16
印　　张：26.25
插　　页：3
字　　数：221,000
印　　次：2019年11月第1版 2019年11月第1次印刷
I S B N：978-7-5321-7057-9/G.0222
定　　价：98.00元
告 读 者：如发现本书有质量问题请与印刷厂质量科联系　T: 021-37910000